Tina —
Enjoy!
Love,
Kathryn

THE GORGON

A MEDIEVAL ROMANCE

BY KATHRYN LE VEQUE

Printed by Dragonblade Publishing in the United States of America

Text copyright 1996, 2014 by Kathryn Le Veque
Cover copyright 1996, 2014 by Kathryn Le Veque

Library of Congress Control Number 2014-033
ISBN 1495358429

KATHRYN LE VEQUE NOVELS

Medieval Romance:

The de Russe Legacy:
The White Lord of Wellesbourne
The Dark One: Dark Knight
Beast
Lord of War: Black Angel
The Falls of Erith

The de Lohr Dynasty:
While Angels Slept (Lords of East Anglia)
Rise of the Defender
Spectre of the Sword
Unending Love
Archangel
Steelheart

Great Lords of le Bec:
Great Protector
To the Lady Born (House of de Royans)

Lords of Eire:
The Darkland (Master Knights of Connaught)
Black Sword
Echoes of Ancient Dreams (time travel)

De Wolfe Pack Series:
The Wolfe
Serpent
Scorpion (Saxon Lords of Hage – Also related to The Questing)
Walls of Babylon
The Lion of the North
Dark Destroyer

Ancient Kings of Anglecynn:
The Whispering Night
Netherworld

Battle Lords of de Velt:
The Dark Lord
Devil's Dominion

Reign of the House of de Winter:
Lespada
Swords and Shields (also related to The Questing, While Angels Slept)

De Reyne Domination:
Guardian of Darkness
The Fallen One (part of Dragonblade Series)

Unrelated characters or family groups:
The Gorgon (Also related to Lords of Thunder)
The Warrior Poet (St. John and de Gare)
Tender is the Knight (House of d'Vant)
Lord of Light
The Questing (related to The Dark Lord, Scorpion)
The Legend (House of Summerlin)

The Dragonblade Series: (Great Marcher Lords of de Lara)
Dragonblade
Island of Glass (House of St. Hever)
The Savage Curtain (Lords of Pembury)
The Fallen One (De Reyne Domination)
Fragments of Grace (House of St. Hever)
Lord of the Shadows
Queen of Lost Stars (House of St. Hever)

Lords of Thunder: The de Shera Brotherhood Trilogy
The Thunder Lord
The Thunder Warrior
The Thunder Knight

Time Travel Romance: (Saxon Lords of Hage)
The Crusader
Kingdom Come

Contemporary Romance:

Sea of Dreams
Purgatory

Kathlyn Trent/Marcus Burton Series:
Valley of the Shadow
The Eden Factor
Canyon of the Sphinx

Other Contemporary Romance:
Lady of Heaven
Darkling, I Listen

The American Heroes Series:
Resurrection
Fires of Autumn
Evenshade

Multi-author Collections/Anthologies:
With Dreams Only of You (USA Today
bestseller)
Sirens of the Northern Seas (Viking romance)

Note: All Kathryn's novels are designed to be read as stand-alones, although many have cross-over characters or cross-over family groups. Novels that are grouped together have related characters or family groups.

Series are clearly marked. All series contain the same characters or family groups except the American Heroes Series, which is an anthology with unrelated characters.

There is NO particular chronological order for any of the novels because they can all be read as stand-alones, even the series.

For more information, find it in **A Reader's Guide to the Medieval World of Le Veque.**

TABLE OF CONTENTS

Chapter One 1

Chapter Two 17

Chapter Three 29

Chapter Four 44

Chapter Five 64

Chapter Six 81

Chapter Seven 100

Chapter Eight 117

Chapter Nine 139

Chapter Ten 155

Chapter Eleven 172

Chapter Twelve 186

Chapter Thirteen 208

Chapter Fourteen 220

Chapter Fifteen 235

Chapter Sixteen 248

Chapter Seventeen 271

Chapter Eighteen 289

Chapter Nineteen 305

Chapter Twenty 323

Epilogue 341

The Great Knights of de Moray Series 349

About Kathryn Le Veque 350

CHAPTER ONE

The Month of May, Year of Our Lord 1235
Chaldon Castle
Dorset, England

T HE SULTRY AUGUST heat was manageable this day. As the sun broke the eastern horizon, the lush English countryside embraced the coming day with open arms. Not only was the advancing day glorious of weather and promise, but the inhabitants of the gentle hills of Dorset were anticipating this day with excitement.

In faith, the day itself could have been wrought with storms and foul weather and still it would have been a grand morn. For on this day, a long-standing celebration was preparing to mount and nothing could dampen the spirits of peasant and noble alike, fine blood and common lines readying the stronghold of Chaldon Castle for the activities of the approaching gala.

The mighty stronghold of Chaldon guarded the road between Dorchester and Weymouth and was being prepared as a new bride for her husband. Proud banners of du Bonne red and white streamed from the mighty battlements, snapping in the steady ocean breeze. The constant hint of salt-air was heavy upon the fortress, licking man and beast alike with dampness as they went about their duties.

Just outside of the open fortress gates lay the field of celebration, a margin of meadow that had been prepared for the events of competition. A large bank of lodges had been constructed to accommodate the noble visitors that would be gracing Chaldon this day, and already a small army of peasants had constructed their vendor's shacks and stalls to provide refreshment between contests.

In the enormous keep of Chaldon that housed the reigning Constable and his family, all was not as sunny as the day appeared. The object of the pending celebration was not the least bit pleased at the moment as he tripped over the clutter of his bower.

"God's Blood," the young man spat. "I cannot find anything in this place."

A smirking face appeared in an adjoining door, features similar to those of the cursing young man. "Temper, temper, my young lord," he cautioned. "You'll chase all of the young women away with your foul temper and nasty disposition."

The frowning man slugged his fist into his smug companion's chest, lacking any power to the blow. "Shut your mouth, Ian. Where in the hell is my hauberk? I cannot find the thing anywhere."

Ian, at least a head taller than his testy younger brother, maintained his smirk as he kicked through a pile of clutter on the floor. "Here it is, lover. Do not fret so."

The younger man snatched the mail hood from his brother, scowling fiercely. "God's Blood, I'd rather get dressed by myself. Go and bother someone else."

Ian snorted humorously, ignoring his brother's demand for solitude and moving for the suit of armor against the broad stretch of wall. Two young squires sat against the cold stone, polishing the armor furiously.

"There is no one else to tolerate me," he said, examining a recently-cleaned greave. "Stephan is with Genisa, probably mounting her for the fourth time this morn, and Summer has been in her solar since dawn, demanding to be left alone. She swears this gala to celebrate your knighthood will drive us to the poorhouse."

The cross young man grunted as he fumbled with his mailed protection. "I did not ask for a party. 'Twas at father's insistence."

Ian returned the greave to one of the young squires and moved to stroke the crafted hilt of his brother's sword.

"Be glad he insisted on celebrating your knighthood at all, Lance," his voice was somewhat subdued. "Stephan received a new sheath for his broadsword. I received a handshake."

Lance glanced to his middle brother, two years older and sixty pounds heavier. Much larger than any of his siblings, he was a mild-mannered lout with a wicked sense of humor. It was a quick wit that Lance had missed terribly when the man had been knighted two years ago, leaving his youngest brother to finish his training alone.

Stephan, Ian and Lance du Bonne had fostered together at Shrewsbury Castle on the Welsh border, far from their coastal fortress of Chaldon. It was an unusual move to keep siblings together to foster, but the three had insisted. The three men had lived together, practiced together, and protected each other from the brutal realities of a careless world. They were a fearsome trio with an unusual reputation of family unity. Some had even wondered if the brothers were able to work one without the other.

But they somewhat disproved that theory when Stephan was inducted into the knighthood at twenty-one years of age; Ian and Lance functioned quite well when Stephan returned to Chaldon. Four years later, Ian received his spurs and also found his way home, leaving young Lance alone at Shrewsbury to finish his training. As the gallery of critics awaited Lance's failure, the lad proved them wrong and honorably earned his knighthood.

In a sense, the festivities planned for this day were in celebration of the du Bonne brother's reunion, not merely the recently attained pair of golden spurs. The three were looking forward to a future of tournaments, leisure and exhilarating adventure.

At this moment, however, Lance could not consider the future beyond locating his boots. As Ian lingered against the wall, continuing his inspection of the squires' handiwork, Lance fumbled about in his cluttered chamber like a huffing bear.

"Damn… I cannot find a damn thing!" he grumbled, managing to locate one boot but not the other. After a moment, he stood tall and shook his fists in frustration. "How is it that everything I need is missing?"

Ian shook his head, moving away from the squires and into the center of the room. "Mayhap if you cleaned the chamber, you could find what you are looking for."

"Enough from you, swill-brain," Lance snarled, crowing with triumph when he caught sight of his other boot. Falling to the mussed bed, he pulled on his footwear. "Stephan said that Genisa was finishing my new tunic. He should have brought it to me by now."

Ian pursed his lips wryly. "I told you that he is most likely with his wife, driving himself into her lovely body until he dies. In fact, I should be so fortunate to warrant such a death."

Lance eyed his brother a moment, his irritation fading as he gazed into the familiar features. "You are still quite fond of Genisa, are you not?"

The mirth in Ian's eyes faded as he averted his gaze. "She is my brother's wife."

Lance rose from the disheveled mattress to collect his hauberk. "You've been in love with her since you met her. Two years ago, I believe."

Ian refused to look at his brother. "I never told you that."

Lance put his head through the mail hood, moving for the open door. Holding out his arms, Ian took the silent request and helped his brother don the remainder of the heavy mail.

"You did not have to," Lance's voice was quiet as he adjusted the protection about his shoulders. "I can see it in your eyes every time you look at her. I can only imagine that the feeling for her blossomed when you first met her upon returning home from Shrewsbury two years ago. Summer swears that you have never looked at Genisa with anything other than love in your eyes."

The mood between the brothers du Bonne was reversing; where Lance had been irritable and sullen only moments before, Ian was now taking on brother's characteristics.

"Our little sister does not know everything."

"Aye, she does. She has wisdom beyond her years."

Ian scratched his blond scalp, uncomfortable with the subject of his lovely sister-in-law. If truth be known, Summer was right. And so was Lance. But he would not admit the truth, not when he loved Stephan far more than his beautiful wife. A sweet fantasy was Genisa and nothing more.

Moving away from his brother, he pretended to busy himself with his Lance's armor. He was eager to change the subject.

"Speaking of Summer," he said casually, "What are we going to do about our baby sister today? Has Stephan made any suggestions?"

Lance shrugged, aware of Ian's bid to shift the subject. "I do not suppose there is anything we can do except be with her constantly. Summer should not be alone for a single moment, Ian."

Pleased that his brother had taken the hint to change the topic, Ian nodded gravely. "Indeed. I do not suppose we could discourage her from attending the tourney altogether, could we?"

Lance snorted. "Not a chance. She has hardly been out of Chaldon as it is and, as with all young maidens, is eager to attend her first tourney."

Ian let out a long, harsh breath. "So be it. We cannot discourage her from attending the festivities," scratching his head again, he seemed to be regaining his good humor. "God help the idiot who is the first to criticize her condition."

"Which is why one of us must be with her at all times," Lance said firmly. "Under no circumstances must Summer be allowed to express herself."

"You mean speak."

"Aye, that's exactly what I mean. We will do the speaking for her."

Ian's gaze was pensive as he watched his brother mill about the piles of disarrayed clutter.

"God's Blood, Lance, what did she do before Stephan returned home from Shrewsbury six years ago?" he wondered aloud. "Who protected her from the ignorant rabble?"

Lance found the pair of protective inner gloves he had been searching for. "She was only three when I left home to foster and had not yet learned to speak," he said. "By the time Stephan returned, she was eleven. Kermit, her childhood tutor, kept her sequestered in the solar most of the time, teaching her to read and figure mathematics. I suppose that is why the solar is still her favorite place; she can hide from the world within its shielding walls. It is the only safe haven away from those who would taunt her."

Ian shook his head in disgust, moving to the lancet window. Unlatching the latticed grate, his gaze wandered over the brightly colored grounds below, inspecting the visitors that had begun arriving yesterday. Many more were expected during the course of the morn, for the tournament was scheduled to begin after the nooning meal.

"She still hasn't recovered from the old man's death, you know," he said quietly, watching the du Bonne standards whip about in the brisk wind. "You were not here when he died last winter, hunched over his books in the solar. Father swore he'd never seen a more dedicated servant. But Summer viewed him more as the grandfather she never knew, not the aged steward with a blind eye."

Lance fumbled with one of the soft woolen gloves, remembering the servant that Summer had been so fond of. He had been a man who had treated her with dignity and respect, ignoring her flaw because he had shared a similar affliction. The beautiful young maiden and the gnarled old man had shared a strong attachment and his death had hurt her deeply.

"Summer says she is going to name her firstborn son after the old steward," Lance said after a pensive pause, still toying with the glove. "God help her husband with a son by the name of Sir Kermit."

Ian snorted, his smile returning. "Little Kermy. How touching." Unwilling to linger on the thoughts of his baby sister and her flaw, he refocused on the day at hand. "Would you hurry? I can see more guests on the horizon and whether or not you are the center of the celebration, I doubt they will be willing to wait for your lazy hide."

Annoyance making a return, Lance scowled at his older brother. "I would have been ready this minute had my chamber not been so completely out of order. With all of the servants we have to cook and serve and clean, how can such a thing be possible?"

"It's possible because you are a complete pig," Ian said frankly, laughing when his brother shook his fist threateningly. As Lance opened his mouth to refute his brother's assessment, a polished, familiar figure appeared in the doorway. The last of the du Bonne brothers had arrived.

"What's so humorous?" Stephan du Bonne moved into the chamber with the grace of a cat, tossing his youngest brother the long-anticipated tunic. "God's Beard, Lance, aren't you finished dressing? The men-at-arms have already formed escorts and are awaiting our presence to lead them in guiding our guests."

Ian snorted with amusement as Lance glowered. "I'll be ready shortly," Lance snapped without force, slugging his giggling middle brother in the arm when the man refused to silence himself. "I was waiting for my tunic."

Stephan cocked an eyebrow; devilishly handsome with pale green eyes and beautiful reddish-blond hair, he was considered the most comely of the three brothers. He also possessed charm that had caused many a woman to swoon.

"It was finished last night," Stephan said, moving to shove Ian away from the window so he could cast his own experienced gaze over the grounds. "Had you not been so drunk, you would have heard Genisa when she offered to bring it to your chamber. As it was, I attempted to deliver it to you after you retired but my knocking could not be heard over the grunts of pleasure coming from within the chamber."

Ian laughed loudly as Lance scowled and turned away, laying the brilliant tunic on the jumbled bed. "I am sure that I wasn't the only one filling my chamber with the sounds of pleasure," he said sarcastically. "And speaking of Genisa, where is my delicious sister-in-law?"

Stephan was moving for the armor against the wall; the squires were nearly finished and the time was past to commence dressing his slothful brother. "Where else? She and Summer have perched themselves on the battlements to watch the influx of guests. It should be quite a spectacle."

Ian's humor faded somewhat as he moved to help his older brother with Lance's protection. "Do you think it wise to allow Summer to mingle with the guests without one of us as her escort?"

"Genisa is with her. Summer will not come to any harm or embarrassment with my wife by her side. Moreover, Genisa prattles so that even if Summer attempted to speak, she would be unable to get a word in."

Stephan sounded confident; but, then again, he always sounded confident. Ian and Lance trusted him. With thoughts of Summer and Genisa and the state of Lance's slothful nature shoved aside, the three brothers prepared for the day with a good deal of mounting vigor. The excitement in the air was a palpable thing.

☙

"DO YOU SEE the Lady Isobel?"

The Lady Genisa Rilaux du Bonne jabbed a slender finger to the green and silver party that had recently passed under the portcullis and into the bailey. Hidden behind the thick walls of the battlements, Genisa and her sister-in-law had been observing the invasion of guests since the early morn. Nearing noon already, the last stragglers were arriving and the bustle of Chaldon was chaotic.

But the chaos had yet to reach the parapet above the bailey, high on the defending walls of the old Norman fortress. The two giddy young ladies had spent a wonderful morning inspecting the guests from their private haven when they should have very well been tending to the masses.

"There, Summer – see?" Genisa poked her tapered finger into the air once more. "Good Heavens, look how fat she has become! Why, I remember when she was the fairest maiden in the shire. Thank Goodness that marriage hasn't turned me into a cow as it has apparently done to poor Isobel."

"You are the f-fairest maiden in the shire, Genisa," Summer du Bonne's soft golden eyes were riveted to the rotund woman below. "My brother surely would not have m-married you if you had been second best."

Genisa smiled, a toothy, lovely grin that had captivated Stephan's arrogant heart. She was indeed a beautiful woman, flashy and blond and finely sculpted. She had been pursued by nearly every eligible knight in the province, and sometimes even the ineligible ones. But the knight managing to capture her heart had been none other than the illustrious Sir Stephan du Bonne, a knight who had amassed a small fortune and a certain degree of fame by way of the tournament circuit. One eve in Stephan's arms had been enough to convince her.

Her gaze was upon him even now as he spoke kindly to the Lady Isobel and her portly husband. Stephan had ridden escort from nearly a half mile out, his powerful frame unmistakable atop his chestnut charger. Even after two years of marriage, Genisa's heart still fluttered wildly at the sight of him.

"Where do you s-suppose Ian and Lance are?" Summer burst into her sister-in-law's thoughts.

Genisa tore her gaze away from her husband's imposing form to glance disinterestedly about the surrounding area. "I do not know," she said truthfully. "They escorted the last party in, the both of them. I can hardly imagine that they would simply disappear when they know all of the guests have not yet arrived."

Summer snorted delicately, her full lips curving into a magnificent smile. "Knowing Ian, they have indeed disappeared. They are p-probably planning to wreak some sort of mischief upon the festivities."

"But this is Lance's celebration. Why would he jeopardize his own party?"

"Who can say?" Summer tossed her exquisite mane of honey-blond hair over one shoulder, stroking the ends absently. "Ever since Lance returned home, it has b-been the same story. Ian leads and Lance follows."

Genisa's gaze focused on her sister-in-law now that Stephan had vanished from view. Staring at the woman's exquisite profile, she thought back to the previous subject of conversation; she knew for certain that she was not the fairest maiden in the shire. From the moment she laid eyes upon her future husband's sister, she knew that she had been living in a fantasy world where she alone was the most beautiful object of worship in all of Dorset. There was another of greater glory.

Genisa learned that the du Bonnes had been harboring a great secret within the stone bosom of Chaldon Castle. The secret of a woman so beautiful, so magnificent, that she was kept sequestered from the outside world of mortals unworthy to gaze upon such loveliness. Her beauty was as fragile as porcelain; long, silken hair the color of honey and a sweet oval face with big, beautiful eyes of an amber-golden color. Delicately arched brows hovered over the thick-lashed gems as defined cheekbones tapered to a delicate chin and delectable mouth. In truth, Summer du Bonne was a treasure that remained hidden from the world.

Although Genisa had not lived that far from Chaldon, as her wealthy merchant father had owned a manse in Swanage, she had never once heard mention of a du Bonne daughter in possession of such unearthly beauty and was angered into a jealous fit by the unwelcome surprise. But that was until she attempted to speak with Stephan's young sister; then she became aware of the reasoning behind the careful shielding of the Lady Summer du Bonne. They did not hide Summer to horde her beauty – they hid her because she stuttered. It wasn't every time; mostly words that began with the letter B or F. But it was pronounced when she did it. Stephan and Ian and Lance tried to protect their baby sister from the reactions of a cruel world and Genisa labored to do the same. She, too, took up the fight to protect Summer.

Her thoughts moved away from her sister-in-law and back to the bailey below, now thinking of her husband's two younger brothers and their tendency for foolery. She responded belatedly to Summer's assertion.

"Stephan will have their hides if they do anything foolish today," she replied. "He and your father have endeavored to make this a successful day."

Summer shrugged, rising from her crouched position and moving across the battlement to the opposite side. Genisa followed and from their perch upon the wall, they could see beyond the fortress into the green countryside beyond.

"Look," Summer pointed into the distance. "Stephan is riding out to greet another party."

Genisa shielded her blue eyes from the brilliant sun. "I cannot see the standards from here. They're too far out."

Summer smiled faintly. "That should be the last of the guests. The tourney is scheduled to b-begin in two hours." Forgetting about the incoming party, her smile blossomed into a radiant gesture. "I have never seen a tourney, Nise. I can hardly stand the excitement!"

Genisa grinned. "It's a wonderful spectacle of arrogance and humiliation. I have seen Stephan compete in at least six."

"And he won every b-bout?"

"Every bout, as you well know. Stephan does not lose." Genisa grasped her sister-in-law by the hand, pulling her toward the portion of the battlement that straddled the portcullis. "We can see the incoming party better from here. If this is indeed the last group, then we must ready ourselves for the afternoon of competition."

"And f-food," Summer said eagerly. "I have b-been smelling roast beef all morn."

"Me, too," Genisa giggled, waving one of the tunic-clad men-at-arms away from the spot she wished to gaze from. The tournament field in the near distance was revealed, several of the guests having already established small tents about the perimeter, and the two women found their attention occupied by the colorful display of shelters. "Look at all of the tents, Summer. There must be hundreds."

Summer cocked a well-shaped eyebrow as she totaled the sea of tents. "I count eighteen. B-but we certainly may have one hundred before the day is through."

Unaware that she had been subtly corrected, Genisa continued to stare out over the bright turf as the flags of various houses were secured to the lodges. One hundred or eighteen was all the same to her; unlike her intelligent sister-in-law, Genisa could not read or write or calculate numbers. The fine arts of needlework and music and painting were all she had ever been required to learn.

Suddenly, her bright expression faded. When Summer glanced at her sister-in-law to say something to the woman, she noted the change in countenance.

"What's wrong?" she asked.

"There's the Kerry tent," she replied, indicating the fanciful shelter of yellow and white. "Good Heavens, I wish they hadn't been invited. I do not know why Stephan insisted on inviting Breck Kerry and his stupid brother."

Summer gazed at the brilliantly colored tarp, its towering standard snapping loudly in the breeze. "Isn't he the knight who b-broke Stephan's wrist last year?" she asked.

Genisa nodded grimly. "He's an unscrupulous knight. Stephan says his tactics are foul and questionable, but his peers tolerate him because his father was a great knight for King Richard the Lion Heart." Pensively, she sighed and leaned forward on the parapet. "I wish he hadn't come. I shall worry terribly about Stephan now."

Summer's gaze drifted over the other tents surrounding the tournament field, an area coming alive with guests and knights and ladies in fine clothing. "Stephan and F-father invited all of the knights on the circuit, men Stephan and Ian have competed against for several years. It would be unfair to invite some and not others for this celebration."

"I know, I know," Genisa sighed unhappily. "Still, I wish he had somehow managed to exclude Breck. I do not want him here."

Summer smiled, attempting to alleviate Genisa's fears. "Not to worry, darling," she said soothingly. "Stephan is the b-best knight on the circuit, is he not?"

Genisa shrugged carelessly, her chin in her hand as she leaned forward on the stone ledge. "So he says," she muttered. "I have only heard him mention a few others, men who give him steady competition. There is one knight I have heard him mention above all others, a man who… look there!" As usual, Genisa had difficulty maintaining her concentration for any length of time and she stabbed her finger into the air, pointing to the road that moved through the town and snaked towards the mighty fortress. "Look at all of the knights in that party. Five in all."

Summer studied the approaching party, beginning their ascent up the wide pebbled road towards Chaldon. She could see the five knights in immaculate armor, riding chargers that were heavy with battle armor. A collection of men-at-arms accompanied them, as well as a wagon, a few servants, and a tiny man riding a mule. Strangely, there were no women to attend the party and Summer found her interest strangely peaked by the all-male retinue.

"There aren't any ladies with them," she said to Genisa. "And look at the standard; black and silver and white. Good Lord, what sort of b-beast is that on the banner? I have never seen such an animal b-before."

Genisa shook her head, her blue eyes narrowed at the approaching group. "Stephan is riding escort," she murmured, attempting to decipher the beast emblazoned across the massive standard. "I have seen the banner before. But, for the life of me, I cannot remember who it belongs to."

"Someone great?"

Faintly, Genisa nodded. "Someone great, I am sure. But I am not sure…."

Her words were abruptly cleaved by a howling roar. Genisa and Summer screamed loudly with surprise and fear, turning in the direction of the harrowing cry. The battlements were practically devoid of soldiers; however, closing in on the ladies with malevolent intent were two armored bodies with the mask of a dead pig where a helmed head should have been.

As the ladies gaped with shock, the pig-masked assailants roared again, fingers clawing at the air. Not surprisingly, Summer and Genisa decided the battlement was no longer the ideal place to linger and they wisely scattered. Lance and Ian had made their appearance and the game was afoot.

Prank or not, there was no real pleasure in being captured by the pig-masked fiends; once, Ian had tickled Summer until she cried fat tears. Another time, Lance had hidden Genisa in a room in the castle and fed Stephan clues of her whereabouts until the enraged husband finally located his hysterical bride, sobbing and sick with apprehension. Stephan had punched Lance so hard that the man had tumbled down a small flight of stairs, cracking a rib.

Their father, Edward, had made weak attempts to curb the activities of his two younger sons after that, but their immature spirit would not be quashed. Even though they continued to harass their sister and sister-in-law with their pig-skin masks, the punishment should the women be captured was far less strenuous these days. Thanks to Stephan's threats, the next time Lance had entrapped Genisa, she had been released after he had forced her to kiss the pig-mask on the nose. And the last time Summer was captured, she had to endure three huge "freckles" made from soot. Mere child's play compared to the punishment their former imprisonment had entailed.

Still, the sight of the horrifying masks was enough to wreak terror into their hearts. In spite of the fact that they pretended to loathe the chase and subsequent capture, in truth, there was a great deal of fun in attempting to elude their antagonists. Even now, racing across the battlements with break-neck speed, there were more giggles than screams.

They made quite a quartet; Summer and Genisa shrieking at the top of their lungs, racing to reach the turret with the flight of stairs that would take them to the bailey, while Lance and Ian, when they should have very well been acting the proper hosts at their celebration, were intent to act like a pair of pre-pubescent boys. The grotesque pig-masks roared, the women screamed, the entire bailey could not help but be aware of the strange chase.

Unfortunately, the turret Summer and Genisa were striving for was blocked by several men-at-arms. Rather than wait for the men to disband and thereby risk capture, the women slithered along a particularly narrow bridge that linked the southern battlements to the western wall and proceeded to race madly for the northeast turret.

Behind them, Lance and Ian were growling like demons, spewing threats in a voice that would have made Lucifer proud. Summer and Genisa dodged around several soldiers, nearly shoving one man off the narrow walkway, but hardly bothering to stop and apologize. A shouted pardon sufficed.

The northeast turret was beckoning, the empty staircase inviting the tormented young ladies. As their pursuers roared and growled, the harried, if not somewhat giggly, young women made it to the gray-stoned turret. Descending the stairs much faster than they should have, they could hear the pig-masked molesters descending the stairs close on their tail.

Unfortunately, as they exited the turret into the upper bailey, a wall of horses and men materialized in front of them and the ladies were forced to skid to a halt. A brief moment of indecision was cut short as another unearthly roar reverberated off the stoned turret behind them. Summer and Genisa turned with horror to note that Lance and Ian were standing in the ground-floor doorway, fingers scratching the air in their general direction and preparing to close in for the capture.

Summer was so exhausted that she was no longer truly concerned with Genisa's well-being; with Stephan to protect her, the woman was better off than her less-defended sister-in-law. Even if Genisa was captured, the pig-men would simply let her go. Were they to catch Summer, however, the penalty would be considerably more brutal. Heels to the ground, Summer summoned the last of her strength and again took off running, but her flight was blocked when a massive figure appeared in her path, armored and more enormous than anything she had ever seen. Unfortunately, she was moving too fast to avoid a collision and with a grunt of pain, she slammed against the armored figure with a good deal of force. Stars danced before her eyes as her forehead came into contact with a breastplate of tempered steel.

As the world rocked unsteadily, she felt massive hands steady her. Oddly enough, Genisa's screaming had stopped and the roaring of the two pig-faced hunters was also gone. It was strangely silent. As Summer put a hand to her head in an attempt to halt the sickening sway, she caught the glimmer of a broadsword.

But not just any broadsword – it was the largest broadsword she had ever seen. Blinking her eyes as the spinning gradually slowed, she found herself staring into the breastplate that had assaulted her skull. Instinctively, her gaze trailed upward, moving across the upper arm and shoulder, scrutinizing a neck that was larger in circumference than her waist. Lodged atop the breastplate and mailed neck was the most fearsome helm she had ever had the misfortune to envision.

And it was looking at her.

CHAPTER TWO

T HE HELM LOOKED at Summer for a moment before focusing on her brothers. Then the broadsword came up, pointing in their direction.

"Remove the masks," the massive knight ordered, his voice rumbling and deep. "I would know who I am about to punish."

"I assure you that punishment is unnecessary," Stephan's voice penetrated Summer's dazed mind. "At least, not at the moment. Trust that I will deal with my brothers at the appropriate time."

The knight did not reply and the broadsword did not budge. Summer, her vision clearing as the pain in her head began to ease, craned her neck sharply to gain a better view of her savior. Through the helm and visor, she could not see his face and, not strangely, found herself curious about him.

There was a long pause as the knight pondered Stephan's words. When he spoke again, his voice was considerably less hostile.

"Ian and Lance," he said. "Forgive me. I should have recognized you in your natural state."

The small, anxious crowd burst into timid laughter. Even Summer managed a weak smile as the massive knight thrust the point of his broadsword forward, piercing the flesh of Lance's mask. With a swift up-parry, an extremely skilled move, the knight lifted the mask from Lance's head to reveal the sheepish expression beneath.

"My lord de Moray," he bowed slightly, slugging Ian when his brother failed to show the same respect. "We are honored by your presence."

Behind the lowered visor, Summer heard the knight sigh. "I have heard women refer to the two of you as pigs," he said, his bass-toned voice muffled behind the tempered steel. "I see that they were not wrong. And I am sure the hounded target currently under my protection is of the same opinion."

Ian, suddenly finding his voice, ripped off the pig mask and moved quickly to his sister, tearing the woman free of de Moray's grip.

"This is our sister, the Lady Summer du Bonne," he said, feeling humiliated for the chaos he and his brother had caused. "And the other lady is Stephan's wife, Lady Genisa."

Bose de Moray hardly heard a word beyond the mention of Summer's name; for the first time, he was able to catch a clear glimpse at the face of the woman he had saved and to say that the angels had granted her the essence of supreme beauty would have been a gross understatement. In truth, he hadn't seen her coming at first; he had been focused on other tasks and had not the time to allow something as common as a scream to attract his valuable attention.

But he regretted his decision not to pay attention. Only when she slammed against his chest had he been aware of her presence and even then, he was only able to sense her panic and his warrior instincts kicked in. The two pig-masked fiends had not been difficult to isolate and his sword was drawn even as he grasped the frenzied woman to steady her. Only now, as the situation became clear, was he able to comprehend her unearthly beauty.

For a moment, he was actually speechless. Her glorious radiance had managed to rob him of his tongue and he swallowed, attempting to regain the power of speech. Gazing upon the woman of porcelain cheeks and unusual golden eyes, he swore the longer he stared at her, the more his language skills threatened to dissolve completely.

"My lady," he sounded remarkably composed. "'Tis indeed a pleasure to make your acquaintance. I had no idea my foolish comrades even had a sister."

Her flawless cheeks mottled with a lovely blush. As a faint smile creased her lips, Bose was absolutely enchanted. But his haze of fascination was disturbed as Ian grasped Summer by the arm, forcibly escorting her away.

"If you will excuse us, my lord, my sister is feeling… fatigued," he said, casting Summer an expression that indicate she dare not disagree. "I will apologize for her clumsy manners, however. I do hope your armor was not scratched."

"She would not have been clumsy had you not been chasing her with your usual tact," Bose returned quietly, not at all pleased that Ian was removing her. "I will forgive her completely. But you are another matter."

With Summer clutched in his grip, Ian paused uncertainly and was preparing a calm, mayhap more placating reply, when Stephan laughed softly and interrupted the exchange.

"Ian fears you already, my lord," he said. "If you threaten him any further, he shall surely hide for the rest of the day and I need him on my team if I am to have a fighting chance against you in the tourney."

Bose continued to stare at Ian and his beautiful sister, gazing at the lady far more than her flushed brother. After a moment, he bobbed his head vaguely.

"The only chance you will have against me at the tourney is if your sister attends the games," his voice was calm. "Surely her beauty will distract me so that a mere knave will be able to best me."

Stephan chuckled again, passing a glance at his pink-cheeked sister. "She shall be there, my lord. I doubt all of the armies in England could keep her from attending her first tournament."

Before Bose could reply, Ian whisked Summer through the crowd and into the keep. Bose watched her mount the ramp into the fore building of the massive keep with a good deal of confusion, wondering why Ian had refused to allow her to respond to his greeting.

For whatever the reason, Bose found himself unexpectedly preoccupied by the brief vision of the lovely Lady Summer. Even when his men began dismantling the troops in preparation for erecting their encampment near the tournament field, Bose was distracted. Stephan, having other duties to attend to, excused himself and his wife with an additional apology on his family's behalf.

But Bose was barely aware of the departure of his host. His mind was still fixated on the image of the golden-eyed maiden, so much so that he hardly heard the familiar voice at his side.

"Farl and Adgar have proceeded to the field to establish our perimeter," the armor-clad knight informed his lord. "Artur went with them and took the horses."

"And Morgan?"

The warrior shook his head. "He's still having trouble with his charger. He's taken the horse directly to the field in an attempt to lessen the swelling of his fetlock."

Bose sighed heavily, forcing himself to abandon thoughts of the du Bonne sister. "No wonder the steed is lame," he mumbled. "He is as old as Morgan is."

Turning for the portal that led from the bailey, they headed toward the gaily decorated field below. A du Bonne servant clad in red and white escorted them from the courtyard, a man assigned to the de Moray party to answer any questions or service any needs. But Bose ignored the hovering servant as he and his companion strolled down the embankment toward the tournament arena.

"God's Beard," Bose muttered as he neared the cluster of bright tents. "The Kerrys are here."

"So I noticed. Did not you see their colors as we rode in?"

Bose shook his head. "Nay, but I certainly should have," he sighed heavily, raising his visor to release the steaming heat saturating his heavily-lined helm. "Tate, I demand you burn their tent to the ground and all occupants within it. I have no desire to go against Breck Kerry this day."

Tate Farnum, young and arrogant with a beautiful crown of auburn hair and milky skin that would have made a woman proud, snorted humorously. "What you mean to say is that you do not wish to compete against Asa Kerry's son."

"Asa and I served together under Hubert de Burgh," Bose said. "Of course I do not want to compete against his spoiled, pimple-faced son. The boy is a menace to the honorable knights competing on the tournament circuit with his unscrupulous tactics and barbaric methods."

Tate nodded faintly, gazing at the bright yellow and white tent. "He broke Stephan du Bonne's wrist last year. Truthfully, I am surprised to see him here at all."

Bose's onyx-black eyes studied the elaborate shelter and waving banners, announcing to the world that the House of Kerry was present. From the subject of Breck Kerry one moment to Stephan du Bonne the next, Bose was reminded again of the delicious Lady Summer. Since it was apparently futile to forget the woman, he struggled to appear casual as he spoke of her.

"What do you know of Stephan's sister?" he asked nonchalantly. "I did not even know the du Bonne brothers had a sister."

Tate liked to believe himself well informed about everything; sometimes, in fact, his hunger for gossip exceeded that of the most curious woman and Bose was constantly chiding him for the fact. But in a situation such as this, it might actually prove useful if he had heard anything about the fair Lady Summer.

"This is the first I have seen of the girl," Tate replied. "But a beauty, to be sure; no wonder the du Bonnes have been hiding her."

Moving into the cluster of tents with their du Bonne servant in tow, the area was alive with squires and soldiers, milling about in orderly chaos as they went about their duties in anticipation for the approaching tournament. Bose ignored the rabble for the most part, his mind still focused on the subject of conversation as he and Tate made their way toward the half-pitched black and white tent well removed from the cluster of shelters.

"How old do you suppose she is?" Bose asked, realizing with dismay that he sounded eager to know.

Tate sensed the curiosity and cast his liege a long glance. "God's Blood, Bose. Do I detect a hint of genuine interest in the woman?"

Immediately on-guard with Tate's knowing query, Bose averted his gaze stubbornly. "Answer the damn question. How old is she?"

Tate grinned; he had served the mighty Bose de Moray for six years, becoming acquainted with a man of little emotion and even less sentiment. He had found service with the dark knight during Bose's years as Captain of the King's Household Guard and had subsequently chosen to follow his superior officer when the man resigned his post shortly after the death of his beloved wife.

The Bose de Moray he had come to know before the passing of the Lady Lora had been a hard man to please, fair and intelligent and incredibly skilled. And even though the man had a face of stone, revealing little of his thoughts and earning the reputation as a man who had not yet learned to smile, still, there was compassion behind the coal-black eyes. But Tate, and others, believed that compassion had disappeared the very moment Bose's wife had perished in childbirth.

Tate had seen the last of his liege's compassion four years ago. From that moment on, it was as if Lora's death had stolen something away from him. The resulting individual spared little time for rest or humor, seemingly possessed to keep on the constant move. Tournaments, competitions, any sort of game that required skill and rewarded money, Bose would find himself a part of. It was as if he had to keep moving, fearful that if he stopped the grief that was following him would catch up.

So he kept running. Tate ran with him, too, as did three other knights who had served Bose when he was Captain of the King's Guard. Men who were more loyal to de Moray than to young King Henry considered it an honor to continue to serve a knight who seemed determined to forget about his past.

"Who is to say?" Tate finally replied. "I would wager to guess that she is no more than twenty years at the most. Far too young for you."

Bose didn't reply as they neared his tent. Just as they closed in on the structure, a large knight with a bushy red mustache raised a massive standard of black, white and silver, announcing that the House of de

Moray had arrived. As Tate continued to eye Bose in anticipation of a reply to his taunting statement, his liege seemed intent to ignore him.

"Farl," Bose boomed. "Make sure my charger's shoes are checked. He was moving strangely, as if a shoe was loose."

The burly knight nodded faintly. "Your squire has taken the beast to Artur, who is examining him as we speak," he replied. "They are under the large gnarled oak near the small ravine to the west."

Bose glanced over his shoulder in the indicated direction, noting the aged oak in the distance and several forms clustered beneath its heavy branches. With a faint nod, he shifted his attention and moved away from Tate to inspect the lashings of his large tent. But the auburn-haired knight followed on his heels; Bose could feel the man behind him, his smirking grin igniting a blaze of annoyance. After testing one of the iron stakes himself, he turned to his smug subordinate.

"Do not you have tasks requiring your attention?" he growled.

Tate shrugged lazily. "A few that can be taken care of in a matter of minutes. I'd much rather talk about the Lady Summer."

Jaw ticking, Bose turned away from his knight and focused on the tent once more. "If you value your life, you will vacate my presence."

Snorting, Tate took a step back but did not depart as ordered. "Come now, Bose," he clucked softly. "If you wish me to find out something about the woman, then all you need do is ask. There is no one better at discerning information than I."

A ticking jaw was now joined by grinding teeth as Bose moved along the tent, inspecting the tarp as Tate lingered several feet away.

"There is nothing more I wish to know," he said as steadily as he could manage. "Go and see to my charger. And send Artur to me when he is finished."

Corners of his mouth still twitching, Tate did as he was told. He knew that Bose's patience was not limitless. Any more lingering on the part of the young knight and he would surely find himself bruised. But he knew, even as he moved away from the black and white tent, that he would seek Bose's answers even if the man was too stubborn to ask his assistance.

Listening to Tate's fading footfalls, Bose knew all too well that the young knight would seek answers to his questions. He would have been a fool to believe otherwise, and a part of him was glad for the inquisitive nature of Tate Farnum. But another part of him was embarrassed for wanting to know about Lady Summer at all.

With a grunt of frustration, Bose began to unpack several of the satchels lining the tent. A small cherrywood table emerged from a large box, as did two collapsible chairs. The more he worked, the clearer his mind became as thoughts of his lovely acquaintance faded from focus and soon he was joined by three male servants who had been procuring food for the nooning meal.

The smell of roast beef was enough to make him forget his troubles entirely as he delved into a trencher of the succulent meat. As the servants unpacked the remainder of the boxes, Bose devoured a huge plate of beef and carrots. He had barely finished mopping up the gravy with a thick slab of bread when the tent flap was abruptly ruffled by a familiar figure.

"I see you waited for me," came the droll salutation. "Good Lord, man, you ate everything but the table."

Bose nodded, his mouth full. "And that is in jeopardy as well."

The knight chuckled softly as he entered the tent, depositing a satchel of personal items against the wall. As the man fumbled about in the leather sack, Bose wiped his mouth against a linen square and eyed his crouched companion.

"He's in there, somewhere. I put him in there myself."

The knight nodded, almost irritably. "Good Lord, that rat has nested in here. I will never get him out."

Swallowing the last of his meal, Bose quaffed deeply from his wooden cup. "Antony is *not* a rat. He is a ferret and far more valuable to me than you are, my aged friend."

The knight shook his head; although Bose had meant the words in jest, they were true. Nothing meant more to the man than his dead wife's spoiled little pet. The small beast was the sole focus of his liege's guarded affection, having kept the fuzzy creature close to his heart since the day of Lora's passing. Certainly, the warrior could hardly fault his lord the lone sentimental attachment.

"His droppings are all over my bag," the knight moaned, his searching hand finally coming to rest on the article of his search. With a squeak, Antony revealed himself from the warm hovel of the older warrior's bag and found himself deposited on his master's lap.

In a rare flash of gentleness, Bose stroked the gray and white ferret. "Greetings, my pooping friend." As the little animal snaked its way up Bose's torso, perching comfortably on his shoulder, Bose held out a small green apple for the beast's approval. "Your dinner, Antony. And eat neatly, if you would. I'll not have apple peel all over my mail."

Having shaken out his satchel of animal waste, the older knight once again pushed the satchel against the shelter wall and made his way to the table. As he drew himself the other collapsible chair, a servant entered the tarp with a full trencher of food. Placing it before the knight, the servant moved to the opposite end of the large shelter and began setting out the furs and bedding.

"Give Antony a piece of bread, Morgan," Bose said as he listened to the hearty crunch of apple in his ear. "I have none to give him."

Morgan Skye cocked a graying eyebrow, dutifully handing over a thick crust. Nearing the ripe age of forty years, he had seen nearly twenty years of service within the crown's ranks. As athletic and spry as men half his years, he continued to compete in tournaments and games when other men his age were well removed from the physical strains of life. When he should have been anticipating the winter of his life, Morgan served as an inspiration to others who considered retiring because of their advancing years.

"Good Lord," he hissed as Bose stole a carrot off his plate. "Get that hairy rat his own trencher and leave mine alone."

Bose repressed a smile as his furry friend devoured the carrot. "Antony loves you, Morgan. How can you be so selfish?"

"Easily. I do not take kindly to an alleged friend defecating all over my baggage."

"What did you expect? He's been sealed within your satchel for hours."

Morgan swallowed his substantial bite, eyeing Bose as he drank deeply of the medium-bodied ale. "Next time, the rat can ride in your possessions. I refuse to carry him any longer."

Bose cocked an eyebrow, the glimmer of mirth in his eyes fading. "My bags are always too full."

Morgan shook his head. "That is a lie and you know it. You insist that the rat ride within my possessions because you are terrified someone will discover your weakness for this hairy beast. It is much easier to explain my attachment to such a pet due to my age or some other sort of nonsense. Who would ever believe the great Bose de Moray capable of fondness for a ferret?"

Bose scratched Antony's nose with massive fingers, his black eyes glittering across the dim tent. "I am not ashamed of Antony."

Again, Morgan shook his head. How many times had they shared this conversation? "Nay, you are not ashamed of the bearded rat. But you are ashamed that a mighty warrior of your station should be firmly committed to a foolish little animal. Why not admit the truth, Bose? No one would fault you for your attachment to your deceased wife's pet."

Bose looked away, his black eyes pondering the dim surrounding of the black and white tent. In the far corner, the servant raised a small flap for ventilation and illumination, but Bose ordered the man to seal the breach. He had a difficult enough time keeping his ferret protected from the world without the additional exposure of an open window.

"What about your charger?" Bose's voice was subdued as he changed the subject. He did not want to argue about the only bit of tenderness within his dark life. "Is the beast lame?"

Morgan mopped his trencher with a piece of bread. "He's got a genuine strain, but I would not go so far as to say that he is lame. Artur has made a healing mash and has the leg securely wrapped. I suppose time will tell."

As Antony crawled about his master's neck, his beady eyes glittering in the faint illumination, Bose poured himself more ale. "Will you avoid the joust altogether and simply concentrate on the melee?"

Morgan nodded, consuming the last of his meal as the faint rumble of commotion of the tournament field grew louder. "One fool with a misaimed blow and my charger would be ruined for good."

Bose digested the statement, bobbing his head in agreement. "I shall miss you, then. But we will be unbeatable in the melee."

Morgan drained the remaining ale from his cup. "Against Breck Kerry?"

"Against them all. We will be invincible this day."

"Even against Lance du Bonne? It is, after all, his day of celebration. Mayhap you should allow the lad to win, just this once."

Bose stared at Morgan a moment; the mere mention of the du Bonne name had been enough to remind him of the elusive du Bonne maiden and, once again, he found himself recollecting her radiant visage.

"Did you know the du Bonne brothers have a sister?" he asked casually, stroking Antony's fur when the animal scampered down his arm.

Rising from the collapsible chair, Morgan grunted as he stretched his tautly-muscled body. "Nay, I had no such knowledge," he cast a glance as he twisted from side to side. "What about her?"

Bose shrugged, laboring to appear blasé in manner. "Nothing, I suppose," he said. "I met her today when we entered the gates. Lance and Ian were chasing her about with pig-masks over their faces, creating a deplorable spectacle. Were I Edward du Bonne, I would lock the lads in the vault for a week or so. That would do enough to age their juvenile spirits."

Morgan snorted at the mental vision of Lance and Ian du Bonne with pig-masks over their faces. "Good Lord, what an exhibition. Were those two not such excellent fighters, I would consider them most useless."

"Useless indeed."

Since Morgan had no helpful knowledge regarding the enigmatic Summer du Bonne, Bose let the subject rest for the moment. Moreover, the melee was rapidly approaching and he needed his focus to prepare for the rough and glorious event. Not strangely, however, it was difficult to force her from his mind as he went about the necessary tasks. It seemed that with every subsequent recollection, it became more and more difficult to rid himself of her consuming memory. God's Beard, he had scarcely met the woman and already he was unable to forget her. But forget he must if he was going to be of any use in the melee and subsequent joust... until he remembered she would be in attendance.

Oddly enough, his words to Stephan came back to haunt him. *The only chance you will have against me at the tourney is if your sister attends the games. Surely her beauty will distract me so terribly that a mere knave will be able to best me.*

He realized it was the truth.

CHAPTER THREE

"COME ALONG, SUMMER," Genisa's squeaky voice was crisp. "The du Bonne men will not wait for us. If we are late, they shall simply leave us behind."

Hovering before a long mirror made of rare polished glass, Summer stroked her honey-blond hair with a heavy horse-bristle brush. Using her hands, she curved the lengthy ends into fat curls, knowing the waves would not remain so entirely tame throughout the day's activities and wondering why she was attempting to make the well-groomed effort.

But it was a joyful effort nonetheless, considering the event of her very first tournament was less than an hour away. Her excitement was thrilling and debilitating at the same time, and she fought to contain both nerves and nausea.

"Summer, what are you staring at? We are going to be late!" Frustrated that her pleas were going ignored, Genisa endeavored to relay the seriousness of the situation. Clad in a gown of ice-blue with her pale blond hair properly secured in a bejeweled net, she looked ravishing. "Certainly, if you brush your hair any more, you are going to pull yourself bald. Put the brush aside. We are expected."

The brush stopped in mid-stroke as Summer continued to gaze at herself, half-listening to Genisa's demands and half-ignoring them. Tardy or no, what mattered most at the moment was her outward appearance and she would not proceed before properly and precisely prepared. As Genisa prodded and pleaded, a soft knock echoed against the chamber door.

"You see?" Genisa raised her hands in the air in a beseeching gesture as she moved for the oak panel. "That is Stephan and he shall the feminine chamber.

"We are waiting to escort you to the field, lad
sister still poised before the mirror. "Are you reac

Genisa looked to Summer, a golden godde
When the woman refused to answer, she sig
darling, we are ready. Aren't we, Summer?"

After a moment's reluctance, Summer nodde
a table beside her. Clutching a delicately embroi
stave off the unseasonable warmth, she smiled bra

"Aye Stephan. We are ready."

He smiled faintly, offering one elbow to his
his wife. Escorting the ladies down the smoke-st
descended the wide stairs into the stone-walle
dismounted the last stair, a rotund, cumbersome
the shadows in a harried burst of fine silks and wo

"Great Gods, ladies," he exclaimed. "The gam
begin."

Summer forced a smile at the ruddy man, hi
of hers. Releasing her brother's elbow, she claime
in a reassuring gesture. "Calm yourself, Father,"
cannot b-begin without you."

In spite of his agitation, Edward du Bonne co
at his youngest child. The beautiful girl his wife h
to, a child so delicate and lovely that he had st
straight days after her birth in awe and won
completely unexpected after three healthy boys,
no feminine names for such an occurrence had be

Edward's wife had been positive that her fo
After all, there was little doubt since the three p

had resulted in a herd of strong du Bonne sons. Therefore, on a warm summer's eve eighteen years ago, Edward had been faced with a most pressing decision. Beyond the grief of losing his wife, he was forced to select a name for the unexpected female offspring who had claimed her mother's existence.

The baron, unfortunately, was not a clever or particularly attentive man and he lacked the concern to name his new daughter. Giving the child over to a female servant and her spinster daughter, he delegated them the task of naming and caring for his newest, if not particularly wanted, child. The two aging women, unable to think of a properly suitable name and fearful of displeasing the temperamental baron with a less than appropriate selection, made the most convenient, if not logical, selection; Summer Evening du Bonne.

A name, in fact, that was perfect for her. She was as warm and beautiful as the summer months, soft and fresh and radiant. Even now as the earl gazed into dark golden orbs, he could scarcely recall ever seeing a finer creature. It was a cruel twist of fate that her beauty was marred by a disturbing speech impediment, for she would have made a very fine marriage match for the du Bonne family. Edward had resigned himself to the fact that his beautiful daughter would never know the experience of a decent marriage, and for that he was truly sorry.

The day was warming as the damp sea breeze caressed the dusty grounds of Chaldon as Edward, Summer, Stephan and Genisa quit the dark-stoned bastion and made their way outside. Summer's hair whipped about her and she struggled to keep it at bay, knowing the over-brushed curls were vanished and wishing she was married if only so she would have been able to net the unruly mass as Genisa did. As a maiden, however, it was customary to keep one's head uncovered to show the beauty of a maiden's hair.

As the small party neared the edge of the bailey, the tournament field came into focus and Summer forgot all about her misbehaving hair. Her focus was completely on the distant cluster of colorful tents, the faint hum of the crowd, and the thunder of the chargers as knights took in a few bouts of last-minute practice.

Somewhere in the distance, a lute and lyre could be heard entertaining the throng and Summer was about to comment on the beauty of the song when a great black banner caught her attention. It was the same black banner that had saved her from a pig-masked fate. She turned to Stephan.

"Is that de Moray's b-banner?" she asked.

Distracted from a game of slap-and-tickle with his wife, Stephan passed a glance at the towering standard. "Aye," he replied, casting his sister a curious glance. "How did you know his name?"

Summer pursed her lips wryly. "Good Heavens, Stephan, you spoke the man's name and it was only obvious that I should hear you," turning from her brother, she once again eyed the flapping colors. "Who is he?"

Stephan took a contemplative breath, adjusting his pinching helm. "God's Beard, where to begin? What is it you wish to know?"

She cocked her head thoughtfully. "Everything. For example, do you know how he acquired his unusual name?"

Stephan shrugged. "Mayhap it is an old, well-used family name."

"B-Bose," Summer repeated softly, drawing out the long "o" until the name sounded like "Bow-z". "Where does he come from?"

"He has a keep outside of Salisbury called Ravendark, and he's been on the tournament circuit for four years," finding a comfortable position for his helm, Stephan once again glanced to the foreboding standard. "Until he joined our ranks, my competition was limited. Now I am lucky if I run a close second to de Moray's talents."

Strangely, Summer felt a good deal of pleasure at that statement. Her brother was praising the man who had saved her from certain torment and she smiled faintly, feeling oddly attached to the fearsome black banner. "What is that on his standard? I do not recognize the s-symbol."

Stephan, disinterested in speaking of a man he would very shortly be competing against, kissed his wife's hand fondly before lowering his visor. "'Tis a Gorgon."

"A Gorgon?"

"Aye," Stephan's voice was muffled behind the steel protection. "They call de Moray the Gorgon because he is massive and dark and ugly. Therefore, the term has become his crest."

Summer's brow furrowed. "I b-believe I have heard of a Gorgon. Isn't that a demon?"

Stephan nodded. "Greek demons. Oddly enough, however, they are female, but the very name means 'dreadful', which describes de Moray perfectly."

Summer's smile faded as she looked to her brother. Somehow, in calling de Moray ugly, it was inferring that he was imperfect. Flawed. Just like she was, in a sense – her imperfect speech against his imperfect looks. But having never seen the man's face through his lowered visor, she had no way of disputing Stephan's claim. After a moment, she turned away and refocused her attention on the field before her.

"How cruel," she murmured. "You should not taunt him for his lack of b-beauty."

Stephan snorted, catching a glimpse of his charger near the small tent bearing the red and white du Bonne colors. "You have yet to see the man, Summer. Just because he saved you from Ian and Lance's foolery, do not permit yourself to have any romantic notions regarding his magnificent knightly appearance. In spite of that fact and other nasty rumors regarding his reputation, he has no shortage of admirers."

Feeling somewhat defensive on the knight's behalf, Summer frowned at her arrogant brother. "Rumors that are lies, I am sure. Sir B-bose is noble and chivalrous, unlike several other knights I know who shall remain nameless. Women are able to sense good within a man regardless of his physical appearance."

"That is not the reason, my ingenuous little sister," Stephan said patronizingly, waving to his squire to let the boy know he was on the approach. "The women who pursue de Moray are simply interested in his wealth and nothing more. With all the winnings he has acquired over the four years of tournament play, he is amply loaded with the stuff and the wealth alone is enough to outweigh the darker implications of his name."

Bidding his family a distracted farewell, Summer watched her brother stroll across the trampled grass, pondering his words. As Genisa moved to Edward's free arm, Summer obeyed her father's insistence that they proceed to the tournament field. After all, the games could not begin without the attendance of the illustrious castle Constable and already they were a half-hour truant.

Let the games begin.

CB

"VERY WELL, BOSE. Ask me any question about the Lady Summer. I can tell you anything you wish to know."

Bose did not look up as he assisted his squire in latching the last of his chest protection. And he furthermore did not look to his confident friend as the young squire finished the final fastens about his massive neck, straightening the mailed hood underneath the plate steel. Only when the lad moved away to collect his master's gauntlets did Bose fix his onyx-black eyes upon the smug, entirely annoying knight.

"I told you that I did not want to know anything else about her. There is no need."

By the corner of the tent, Morgan looked up from repairing his well-used scabbard. The end of the aged leather was fraying and he was distraught with worry; however, his fret did not prevent him from overhearing Tate's thoroughly self-satisfied statement.

"Who is Lady Summer?"

"No one," Bose grumbled.

"A certain lady who seems to have captured our illustrious leader's attention," Tate supplied with restrained humor as Bose looked away, fumbling with the gloves offered by the squire. "Although he refuses to admit anything, I am quite confident that he has a moderate interest in her. Am I incorrect, my lord?"

Bose maintained his silence as Morgan rose from his corner seat, his brown eyes wide with genuine surprise. "God's Blood, Bose. Is this true? Have you finally found interest in a woman?"

Yanking on a glove in a distinct exhibition of annoyance, Bose's black eyes blazed with threat and hazard. "Not in the least. And if Tate isn't careful, he shall find himself impaled in the melee by my very own weapon. Do I make myself clear, Farnum?"

Much to Bose's aggravation, Tate merely snorted humorously to the deadly threat and turned his attention to a still-surprised Morgan. "You should see her, old man. As beautiful as when the world was new," spacing his hands a foot or so apart, he outlined an obvious female figure. "And her form is in fine shape. Fine, fine shape. My God, I do believe I would have her myself had our liege not expressed interest first."

Morgan stared at the snickering young knight, hardly believing what he had heard. To declare that the omnipotent, focused Bose de Moray was interested in a woman was beyond his scope of comprehension. A smile of hope creased his lips. "Who is she?"

Casting Bose a long glance from the corner of his eye to make sure the man was paying attention, Tate crossed his arms smugly. "She is the Lady Summer du Bonne, a mere eighteen years old one week ago today. She is unmarried, unpledged, and unattached. And from what I have been able to discover, something of a hermit. Her father keeps her under constant isolation for reasons I have been unable to ascertain."

Although his manner indicated a lack of interest, Bose was nonetheless listening carefully to Tate's information. As his squire secured his remaining gauntlet, he struggled between the instinct to demand more of Tate's knowledge on the woman and the urge to deny the situation. Bewildered and confused, for the moment, denying his interest was the only manner of self-preservation he could think of...at least, until he could come to better understand the chaos for himself.

"I am not surprised to discover you been wasting your time in pursuit of useless knowledge when there is a tournament to be had."

Determined to move from the subject, he gestured sharply to Morgan. "Did you finish repairing your scabbard? And what about your horse? Have you checked on the animal since Artur wrapped his leg?"

Morgan's gaze was even at his brusque lord; since it was rare that Bose display any emotion whatsoever, he was able to deduce by his sharp mannerisms that Tate's ramblings held a measure of truth. But how much truth? If for no other reason than to satisfy his curiosity, Morgan was determined to find out.

"Whether I tend the beast now or at tournament time will be of little difference in how correctly the leg has healed. Clearly, I have done all I can," turning to Tate, he met the man's twinkling eyes. "Is that all you discovered about the Lady Summer? What of her schooling, her beau?"

Tate shook his head, struggling not to look at Bose as he spoke. "Apparently, she did not leave home to foster and from what I have been told, she has not entertained a single suitor. Most strange, considering the woman is lovelier than any female I have yet to witness."

Morgan cocked an eyebrow. "Lavish praise coming from a man who had known his share of feminine companionship," he said. "But I do believe your clues are obvious – there must be something wrong with the woman. Mayhap beneath the beauty and grace, she harbors the temperament of a shrew."

Tate sensed the game, taking the lead. "God be merciful, I should have realized. 'Tis the only explanation. Mayhap… mayhap she harbors a hideous defect. Like a third leg hidden beneath her gown, or a chest carpeted with hair."

Morgan made a distasteful face. "Good Lord, I can hardly imagine running my lips over breasts as hairy as mine," suddenly, his unpleasant expression turned to one of overstated dismay, his eyes bulging with mock horror. "What… what if she is not a woman at all? What if she is truly a man, merely dressing as a woman?"

"An incubus!"

"A demon!"

"A sorceress! Good Lord, a sorcer*er*!"

"A…!"

"Enough!" Bose finally roared, out of character for his normally restrained disposition. Turning away from the sword he had been fumbling with, his dark face was lined with irritation. "I have heard enough from the two of you. No more talk of hairy chests or men wearing women's clothing. And I do not want to hear another word regarding Summer du Bonne. Do you comprehend?"

Unable to keep the smile from his lips, Morgan snickered softly and clapped a companionable hand on Bose's shoulder before returning to his own equipment. "Indeed, my lord. Not another word."

Bose's black eyes were piercing as the older knight continued to snort disrespectfully. "I do not jest, Morgan. Not another word."

Morgan eyed the man, nodding his head with earnest agreement. "I indicated that I understood, Bose. There is no need for threats."

"Aye, there is. You are pushing me to the brink and should be amply forewarned."

"I have done nothing of the kind. What has happened to your sense of humor?"

Bose continued to stare at the man long and hard a moment before turning away. "It is intact given the proper circumstances, and considering we have a competition in fifteen minutes, I hardly find your amusement valid." He lifted his arms as his squire secured his scabbard for the melee, long and free and at the ready, as he cast a final glance at his two comrades. "Tate, get mounted. Morgan, if you are not going to compete, you and Artur discover from the heralds who is to be on our team for the melee. I would know these fools who intend to ride upon my glory."

With a smirk, Morgan quit the tent. Tate maintained his position a moment longer, wondering if Bose intended to press him for more information regarding the fair Lady Summer without Morgan's presence. Even though he was well aware that Morgan was Bose's closest friend, still, it would somehow be easier to discuss the lady between two men rather than three.

But Bose apparently had no intention of pressing the issue further and Tate wisely left the tent, heading for the gnarled oak where his squire had prepared his charger. Bose's massive beast was prepared as well, muzzled to prevent him from attacking his handlers.

As Tate mounted, making sure the banner decorating his horse's body was properly secured beneath the armored tack, he wondered if he shouldn't attempt to ascertain more about the young maiden who had captured Bose's eye. The further his lord denied such interest, the more Tate knew the fair lady had indeed succeeded in snaring the man's attention.

The silver peals of the trumpet could be heard, calling all spectators to the lodges and announcing to the competitors that the event was about to commence. Forcing thoughts of Bose's lady aside for the moment, Tate straightened the decorative plume atop his helm and reined his charger toward the arena, his excitement mounting. He knew that Bose's remaining two knights would already be at the field, awaiting his company. And with all of the houses preparing to combat in honor of Lance du Bonne, the day would prove to be exciting and profitable.

Tate looked forward to certain victory. With Bose de Moray on his team, there was no question.

CB

COLORFUL KNIGHTS OF every house were lining up on opposite sides of the tournament field, emblazoned with standards and fancy armor and brilliantly-colored lances. Seated between Genisa and her father, Summer was overwhelmed with the sight and spectacle before her. Never in her life had she seen so many knights, all lavishly dressed as if they were preparing to attend a feast rather than a battle.

Magnificent shields were lodged over the left knee of each knight, positioned for ease and access. War implements crowded the armored saddles; swords, axes, maces, flails and war hammers gleamed wickedly under the brilliant afternoon sun. The horses themselves were covered with beautiful banners embossed with the colors of their knight and, in some cases, his crest.

As two teams prepared for the coming melee, Summer scrutinized every knight who happened to thunder past the lodges, or every warrior who seemed to be gaining a bit of practice before the competition began. She was wide-eyed with wonder.

"Do you see that your father's heralds have divided the knights into two teams?" Genisa was saying. "The two teams will charge one another and fight until only one man is left. That is why they call it the melee."

"It is quite a brutal spectacle, Summer," Edward's high-pitched voice was an annoying buzz over the excitement of the crowd. "Certainly, there are codes the knights must adhere to; they must not intentionally try to kill their opponent, and they must not strike a man when he is down. Once a knight is off his horse, he is out of the competition. The object, of course, is to remain mounted and try to keep your head on in the process."

Summer knew all that; she had heard her brothers explain tournament rules a thousand times. On her other side, Genisa piped up again.

"The team that loses becomes the prisoners of the victors and must pay them ransom," she said. "That is how the knights make their money."

"Or lose it," Summer responded dryly.

Genisa giggled, nodded. "Stephan lost a good deal last year at the tournament in Swindon. Not only was he on the losing team in the melee, but he lost to Bose de Moray in the joust as well. He was so angry with the money he lost that he cursed de Moray for an entire week."

Summer smiled, her thoughts once again turning to the mysterious knight who had saved her from her brothers' foolery. Glancing to the east side of the field, her golden eyes searched for the black and white standard she knew to be de Moray's. But there was no black and white on that team, only innumerable brilliantly sewn hues, including those of the du Bonne red and white.

Shifting her attention then to the west side of the arena, the distinctive black and white standard of the House of de Moray was evident. An odd, fluid warmth pulsed through her veins as she drew deep the sight of the striking banners; with all of the scrutinizing she had been doing of every man and beast within the confines of the field, she wondered how she could have missed the de Moray colors.

It began to occur to her that her brothers and de Moray were on opposite teams. Pondering the dilemma, Summer's attention was drawn to the perimeter of the field opposite the lodges. Even with the multitude of men and horses milling about, the squires and stable hands and grooms and servants scurrying to and fro, still, she found herself drawn to a particular figure making his way toward the eastern siege line.

"Look, Summer!" Genisa's high-pitched voice startled her. "There is Sir Bose. See him? Over there, on the massive black charger."

If only to quiet the woman, Summer nodded her head sharply. But Genisa, too, seemed to be entranced with de Moray's appearance and she poked a finger in his direction.

"He is hardly wearing any trappings, as the other knights do," she said. "No plumes or fanciful helms. Only his banner across his charger's haunches. In every competition I have ever seen him in, his dress is always the same. He is much more understated than the rest."

"Mayhap he doesn't wish to draw attention to himself," Summer said quietly, her heart thumping against her ribs with the thrill of seeing de Moray. "He seemed rather understated today, when we met."

Genisa shrugged, reclining against the cushioned chair. "I have never met him before, to be truthful, nor heard much about him. Today was the first Stephan has truly spoken in depth of him."

Mercifully, the woman quieted herself and Summer was permitted to gaze openly at the distant knight uninterrupted. She observed every fluid motion of his massive arms, bringing about his shield emblazoned with the mighty Gorgon crest and poising it over his left knee. There were three other knights from his house competing on his team, and the men seemed to swarm about him when they noticed his presence. A little man on the ground handed him his lance and he collected it easily, a great black and white spiral pole.

Summer watched, enthralled by the only knight she had ever met aside from her brothers, until Genisa once again screeched in her ear.

"Summer!" she burst. "Look; the herald is taking the field. The game is about to commence."

Rubbing her ear where Genisa had nearly punctured the drum, Summer noted that indeed the herald was taking the field. On her left side, Edward leaned close.

"See the sword in the man's hand?" he gestured to the red and white clad servant. "That is my sword. Grandfather fought on the Lion Heart's crusade with that weapon."

Summer recognized the sword; it held a decorative place of honor above the massive hearth in the main hall. Edward, sensing his daughter's excitement, took her hand and squeezed it tightly in an extremely rare show of encouragement. In spite of the surprise of the uncommon display, Summer gripped her father's hand with natural ease, smiling happily at him as the herald demanded readiness from the opposing sides. All visors went down in varying order in answer to the herald's demand, indicative of the combatant's state of preparedness. As several other heralds positioned themselves about the arena in preparation for refereeing the event, the primary herald held the sword high.

"In the king's name, do your battle!"

The sword came down. With a roar that made Summer's hair stand on end, dozens of lances came down from their upright positions and hovered parallel to the ground, pointing menacingly at the men on the opposite side of the field. The thunder of chargers filled the air as spurs dug deep into the sides of the beasts, urging them on to victory. Great clumps of earth were kicked up by the excited steeds, pelting the spectators who happened to be standing too close.

Summer hadn't realized she had let out a small cry as the opposing waves of knights crashed into one another in a great roar of flesh and metal. Poles snapped, sending colored pieces of wood hurling into the air as the grunts and shouts of men in mock-battle penetrated the damp sea air. A few men were felled in the initial clash before they had scarcely had a chance to fight and the crowd in the lodges went mad with glee and terror.

Summer continued to observe as flails sang through the air, pummeling unfortunate opponents with their spikes and weight. The echoes of heavy broadswords filled the air as knights did battle against one another, sharpening their combat skills and showing off for the crowd. Already, chargers were going over on their sides and Summer gasped as brave young squires rushed out to the field to assist their fallen masters.

"The b-boys will be killed!" she insisted to her father, as if he hadn't noticed the actions of the foolish young lads. "Make them stay away until this is finished!"

His expression was intolerant. "Summer, 'tis their duty to remove their fallen masters from the field. Otherwise, the men would be trampled under the feet of others."

Distressed, Summer returned her apprehensive gaze to the field, watching as a strong young squire dragged his armored liege from the battle. But the man's charger, still on the ground in the midst of the chaos, was too injured to rise and Summer came to the conclusion that the melee wasn't exciting any longer. It was brutal, barbaric, and reckless.

The thrill of her first tournament began to fade as she watched several more men go down, one of them bearing de Moray's colors. Some were able to walk from the field on their own, others had to be carried off. Chargers limped away, others dashed away, kicking up their heels and crashing through the barriers. As Summer became disillusioned with the battle before her, others in the lodges were shouting for more.

Summer's stomach churned as a knight bearing colors of yellow and red fell to the ground, blood streaming from the slit in his visor. His squire was too small to carry him away and began to shout for help, waving to the heralds milling about the battle's perimeter. But the heralds refused to assist, demanding that other squires move in to aid the lad. As Summer watched, the small squire and two other young men carried the injured man from the field.

The game was no longer entertaining. Summer could not imagine what Genisa or her father found amusing within the vicious sport of the melee, men hacking and bleeding and fighting all in the name of glory. In faith, she hadn't known what to expect from the event; somehow, she imagined chivalrous knights doing delicate battle, denting armor and little else. Certainly not this blood sport before her, knights savagely fighting until only one man was left standing.

She did not want to watch any more.

CHAPTER FOUR

"**F**ATHER, I DEMAND you stop this now!"

Edward tore his gaze away from the exciting spectacle, shocked to discover his daughter near tears. His brow furrowed unsympathetically. "Summer, what *is* the matter?"

"This," she jabbed a slender finger toward the bleeding, writhing mass in the center of the field. "Men are d-dying in there!"

Edward forced himself to pat his daughter's hand in a feeble attempt to calm her. "No one is dying. It is all a great competition of skill and talent."

Summer yanked her hand away from her father, exasperated that the man failed to see the seriousness of the situation. Turning to Genisa, she attempted to gain a measure of support for her protest. "And you? How can you enjoy this travesty?"

Genisa looked shocked and remorseful at the same time. "What's the matter with you, Summer? I thought you were excited about this."

Sensing she would receive little backing from her sister-in-law, Summer frowned with dismay; no one seemed to understand her concern and that, in turn, greatly distressed her. As she contemplated the blood-thirsty side to Genisa and her father she had never known to exist, another harrowing cry emitted from the battlefield and she turned in time to observe a massive green and yellow charger list heavily to one side. Bearing down upon the toppling beast was none other than the mighty Gorgon himself.

All thoughts of terror faded for the moment as Summer watched Bose wield his broadsword high, bringing down blow after powerful blow upon a man astride the collapsing destrier. In fact, it seemed that Bose was actually pushing the horse and rider to the ground with his tremendous strength, and Summer winced when the final blow from Bose's powerful sword sent the man to the ground once and for all.

It had been quick, bloodless and swift. Somehow, Bose's battle hadn't been a fight to the death and Summer found her distaste for the game oddly eased. As she continued to watch the massive warrior astride the black and white charger, Bose turned to the man next to him and plowed through the unfortunate knight as if he were no more than a child.

Summer observed with a mixture of fear and fascination as Bose bloodlessly unseated yet another hapless victim. With an additional rival sent to the earth, he appeared to pause slightly to discern just who would be his next casualty. As Summer watched, he moved directly for a red and white charger.

"He's going after Stephan!" Genisa's cry suddenly mingled amongst the shouting of the crowd. "Stay away from him, you beast! Stay away from my husband!"

Summer watched intently as Bose and Stephan exchanged brutal sword blows. Metal against metal, strength against strength, the two men battled furiously as their chargers screamed and snapped at one another. Genisa gasped with terror as Summer continued to observe, frozen in a world of awe and apprehension as the ruthless battle waged before her.

As other horses crashed to the ground and knights were summarily dishonored by being unseated from their mounts, Stephan and Bose appeared to do battle much longer than was usual for a single bout. They continued to hack away at one another as their horses turned circles upon the earth, screaming and grunting in the heat of battle.

Summer forgot her distaste for the melee; watching Stephan and Bose compete in a fierce battle was exactly as she had imagined the tournament to be. Now, finally, she was glimpsing the essence of the games within the powerful blows and deft skills of her brother and Bose de Moray. No injured horses, no flowing blood, only talent and knightly prowess as it was meant to be. This, she decided, was definitely worth watching.

Summer was hardly aware when the field cleared, leaving Stephan and Bose to do final battle as if they were Lucifer and Gabriel. With their comrades shouting encouragement from the sidelines, Summer could do nothing more than watch the brilliant demonstration of mastery, knowing how fatigued the warriors must be but neither willing to concede defeat. Certainly, Stephan considered himself the best competitor in the realm. And, undoubtedly, Bose considered himself the same. More hacking, more grunting, until finally, a broadsword clattered to the earth.

It was Stephan's.

Genisa whimpered as her husband struggled to regain the mace secured to his saddle, dodging some of Bose's heavy blows but absorbing others. It was only a matter of time before Bose was able to unbalance Stephan enough to give him a hard shove and send him smashing to the earth. As a roar of victory went up from the lodges and sidelines alike, the knights on Bose's team congratulated their victor for a job well done and Summer could not help but cheer for him as well.

Her applause, in fact, was the only praise Bose heard. Aye, he had seen her seated at the edge of the lodges with Stephan's wife and Lord du Bonne. He could not keep his eyes from her as the competition began, coming dangerously close twice to being pummeled. But in the heat of the battle, he had overcome the distraction caused by the lady's lovely presence and had delved into the melee with his customary vengeance. One man, two men, five… all of them had succumbed to the Gorgon's mighty sword.

Including Stephan; Bose had already disposed of Ian when he sought out the man's older brother, purposely targeting him in the midst of the chaos. He knew that Summer would be monitoring her brother's progress and Bose intended that she should see him as well, even if he was intent to do away with her beloved sibling.

Even as he saw her sitting in the lists, a faint sea breeze gently lifting tendrils of honey-blond hair, he had no idea what sentiment was

stirring deep within his heart, but he knew enough to realize that they
were emotions he had only experienced once in his life, when he had
met his Lora. He felt sick to his stomach when he realized that even the
initial attraction he had held for his wife was nothing compared to what
he was feeling for Summer du Bonne. What he was experiencing for her
was something different altogether.

It was a confusion that grew and eased all at the same time when he
briefly considered allowing Stephan to win the bout simply so his sister
would not be disappointed. Stephan had fought admirably until the
end, when he suddenly listed dangerously and Bose was forced to end
the match. Had he grasped Stephan by the arm to right the man, it
would have appeared extremely suspicious. Therefore, he did what was
required. He shoved Stephan to the ground.

And his sister had cheered. Even now as he turned in the direction
of the lodges, he could see that she was clapping boldly for him, her
exquisite face graced with a smile. When Stephan rose unsteadily to his
feet, Bose was scarcely aware of the man's words of praise.

"Congratulations, my lord," Stephan said amiably. "I do suppose
now I am required to pay your ransom."

Bose continued to stare at Summer, smiling broadly underneath the
red and white canopy. God help him, the longer he stared at her, the
more forcefully his heart pounded. After a lengthy moment of gazing
upon her beauty, he tore his eyes away from the captivating vision long
enough to focus upon his opponent.

"No ransom, du Bonne," his baritone voice was quiet. "I would ask
a favor instead."

Stephan raised the visor to his three-piece helm, his flushed face
curious. "God's Blood, man, by all means. What is this favor?"

Bose felt like a fool; an immature, giddy fool. Beneath the visor, he
could feel the embarrassing flush and it took far more courage than he
imagined to bring forth the request.

"Your sister...," his voice was barely audible. "Does she have a
champion this day?"

Stephan stared at him a moment. Then, slowly, he shook his head. "Nay, she does not."

Bose swallowed. "Would you be so kind as to ask her if she would permit me to wear her favor? I would be greatly honored."

Stephan continued to gaze at the man, torn between the thrill of his interest and the desire to protect his baby sister. Yesterday, he had given little thought to de Moray's flattery toward his sister when they had been unexpectedly introduced and found himself sorely regretting his lack of foresight. From the sheer tone of the knight's voice, he should have understood the interest.

But he had not. In truth, it had never occurred to him given de Moray's stand-offish reputation; never once had he seen the man with one of the many women who were intent to pursue him. Which was why Bose's expressed interest came as something of a shock; God's Blood, how Stephan wished another man had voiced his regard for Summer, a noble knight who could be easily discouraged.

De Moray, however, was another matter. Stephan had first heard the rumors regarding the man's reputation shortly after the knight had joined the tournament circuit; dark, evil implications that were difficult to ignore. But Stephan had never given much thought to the vicious gossip until this moment.

After a brief pause, Stephan shook his head slowly. "I am afraid I cannot grant your request, my lord. If you will name your ransom, I shall be more than willing to pay."

Beneath the visor, Bose was not shocked by Stephan's denial. But he was extremely disappointed. Struggling to keep an even manner, he raised his visor beneath the light of the radiant sun; rivers of sweat bathed his stubbled face as black eyes focused intently upon their bright green counterparts.

"Instead of naming my ransom, I would make an additional request that will take the place of any monetary compensation. If you will not solicit your sister on my behalf, might I know the reasons behind your decision? Is there something I have done to offend you and am unaware of the occurrence?"

The heralds were moving toward the two men to ascertain why they were still lingering on the field. If there was a dispute, the heralds would be required to settle it. Stephan eyed the men in the red and white tunics, attempting to formulate a quick reply before there were more ears upon them.

"You have never offended me at any time, my lord, and I consider it a great honor that you have expressed interest in my sister," he said rapidly, quietly. "But I must again refuse to divulge the reasonings behind my decision, as they are of a private nature."

Bose's raven's wing eyebrows drew together in puzzlement. "I do not understand, Stephan. Is she already pledged?"

The heralds were nearly upon them. Stephan turned to Bose during the last brief moment of privacy, his green eyes piercing. "She shall never be pledged. I would kindly ask that you dismiss her from your thoughts and seek your attentions with another. Leave my sister alone."

With that, he turned on his heel and marched from the arena. The crowd cheered weakly for the loser of the melee as Bose remained on the field, waving off the urgent queries of the heralds and entirely consumed with the gist of Stephan's reply. As a noble knight, he should have respected the man's wishes and simply ridden from the field without another thought to the lady. But as Stephan's words settled deep, he found he was more confused than ever.

His black eyes sought the lodges again, pensively; the lady was still smiling at him. God help him, he should have turned that moment to retreat from the arena. But the more he stared at her distant, lovely face, the more he realized that he was unwilling to accept Stephan's answer. *She shall never be pledged.* Just what in the hell did that mean?

Bose was a very private fighter, well removed from the adoration of the crowd and the praise of his admirers. He never participated in the parade of knights that usually commenced before the tournaments, instead, leaving the pomp and circumstance to those more willing to accept public accolades. Given his pattern, it was unusual for him to turn his charger in the direction of the lodges. His own men saw him advance toward the lodges, wondering if he had suddenly gone mad from a blow to the head and had forgotten which direction to take back to their tent. Other knights saw him as well, finding it extremely odd that Bose de Moray should bother himself with a female admirer. For as long as any of them had known the man, he showed little concern for anyone other than himself or his men.

Summer could hardly believe that Bose was moving toward the lodges, his visor raised and his black eyes focused upon her. As he drew near, she found herself studying features that had eluded her until this moment; they were not as horrible as her brother had described them to be. She could see his eyes, as sharp and as black as a moonless night, emerging from beneath ruggedly arched brows. His partially obscured face was lined with sweat, his nose straight and true, his lips full and masculine.

He moved closer and she was able to complete her assessment of his physical features; nay, he was clearly not as unattractive as Stephan had described him. He was terribly masculine in appearance, brutally handsome in a harsh sort of way. She rather liked looking at him.

She was so involved with her observations that she was startled when he drew alongside the raised platform, the snorts of his charger jolting her from her train of thought. Black eyes fixed upon those of dark gold and, for a moment, neither one dared to break the spell. After a moment, Summer offered a timid smile. He smiled back.

"Did you enjoy your first melee, my lady?" he asked politely. "As I have understood, it was your first."

Summer rose to her feet, her smile broadening. Before she could speak, however, Edward and Genisa thrust themselves forward, intercepting Summer's reply.

"She was terrified at first, my lord, but she calmed when you and Stephan battled for victory," Genisa's shrill, squeaking tone was irritating. "Congratulations on your win, although my husband undoubtedly feels otherwise."

Bose looked to the woman, pretty and flashy with big teeth and a sensual smile. But, already, her high-pitched voice annoyed the hell out of him.

"In fact, he has already congratulated me on a fine match, Lady du Bonne," he said respectfully. "But his younger brother, I am sure, feels otherwise. I sent Ian to the ground within the first minute or so."

"A magnificent defeat, my lord," Edward agreed. "We've not yet met, but I am Edward du Bonne. I have heard a great deal about you, as my sons' most formidable nemesis."

Bose bowed his head slightly in thanks, his onyx eyes fairly glittering at Summer. "Where it is my pleasure to vex your sons, most assuredly, my intentions toward your daughter are precisely the opposite," when Summer blushed profusely, he could not help but smile. "Might I have a word in private with her, my lord?"

Edward's smile faded and Bose caught the nervous glance he cast to his daughter. "I… that is to say, my daughter is a proper maiden, my lord. I am uncomfortable with your term 'private'. Mayhap it would be best if you said your farewell at this time; undoubtedly, you are tired and wish to rest after your thrilling victory."

Sensing that Bose was focused on the baron, the crowd began to filter from the lodges to take in a bit of the merriment intended to accompany such an event. Jugglers, men who breathed fire, and other entertainers perused the grounds, vying for attention and coinage. Since the melee was over for the day and the joust would not commence until the morrow, there were a hundred other diversions to occupy the guests until the evening feast.

But Bose ignored the throng as they vacated the stands, still focused on the baron and his evasive answer. Feeling his annoyance mount, since he had yet to be given a valid reason as to why he must steer clear of the lady's company, he fixed the short, fat man with a heady stare.

"When I used the word 'private', I simply meant to infer having a confidential conversation with my lady, not to whisk her into a darkened tent and have my way with her," as Genisa gasped with the shock of his bold words, Bose drew in a deep breath and attempted to calm his irritation. "I assure you, my lord, I have no intention of vexing or molesting your daughter. A brief word is all I ask. You may stand where you are and observe the entire happenstance. In fact, I would encourage you to do so for your own peace of mind."

Edward's gaze was unusually hard and unusually soft at the same time. He knew little of Bose de Moray other than what his sons had seen notable to mention, nearly all of their tales revolving around the man's uncanny strength and knightly ability. Still, he was unsure and reluctant.

"As well I appreciate your noble offer, I find I must decline yet again," he said quietly. "We thank you for your query, sir knight, but my daughter is not interested."

"Did you ask her?"

"N-Nay, he...."

Summer's budding reply was abruptly cut short by Genisa's grating voice, overshadowing her sister-in-law's attempt at speech.

"I am afraid this day has been most taxing on Summer and myself," she said quickly, grasping her sister-in-law firmly by the arm and practically dragging her toward the exit. "If you will excuse us, sir knight. My lord baron."

Bose watched, his black eyes glittering, as Genisa literally yanked Summer down the small flight of stairs leading from the lodges. Onyx-black orbs locked with those of dark gold and he could literally read the pain and sorrow within her shimmering eyes. Her expression, so recently lined with warmth and excitement at the sight of him, was drawn and taut and, he thought, bordering on tears.

He watched her retreat until she disappeared from sight. When Summer had faded from view amongst the vendors and crowd, he returned his attention to the rotund baron. From soft black one moment to blazing embers the next, his gaze was anything but tolerant upon his host.

"My lord," he began, his baritone voice as steady as he could manage for the fury and confusion building in his heart. "I realize you do not know me; therefore, I do not fault your protectiveness where your daughter is concerned. But I am a noble knight with an established reputation, and believe me when I tell you that my intentions toward your daughter are entirely chivalrous."

Edward, normally weak-willed and fairly pliable to the desires of others, met his gaze with wavering courage. "You must understand, my lord, that I find no fault with you at all. In fact, your interest pleases me greatly. But Summer is… courting her is out of the question. I sincerely wish I could elaborate, but I cannot. 'Tis a private matter I prefer not to discuss with a stranger. Please obey my wishes and end your pursuit."

Bose emitted a harsh sigh, leaning forward on his saddle in a gesture of exhaustion and disbelief. "God's Beard, I did not say anything about courting her. I merely wanted to speak with her."

"But why?"

He looked at the man a moment before averting his gaze, staring off toward the rapidly approaching sunset. After a moment of deliberation, he waved his hand in a careless gesture. "I am without a lady to champion for this tournament. I merely wished to ask her for a favor."

Edward stared at the knight, shaking his head after a moment. "I am sorry," he said softly, moving away from the dais and down the stairs before Bose could say another word.

Bose remained before the empty lodges for quite some time afterward, wondering why on earth the House of du Bonne had refused to allow him to speak with the fair Lady Summer. First Stephan and now the father. Both of them reacting strangely toward the request, as if Bose had somehow demanded the maiden be allowed to bear him a son out of wedlock.

The problem, however, was clear; he simply wasn't good enough for her. She was far too beautiful for him, an aged widower with nothing by way of bloodlines or family ties to offer her. Of course that was the true reason; she was well beyond his grasp.

With a heavy sigh, he turned his charger toward the edge of the field where his men were already collecting ransom from their humble prisoners. Once a ransom was paid, the man was free to go and prepare for the coming joust. Though the thought of money to be had usually pleased him, he realized that there was nothing to be pleased with this day.

Victory or not, he shouldn't have even come.

☙

"STOP DRAGGING ME about, Genisa!" Summer snapped when the lodges were well out of sight. Yanking her arm free, she glared irritably at her sister-in-law. "Let go of me!"

Genisa appeared properly contrite in the face of her husband's angry sister. "I do apologize, Summer, but you are fully aware that I only have your best interests at heart. We had to leave before…."

"B-Before I embarrassed everyone with my stammering speech," Summer supplied harshly, humiliated and furious. Sighing heavily, she turned away and allowed her pouting gaze to rove the grounds. She wanted to be normal. She wanted to laugh as other maidens laugh, to encounter the thrill of her first beau, and to know all else that noble maidens usually experience. The fact that Genisa and her father had chased Sir Bose away as if she carried the plague cut a path of anguish deep into her heart; more than ever, the true reason behind their shielding actions was obvious and Summer found herself wanting to be away from her overbearing sister-in-law.

Her voice was quiet but firm as she eyed her apprehensive sister-in-law. "Go away, Genisa. Please go away and leave me alone."

Genisa's expression washed with genuine remorse. "Summer, I am truly sorry. But you know as well as I that… we must make sure you are kept silent and protected."

"Protected? Ha!" Summer snorted. "You mean properly hidden."

"Hidden?" Genisa repeated, sincerely confused. "Not hidden, Summer. *Protected.*"

"Call it what you will, Genisa. Regardless of the term used, it means the same thing. Isolating me from the world."

"Not by choice," Genisa's voice was quiet. "There are those who simply do not understand your flaw."

Although Genisa had meant to describe her affliction and nothing more, Summer interpreted her statement as an insult. Cheeks flushing with shame, she whirled on her sister-in-law in a vicious billow of golden satin. "My flaw is that I cannot speak a sentence without f-faltering at times. Your flaw is that you talk too much and your voice grates upon my ears like the b-bray of an injured goat. Now tell me; whose flaw is greater?"

Genisa gasped, her mouth opening with outrage. "How cruel you are. I was merely trying to protect you, Summer!"

"Do not protect me!" Summer practically screamed, oblivious to the curious glances upon the two shouting ladies. "I do not want your protection! In fact, I do not want you near me at all!"

Genisa's mouth gaped further, her cheeks mottling a hot red. "You ungrateful wench. How dare you spurn my concern!"

Summer let out a strangled groan. "Concern for what others will think of your reputation with a sister-in-law who stutters," when Genisa attempted to lodge a stern protest, Summer simply turned on her heel and marched in the opposite direction. "Go b-back to Stephan, Genisa. I do not need, nor do I want any more of your p-protection."

Genisa called to her and attempted to follow, but Summer gathered her skirts and dashed off as if the Devil himself were nipping at her heels. In and out of vendor shacks she ran, renting a wild path through the cluster of visitors in an attempt to elude her sister-in-law. She wanted to be free of the woman, if for no other reason than to compose her thoughts.

By the time she entered the perimeter of tents housing opposing knights, Genisa's shouts had faded and Summer slowed her pace, wiping the steady stream of tears from her cheeks. The day was waning as the sun set steadily in the western sky and high above, seagulls called loudly in their search for food.

Summer ignored the gulls, the cooling sea breeze, and the distant roar of the crowd populating the vendor stalls and surrounding area. In spite of the clusters of unfamiliar tents, she knew the area well and realized, eventually, she would emerge onto the road leading to Chaldon. So she wandered, staring at the ground and going out of her way to avoid a knight or squire or servant within the field of the tightly clustered shelters.

She did not want to speak with anyone. Nor did she particularly want to see anyone, given the fact that the only man she possessed a desire to see was probably lodged within the warm comfort of his tent, congratulating himself on a fine victory and putting her out of his mind.

Toying with the ends of her hair absently, her expression molded into that of a permanent pout, she wandered to the base of a gnarled old oak and deposited herself at the roots. The pungent smells of roasting meat filled the air as the evening meal drew close, but Summer wasn't hungry in the least. There wasn't a food or drink in the world that could ease the ache she was experiencing at the moment. It was an ache that only intensified when she caught sight of the striking black and white tent in the near distance.

The proud Gorgon banner flapped sharply in the brisk sea wind, silently saluting the onset of a mild evening. Summer ripped up clods of grass, venting her turmoil and wondering why God had saddled her with so horrible an affliction. She oft made a conscious effort not to stammer her speech, speaking slowly and distinctly. And sometimes, her efforts worked. But more often than not, she would forget her slowed pace and return to her natural pattern and stuttering syllables.

Sir Bose wasn't to blame for his unwillingness to defy her father's denial. In truth, she did not blame him; she blamed her father for his sense of pride, unwilling to expose his daughter to a potential suitor and thereby release the secret of her speech impediment. And once Sir Bose discovered her imperfection, certainly, he would formulate his own rejection.

But, Dear God, somehow she wished he would be able to overlook her flaw in lieu of her better qualities. As if, somehow, he would be able to tolerate her stammering in lieu of coming to know the woman beneath the defect. Dear God... she wished he would be different from the rest.

The sun descended in the western sky, turning the colors from blue to orange to gold; still, Summer continued to sit beneath the old oak tree in gloomy silence. As dusk drew nigh and the damp sea breeze turned cold and wet, still, she sat and pondered her impending future. Realizing that, indeed, she appeared not to have one at all.

♋

IN SPITE OF the fact that the evening meal should have been a victory celebration, there was very little happiness at all. Within the encampment of the House of de Moray, the mood was oddly sullen and strangely quiet. As the knights in Bose's service commenced their meal of mutton, onions and sweetened carrots, there was far less joviality than usual. Little talk, meaningless banter, and at the head of the silence sat none other than Bose himself.

A trencher of half-eaten mutton sat before him, cooling and scarcely touched. On his right, Morgan picked through his meal in respectful silence, eyeing Tate now and again to make sure the knight had every intention of keeping his mouth shut on the subject of Lady Summer. To make sure they all kept their mouths shut. There was not one man among the morose crowd that wished to broach the truth.

They had all seen Bose ride to the dais with the intention of speaking to the beautiful young woman. And they had all seen the lady escorted from his presence. What could have been a potentially pleasing situation turned dark and moody the moment the lady left his company.

Even after the lady had long since vanished, Bose had remained silent and pensive and isolated, poised before the lodges that had once been filled with people screaming his name. There was no one left to congratulate the victor; not even the only woman from whom he would have gladly accepted the accolades. So he turned away from the vacant seats and returned to his encampment, empty-handed and closed mouth.

There was not one man in the tent that hadn't suspected Bose's purpose when he boldly approached the dais. Knowing their lord as they did, his reserved nature and disinterest toward life in general, it must have taken a tremendous amount of courage for him to initiate the action. And further knowing the man as they did, there wasn't one man in the tent immune to the sting of rejection their liege was experiencing.

Beyond Morgan's pensive silence and Tate's deliberate quiet, Farl McCorkle eyed his liege with a good deal of sympathy. A massive, burly Irishman, he had served with Bose for several years within the Household Guard. His bushy red eyebrows and overgrown mustache almost gave him the appearance of an unkempt heathen; in truth, there was no finer warrior in the heat of battle and Bose considered himself fortunate to warrant the man's loyalty.

Seated next to the crusty Irish knight was a diminutive warrior by the name of Adgar Ross. Where his Celtic counterpart was brawny, loud and curt, Adgar by contrast was quiet, well-manicured and faintly handsome. Nearly as old as Morgan, in spite of his small stature and meek manner he was a fierce fighter and an intelligent tactician. Bose and Adgar had carried on many a conversation regarding battle methods and maneuvers before competition, establishing a winning pattern that carried through to this very day.

Aye, Farl and Adgar were worth their weight in gold as far as Bose was concerned. As in the melee today, they had been powerful contenders who had lasted admirably. But this night, their usual advice and commentary regarding the day's match was unwanted by their brooding liege. Having been advised of the circumstances regarding a certain young lady, the two knights maintained their respectful silence just like the others.

That is, all except for Artur. Bose's great-uncle wasn't a knight, nor had he ever been. He was a tiny old man born with a crippled arm that had prevented him from training as a proper knight. In spite of his defect, Artur possessed the extreme de Moray trait of determination. He had fostered in a fine household and although unable to participate in actual knightly training, he nonetheless learned all he was able and soon took to training knights himself, working in apprenticeship with a collection of powerful warriors.

Artur had helped train Bose's father, and Bose himself when he had come of age. Throughout his grand-nephew's years of service as Captain of the Guard, Artur had been at the forefront of organizing and instructed the captain's men. Bose refused to be without the little man – he may have been stubborn, private and independent, but he was extremely loyal to those closest to him. 'Twas a tightly knit group encompassing the House of de Moray, protective and strong, and if Bose never accomplished another feat of glory in his life, he would have gone to his grave extremely proud of the life and relationships he had nurtured.

"Why would not the baron let you speak with his daughter, Bose?" Artur finally asked the fateful question they had all been pondering for the better part of an hour. "Did you offend him somehow?"

Morgan and Tate looked to each other, waiting for their liege to explode. Although Bose wasn't a naturally violent man, he had been known to break furniture on occasion when pushed beyond his limits. Farl simply pretended he hadn't heard the question while Adgar focused on his half-finished meal. When his grand-nephew did not answer right away, the old man pushed.

"What did you do, Bose?"

On his fourth cup of ale, Bose contemplated his pewter chalice in silence. After a lengthy pause, during which Artur grunted an additional measure of encouragement, he grasped the cup and drained the contents. Morgan refilled it immediately.

"In faith, I do not know," his baritone voice was hoarse with fatigue and alcohol. "I suppose I am not considered a fine enough prospect for the baron's lovely daughter."

"Posh," Artur spat, shuffling across the floor and shoving Tate from his chair. Taking the man's seat, he focused intently on his brooding nephew. "You are as fine a knight as has ever lived, Bose, and certainly a suitable match for a baron's daughter."

Faintly, Bose shook his head. "It's not the fact that she is a mere baron's daughter. She is so damn beautiful that surely they are awaiting a more… attractive prospect."

"Rubbish!" Artur crowed, jabbing a gnarled finger into the man's chest. "There's nothing wrong with your appearance. So you have a few scars; so what? There's not one perfect individual upon the face of the earth, including Lord du Bonne's daughter, I'd wager. Surely the girl has a flaw."

"Not this girl."

Artur shook his head in exasperation. "You are too quick to praise and too quick to concede defeat. The Bose I know would not have given up as easily as this. Are you so lacking in confidence that you will not fight for what you want?"

Bose's brow furrowed with confusion and he took another hearty draw of ale. After a lengthy hesitation, he emitted a loud sigh. "God's Beard, Artur, I never said I wanted the girl. I merely wished to ask for her favor and suddenly, everyone is acting as if my marriage proposal was rejected."

"'Tis because you are acting in the same manner. I would tend to believe that you want more than a favor from the girl."

Looking into Artur's face for the first time, it was an effort for Bose to scowl convincingly. "You are mad," he hissed, draining his cup and rising from the table. Still clad in his mail tunic and plate armor, he wandered away from the table. "How would you know what I am feeling? You've never even seen the woman; you are basing your observations on what these fools are telling you. They insist I am somehow in love with a woman I do not even know, and you believe them."

"I believe my eyes and ears and instincts. And they are confirming what I have been told."

Bose grunted with frustration, turning away from the collection of men huddled about the small cherrywood table. "You are all mad. The woman means absolutely nothing to me."

"Then why are you so troubled?"

Bose stared at the half-open tent flap, his frustration fading as he pondered Artur's softly-uttered question. God's Beard, why *was* he so troubled? He'd never spoken to the Lady Summer; he'd seen her barely twice and the relationship they shared was purely one of smiles and glances and nothing more. There was no physical contact involved, no stolen kisses, nothing whatsoever to warrant a strong emotional attachment.

… then why *was* he so troubled?

"I am not troubled by the lady," his reply filled the drawn-out pause. "'Twould seem that my collection of knights is intent to exaggerate the situation and for that, I am indeed distressed. Now hurry and finish your meals and be out of my sight."

The order was taken literally. Those with food remaining on their trenchers began to shove huge bites into their mouths. But Artur continued to stare at the dark warrior and knowing that there was far more supporting the refusals of his interest in the lady than he was willing to voice.

"It's Margot, isn't it?" the old man's voice was quiet. "She has managed to convince you that any normal interest you should experience for a woman is a direct insult to Lora's memory."

Bose looked to his grand-uncle, the onyx-black eyes smoldering with restrained emotion. "She has not convinced me of anything. And you will not bring Lora into this."

"The old bitch has you chained to her daughter's memory as if you were an eternal prisoner." Artur was unafraid of his hulking nephew's wrath; when speaking of Margot or Lora, the calm persona that was the epitome of Bose's character saw a rapid collapse. Artur was genuinely distressed over the peculiar power Margot seemed to wield against her son-in-law, a strength Bose oddly refused to acknowledge.

"Do you not see what she is doing to you, Bose?" the old man hissed pleadingly. "She is controlling you through her dead daughter and you are allowing her to do so."

Bose's cheek ticked faintly as he eyed his uncle a long moment. "I will not discuss this with you, uncle. Not tonight."

"So you are not. 'Tis I who am discussing it with *you*. Margot has persuaded you to live only for Lora's memory and not for the future that lies ahead. What if this Lady Summer is someone with whom you could arrange a satisfactory contract? Will you give it all up for the ramblings of a bitter old woman and the memory of her dead daughter?"

Bose's face mottled a dull red. Had he not forced himself to turn away, he most likely would have said or done something unreasonable.

"Good knights, if your meal is concluded, then be gone with you," he said quietly. "The joust is on the morrow and I will insist my men retire early."

Tate needed no further encouragement. He had already provoked his liege well beyond the limits this day and from his liege's current mood after Artur's pestering, suspected it would be wise to make himself scarce. Farl and Adgar abruptly lifted themselves from their chairs, determined to finish their food elsewhere. This was not a place they wanted to be.

Only Morgan and Artur were left, alternately staring at each other and the massive man frozen near the shelter opening. Seeing that it would be of no use to press the topics of Margot or the obscure Lady Summer, Artur wisely concluded to rest both subjects. All thoughts of Bose's manipulative mother-in-law aside, he would again press the focus of the mysterious woman with the next opportunity.

"Where's Antony?" Bose shifted the focus.

Artur looked around, disinterestedly at first, but with more conviction when Morgan leapt from his chair and joined the search.

"He was here when we commenced with our meal," Morgan replied, sifting through the bedding at the opposite side of the tent. "I fed him a piece of bread."

Bose's brow furrowed as he began to search, looking under the table and chairs, rummaging through the boxes and satchels. But as the search progressed and still no ferret, Bose realized that his clever friend must have escaped the tent.

"God's Beard," he hissed, more frightened that Antony would come to harm than he was for the fact that his secretive pet would be discovered. "I have got to find him. Come along, Morgan, and help me search. He knows you."

Without hesitation, Morgan quit the tent in pursuit of his liege, leaving Artur to finish combing the far reaches of the tent. But the old man realized that the black-eyed animal was not within the boundaries of the black and white shelter. If he did not end up as mashed guts beneath the hooves of a charger or the main course of a peasant's meal, it would be a miracle.

But Artur believed in miracles. Slowing his search, he lowered his weary body to Bose's comfortable chair and sighed deeply, listening to the cries of the nightbird. Even as his thoughts were focused on his nephew's attachment to the pet, somewhere in the midst of gray and white fuzz again came thoughts of a certain young lady. He wondered if the lady liked ferrets, too.

CHAPTER FIVE

"D AMNATION!" CAME THE foul roar. "You did that on purpose!"
"Quit your bellowing and allow me to finish."

Small, piercing blue eyes glared daggers at the aged physic as the man finished the last of the stitches. When he was finished, the injured man with the unruly mass of bright red hair snatched the pewter hand mirror from the table beside him and peered intently at his reflection.

"Damnation," he spewed again with far less volume. "It will leave a scar. Just inside my hairline."

"With all of your hair, who will notice?" A younger man with a lighter shade of the same color hair lounged against the furs on the floor, staring up at his older brother. "Be thankful the gash was not across your cheek."

The man bearing the stitches tossed the mirror aside in disgust, ordering the physic away with a curt command. When the aged healer quit the tent with his usual slow pace, the injured man poured himself a healthy draught of ale.

"Easy on the drink, Breck," the younger man said. "You know your head will be aching come the morning if you consume too much. And you must be clear-headed for the joust."

"Aye," Breck mumbled into his cup. "Clear-headed to return de Moray's favor."

The man on the floor snickered softly. "Your own helm gashed your scalp."

"With de Moray's assistance," Breck turned to face his far less serious younger brother. The man simply would not realize a grave situation if it walked up and slapped him in the face. "Think, you idiot. I would not have slashed my scalp had de Moray not shoved me to the ground. I was lucky I wasn't trampled."

Duncan Kerry laughed again, much to his brother's annoyance. "Had he wanted you to be trampled, you would have been."

Breck stared at his brother a moment before turning away, pondering the world outside of the lavishly furnished tent. Beyond were a sea of vibrantly hued tarpaulins of various houses and provinces. Men he had fought against before, a number of times, and men he had beaten on more than one occasion. A plethora of losers prepared to bow at his mighty feet. Except for de Moray.

It was always the same with him. A brutal fight, a decisive defeat – Breck's defeat. Aye, he'd come close to beating de Moray on occasion, but never close enough. Never close enough to inflict enough damage that would send the powerful knight to the ground. Whether it be in the melee or joust, the story was consistently similar – Bose's victory and Breck's rout.

Today was no exception. Breck had fought admirably until the end, finally put down by none other than de Moray himself before the man moved on to do final battle with Stephan du Bonne. More angry than injured, Breck had left the field in disgrace, watching the final duel as the crowd roared wildly with approval. Approval that should have been meant for him.

It had been a bitter defeat to concede. Breck and Duncan were considered powerful contenders on the circuit, following in the legacy of their recently departed father. Breck knew that his tactics were looked upon by some of the other knights as brutal and unscrupulous. It was a mere difference of opinion, of course. Breck saw nothing inequitable in striking a fallen man in the melee, provided he wasn't seen by a herald and disqualified, or using quick, sudden movements in the joust to unseat or injure his opponent.

"I do not suppose the heralds would allow me to use my spear-tipped joust pole as opposed to the crows-foot point," he muttered casually, far calmer than he had been moments earlier. Turning to cast a devilish, glance to his brother, he raised his red eyebrows quizzically.

"Nay? Well, then, I must think of another way to defeat de Moray."

"God's Toes, Breck, what were you going to do with the spear-tip? Gore him?" Duncan sat up from his pile of furs, shaking his head. "Even for you, that is a rather barbaric maneuver. Moreover, the very second you planted the spear, his knights would be all over you. You would never have a chance against them."

Breck shrugged, listening to a dog bay somewhere in the distance as the moon rose. "As I said, I'll have to think of another way to best him," he began to pick at his big, crooked teeth. "Did you see him ride toward the lodges today after his victory? He appeared to speak with Lord du Bonne."

"Or gawk at the Lady Genisa," Duncan licked his lips lewdly. "I pray every night that Stephan du Bonne will meet his end so that I may claim his lovely leftovers."

Breck snorted, still picking at his teeth. "I suspect you'd have to fight Ian and Lance for the privilege. In fact, I have oft wondered if she services all three brothers as well as they treat her," shaking his head, he examined the contents of his teeth in the tips of his dirty fingernails. "Nay, I doubt Bose was gawking over Genisa. And I doubt even the baron's summons could have coerced his reluctant nature to move toward the lodges. I suspect, dear brother, that the unknown lady seated between Genisa and the baron was the reason for his interest."

Duncan cocked an eyebrow. "Why would you say that?"

"For the reasons I have already given. Mayhap there is something between the two."

Duncan shrugged carelessly. "And if there is?"

The dusk deepened as Breck explored his unclear, if not somewhat evil, line of thought. "I do not know. Mayhap… mayhap we should discover who the lady is."

"Why?"

"Simple curiosity, I suppose. I wonder if she is aware of de Moray's darker reputation."

Duncan pursed his lips. "There is not one man among us without some sort of sinister, darker reputation. Moreover, any gossip regarding de Moray is just that – gossip. In four years no one has been able to discover much about him."

Breck appeared particularly thoughtful. "I'll bet the lady knows something about him. Mayhap she could prove to be useful."

His brother snorted. "How? To divulge more damaging information regarding the truth behind de Moray's shady reputation? Or do you plan to use her against the man in a literal sense, mayhap?"

Breck did not reply for a moment. Then, he turned from the open portal and focused on his brother. "As I said, I do not know at the moment. But certainly, we should explore all of our options."

Duncan stared at his brother a moment before pursing his lips wryly, rising from his pallet with a grunt. "You are mad. There are dozens of knights we compete against with wives and ladies and you've never once made mention of using a particular woman to subdue her knight. And now you speak of the most powerful knight of all. Just how in the hell are we supposed to accomplish such a task?"

Breck moved for the half-empty ale pitcher, pondering the possibilities. "Who can say? Mayhap an opportunity will present itself. Or mayhap not. However, I am willing to weaken de Moray any way I can. He has been a thorn in my side long enough."

Duncan wandered to the leaning table to pick at the remaining mutton, thinking his brother to be foolish and reckless with his thoughts of betrayal against de Moray.

"The only reason Sir Bose hasn't speared you through the gut is because he and father were friends once," he said. "He tolerates you and nothing more. Were you to push him, there's no knowing how the man would react. And you seem to forget that he employs four very powerful knights, men willing to kill for him without hesitation. Have you considered that?"

Breck pretended that he hadn't heard him. "She was certainly beautiful," he muttered, taking a swig of ale directly from the pitcher. "I have never seen her before. I wonder who she is?"

Duncan rolled his eyes in frustration, commandeering a small stool and sitting before the cold meat. Chewing on a slab of fat, he eyed his foolish brother. "If she belongs to de Moray, I say leave her alone. To make an attack on a knight on the field of competition is one matter, but to molest his lady is quite another. Forget whatever it is you are thinking."

Breck heard him. He did not want to hear him. Even so, he knew very well he should listen to his younger, more level-headed brother. But he could not seem to.

∛

THE HOOT OWL was directly overhead. Although Summer could not see the bird, she could certainly hear him. Asking the constant question; *Who, Who, Who?* Who indeed, Summer mused bitterly. Who would be foolish enough to remain alone, unescorted, in the midst of the knights' camp well after dark? And who was content to wallow in the self-pity and confusion that had refused to abate for well over an hour? Who, indeed.

Summer continued to recline against the ancient oak, ignoring the pesky owl and listening to the faint rumble of the surrounding camp. The sea breeze had increased in intensity, casting a chill in the air and Summer rubbed her arms to keep warm, the golden silk providing little protection against the damp wind.

Even so, she had little intention of leaving her quiet haven beneath the great tree. Although her thoughts had calmed somewhat since fleeing the field, there still remained a distinct measure of anger toward her selfish, proud family.

Clearly, she had struck home with her accusations. Genisa had most likely returned to the keep to inform the rest of the family that Lady Summer was aware of their "alleged" protective actions. Her thoughts darkened as she pondered her relationship with her family from now on.

Toying with the grass absently, she was so consumed with her gloomy visions that she was gradually aware of glittering black eyes staring up at her. Even as she found herself gazing into the tiny orbs, she wasn't quite sure what she was looking at; only when the eyes blinked, rapidly, did she realize that she was no longer alone beneath the aged, sheltering oak.

Summer sat up from the tree trunk, not particularly afraid of the small, dark eyes as they studied her curiously. Sitting very still so as not to startle her little visitor, she was eventually rewarded when the small gray and white ferret emerged from the shadows and into the weak moon light.

It was a beautifully maintained little beast, clean and bright and well fed as it scampered onto her lap. Sensing from the behavior and condition of the animal that it was exceptionally tame, she began to stroke the silky fur.

"My goodness, little one," she cooed in flawless speech. "Who do you belong to?"

Tiny whiskers licked her arm as the ferret moved up her torso, sniffing her skin and wiggling its little nose. Summer giggled as tiny claws tickled her skin, collecting the ferret into both hands as to better inspect the best. Golden orbs met with curious, rodent black and she smiled brightly, noting the beautiful shadings of gray and white upon the fuzzy coat.

"I would suspect that someone is missing you right now," she said softly, tearing her eyes away from the pet long enough to glance to the glowing encampment. There appeared to be no lady in frantic search of her pet. With a shrug, Summer rubbed noses with her newest friend. "I suppose I should discover who you belong to. After we've become acquainted, of course."

Within her soft hands, Antony was quite content to allow his rescuer to gently caress him. But his attention was finite and he worked his way to her shoulder, perching atop the tender skin and sniffing the brisk sea air. Summer giggled as he scampered along her neck, losing himself in her hair and eventually coming to the conclusion that her thick mane was a wonderful, warm haven in which to hide from the frightening world.

Summer attempted to coax the furry creature from her hair, but he ignored her and she suspected the hooting of the owl had something to do with his reluctance. She did not blame him in the least and was content to allow him to remain for the time being. The restless creature, however, eventually emerged from the silken blond cave and worked his way down her arm, moving to the comfort of her lap once more.

Summer continued to stoke her new companion, thoughts of finding its owner fading by the moment. She'd never had a pet, not even a bird in a cage, and she realized that she could come to love the little animal deeply. He was sweet, well-behaved and clean, and she wasn't the least bit sorry that she was stealing someone else's property. If they were careless enough to allow him to escape, then they did not deserve the responsibility or the pleasure accompanying such an animal. She kissed and cooed to the little animal.

"He has never been quite so affectionate with me."

The baritone voice startled Summer and she looked up as a massive form stepped from the shadows into the moonlight, his hands raised in supplication. She must have recoiled or otherwise displayed fright, because the figure came to a halt.

"I am sorry if I frightened you, my lady, please forgive me," Bose said quietly, keeping his hands raised to prove he was no threat. "I heard your laughter from the trees and followed the sound. I wasn't spying on you nor do I intend you harm, I swear it."

Summer continued to stare at him with big eyes, surprised by his appearance, unsure what to say. Even though the man was without his helm, she remembered those features. She had seen him, earlier that day as he had asked permission from her father to speak with her. It was Bose de Moray in the flesh and delight mingled with her surprise, becoming nervous apprehension. Here they were, alone, and she was uncertain. Uncertainty sealed her lips. She just sat there and looked at him. She'd never been in this position in her life.

Bose sensed her hesitance. He, too, was struggling to overcome the shock of coming across Lady Summer, with Antony in her hands no less. He still wasn't even sure he wasn't dreaming it. Eager to ease her anxiety, he lowered his hands while maintaining a distant, unmoving position. For a moment, all he could do was look at her. He'd never seen anything so beautiful in his entire life.

"Antony has never been as loving with me as he apparently is with you," he said quietly, wondering why his voice was tinged with an odd quiver. "He escaped this night and I was frantic with worry for him. How fortunate for me that you have found him."

Summer tore her eyes away from Bose long enough to gaze at the fuzzy creature in her grasp. Obviously, the little beast belonged to the knight. Without hesitation, she extended her hands to offer Bose the animal. He eyed her a moment, his black eyes blazing with warmth, before slowly shaking his head.

"He likes you better, I can tell," his voice was soft. "Please… you will keep him."

His tone was soothing, his manner gentle. Summer's brow furrowed and her lovely face washed with a curious expression, looking to Antony as if the ferret could confirm his master's directive. Bose continued to stare at her a moment before slowly crouching in an attempt to make himself appear less threatening. He wanted to be on her level.

"I did not mean to disturb your peaceful evening," he said quietly. "I would be honored if you would allow me to join you."

Summer continued to stare at him, knowing that he had been carrying on a once-sided conversation until this point. Sooner or later, he was going to expect a reply. But she did not want to make a fool of herself, as she wasn't certain she could reply without stammering all over herself. It seemed to get worse when she was upset or nervous. As she pondered her next move, Antony abruptly scampered across her lap and onto the ground. Mounting Bose's arm, he scurried to his familiar post atop his master's broad shoulder.

"Ah, my treacherous little friend, so you think to return to me?" his thick fingers scratched affectionately at the animal. "For certain, I thought I'd lost you. But it would seem that you and I had the same idea to find a certain young lady."

Summer watched him play with the pet, blushing furiously when he turned his gaze upon her. Averting her eyes, her respiration began to come in sharp pants. *Say something, you foolish wench!*

"I did not receive a reply from you earlier, when I asked if you had enjoyed your first melee," he said, drinking in her exquisite profile and finding that the peculiar quiver in his voice had spread to his limbs. "Your brother's wife seemed most anxious to answer for you. Does she do this habitually?"

Summer stared at her hands. Then, she nodded faintly. "S-She does."

Bose's gaze held even, although there was no mistaking the stammer in her softly-uttered reply. As an inkling of suspicion came to mind, a curiosity took hold and his stare grew in intensity.

"I have heard Lady Genisa possesses the ability to talk God off his throne," he said casually. "I see that the rumors were truth."

A faint smile creased Summer's beautiful lips. "Indeed, my lord," she nearly whispered. "Genisa is most chatty. And most overb-bearing at times, although she means well."

Then it was true. Bose came to realize that he had not imagined the catch in her speech. He also knew why the lady had remained so silent in his presence, why her sister-in-law and father has answered for her, and why Ian had dragged her away when a conversation was imminent. It made his heart ache for her, because what they did not know was that Bose understood such things. God help him, he understood a great deal.

"I see," his baritone was scarcely audible as he replied belatedly to her statement. "Since she is not here to answer for you, then I would expect to hear your thoughts personally. Did you, in fact, enjoy the melee?"

Summer continued to stare at her hands, the ground, and finally Antony as he scampered down Bose's arm and clamored up her thigh. Petting the fuzzy creature, he heard her give a faint sigh before she gave him her full attention.

"Nay," she replied frankly. "I thought it was a horrible d-display of savagery and male pride. I never want to see another melee as long as I live."

He met her gaze a long moment, his lips creased with mirth. Before he could control himself, he was howling with laughter such as he had never known and Summer watched him, horrified and ashamed, knowing that he was laughing at her affliction. With a whimper of anguish, she bolted to her feet and gathered her skirts. But massive hands were suddenly holding her firm. Somehow, he had covered the distance between them and was now grasping her. His grip was like iron.

"Where do you go?" he demanded softly.

"Let me go!" she cried. His fingers were like iron, biting into the soft flesh of her arms and much to her dismay, Summer felt the sting of tears. Throwing herself about, she struggled fiercely to release his hold before she disgraced herself further. "Release m-me immediately!"

Instead of complying, Bose's grip tightened. Summer gasped as bolts of pain coursed through her arms and her struggles came to a halt. Golden orbs locked with onyx-black and Bose could literally read the shame and terror brimming in the depths.

"You believe me to be laughing at you?" When she refused to reply, he shook her gently. "Answer me. Do you believe me to be laughing at you?"

After brief consideration, during which she realized that she had little choice but to respond to him, Summer nodded once. He released her and she stumbled away from him, her eyes wide and accusing. But she did not run.

"I wasn't laughing at you, my lady, I swear it," his voice was soothing and sincere. "'Twas your words I found humorous and nothing more. You are entirely correct in your description of the melee. 'Tis a contest to promote the male ego."

She continued to stare at him, the shame and fury fading from her expression. Near the tree, Antony continued to scamper about and above her tumultuous thoughts, Summer realized that she had virtually thrown the animal from her lap in her haste. Embarrassed, she lowered her gaze and returned to the tree.

"I am sorry, Antony. I did not mean to be brutal," her apology was whisper-soft as she scooped up the fuzzy creature. Rubbing noses with her newest friend, she could feel Bose's massive presence over her shoulder.

She did not know why she should believe him; the man was a stranger. But there was something in his tone that relaxed and enchanted her at the same time. True, she had wanted to know of his reaction to her defect; even so, the process of discovery was a frightening, overwhelming thing.

"My f-father would not allow you to speak with me today for obvious reasons, my lord," slowly, she turned to Bose, raising her eyes to meet with those of piercing black. "You must understand that they do not wish for my… imperfection to b-become public knowledge. They do their best to protect me."

Bose met her gaze, feeling anguish for her plight. "That is why Stephan refused to allow me to speak with you after I won the melee." He watched her nod her head. "And your father. That is why he discouraged me, as well."

Again, she nodded. He studied her closely as she continued to clutch Antony, knowing from experience of the shame she had encountered. After a moment, he reached out and gently stroked the animal within her grip, succeeding in capturing her hooded gaze.

When their eyes met, he smiled his charming, lop-sided grin. "In their defense, I will say that I can understand their fear. However, regardless of their shielding instincts, there is nothing on this earth powerful enough to discourage my attention toward you."

He watched with delight as her golden orbs widened with surprise. In spite of the colorless moon glow, he caught an unmistakable mottle to her cheeks.

"Why would you say this, my lord?" she asked breathlessly.

"Because it's true. You, my lady, are the embodiment of the perfection God has intended for all womankind. I knew it from the first moment I saw you. And if your father and brother believe that an insignificant speech irregularity is going to discourage me from coming to know you, they are sadly mistaken."

Summer's expression grew more intense, filled with astonishment. It was all she had ever hoped to hear, but in faith, never truly expected to. Indeed, she wondered if she was dreaming as she gazed into sharp black eyes, gentle and warm as they blazed upon her.

"You are serious?"

"Never more so."

A well-arched blond brow rose. "You are... you are not embarrassed by my speech? You do not f-find it repulsive or discomforting?"

"Not at all. In fact, I am used to it."

"*Used* to it? What on earth do you mean b-by that?"

He continued to stare at her. In fact, he'd done nothing but stare at her since the moment they had met. "Because my mother spoke as you do."

Summer gazed at him as if she did not fully understand his words. Then, as reality settled, her jaw popped open. "Your *mother*?"

He nodded and turned away to regain his seat underneath the massive oak tree. Without hesitation, Summer followed and deposited herself next to his outstretched legs. He crossed his ankles, smiling at her awed expression.

"You find that surprising?" he asked. "Surely you did not believe yourself to be the only individual who has ever suffered from such an affliction?"

She blinked in thought; in faith, she'd never considered such a concept and after a moment, she shrugged. "Sometimes I feel as if I am," she said softly. "B-but, I suppose, now that I think on it, it would be selfish of me to consider that God saved this imperfection for me alone."

He laughed softly, displaying a row of even white teeth. The right side of his mouth was far more pliable than the left, the cheek moving stiffly, and even within the dim illumination of the moonlight Summer could see three fierce scars, in parallel succession, gracing his chiseled cheekbone and disappearing into his hairline. She found herself wondering what animal could have caused such scars.

"I would hardly call it an imperfection where it pertains to you, my lady," he said, his laughter fading as he interrupted her train of thought. "For certain, I have never seen such magnificence."

With a shy smile and a fierce mottle of red flooding her cheeks, Summer forgot all about his lopsided grin and lowered her gaze, staring to her lap and listening to his soft chuckle, casting him another coy glance when he continued to snort. As Antony once again moved from her grasp and onto his master's massive legs, she realized she was growing quite comfortable with the presence of the beast's gentle master.

"Is your mother still living, my lord?" she asked, attempting to divert the focus from her reddened face.

"Nay, she is not," he replied, without sorrow. "My mother passed away several years ago. And yours?"

"She died shortly after my b-birth," Summer answered, also without sorrow. "My father tells me I resemble her a great deal."

"Then she was a beautiful woman," Bose said sincerely.

Summer nodded in agreement to his assertion of her mother's grace, coming to feel comfortable enough that she could look the man in the face without averting her gaze shyly or uncertainly. Above their heads, the owl hooted again and Antony paused in his busy inspection of Bose's leg, looking into the darkened branches of the tree. Summer watched the ferret and Bose watched Summer.

"He is most threatened by the owl," she said. "Mayhap we should return him home."

"'Twill be my pleasure to escort you safely back to Chaldon," Bose replied, then paused a moment to eye her strangely beneath the silver moon. "Tell me, my lady; was there a reason why you were loitering about the knights' camp this eve? Considering how protective your family is, I can hardly imagine they let you wander about the encampment alone."

So much for her fading blush. Her cheeks ignited with color again and Summer lowered her gaze yet again, toying with the grass beneath her hand. She did not want to tell him why she was here, running from her family.

"I shall answer your question, my lord, if you will answer m-mine," the golden orbs came up from the grass, ensnaring him within their power. "Why did you wish to speak with me after the melee?"

"To ask for your favor. Now, why are you wandering alone amongst the shelters?"

"Do you still wish for my favor?"

He cocked an eyebrow, aware that she was deliberately attempting to evade his question. "Without a doubt. Unless, of course, the reason why you were lingering about the tents is because you were waiting for your lover to appear."

She frowned. "Ridiculous. I do not have a lover."

He sat forward, away from the trunk, resting his arm on a propped knee. "If you give me your favor, there are those who would believe that I am your lover."

He watched as Summer rose to her feet and fumbled with the sleeve of her gown. Abruptly, a blur of white was dangling from her fingers. It took Bose a moment to realize she was extending a kerchief.

He was on his feet faster than he could ever remember moving. Summer smiled, a bashful, beautiful gesture, as his timid fingers came up to clasp the delicate material.

"'Tis my handkerchief," she said quietly. "It is all I have at the moment that I may offer as a favor."

Gently, the kerchief fell from her fingers and into his grasp. His expression laced with wonder and pleasure, he brought the small token to his nose and inhaled deeply.

"God's Beard," he groaned before he could stop himself. When Summer's expression washed with concern, he struggled to explain his reaction. "It... it smells wonderful, my lady. The essence of roses, I believe."

She nodded, her smile returning with relief. "My b-brother bought me the perfume on a trip to London last year. The merchant told him that it had been Princess Eleanor's f-favorite fragrance."

"Princess Eleanor?"

"King John's daughter, Eleanor, b-before she married Lord Simon de Montfort. Apparently, Lord Simon preferred his wife to wear gardenia and she relinquished her roses to please him."

He gazed at her a moment, a faint smile tugging at his lips. "The man was a fool. There is surely no finer fragrance."

She blushed pleasingly; in fact, the faint pink cast had hardly left her cheeks since his appearance. But her uncertainty was gone, so much so that he felt very comfortable and very bold when he gently took her hand in his massive gauntlet, bringing it to his lips for a tender kiss. He simply could not help himself.

Nor could Summer help the wild surge of excitement that fired through her body. The only men who had ever kissed her had been her brothers, chaste kisses to her forehead or hand. But Bose's kiss, as simple a gesture as it was, spoke of untold passion. Her heart was thumping painfully against her ribs.

"M-M-My lord," her stammering was noticeably worse due to her quivering nerves. "T-The hour grows late. I should return to the keep before my b-brothers come looking for me."

He smiled, feeling her hand trembling against his fingers and experiencing the resurgence of sentiment within his heart that he had once believed deeply buried.

"As you say, my rose lady," he kissed her hand again. Collecting

Antony into one hand, he tucked her palm firmly into the crook of his elbow. "I am forced to agree with your suggestion that we return to the keep. I should not want your brothers to find us out in the wilds, alone. Certainly, their punishment would be severe."

Summer's knees were shaking so that she could hardly walk, but somehow she managed to follow his lead. "M-My b-brothers are afraid of you," she said, unable to keep the quiver from her voice. "T-They...t-t-they..."

He smiled, knowing it was his kisses that had affected her speaking manner and enormously pleased with her reaction.

"Slow yourself, my lady," he said calmly, continuing their casual walking pace purely to maintain a level of normalcy about them. If she were to notice that he was unconcerned with her stammering, it might ease her embarrassment and help her regain control of herself. "Relax and take a deep breath. There now, that's good. One more. Better?"

Summer nodded, maintaining her deep, even breathing; she had been horrified with her worsening condition until she realized Bose wasn't the least bit concerned. In fact, he was willing to help her through her difficulty. After several moments she looked to Bose with appreciative eyes.

"T-Thank you," she said softly. Bose swore the small hand about his elbow tightened. "You are very patient."

He smiled his faint, lop-sided grin. "As I told you, I have experience with your sort."

She cocked an eyebrow, sensing his jest. "Is that so? And what sort is that?"

His smile broadened and he handed her the ferret. "The right sort, my lady. The right sort," when she smiled faintly, his free hand closed over the small fingers clutching his elbow. "By the way; you never did tell me what you were doing in the knight's camp."

Her smile broadened as she watched the grass pass beneath their feet. "W-Waiting for my lover."

"You said you did not have a lover."

Her golden orbs found the silken kerchief, still tucked within the folds of his massive gauntlet. As Antony demanded to be set loose into her hair, she put the animal to her neck and reached out, tugging at the white fabric peeping from beneath Bose's armored glove.

"I suppose I do now."

He met her gaze. "I suppose you do."

CHAPTER SIX

"**G**OOD GOD, SUMMER! You gave him your favor?"

It was just after the dawn of a new morning. Seated before three very angry brothers, Summer maintained her courage.

"I did," she said, gazing defiantly into Lance's blazing blue eyes. "We shared a very nice conversation and when he asked for my favor, I gladly gave him my handkerchief."

"And he gave you that… that hairy rat as a token of his esteem?"

Antony, hovering in the folds of Summer's unmade bed, was intimidated by the loud voices and angry gestures. As small black eyes peered from beneath the bedrug, Summer looked to the tiny creature as if to apologize for the uproar.

"He said that Antony liked me b-better," she replied evenly. "And I could hardly refuse his generous gift."

Standing by the lancet window of his sister's bower, Stephan gazed over the tournament field without emotion. As the day emerged bright and clear, the final touches to the joust barrier were being completed by the carpenters and the lodges were being readied for the second day of guests.

His thoughts, however, were far removed from the arena below. He was concentrating on his sister's first display of rebellion, the harsh words to his wife that had reduced the woman to tears. Oddly enough, he wasn't angry. Summer was a bright, intelligent girl and it was only natural that she desired more of a public life once she had sampled a taste. But the fact that her desires seemed to center around Bose de Moray was disturbing to say the least.

"I told him to stay away from you," Stephan muttered, his tone far more relaxed than his youngest brother's. He moved his attention away from the window and back to his sister. "Did he tell you that I asked him to stay away from you?"

"Nay," Summer shook her head; although he was outwardly calm, Stephan's temper was legendary. And he had a knack for holding a grudge as well. Combined, the two factors frightened her more than Lance's wild raging and Ian's brooding silence. "He said that he asked to speak with me, but that you had denied him."

Stephan stared at her a moment before returning his focus to the field below. "Is that why you ran off last night? To be with him?"

Summer gazed at her brother a long, heady moment. "Nay, Stephan, I did not. I ran away last night because your wife and our father greatly embarrassed me in front of Sir B-Bose. It was purely coincidental that he found me later on, seated beneath Grandfather's oak tree."

"You were at Grandfather's oak tree?" Lance repeated incredulously. "Good God, Summer, that's located in the heart of the knight's camp! What on earth were you thinking, girl?"

"I was thinking to be alone, Lance!" she shot back, her composure slipping. "It's p-perfectly acceptable for me to be alone, wherever or however I chose!"

"Not in an encampment full of knights," Lance jabbed a finger at her. "And what about that, anyway? Did you and de Moray do anything other than talk? Or, mayhap, did he pick up where another knight left off?"

Summer bolted from her chair, furious and insulted. "How dare you accuse m-me of… of… damnation, Lance! You k-know me better than that!"

Stephan pushed himself away from the window, placing himself between his two siblings. "Lance did not mean to infer that you were… God's Blood, Lance, apologize for your slanderous statement," he frowned at his youngest brother. "Whether or not you meant to accuse your sister of wanton actions, your statement was uncalled for."

Ruddy-cheeked, Lance sighed heavily and turned away. "I did not mean it the way it sounded, Summer," he said, his voice taut with emotion. "It's just that… Good God, we spent hours searching for you last night, looking in all of the usual places. We stayed clear of the knight's camp simply because we knew you would not venture into the heart of such an establishment. And then, when you finally decided to return from your wanderings, you went directly to bed without a word as to where you had been. It was frustrating to say the least."

"And frightening," Ian put in, his tone even and relaxed. Where Lance could splinter the walls with his shouting, Ian, like Stephan, scarcely raised his voice. "We were worried for you, love. We'd been searching for hours when next we realized, one of the sentry's informed us that you had returned under de Moray's escort. Since you went directly to bed and refused to speak with us, we spent the entire night tossing and turning, wondering what had happened. Can you see our point, Summer?"

Her anger somewhat cooling with her middle brother's manner, she was nonetheless hurt by Lance's implication. "Nothing happened, Ian. Sir B-Bose was a perfect gentleman."

Stephan eyed his sister a moment, carefully scrutinizing her defensive, emotional demeanor. "Let's start at the beginning, sweetheart. After you ran away from Genisa, where did you go?"

Summer shrugged, tearing her hostile gaze away from Lance and moving toward the long, latticed windows overlooking the eastern wall. "I wandered until I came to rest under Grandfather's oak. Sir B-Bose found me there and we had a wonderful conversation."

"Then he knows about your speech?"

She cast her brother an impatient look, as if he were a simpleton. "Of course he knows. And he doesn't care. His mother was stricken with the same affliction and he is perfectly comfortable with the fact."

Ian and Lance glanced to Stephan, the men exchanging various degrees of surprise. After a lengthy pause involving deeper deliberations and speculation, Stephan turned away from his mildly-astonished brothers to refocus on his sister. Stroking his chin in a thoughtful gesture, he labored to formulate a careful reply.

"I see he told you something of himself then," he said, watching her expression closely. "Did you learn much about him?"

She sighed, her slender fingers toying with the wooden lattice as she gazed over the compound. "He spoke of his mother. We did not speak of much, truly."

Listening to her explanation, Stephan's fears were somewhat allayed but not his fury. He had specifically asked de Moray to stay away from his sister; obviously, the man was unwilling to obey his request. Before the situation grew out of hand, it was becoming apparent that drastic measures would have to be taken to cleave any further contact.

Drawing a deep breath for strength and courage, he moved toward his sister. "Summer, in spite of your pleasant contact with de Moray, I believe it best that you stay away from him. I'll return the pet and collect your favor and…."

She whirled on her brother, her calm deportment vanished as her eyes widened with immediate outrage. "You'll do no such thing. I f-forbid you to control my life in such a manner."

Stephan sighed, struggling to keep his demeanor composed and caring. "I am not attempting to control you, sweetheart, merely protect you. You must trust that I know best in such matters."

"No!" she practically shouted. "You are not my f-father, Stephan du Bonne. If I want to bestow Sir B-Bose with a favor, then it is my decision and not yours."

Stephan's jaw ticked faintly as his composure slipped a notch. "Father will agree with me and well you know it. Summer, you must trust me in these matters. I know far more than you when it comes to the trials of courtship."

"Who said anything about courtship?" Summer demanded. "I gave the man a k-kerchief, not a wedding promise!"

"Listen to him, Summer," Ian said quietly. "He's only thinking of your best interests, love. We all are."

Summer looked to her brothers. The flush mottling her cheeks deepened and her pretty jaw ticked wildly with emotion. *Damn them!* They were always trying to run her life, forcing her to their demanding will in every matter large or small. And as an obedient sister, she obeyed them implicitly.

But not this time. She was determined to do as she pleased, if only this once. She liked Bose; he was kind and noble and chivalrous and she could hardly understand her brothers' collective resistance to her interest. As she continued to gaze into their stern, if not somewhat compassionate expressions, her anger inevitably gained speed.

"I thought you would be pleased that I f-found someone to tolerate my difference," she said quietly, with thinly-reined fury. "Instead, you seek to isolate me from him as well. Will this never stop, Stephan? Will I not be adequate for any man?"

Stephan's expression softened dramatically. "God's Blood, Summer, it's not your inadequacy at all. You are perfect, sweetheart, truly. It's Bose we are concerned with."

"W-Why?"

Stephan stared at her a moment, noting her volatile emotions, feeling her shame and curiosity and anguish. Of course she resented his interference; he'd never given her a valid motive behind his brotherly concerns. Mayhap if she were to discover the basis for his objection, she would come to realize his earnest stance.

"Do you remember yesterday when I mentioned that Bose de Moray possessed less than a desirable reputation?" he asked.

Summer nodded firmly. "Aye. And I told you that I would not believe the slander, whatever it was."

Stephan maintained his gaze a moment before lowering his eyes, scratching absently at his chin. "Allow me to inform you what has been said before you make any rapid decisions. When de Moray came to the tournament circuit four years ago, it was rumored that he left his post as Captain of the King's Guard under mysterious circumstances," raising his somewhat hesitant gaze, he fixed his sister in the eye. "It was said that he killed his wife in order to gain her wealth. I am unaware of the circumstances, for the speculation is purely rumor. But as hearsay would have it, it is said that his wife was well and whole one day and dead the next. Immediately after her death, de Moray resigned his post and fled London. He hasn't returned since."

Summer's anger and outrage transformed into shock of the deepest level as Stephan's words permeated the fragile membrane of her soul. Mouth open with disbelief and horror, her head slowly wagged back and forth. "I… it's not true, Stephan. I cannot b-believe it would be true."

Gently, Stephan put his hand on her shoulder. "The rumors are said to come from a most reliable source."

Brow furrowed with incredulity, Summer's pain and shock was evident. "Who, for God's sake?"

"His wife's mother."

Summer simply stared at him. Stephan gave her a brief, sympathetic smile before removing his comforting hand. Wisely concluding that it was time to leave their sister to her own thoughts, the three brothers moved for the chamber door. Although stunned, Summer still considered the subject very much open for debate.

"The man I spoke with last night was not capable of such an act," she said quietly, her voice strangely tight. "I c-cannot believe you, Stephan. I simply cannot."

The three brothers paused by the door, the two younger men looking to their older, wiser brother to refute her statement.

"Even if you do not believe me, I ask that you trust me all the same," he said quietly. "Have I ever lied to you, Summer? Have I ever done you wrong?"

Golden eyes met those of soothing green, the pain from her gaze cutting deep into his heart. Bose de Moray had been the only man she had ever truly known outside of her immediately family, a dashingly dark knight who had stolen her naive little heart with his gallant actions and gentle pursuit. A heart Stephan was now smashing to pieces.

"Nay, Stephan," her reply was soft. "You've never done me wrong."

Stephan opened the door, ushering his brothers through. Now that the crisis was past, it was time to focus on the approaching joust and they were eager to move from a most depressing confrontation with their young sister. Just as Stephan moved to close the door, Summer's quiet voice brought him to a halt.

"I'll tell him, Stephan," her whispered words were barely audible. "If I am to take b-back my favor, then I would do it myself."

Although against the idea, Stephan nonetheless nodded with hesitant agreement. "After I have donned my armor, we shall seek him. Acceptable?"

Summer could hardly manage the energy to acknowledge him.

"I shall speak with him alone," she murmured, gazing toward the latticed window and listening to the faint sounds in the bailey. "Do you understand?"

Again, Stephan nodded, knowing how hard this was for her. "As you say, sweetheart," he replied softly, closing the door as he spoke. "Genisa will be here in a few minutes to help you dress."

The door latched shut with a faint click, leaving Summer alone with her tumultuous thoughts. Although her first instinct was to refute her brother's statements, she was forced to admit that, indeed, Stephan had never lied to her. He had always protected her.

Until yesterday, she had been quite content to remain protected. But that was before the appearance of Bose de Moray; suddenly, Summer sensed there was more to life than her isolated existence at Chaldon. The massive knight with the onyx-black eyes and lopsided grin had affected her.

Sighing heavily, Summer unlatched the lattice and gazed onto the bright countryside below, catching sight in the distance of Bose's black and white tent. Leaning against the cold stone, she closed her eyes to the soft sea breeze caressing her face. Aye, she would speak with him, requesting her favor returned unless he had an answer to her brother's disturbing suggestion.

Do not let the rumors be true. For once, let Stephan be wrong.

CB

"TELL ME MORE, Bose. After you found Antony with Lady Summer, what happened?"

Standing with his arms aloft as his Squire of the Body went about securing his breastplate, Bose refused to look at an overly eager Tate.

"Nothing happened. We exchanged a few pleasantries and I escorted her back to the keep. God's Beard, Tate, I already told you this. I told you last night and this morning, too. There is nothing new to add."

"But you gave her Antony, for God's sake. If there was hardly more than a few pleasantries exchanged, what on earth possessed you to gift her with your beloved ferret?"

Bose continued to watch the lad as he straightened the mail beneath the plate protection. "As I told you, she had found Antony wandering loose among the tents. When I happed upon them, they were getting along quite famously and it was obvious that he preferred her gentle touch to mine. I can hardly blame the beast."

Tate pondered his answer a moment, thinking the calm reply to be unemotional. "What is she like, then?" he persisted. "If you delivered her your most prize pet, surely she is entirely wonderful."

Bose let out a slow, weary sigh as Tate fidgeted like a giddy young boy. "She is. A delightful, wonderful woman."

In the corner, already dressed for the approaching joust, Morgan shook his head in a patient gesture. "You already told him that. For the love of God, Bose, tell him more before he bursts a vein."

Tate grinned at the older knight, knowing the man wanted to know the gory details of the encounter just as badly as he did but was far too dignified to say it. Instead, he would allow Tate to make a fool of himself.

"There's nothing more to tell, I say," Bose insisted as his squire carefully secured the final latch. "We met, we spoke, and I took her home. End of story."

"Except for the favor," Morgan reminded him, chuckling softly when Bose cast him a menacing glare.

"Ah, yes, the favor," Tate delved into the delightful little detail. "Tell me how you acquired it. Did you demand it from her? Beg? Plead? How did she give it?"

"With her hand," Bose supplied drolly.

"That's not what he meant," Morgan put in.

"I know what he meant," Bose snapped in his first show of irritation, lowering his arms as his squire finished the smaller details of armoring. "There is nothing more to tell, truthfully. I asked, and she was gracious enough to comply. As I said before, she is a beautiful woman with a beautiful personality. And if you behave yourself, I just might introduce you someday."

Tate snorted, crossing his arms and stepping aside as the young squire handled the massive broadsword. "God's Blood, she is so beautiful I'd surely turn into a blathering idiot at the sight of her. How did you speak with her and not collapse completely?"

"It wasn't easy," Bose admitted, adjusting his broadsword as the squire secured it loosely. "She has the most amazing golden eyes. And she possesses a surprisingly droll sense of humor."

Morgan watched his liege, elaborating on last eve's encounter far more than he had all morning. Knowing that by the sheer tone in Bose's voice, the man was smitten. "And, naturally, she enchanted you."

"Naturally," Bose agreed, although it was done without a hint of remorse or emotion. "I would've had to have been a corpse not to have responded to her charms."

"Did you kiss her?" Tate could hardly refrain from asking.

Bose cocked an eyebrow, a restrained scowl crossing his rugged features. "Aye, Tate, I kissed her and ravaged her and left her for rubbish." When Morgan laughed softly at the sarcastic reply, Bose shook his head at Tate's foolish question and moved to claim his helm. "God's Beard, you've got me bedding the woman already and we've only just met."

But Tate was undeterred by his lord's irritable response. "Were it me, I most definitely would have bedded her by now."

Bose grasped his helm in one hand. "That is the difference between us, my friend. I have more respect for a woman than you do."

Tate shrugged as if in agreement. The joust was rapidly approaching and Bose had been selected in the draw as the first combatant against none other than Breck Kerry. Knowing the man needed his concentration for the coming event, Tate stopped his questions. There would be time enough later to pester Bose with his curiosity.

Farl, Adgar and Artur were already outside, making sure the mounts were properly prepared. As the three men inside the tent exited the shelter, Farl appeared in the opening and nearly ran Bose down in his haste. Bushy red mustache twitching, his faded green eyes focused intently on his liege.

"You have a visitor, my lord," he said with more excitement than he had exhibited in a long while. "A *lady* visitor."

Bose's usually emotionless face slackened. "What lady?"

Farl's weathered eyes crinkled with mirth. "A certain young lady with a ferret that looks remarkably like Antony."

Bose was out of the tent before he could draw another breath, ignorant of the equally-eager entourage behind him. Rounding the corner of the black and white shelter, the young woman and her brother came into view and at that moment Bose was reminded of the crowd gathered in his shadow; he swore he heard a collective sigh of appreciation go up. Momentarily distracted from her radiant presence, he turned to scowl fiercely at the collection of loyal knights.

"Away, vultures," he growled. "I would speak to the lady alone."

Farl turned to obey, plowing into Tate and nearly taking the man to the ground. Grasping hold of the bewitched young knight, he pulled him along as he made haste away from Bose, leaving Morgan to casually vacate his liege's company. After casting the lady a lingering glance, the older knight wandered away and Bose drew in a deep breath for strength and composure, turning once again in the direction of the lady.

God's Beard, she was more beautiful than he had remembered.

Approaching as casually as he could manage, he was well aware when Adgar abruptly moved past him, discreetly dispersing the squires and servants who had collected in a crowd to stare at the magnificent lady. Only Artur remained, speaking with Stephan as Summer's golden gaze fixed upon the approaching warrior.

Bose acted as if Stephan were invisible as he came to a halt before Summer. "My lady," he said as smoothly as he could. "I did not expect to see you again so soon. To what do I owe the honor of your visit?"

Summer met his smile, her gaze oddly hesitant. She tore her eyes away from Bose's sharp black orbs, looking to her brother to silently beg the man's departure. Bose, too, looked to Stephan, not surprised to note his hostile expression.

"Stephan," he greeted steadily. "I see that you are prepared for the joust. The fourth round, is it?"

Stephan had no intention of replying until Summer's beseeching gaze coerced him into a strained response. "Aye."

Bose nodded faintly in acknowledgement, unoffended by the man's lack of manners. If the situation were reversed and it had been Stephan du Bonne disrespecting Bose's wishes by pursuing his young, beautiful sister, Bose would not have been quite so composed. Deadly would have been closer to the mark.

Therefore, in lieu of meeting Stephan's challenging gaze since he honestly could not fault the man his outrage, he returned his attention to Stephan's exquisite sister. The twinkle reappeared in his eye as he once again drank in the sight of her loveliness.

"Is there a reason for your visit, my lady?" he asked pleasantly. "Or did you come to distract me from the day's event?"

The familiar blush returned to her cheeks, far more radiant under the early morning sun than it had been beneath the cold gray moon.

"I came to speak with you, my lord," she said quietly. "Stephan was gracious enough to escort me even though he is extremely b-busy with preparation for this morn's joust."

It was a hint for Stephan to leave her alone with the massive knight, but her brother refused to heed the roundabout request. His eyes still riveted to Bose, there was no mistaking the tension in his voice as he spoke.

"Summer, I have a need to speak with Sir Bose before you commence with your conversation," he said evenly. "Please leave us alone for a moment."

With great hesitance, Summer cast her brother a long glance before quietly excusing herself, moving several feet away. Artur, seeing his opportunity arise, made sure Stephan maintained his focus on Bose before discreetly moving toward the lady. Bose's focus was on Summer's brother.

"You wanted to speak with me, Stephan?" Bose braced himself.

Stephan did not hold back. "I have been led to understand that you disobeyed my request that you leave my sister unmolested," his voice was as cold as ice, biting and hard and severe. "Fair enough. I cannot fault you a true desire to pursue the object of your interest. What I say now, I say not because your rebellious actions have offended me. I say it because my sister's welfare is my utmost concern."

Bose nodded his head. "Continue."

Stephan's voice was reduced to a threatening whisper. "I know nothing about you. But what I have heard through rumor and hearsay I must say I find exceptionally disturbing. Although I do not pass judgment on you, I must trust my instincts where my sister is concerned. You will stay away from her, as I have asked, or I shall take steps to ensure she no longer has any further contact with you. Do you understand?"

Even though Stephan had not defined the rumors, he did not have to; Bose knew what he was speaking of. It was difficult to maintain his composure as he met Stephan's unfriendly gaze.

"Is that why you came?" he asked quietly. "To threaten me with violence if I do not sever all contact with your sister?"

"I came to demand you stay away from her."

"And what of your father? Surely he has supreme say in all matters regarding the lady."

"My father agrees with me, which is why I have been chosen to deliver the message, warrior to warrior. Mayhap you will understand the message more clearly."

"I understand perfectly. But you, sir, do not."

Stephan frowned. "And what does that mean?"

Bose regarded the man a long moment, his black eyes glimmering with sorrow and fury. "You profess not to judge me based on rumor but by your actions, you have done precisely that," turning away, he immediately focused on Summer, blushing profusely as Artur attempted to carry on a one-sided conversation. "Your sister wishes to speak with me. If there is to be any true cleaving of this infantile relationship, then I would hear it from her alone. Good day to you, my lord."

Stephan let him go, somewhat off-guard by his accusation of bias but realizing the man to be correct. With a lingering glance to the backside of the massive knight, he moved a respectable distance away as conversation commenced between Bose and his sister. Once de Moray heard the same message from Summer's lips, surely the man would have no choice but to comply.

Bose knew Stephan to be watching him as he approached Summer, chasing Artur away with a good-natured insult. As the old man fled, Bose refocused his attention on Summer with a sinking heart; in light of his dialogue with Stephan, he knew the general theme of the impending conversation.

"What is it you wished to say to me, my lady?" he asked pleasantly.

Summer's beautiful face was upturned, her golden eyes boring into him as the gentle morning light caressed each feature with warmth. "I would ask you what Stephan said f-first."

Bose's expression did not change, although he paused a brief moment to collect his thoughts. "He has asked that I stay away from you. Do you wish this as well?"

Do you wish this as well? His sorrowful words echoed in Summer's mind and she took a deep breath, glancing to her stiff brother perched upon the distant rise. Her gaze lingered on the man before returning her focus to Bose.

"Would you walk with me, my lord?" she asked softly, heading in the direction of her Grandfather's oak.

Without hesitation, Bose complied, feeling the least bit like an eager squire trailing after a beautiful, unreachable lady. God's Beard, he'd walk all the way to London if she asked him to. He'd do anything she asked of him.

The grass was soft and moist beneath their feet as they strolled in silence toward the massive oak tree. Bose kept his gaze ahead, catching a steady glimpse of her persimmon-colored gown from the corner of his eye. As they proceeded to walk and Bose continued to ponder her beauty, he was jolted from his thoughts when her gentle voice filled the air between them.

"I have been told to retrieve my f-favor," she said, not looking at him. "And I have been f-further told to return Antony to your care."

Bose was prepared for her statement. "I see. Were you given a reason for these actions?"

Beneath the great sprawling tree, Summer came to a halt and turned to face him. "Stephan has relayed a most disturbing bit of information and I know of no other way to approach the subject than to plainly ask you," taking a deep breath, she fixed him in the eye. "Please forgive my cruel question, my lord, b-but I find I must know the truth."

His gaze lingered on her a moment, trying not to appear unnerved. Crossing his arms, he forced himself to maintain an emotionless facade. "Ask then, my lady. I shall answer truthfully."

Gazing into his scarred, rugged face, Summer felt brutal and foolish at the same time. After her brother had informed her of de Moray's villainous reputation, she had spent the better part of the morning coming to grips with the information. Although her heart strongly refuted the lies, her mind was convinced that Stephan was merely protecting her best interests.

"Please do not think me heartless, my lord," she whispered, almost pleadingly. "I certainly do not mean to be."

A faint smile tugged at his lips; for certain, he could see that she was extremely upset by the entire circumstance. "How can I think you heartless if I do not know the question?"

With a heavy sigh, Summer lowered her gaze. "M-My b-brother s-said… h-he said…."

Her stuttering grew particularly bad. "Slow yourself, lady," his tone softened. "Slow down and take a deep breath. There is no need to be nervous."

Swallowing hard, Summer's expression was painful. "I-I am n-not, truly. I-It's just that S-Stephan's words upset me so."

"What words, love?"

All twitching, agitation and disquiet came to a halt. Summer's wide-eyed gaze came to rest on Bose's piercing black orbs and, for a moment, she forgot how to breathe. *He had called her love.* The world around her could have exploded to cinder and still, she would be riveted to Bose's wonderful face. Nothing else seemed to be more important than the emotions she was experiencing at this very moment.

"That you killed your wife."

"I did not kill my wife."

Summer's mouth worked as if she were attempting to speak, but no words came forth for the moment. "But… she is dead?"

"She is. A result of childbirth and nothing more."

The truth. Clean, clear, and concise. Four years of rumors dashed in one swift motion. Summer stared at him, wanting so desperately to believe him.

"But what of the rumors?" she wanted to know. "Stephan indicated your mother-in-law to be the source of the hearsay."

Bose's gaze was steady. "The woman blames me for my wife's death, insisting that the son I planted killed her with his size. Angry that I chose to divert my grief by joining the tournament circuit, my mother-in-law spread the rumors in hopes of ruining my chances of being accepted as a true contender."

"And you never sought to dismiss them?"

"They never mattered until now."

Again, there was no hesitation in his answers and by the expression on his face, Summer realized that any lingering doubt was dissolved. He had answered her completely and she believed him without reserve. Unable to control her relief, she emitted a sigh of such power that her entire body deflated; she surely would have tumbled to the ground had Bose's steadying hand not held her firm.

"Good Lord," Summer breathed, hand to her forehead. "I felt like such a fool for asking. I did not want to, but Stephan…."

"Summer," Bose interrupted her prattling statement. When she looked into his eyes, she could hardly explain the glimmer of joy and mirth within the onyx depths. "Do you realize you've spoken the last several sentences with hardly a stammer?"

Her brow furrowed and she opened her mouth to speak, abruptly pressing her lips tight when the truth of his words sank deep. She had indeed spoken the last three sentences without a stammer.

"Impossible," she whispered, her eyes wide with shock and disbelief. "I always stammer."

He smiled, a broad delightful gesture. "I shouldn't have said a word. We could have continued the conversation endlessly and you would not have realized the event of a miracle."

"Miracle?" she shook her head, baffled and unbalanced by the entire conversation. "But… it's simply impossible. I always s-stammer. I always will."

He stared at her. "Sometimes, we do things because others expect us to. Or we complete certain actions purely out of repetition or self-pity. Is it possible that you stammer because your family has pitied you and coddled you so that you've known nothing else? A childhood affliction that you've continued simply because it was expected of you?"

Bewildered, she shook her head. "I… I do not know," cocking her head with confusion, she peered at him curiously. "Are you saying my f-family is to blame for my problem?"

He cocked an eyebrow, eyeing Stephan lingering impatiently atop the distant rise. "Of course not. All I am suggesting is that you do what is expected of you. I have treated your affliction with understanding and a casual manner, therefore, you are less inclined to realize the obvious."

"Which is?"

"That you stutter out of habit. And because you are expected to."

She stared at him in astonishment. In faith, she'd never given his logic any measure of consideration and had no idea how to respond. "T-T…This is what you would believe?"

He shrugged faintly. "I did not say that. I am merely suggesting the possibility," his voice softened as his gaze raked her delicate features. "My father once said that my mother never stammered when she spoke to animals or pets, or when she muttered to herself when she was alone. And she never stuttered whilst she was singing, and she had a lovely voice indeed. My father managed to break her of her impediment somewhat late in life by putting their conversations to song. Can you sing?"

She flushed about the ears. "Not a note."

He smiled, a wonderfully lop-sided gesture. "Then we shall have to discover another method to rid you of this habit."

How on earth they had moved from the subject of Bose's evil reputation to the focus of her speech, Summer wasn't sure. But just as the man had been truthful and correct in every matter thus far, he also seemed to know a great deal about her flaw. Certainly, his speculations left food for thought and Summer found herself upswept with his suggestion. The more she thought on his words, however, the more she realized her stuttering had dramatically lessened the very moment he addressed her fondly.

Flush deepening with the wonder of a new discovery, she was off course of the original subject and fading fast. Bose, however, was still acutely aware of Stephan's menacing presence and he dropped his hand from her arm, nearly grasping at her again when she wobbled threateningly.

"I believe your brother is waiting for you, my lady," he said quietly. "In spite of our recent conversation, would you still like your favor returned?"

Eyeing her brother, Summer sighed sharply. "Nay," she said softly. "You will keep it. And you will do me a f-favor, as well."

He was unable to keep the smile from his lips. "Anything at all, my lady. All you need do is ask."

"Triumph over my brothers," she said, returning her attention to his inquisitive, if not somewhat pleased, expression. "Beat everyone t-this day and win the joust."

Biting back a broader smile, he bowed gallantly. "Your wish is my command, my lady. I shall endeavor to fulfill your desires."

His grin was infectious and Summer smiled in return. "Thank you, Sir Bose. F-For everything, I thank you."

"'Tis my pleasure to serve you, Lady Summer."

She reached out a small, delicate hand and grasped his massive gauntlet. Bose's heart leapt wildly against his ribs and, unable to help himself, he brought her hand to his lips for a lingering kiss. It was sweet and warm and wonderful. As Summer smiled radiantly, they could hear a faint shout in the distance. Bose did not look to see who it was; he simply kept staring at Summer.

For decency's sake, he attempted to release Summer's hand, but she refused to let him go and eventually, they both turned in the direction of the shout. Thinking it must have been Stephan, they were surprised to see it had not come from him. Bose continued to hold Summer's hand tightly as Morgan interrupted their gentle encounter.

"Forgive me, my lord," the well-groomed man said. "Another party has been announced nearly a mile out, bearing your household name and colors."

Bose's brow furrowed. "What nonsense is this? Who could be approaching, bearing my banner?"

Morgan cleared his throat, hesitant to continue in the presence of the lady. But he was given little choice. God help him, he wished he were bearing any news other than the information about to spill forth.

"Margot has come, Bose."

CHAPTER SEVEN

"**W**HY ARE YOU here?"

Margot was not surprised by the enmity-laced question. Her faded blue eyes narrowed at her powerful son-in-law, fury matching fury, hate matching hate. She had no love for the man who killed her daughter.

"I begged you not to go to Chaldon during this time of mourning," she said bitingly. "The anniversary of Lora's death was yesterday and I specifically asked that you spend it at Ravendark, reflecting upon her memory."

Bose's lips were pressed into a tight line of displeasure. From outside the black and white tent, the roar in the distance told him that the combatants had taken to the lists and were practicing for their coming bouts. When his presence was required on the field in preparation for the approaching games, he found himself locked in verbal combat with an aged shrew he could scarcely tolerate. But for Lora's sake, he was compelled to abide the harshness.

"You did not ask that I remain at Ravendark, you demanded I stay," he replied, struggling to keep his emotions in check. Margot had the uncanny ability to snap his composure. "As I explained to you, Lora is well aware that I have been mourning her death consistently for the past four years. Whether or not I remain locked inside my chamber, wailing like a fool, does not mean that I am any less sorrowful for her passing."

Margot's thin jaw ticked dangerously. "Were you any more of a man I would expect you to cease this foolish tournament obsession and devote the remainder of your worthless life to her glorious memory."

"Margot, I will not discuss this with you," he said as evenly as he could manage. "I have a joust coming very shortly and your unwelcome presence is distracting. Tell me why you've come and be done with it."

Thin and frail and quaking with age, Margot's feeble appearance concealed a ferocious tongue and bitter soul. Her eyes flashed angrily at the man she possessed like a hostile demon, sinking her claws deep into his soul as if to never let him go. He was hers; a possession, a whipping post, a limitless source of vengeance and pain.

"I already told you," her feeble tone was laced with malice. "I asked you not to continue your usual pursuits during the anniversary of Lora's death. We should spend the time together, you and I, paying homage to her memory."

"So you followed me to Dorset because I am not mourning to your satisfaction?" he shook his head bitterly. "You make my life miserable enough at home. What makes you think I want you here, wreaking havoc and causing misery? 'Twas certainly not your right to commandeer the men I left behind to protect my keep and demand they escort you to Chaldon."

"'Twas indeed my right as your mother-in-law," she snapped. "You and I should be together during this time of sorrow. Since you coldheartedly chose to continue with your worthless occupation, I had no choice but to follow and ensure that you do not forget my daughter's memory. Here I am, and here I will stay."

His face twisted into a wry, disbelieving expression. "Why, for Christ's sake? You would do well to simply return to Ravendark and mourn alone because I, for one, do not want you here. And I certainly do not need you to tell me where and how I shall grieve the passing of my wife. I believe I have grieved quite enough over the past four years to satisfy you."

Margot's eyes glittered furiously. "You know nothing of grieving," she hissed. "You quit your post as Captain of the Guard simply because you could not bear the memories associated with the position and I agreed wholeheartedly with your judgment at that time. But instead of retiring to the keep granted you by King Henry to ponder your lonely future and bygone dreams, you chose to pursue the debauchery of life upon the tournament circuit. This, Sir Bose, I hardly call grieving and if you believe for one moment I am satisfied with your supposed display of sorrow, you are sadly mistaken."

His jaw ticked faintly as he studied the embittered woman he had once liked a great deal. But time and death had changed the situation between them, a brittle relationship where there had once been genuine affection.

"So, instead of attempting to move on with my life in spite of tragedy, you would have me isolate myself from the world to live on broken dreams and a dead wife," shaking his head, he sighed heavily. "Margot, I had to do what was best for me and you are well aware of the fact. I have made a good deal of wealth upon the circuit, enough to keep you in comfort for the rest of your life. As Lora's mother, it is my obligation to take care of you. But I forbid you to criticize the method by which I have obtained my wealth or the method by which I grieve; the tournament circuit has offered me a good deal of support and distraction in both categories, of which I have greatly needed. If you do not understand my motives or ideals, that is your misfortune."

Her thin lips drawn tight, a faint mottle lingered upon her wrinkled cheekbones. "'Twas Lora's misfortune to have married you at the first."

He refused to be baited by the familiar insult Margot resorted to every time the conversation veered against her. Turning from the vicious woman, he ordered his manservant to see to her comfort and hastily quit the tent; he simply could not deal with her any longer.

On his heels, the skilled squire followed closely, laden with his liege's spare pole and other weaponry. The primary pole was already at the field with the fully armored charger, awaiting the appearance of the mighty lord.

The joust field came into view shortly, the bright joust barrier carving a path down the middle of the field laden with the colors of the competing houses. There were several knights prancing about the field, gold and green colors, blue and yellow, and three red and white. The moment he laid sight upon the du Bonne red and white, all thoughts of Margot faded. There was a far more distracting presence in the stands than the lingering memory of his mother-in-law and her dead daughter.

A faint roar went up from the crowd, distracting him from his thoughts as he realized the cry was meant for him. Artur appeared, babbling about the climate of the day and other insignificant notions, knowing his nephew had just endured a hellish go-around with Margot and attempting to distract the man with talk of the coming event.

But Bose waved the old man away. The moment he caught sight of Summer in her persimmon colored dress seated beneath the large red and white canopy, he was quite adequately distracted.

෪

SILENT AND ATTENTIVE, Summer had all but ignored her sister-in-law and her father since her arrival to the lodges. Since the very moment Stephan had escorted her from Bose's presence, her brother had been furious that she had refused to reclaim her favor and she, in turn, had responded to his anger. A few bitter words between them, unusual between the affectionate pair, had been a direct catalyst to even greater hostility.

Red-faced and tight-lipped, the eldest du Bonne brother proceeded to roughly escort his rebellious sister to the lodges where Genisa and Edward awaited the commencement of the games. With a halting explanation of her behavior to his father, Stephan quit the lodges in search of his charger. With the joust set to begin, he had more pressing details to worry over than his sister.

He had made her well aware, however, that he would deal with her at a later time. Edward had never dealt the punishment for his children; Stephan always had. As long as the eldest son handled the unruly brood, Edward was assured that all would be dealt with in a fair and diligent manner. In truth, Stephan was like a crutch; the more used, the more needed. Not strangely, Edward would never dream of interfering in his heir's method of discipline or justice; whatever his son decided was good enough for him and he supported the man.

Therefore, Edward pretended to disregard his daughter's rebellion as she took a seat in the lists and Summer ignored him back. Genisa eyed her sister-in-law with a great deal of bewilderment. She couldn't understand why the woman should suddenly transform from a respectful sister into a defiant vixen. The sweet young lady who had sat with her atop the battlements yesterday morn had changed overnight.

"Summer?" she whispered hesitantly, tugging on the woman's sleeve when she failed to obtain a response. "Summer? Is something the matter?"

Summer turned to her sister-in-law with an expression Genisa had never seen before. It was so... cold. "Nothing is the matter, Genisa. Nothing in the least."

Genisa's pure blue eyes were somewhat sad. "Then why is Stephan so angry with you? Summer, why won't you tell me what's happened? Does it have something to do with Bose de Moray?"

Summer's cool stance wavered slightly. "Your husband is angry b-because I have made my own decision regarding Sir Bose and he does not agree."

"Decision about what?"

Summer's attention moved to the field as a knight clad in magnificent red and black thundered by the lodges, a massive carved eagle protruding from his newer helm. The crowd roared its approval and she watched the knight as he turned at the end of the field and lost himself amongst the other contestants.

"Sir B-Bose asked that I supply him with a favor and I did," she finally replied. "Stephan is angry."

Genisa's brow furrowed. "Why, that is foolish. My husband seems to forget that we met the very same way, at a tournament in Richmond. He gallantly asked for my favor and I supplied him with a piece of my gown."

Summer looked to her sister-in-law again, her expression somewhat less harsh as she recalled the event. "I remember. He could not stop speaking of you."

Genisa smiled, noting that Summer sounded a good deal more like her usual self with that short, gentle reply. "And I could not stop speaking of him, either." Another knight roared past the lodges, clad in green and yellow and both women turned to watch the man ride by. "Good Heavens, I'd wager to say that a good portion of the married knights have met their wives at tournaments. I find Stephan's attitude so ridiculous that I believe I'll tell him so."

Her stiff manner fading with Genisa's support, Summer was once again relaxed and smiling as opposed to rigid and resentful. After all, her sister-in-law had nothing to do with Stephan's unbending attitude. She softened further.

"Nise," Summer looked to the lovely woman. "I do apologize for the terrible things I said yesterday. You do not b-bray like an injured goat and you do not talk too much."

Genisa's smile broadened and she reached out, clutching Summer's hand tightly. "You already apologized to me, darling. This morning when you allowed me to help you dress for the day. There is no need for spoken sorrows between family."

"Aye, there is. I truly d-did not mean what I said. I was… confused, I suppose, and upset."

"I know," Genisa squeezed her hand. "I realize it must be difficult for you, having your first taste of the real world. You've been isolated so long for your own protection that it is only natural that your first experience of excitement left you feeling deprived of a normal life."

Summer cocked an eyebrow. "How insightful, Genisa. Especially f-for you."

Genisa wasn't insulted in the least; Summer knew her well enough to know that her view of the world moved scarcely beyond the surface of her frivolous thoughts. "They are not my words, but Stephan's. When you ran off last night, he was very worried and spent a good deal of the time trying to rationalize your state of mind."

Summer lowered her head shamefully, shrugging after a time. "I do apologize for f-frightening everyone, but at the time, it was as if… as if I had to break free." Suddenly, the crowd emitted a mighty shout and Summer's head came up to locate the source of their excitement. It took her no time to witness Bose's arrival at the edge of the field, mounted astride his mighty charcoal steed as several men hovered about to adjust his armor.

Instantly, her heart thumped against her ribs and she could feel the familiar heat rush to her cheeks. "B-But I do not regret my actions. Had I not run from you, I would have never met Bose."

Genisa noted her sister-in-law's expression as she beheld her favored knight; literally, she could read the wonder and appreciation in the woman's eyes and it was not hard to recall the same excitement at the time she had first met Stephan. "You have only just come from him, have you not?" she asked. "What did you speak of?"

Summer continued to watch the distant knight, pondering Genisa's question in spite of her distraction. "Nothing terribly exciting," she said, skirting the issue. "Stephan demanded I reclaim my favor, as I said, b-but I refused to do so. Instead, Bose and I had a wonderful conversation until a situation arose that he was required to deal with."

"Situation? What was that?"

Summer shook her head faintly, her eyes riveted to the black and white warrior. "T-truthfully, I do not know. He excused himself so quickly that I never had a chance to ask."

Genisa mulled over the answer, watching the countenance of her sister-in-law's demeanor. "Was he wonderful, Summer?" her voice was soft, encouraging. "Was he completely, utterly wonderful?"

Summer nodded, her gaze never leaving the massive knight. "More than wonderful, Nise. He is everything a knight should be. Everything a man should be."

A grin graced Genisa's lips. "When the two of you spoke, was it kindly? Did he notice your stammer?"

Eyes still fixed upon Bose, Summer nonetheless cocked a droll eyebrow in response. "A deaf man would be able to detect my stammer. He told me, in fact, that his mother suffered the same condition." The intensity of the crowd rose again as Bose gathered his reins and paced about at the edge of the field, working off the nerves of his excitable charger. Summer's stare never left him, a faint smile upon her lips. "Look at him, Genisa. Look at him and tell me that you do not b-believe him to be wonderful, too."

Genisa, her own smile broadening, tore her gaze away from Summer's awe-struck expression long enough to refocus on the black and white knight. "He is indeed wonderful, Summer."

Summer barely heard the softly-uttered words, her thumping heart creating a deafening rush in her ears as she stared at her champion. He handled the enormous destrier with a good deal of skill and grace, *Chivalry* the French used to call it. Before the term meant knightly goodness and strength, it meant the precise skill of handling a war-horse. With thigh pressure, soft noises and delicate rein movements, the ability to control one's horse masterfully was a truly impressive skill.

And Bose most definitely possessed the skill. Summer continued to watch him, entranced, when suddenly he whirled his horse in a wild circle and abruptly dug his heels into the animal's sides. Throwing up great clods of earth, the vicious charger was suddenly bearing in her direction and Summer gasped with surprise and glee, knowing he was coming to impart a few words to her before his bout began.

Summer rose to her feet in anticipation, her hands clasped to her breast and her eyes wide. But just as she managed to leave her seat, a familiar chestnut charger bearing red and white standards suddenly veered into Bose's path, the horses nearly colliding in what would have surely been a devastating accident.

Bose was nearly unseated but managed to regain his balance quite nicely, raising his visor to his interceptor. Banking his fury with almost being pitched from his warhorse, he braced himself for the discouragement he knew was sure to come.

Stephan, however, was not so adept at hiding his anger. Visor secured, Bose could easily imagine the expression behind the menacing voice. "I told you to stay away from her, de Moray," Stephan growled. "I meant it."

Bose continued to struggle with his nervous charger. "But she does not share your opinion. And I continue to carry her favor."

"I know you do. However you managed to convince her that your reputation and intentions are completely innocent, know that I am not as gullible as she is. I'll not have an alleged murderer pursuing my sister and you would do well to heed my warning."

A flicker of emotion crossed Bose's face, as quickly vanished. "I am well aware of the rumors spread about my dark past, that I murdered my wife to gain her inheritance. But I swear upon God's Holy Order that the rumors regarding such nonsense are completely false."

Beneath the visor, Stephan continued to glare at him. However, it was difficult not to sense his candor; Bose's tone was steady, his manner calm. There was nothing within the bottomless black depths that suggested anything other than the undeniable truth.

Stephan was not an unreasonable man. But four years of gossip had imbedded itself within his thoughts more deeply than he cared to admit. In his defense, however, within that time Bose had done nothing to reject the wild myths, feeding them instead with his stand-offish manner and self-isolation.

Whereas the majority of circuit knights were friendly and cordial to varying degrees, Bose severed himself from all social contact. No one truly knew the man, making it extremely easy to consider the hearsay. Unlatching his three piece helm, Stephan slowly raised the gleaming visor.

"Why tell me now?" his voice was oddly strained. "The information has been prevalent for four years, de Moray. Why vindicate yourself now?"

Bose's gaze trailed to the luscious woman standing atop the lodges, her long hair gently wafting in the breeze. "I never cared what others thought until now," tearing his eyes away, he refocused on the wary brother. "Believe me, Stephan. I never killed my wife. 'Twas a vicious rumor invented by my mother-in-law to damage my chances on the tournament circuit. My wife died in childbirth and her mother has made it her goal in life to wreak misery upon me."

Stephan regarded him for a moment. "But I have also heard tale that you resigned your position as Captain of the King's Guard in disgrace because of your wife's death. What do you say to that?"

"I resigned my post because of the memories associated with it. I had met my wife while serving as Captain of the Guard. Our Henry was quite disappointed in my departure, in fact. He was terribly fond of me."

Stephan continued to meet his gaze, fighting against the mounting indecision gripping his heart. As an honorable knight, he should believe the man without question and allow him to pursue the woman of his choice. But as the protective brother, he could not give himself permission to accept the knight's explanation. At least, not yet.

The peal of the trumpet sounded over the field, announcing the approach of the first bout. Bose's gaze was torn between Stephan's dubious expression and Summer's distant form.

"Just a word, Stephan, before the joust," his voice was nearly a whisper. "One word and I shall vacate immediately. Please."

Stephan sighed faintly, irritated with his confusion and wondering why he could not seem to overcome the gossip he had professed to disregard.

"Nay," his eventual reply was muted. "Not now. Mayhap… later. I must think on it."

Bose emitted a heavy sigh, disappointed. "Very well," his voice was calm and resigned. "I shall obey your wishes this time. However, I…."

His word were abruptly cut short and Stephan watched, startled, as the knight's normally expressionless face took on a countenance of such ferocity that Stephan immediately turned to see what had disturbed him so.

Breck Kerry was poised before the lodges, speaking with Summer.

CS

SUMMER HAD NEVER seen him coming. One moment, she was gazing at Stephan and Bose in deep conversation and in the next, a knight bearing green and yellow standards was immediately before her. His armor was beautiful, his banners unsullied with dirt or flaw, and atop his elaborate helm was the image of a great horned beast.

Startled by the unexpected appearance, she took a step away and openly studied the man. For a moment, no one spoke, and then the knight reached up to raise his visor. A pale, pock-marked face and small blue eyes gazed back at her intensely. When he smiled, it was only to reveal large, slightly green teeth.

"My lady," he said, his voice medium-pitched. "My name is Sir Breck Kerry. I am competing in the first round and was hoping if you have not yet given your favor to anyone, that you would graciously consider my solicitation."

Summer did not like any aspect of the pale-faced, foul-breathed knight. Not his manners, nor his looks, nor the strangely annoying quality to his speaking tone. When she cleared her throat in a firm attempt to discourage him, Edward suddenly appeared at his daughter's side, his round face taut.

"The lady is not dispensing favors, Sir Breck," he said with more fortitude that Summer had heard in a long while. "Choose another."

Breck, however, was undeterred and dipped his head gallantly in the baron's direction. "My lord," he greeted. "My brother informed me this morn that the delightful creature seated next to you at yesterday's melee was your only daughter. Since I was unaware the du Bonne brothers had a sister, I was merely attempting to introduce myself."

Edward eyed the aggressive knight; he knew him to be the man who had broken Stephan's wrist last year and in spite of his callous attitude in matters pertaining to his children, found himself leaping to Summer's defense....

"They do indeed," he replied coldly. "If you will excuse us, sir knight, the joust is about to commence."

Breck continued to eye Summer, then Genisa when the woman took a position beside her sister-in-law and clutched her protectively. His small blue eyes raked Genisa suggestively before returning to Summer.

"I understand your father's concern, Lady Summer. Even so, my intentions are purely honorable," he said with mock sincerity. "Have you indeed given your favor this day?"

Before anyone could stop her, Summer stepped forward in a fit of disgust. "I have given my f-favor to Sir Bose," she said. "Now, please go. I have no desire to speak with you."

The smile on Breck's lips faded with unnatural swiftness. He continued to stare at her, digesting the flaw she had been unashamed to display with her insolent tongue. Instantly, his excitement and lust banked as he pondered her defect; God's Blood, what a tragedy her condition exhibited for, certainly, she was terribly beautiful. But with her flagrant stammer, she was as worthless as a three-legged cow and his disappointment settled.

His discouragement, however, was of little matter; the fact remained that the lady and Bose were attracted to one another, so much so that she had given him her favor. And the fact that Breck had sworn to avenge his failing in the melee against Bose merely fed his determination to sway her opinion against the mighty knight.

"I... I apologize if I have offended you, my lady," he said as genuinely as he was able. "I had no idea that you and Sir Bose were... well, that is to say, I am distressed to learn that you have allowed a knight of such questionable character to bear your favor."

Summer's gaze was unnaturally piercing. "Sir Bose is a perfect knight and I am proud to have him b-bear my favor."

Breck gave her his best anxious expression. "But he is a... God's Blood, dare I say it? His reputation toward the fairer sex is certainly not the most solid."

Summer cocked an eyebrow, angered and shaken with the knight's implication. Good Lord, did everyone know of the lies regarding Bose's past? Cheeks flushed, she tried her best not to shout her defensive reply.

"And the rumors you refer to are nothing but a pack of malicious f-fabrications," she said, her voice acquiring an odd quiver. "Sir Bose never killed his wife. She died in childbirth."

Breck's eyes widened with mock concern. "And he told you this version of the truth, my lady?"

"He did. And you will believe him w-without question."

Breck blinked innocently, as if digesting her forceful statement. Clearing his throat delicately, in a fashion suggesting he was shocked by the entire conversation, he shook his head feebly.

"My lady, did it not occur to you that he would parlay any conven-ient tale so that you would disbelieve the reality of his darker reputation? Surely you realize that a smitten man will do or say anything to gain your trust," his gaze moved to Edward, round and short and perspiring under the bright morning sun. "My lord, you must protect your daughter from de Moray's evil. I fear that...."

Breck's words were abruptly cut short by the powerful thunder of hooves, startling his warhorse and causing the animal to dance about nervously. Summer was vaguely aware of a red and white banner before her as the brilliant sunlight reflected off portions of plate armor, nearly blinding her.

Amidst the red and white and bolts of silver, however, she caught a glimpse of black and white. The very next she realized, Breck Kerry lay on the ground and Bose was already dismounted, stalking the downed knight.

The tension in the air was unmistakable as the crowd in the lodges jockeyed for a better position from which to watch the extra-curricular event. Summer was aware that Stephan had placed himself between his sister and the green and yellow knight, his powerful warhorse snorting and foaming. She heard Genisa gasp as Bose reached down and grasped Breck by the neck, heaving the man to his feet in one effortless motion.

Summer was truly shocked by the swiftness of the entire event, but her surprise had not robbed her of her senses. Grasping her skirts, she dashed to the edge of the platform where Bose was preparing to deal Breck a harsh lesson.

"Bose!" she cried softly. "What are you d-doing?"

At the sound of her sweet, shaken voice, Bose's helmed head immediately turned in her direction. With Breck still clutched in one massive gauntlet, he raised his visor with the other.

"I am preparing to punish him for speaking to you," he said frankly. "Did he offend you, my lady? Was his manner bold and intolerable?"

Gazing into his piercing black eyes, Summer's astonishment faded as a tremendous sense of flattery took hold. Aye, Stephan and Ian and Lance had punished her tormenters and old Kermit the tutor had been quite free with his cane when he deciphered a slanderous insult toward his young charge. But her thanks for their shielding behavior had never mounted to the warm, fluid excitement she was feeling with Bose's chivalry.

She could not help the smile that creased her lips. "Nay, my lord, he was not b-bold or aggressive toward me. Truly, there is no need to punish him, though I thank you deeply for your concern."

Bose paused a moment, his face unreadable, before releasing Breck completely. The knight stumbled back, rubbing at his neck and glaring daggers at the massive warrior at least a head taller than himself.

"Damn you, de Moray," he hissed. "Your foolish heroics were uncalled for. There is no law against my speaking to the lady."

Planted between his sister and the two scuffling knights, Stephan cocked an eyebrow as he joined the conversation. "Nay, Kerry, there is no law against you speaking with my sister. But I will only tell you one time; stay clear of her. If I ever see you speaking or even so much as looking in her direction, you'll most certainly not like my reaction."

Breck's gaze was even as he beheld Stephan with small blue eyes. "Yet you would allow de Moray, a known murderer, to bear your sister's favor. Most strange, Sir Stephan."

Although Bose did not react, Stephan drew in a long, intolerant breath. "If I must make a choice between the two of you, I suppose I would rather see Sir Bose bear my sister's favor," unwilling to say any more, he reined his charger in the opposite direction and motioned to the heralds at the corner of the field. "I believe you gentle knights are scheduled to joust. Mayhap you can settle your dispute with the aid of a lance in your grip."

Bose immediately turned away from Breck and regained his steed, mounting effortlessly. Breck, still shaking off the shock of having been unseated quite brutally, moved slowly to his snorting mount and cuffed the horse when it snapped at him. Emitting a yelp when his unprotected wrist made contact with the strip of armor secured to the horse's face, he grumbled and grunted angrily as he mounted his charger.

As the two opposing knights fumbled with their destriers and equipment, Stephan returned his attention briefly to his sister. Summer smiled faintly at her eldest brother.

"Thank you for your intervention," she said softly, fumbling for an apology. "And I...I am sorry for my hateful words, Stephan. I never meant to b-be...."

He put up a quieting hand, matching her smile in spite of the anger and arguing that had taken place earlier. No amount of fury and quarreling could dampen the true sibling affection they held for one another and Stephan knew that in spite of his bewilderment regarding de Moray, Summer would most likely have a champion for the rest of the tournament.

"I know, sweetheart," he said, touching her pink cheek. "Do not fret; we shall discuss it later," turning to his wife, he quickly motioned her over. "Come here, love, and give me a kiss. I have got to vacate the field before I am mistakenly gored by an eager competitor."

Obediently, Genisa rushed to her husband and kissed him sensually on the lips. His eyes closed at her tender touch and, smiling, he kissed her again. Gently caressing her silken face for a brief, distracted moment, he nonetheless cast a final glance at Bose before slamming his visor shut and spurring his charger across the field in a rush of flying dirt and grass.

Summer and Genisa watched Stephan depart in proud silence, their smiles fading as Breck Kerry gruffly rode past, rubbing at his shoulder and adjusting his helm. As Genisa sighed dreamily and returned to her cushioned seat, Summer turned her gaze to the last of the trio that had yet to depart.

Bose sat atop his charger, fumbling with the neck of his helm. Summer continued to stand at the edge of the platform, her heart beating wildly against her ribs as she watched him. His visor was up and he was looking at her, his face emotionless, until he finally appeared satisfied with whatever his thick fingers had been toying with.

Summer's breathing quickened as the charcoal gray charger moved slowly to the edge of the lodge, the beast amazingly calm and showing little of the agitation it had displayed earlier. Bose's thigh grazed the edge of the platform, by Summer's feet, as his rugged features gazed up at her intently.

"Are you certain he did not insult you?" he asked quietly, with genuine concern. "Breck Kerry is not one of the more chivalrous knights on the circuit."

She shook her head. "'Tis sweet of you to ask, b-but again I say he did not," her gentle expression faded somewhat. "However, he said some terrible things about you. I was going to punish him myself before you rode to my aid."

Bose cracked a smile, a charming lopsided gesture. "Your vengeance on my behalf will be unnecessary, my lady. Beating him in the joust will be punishment enough."

She matched his smile, lifting an arrogant eyebrow. "You promised to b-beat them all, my lord. I will hold you to that vow."

"And I shall," again, the piercing notes of the silver trumpet filled the brisk sea air and Bose turned in the direction of the heralds, obviously impatient to get on with the game. With a faint nod, as if acknowledging the silent gazes fixed upon him, he returned his attention to Summer one last time. "I am afraid my time has come. I do hope you enjoy the joust far more than the melee."

Summer tore her eyes away from him long enough to note that Breck had taken up station on the opposite side of the field, retrieving his lance and shield from a young squire. "So do I," she replied, once again fixing him with her golden gaze. "Take great care, my lord. I should not like it if my favor b-brought bad fortune upon you."

Bose suddenly dug into the fold between his breastplate and armor, drawing forth a familiar small white kerchief. Bringing it to his nostrils, he inhaled deeply, closing his eyes at the blissful evocations of the rose scent. With a smile, he opened his gaze to Summer's beautiful face. Kissing the white linen, he returned it to its safe, armored haven.

"Although I should like to have the final encouragement Stephan obtained, I will refrain from asking," he said with a twinkle in his eye. "Your brother did not want to me to speak with you before the joust and were I to steal a kiss as well, I would undoubtedly incur his wrath. Ian's and Lance's, too, I suspect."

A faint pink mottled Summer's cheeks as her gaze lingered on her strong champion for a moment. Averting her eyes, for she knew he was required at the far side of the field to obtain his lance, she turned for her cushioned chair.

"B-But you would not incur mine," she said softly.

Bose watched, his entire body flooded with a surge of excitement and encouragement, as she elegantly took her seat. Her cheeks were flaming madly and she refused to look at him, and he slammed his visor closed, digging his spurs into the smooth black sides of his charger. Reliving her words the entire jaunt back to his starting position, there was no doubt in his mind that he would win this tourney.

CHAPTER EIGHT

ARTUR AND THE knights were waiting for him when he returned to the starting post. They had all seen the confrontation between Bose and Stephan, and the subsequent encounter between Bose and Breck. Therefore, it stood to reason that they were also well aware of the ensuing conversation between their liege and the lovely lady after the scuffling had subsided. There wasn't a man among them not extremely curious to know what had transpired; Bose de Moray in the middle of a contest for a lady's affection was an unknown event.

But the moment Bose joined the ranks of his men, the group was wise enough to bank their curiosity in lieu of preparing their liege for the coming bout. If Bose suspected the wild interest, which of course he did, it was apparent he was unwilling to elaborate on the subject. Retrieving his pole from Tate, Farl handed the man his shield as Artur fussed over the destrier's impeccable armor.

"This beast's chamfrom is off-center," the old man grumbled, struggling with the face armor of the horse. "And your caparison is nearly disheveled. How did this happen?"

Bose adjusted his lance, balancing the pole under his arm as he tightened his gauntlets. Tate and Morgan straightened the banner across the horse's body that Artur had accused of being disheveled, although the wide standard was in exceptional shape. To their liege's aged uncle, however, nothing within their midst was ever perfect. His biggest delight in life was to find fault with every matter. It made him feel more useful.

"Tate," Bose caught his knight's attention as he continued to adjust his glove. "Fetch Stephan du Bonne to me immediately. I have something I must say to him before I attend the field."

Tate nodded briefly and was gone, momentarily deterred from pestering his lord as to the current status with the lady in the lodges. But Morgan was not so encumbered; without Tate to take the offensive, he was left on his own and his curiosity was nearly killing him.

When Bose finished with his gauntlets, the older knight handed him his sword. "She is a beautiful woman, Bose. I'd kill Breck Kerry, too, if the bastard attempted to steal her from me."

Through his lowered visor, Bose found Summer's persimmon colored gown on the lodges and the pounding of his heart flooded his eardrums. It was a moment before he was able to reply. "Have you ever been in love, Morgan?"

Morgan stared at him, his dark brown eyes soft with deliberation. After a moment, he smiled weakly. "Once, when I was young. Her name was Lily and she wanted absolutely nothing to do with me."

"Wise woman," Bose muttered. He continued to gaze at Summer's distant form. "Do... do you remember the thoughts and sensations, Morgan? Do you recall the feelings you experienced? Like nothing you've experienced before?"

"Or since," Morgan eyed the normally-reserved man. "Why do you ask? Are you thinking that mayhap you are feeling more than simple attraction for the lady?"

Bose's gaze never left the remote figure on the lodges. After a brief silence, he slowly shook his head. "I do not know," his voice was nearly a whisper. "The only measure of wisdom I possess in the matter is the fact that I believed all my emotions pertaining to the opposite sex to have died in childbirth four years ago. Since yesterday, however, they seemed to be resurrecting themselves whether or not I am willing to accept them."

Morgan listened to the confession with a faint glimmer to his eye; for Bose to be conversing on a matter of personal conviction was an event of the enormous significance. It was one Morgan did not take lightly; he clapped his liege on his thickly armored leg in a gesture of commiseration.

"If she brings about sentiment you thought to have perished, most certainly I would not oppose the obvious," he said, eyeing Artur as the old man fussed with the caparison over the horse's rear quarters. "You've known her less than a day, Bose. What you are experiencing could be nothing more than infatuation. Give yourself time before you decide whether or not to run from your feelings."

He meant it in half-jest, half-not. Beneath the lowered visor, Bose smiled thinly. "My feelings for Lora were gradual, Morgan. A slow, steady pace of discovery," turning his armored head in the direction of the lodges, the helmed head slowly wagged back and forth. "What I feel for Lady Summer is something I have never before experienced. In fact, I believe it to be more powerful than I am at times."

"And this frightens you?"

"It scares me to death."

Artur, finished with the banner across the charger's haunches, moved forward in his complete inspection of Bose's armor. The heralds were impatient to begin the bout and Breck Kerry had already taken the field in full regalia. The crowd in the lodges grew restless and Morgan knew the private conversation between him and his lord was ended for the moment.

"Remember, Bose," Artur fixed on his mighty nephew, oblivious to the fact that he had all but shoved Morgan out of the way in his haste to make conversation with the armored warrior. "Breck breaks low and to the left at mid-point. You'll have to compensate if you do not want to be unseated on the first run."

Forcing himself from the conversation with Morgan, Bose listened to his uncle's sound words. "I know, Uncle Artur. I have fought the man before, many a time," his helmed head suddenly bobbed about as if he was eagerly searching for something. "Where's Tate? I want to speak with Stephan before the round commences."

Farl and Adgar, standing ahead of their liege by the edge of the field, were attempting to explain to the heralds why their lord was delaying. He could see that the heralds were eager to begin the bout and he knew he would be unable to delay any further. Stephan or no, the crowd was expecting his appearance.

The massive charger moved forward, sensing the excitement from the rumbling crowd. Artur scampered alongside the dancing beast to impart his last few gems of wisdom.

"If he doesn't unseat you on the first pass, the second run will be aimed at your head," the old man huffed and panted. "Well you remember what he did to Sir Rolf at last year's tourney in Wrexham?"

"Broke his neck," Bose answered unemotionally. "The man has no use of his arms and legs and can scarcely breathe."

Artur's black eyes were intense. "Mind he doesn't break your neck as well."

Bose did not reply as they reached the edge of the lists. The crowd, noting the circuit champion was preparing to take the field, began to roar with anticipation. The heralds moved to their respective positions along the joust course as the lead herald moved to the center of the barrier, raising his hands to quiet the unruly, eager throng.

When the commotion died to a muted roar, the chief herald lowered his quieting hands and drew forth Lord Edward's sword.

"Let Sir Bose and Sir Breck come forward!"

The crowd began to stir again as Breck, who had been prancing about at the far end of the field, took position beyond the end of the joust barrier and raised his lance to a full upright position. Bose watched the man's arrogant stance from his location at the opposite edge of the field, experiencing the resurgence of the jealously and anger. He was going to enjoy unseating the idiot. And the man would be fortunate if he did not find a lance aimed at his head.

Farl and Adgar were beside him, watching their liege's opponent with a good deal of loathing. They had all competed against the man, innumerable times, and there was not one among them who had not been subjected to the knight's unscrupulous tricks.

"If you cut him high on the first run, he shall miss the move because he shall be expecting you to counter his low maneuver," Farl's Irish accent was heavy with disgust. "You'll be able to take his damn head off."

Bose was silent, as was usual before a bout as he utilized his concentration for the upcoming strategy. Adgar and Morgan, standing on the opposite side of Farl, exhibited varied expressions of loathing.

"Pimple-faced idiot," normally mild-manner Adgar was grim. "I drew Duncan in the third round. Best the eldest, Bose, and be done with it. I have a penchant to do the same to his whelp brother and we can defeat the Kerry lads in one mighty blow."

Bose listened, digested, stored for future reference. The chief herald, however, was expecting the presence of his second competitor and Bose's grip tightened on the reins as he prepared to spur his charger forward. But the moment he moved to do so, a shout in the distance halted his progression.

His head turned stiffly in the direction of the shout, a feat made difficult within the confines of his helm. Moving toward him across the trampled green earth was Stephan du Bonne astride his chestnut charger. Tate ran alongside in his mail and portions of leg protection, his fair face glistening with sweat.

Stephan reined his horse to within several feet of Bose, his handsome features inquisitive. Considering Bose was required upon the field this very moment, it was surprising that he should delay in any manner. But the man was determined to have his say and Stephan had a suspicion as to the subject. He would oblige the man by listening. Mayhap, in a sense, he would be making amends for his lack of faith in the truth of Bose's reputation.

"My lord?" there were a dozen men between them, mostly de Moray's men in colors of black and white. But Stephan ignored them as he focused on their mighty liege. "You wished to speak with me?"

"Indeed," Bose directed his horse a few feet in Stephan's direction, knowing the heralds must be nearing seizures of anger by his lack of readiness. "I am afraid I must make this brief and I apologize for taking you away from any pressing business. I… I simply wanted to thank you."

Stephan's visor was raised, a blond eyebrow lifting slowly. "For what?"

Bose was apparently unconcerned with the dozens of ears witnessing their conversation. "For allowing me to speak with the lady. Although you had originally denied me, still, I thank you for relenting your stance. Your generosity is commendable."

Stephan stared at him a moment, listening to the increasingly agitated roar of the congregation as their champion delayed his arrival to his joust position. "'Twas your right, I suppose, after you subdued Kerry," his bright green eyes sought the impatient knight in yellow and green standards at the far sight of the field. "I suppose you must subdue him again."

Bose had said what he had intended, feeling satisfied that he had made his thanks known. Somehow, it was important to him. Knowing that without Stephan's approval, the chances of courting the man's lovely sister were slim and he was determined to earn his support. After a moment, he dipped his head again in a gesture of gratitude.

"I suppose I must," he said, gathering his reins. "And if I do not arrive shortly, I fear the crowd will rip Kerry's pole from his grasp and gore me in a fit of impatience."

The last few words were muffled as he dug his spurs into his charger's heaving sides, the crescendo of the crowd and the thunder of hooves all but drowning out the bass-toned voice. Stephan watched with an odd mixture of envy and understanding as the multitude of spectators welcomed the previous day's melee champion.

Bose assumed a prepared stance, his lance in the customary upright position and his shield poised as the chief herald moved to the edge of the lodges with Lord Edward's sword. Since Bose had delayed the match by several minutes, they were eager to commence the bout immediately. As the squires vacated the field and hovered about the edges, the crowd quieted dramatically in great anticipation.

Fortunately, the wait had ended. As the sun traversed the sky-blue field above in its hunt toward the nooning hour, the chief herald raised the sword high into the crisp sea air of Dorset.

"For honor and glory, charge!"

༼ ༽

SUMMER COULD HARDLY stand it. The herald's shout to commence startled her and the thunder from the chargers was more than she could bear. In spite of her unease, however, she was unable to look away from the spectacle before her.

The green and yellow lance splintered on Bose's shield, sending daggers of wood exploding in all directions. A piece of coated pole landed a foot or so away from Summer and she stared at it a moment, forcing herself to breathe as she realized Bose had made it through the first pass unscathed.

Even though the recoil motion with the contact sent the chargers reeling onto their hind legs, both knights remained seated and finished the first pass. Summer turned her relieved gaze in the direction of her champion as the lodges around her were literally mad with delight.

"Nobly done!" Edward shouted from his elaborate chair, cushioned with a fine satin pillow. "A fair break, indeed."

Summer was distracted from Bose's undamaged vision by her father's cries of pleasure. She cast the man an intolerant glance, suggesting she did not agree with his assessment. He caught her expression, his fair face folding into a smile.

"What is the matter now?" he asked jovially. "You do not like the joust, either? It does not possess the violence of the melee and for that, I should think you would be appreciative."

Summer's gaze lingered on her father a moment and she shrugged. "I do not believe appreciative would be the word I would choose to describe my opinion," she passed a glance at Genisa, who was completely unruffled by the spectacle. "How can you be so entirely c-calm throughout this savagery?"

Genisa patted her arm. "'Tis easy, truly. Stephan is not competing at this moment, therefore, I am calm. My demeanor will change considerably when he takes the field, I assure you."

Summer shook her head, not particularly surprised when her father turned away to involve himself in the food his servant delivered. The man was barely beyond a word of comfort and she was accustomed to his indifferent manner in all aspects. Therefore, she returned her attention to the field as Breck was handed a fresh lance.

"Do not worry so, Summer," Genisa's voice was soft, nearly humorous. "Sir Bose is the very best. Even Stephan says so."

Summer cast her sister-in-law a dubious glance. "I do not think I like the tournament, Genisa. I b-believe this shall be my last spectacle."

Genisa smiled slyly. "But what if you marry Sir Bose? He is a member of the tournament circuit and you, as his wife, should travel with him."

Summer's doubtful expression softened as a faint flush mottled her cheeks. "Good Lord, Genisa, what would lead you to believe that B-Bose would want to marry me? We've only just met."

"And he hasn't left you alone for a minute. I'd say his attention has been a distinct sign of serious interest."

Averting her eyes uncertainly, Summer fixed on the field before her. "I cannot b-believe his attention toward me is anything other than normal chivalry. Why would he want a wife who stammers?"

Genisa's reply was cleaved as the chief herald shouted another start. Summer's apprehension returned full-bore as Bose and Breck charged each other on opposite sides of the joust barrier. The rumble of destriers filled the air as the opposing knights rapidly closed the distance, lances leveling and shields fixing as they drew closer and closer still.

The crowd in the lodges was taut with anticipation as the competitors swiftly shortened the gap. An expectant hush settled as the second run appeared to be going smoothly. But the illusion dashed when Bose suddenly jerked off-center in the saddle, a last minute move with no apparent reasoning until deafening sounds of metal against wood filled air.

It was not a normal sound to be associated with a joust. As a horrified crowd looked on, Bose's helm went spinning from his head, flying through the air in a violent burst of twisted steel. The dented piece of protection that had once been on Bose's head smashed into a supporting post near the center of the lodges, sending people scurrying with screams.

But no one screamed louder than Summer. Convinced she had just witnessed Bose's beheading, she screamed in horror and covered her eyes. She could feel Genisa grasp at her, a faint trembling voice of comfort in her ear, but she was unable to comprehend the meaning of the words. Somewhere above the hysteria, she thought she heard her father's voice, demanding she cease her screaming and look to the field. But she kept her hands over her eyes, sobbing. She couldn't bear to look.

"Look, Summer!" Genisa's voice was in her ear, stronger than before. "Sir Bose is at the end of the field; he's still mounted!"

As if by magic, Summer's hands came away from her face and she bolted to unsteady feet, her golden gaze coming to bear on the near side of the field. Indeed, Bose was still seated astride his warhorse, his black hair spiky with sweat beneath his askew mail hood and his face pale. But he was alive and Summer was so swept with relief that she was weak with it.

But her relief was cut short when Bose turned in her direction. Blood streamed down the right side of his face, coating his mail and disappearing beneath his plate armor. The chief herald stood alongside him as well as several of his knights, concern and fury evident in their expressions as they evaluated his ability to continue the event.

Bose's unnaturally tight expression listened intently to the herald's words and he nodded now and again, eventually shaking his head as if to disagree with what was being said. Summer watched with her breath caught in her throat as he conversed with the distressed men about him. When it became apparent that he planned to continue in spite of his wound, Summer could not help her reaction. With all of the volatile emotions she had sampled over the past few moments, there was truthfully no other outlet for her tension and strain. The tears returned with a vengeance.

In spite of his spinning head and ringing ears, Bose was acutely aware of Summer's hovering presence by the edge of the platform. Although he had convinced the heralds and his men that he was indeed capable of finishing his bout, he was truthfully having a good deal of trouble focusing his eyes and could scarcely remain balanced atop the saddle. But the fact remained that Breck Kerry's vicious tactics could not go unanswered.

Bose was well aware that Breck was retaliating for the earlier justice dispensed on Summer's behalf and he was equally aware that Breck had fully intended to do more than unseat him. There was no doubt the lance had been aimed at his head in a last-minute maneuver that left Bose hardly able to compensate. Even though he had been able to dodge the full effect of the blow, he had still been caught on the side of the helm.

Unfortunately, his head protection was smashed and distorted and there was no possibility of wearing the damaged equipment until it could be properly repaired. Better the helm destroyed than his skull. He ignored Morgan's and Tate's protests as he prepared to take his third run without his head armor.

Even as he disregarded the pleas of his loyal knights that he at least borrow another helm, he found he could no longer disregard Summer's distant form. Her hands were to her mouth and although he tried not to look directly at her as he struggled to straighten his mail hood, he could only imagine that she must be terrified. If the melee had served to jade her opinion against the civility of tournaments, then he could only assume that his near-beheading had only further served to increase her distress.

When he righted his hauberk as best he could in spite of the stinging gash to his scalp, he could not help but look to his favored lady to make sure she was calm enough to witness his third run. Even though his eyes were hazy and out of focus, he could nonetheless see her reddened face and terrified eyes.

Bose's heart sank as he viewed her expression; he realized he could not continue until he eased her distress. Even though his primary concern should have been the imminent unseating of Breck Kerry, still, he found he could not focus on the coming run until his lady was adequately calm. He did not like to see her so terribly, though understandably, upset.

Morgan and Tate continued to prattle about their lord's foolishness should he decide to finish his bout without adequate protection; they might as well have been speaking to the birds for all Bose heard them. Asking the anxious heralds to return to their positions, he ignored his troubled men and reined his charger in the direction of the lodges.

Summer saw him coming towards her, sobbing softly into her hand and unconcerned with the fact that she was making a spectacle of herself with her emotional display. Bloodied, dizzy and all, Bose directed his charger next to the lady's feet and smiled wanly into her frightened face.

"Do not weep so, my lady," he said softly. "As you can see, I am well enough to finish this bout for your glory. I promised to win the joust, did I not?"

She sobbed pitifully. "I d-do not w-want you to compete any longer," she gasped. "I-I…I-I w-want you t-to l-let me tend your wound."

Genisa rose from her chair, lingering behind Summer with a comforting hand to the woman's shoulder. Her bright blue eyes were laced with concern as she focused on the scarred, bloodied knight.

"I must agree with her, Sir Bose," she said timidly, knowing her opinion had not been solicited. "Your head is bleeding and must be tended. Moreover, you surely must be feeling ill as a result of your brutal blow."

Bose sighed faintly, his gaze moving from Stephan's lovely wife to Summer's pitiful expression. He could feel himself weakening, willing to overlook a matter of honor purely for the fact that his pride was causing Summer a great deal of distress. And with the added plea of another concerned lady, he was not immune to the feminine pressure.

"I appreciate your concern, Lady Genisa," his bass voice was soft. "'Tis true that I have felt better, but I am fully capable of doing away with my opponent. If you would ask your sister-in-law to sit, I shall be but a moment and then I will happily submit to her nursing."

"Nay!" Summer's hand came away from her mouth and she moved forward, the same hand touching his great mailed head before she could control herself. "You are injured, Bose. P-P-Please do not do this. P-Please!"

Gazing into her pained golden eyes, Bose realized he was willing to relent. She was distraught and he felt a tremendous sense of pleasure and satisfaction with her concern for his welfare. But the fact remained that Breck was waiting impatiently at the end of the field for the conclusion of their bout and the heralds were expecting him to take immediate position. Hating himself for his determined sense of knightly honor, he took her hand and kissed it gently.

"My lady, I promise this will only take a moment and I swear to you that when I have finished, I will submit to your healing hands completely," when she shook her head again, he smiled bravely and kissed her hand again. "I promise that I will unseat him on this pass. For the fact that he has frightened you so terribly, I will do this and take great pleasure in his humiliation."

He was smiling encouragingly at her, attempting to offer a measure of comfort and ease when he, in fact, was the injured party and in dire need of the same comfort. Genisa whispered in Summer's ear, telling her to let the man finish his bout. Genisa understood the pride of a knight, knowing that honor and dignity meant everything in a world of battles and glory and death, and where vengeance was a part of that honor.

Summer simply did not understand all of the elements composing the soul of a true knight, but she was somewhat aware of the fact that

Bose felt a need to unseat his unscrupulous opponent for the very reason that he would not allow the man to dishonor him with his unethical tactics. To concede the round, even with a gashed head and reeling senses, would be to admit that his adversary had managed to weaken him.

Summer's weeping faded as she allowed Genisa to gently pull her from Bose's grip. The knight was grateful for the married woman's assistance and, with a confident wink to his quivering lady, drove his charger to his assigned position.

"Come and sit, Summer," Genisa gently directed her back to her cushioned chair. "He shall be finished in a moment and then you will be able to tend his head."

Touching the hand he had so tenderly kissed, Summer plopped limply into her chair, silently cursing herself for not being firm enough in her demand that he abandon his bout, yet knowing in the same breath that knightly honor was a rigid, consuming thing.

"You are far too emotional, Summer," Edward looked up from the last of his food, licking the fruit juice off his fingers. "Blood and injury is simply part of the sport. The element of harm makes it far more exciting."

Summer cast her father a long glance, accustomed to his insensitive perspective and not particularly affected by his words. He was an odd man, truly, and although she tolerated him for the mere fact that he was her sire, their relationship lacked any true measure of affection. Old Kermit the tutor had been more of a father to her than her own and she had felt his death with the same intensity of sorrow. The man seated across from her slurping the last remnants of food from his flesh had always been more a stranger than a relative. And he liked it that way.

"Forgive me if I embarrassed you, Father," she said quietly, feeling herself calming as the knights on the field prepared for the last run. "But I cannot help my d-disgust for this tournament."

Edward eyed her as his manservant poured a third chalice of fine Bordeaux. "Mayhap that is true, but you are still intent to watch de

Moray as he attempts to level Breck Kerry," wiping his hands on his sleeves, he accepted a goblet from the submissive servant. "Stephan told me of him, Summer. I am not sure if I approve."

Summer cocked an eyebrow at her father as Genisa visibly shrank; given her sister-in-law's conversation with Stephan earlier, Edward's disapproval would not be well met. "He is a kind, chivalrous man and I am greatly honored b-by his attentions," Summer said evenly. "B-Before you approve or disapprove, speak with the man yourself and draw your own conclusions. That is, if you can m-manage the effort."

Edward's brow rose dramatically. "What's this? Insolence from the daughter I have protected throughout her life from the cruelties of a vicious world?" feeling the fine alcohol coursing through his veins, his outrage gained speed. "Be glad I did not leave you to the elements on the day of your birth for causing your mother's death. You would do well to bank your defective tongue, wench, and be grateful for my mercy."

Genisa closed her eyes as if to ward off the harshness of Edward's words; wine always affected his tongue, turning the normally even-tempered man into a vicious brute. Considering how rare his contact with his children, it was unfortunate that whatever encounters occurred when he was drunk were cruel and mean-spirited. Edward emerged from his private little world so infrequently that it was truly tragic for the rare occurrences to be marred by hateful words.

Summer, however, was unaffected by his statement. She was more interested in the chief herald preparing to signal the third pass and she found her attention focused on the gaily-colored lists. She refused to allow her father to distract her from the situation at hand.

The herald dropped his flag and in that instant, her heart leapt into her throat as Bose and Breck commenced their run, charging toward one another with blinding speed. Closer and closer, thundering knights drew near and Summer was riveted to the massive warrior jousting without a helm, his face half-hidden behind the Gorgon shield.

In an act of self-defense as well as an act of retaliation, Bose made sure his lance remained level and straight as if he were unaware of Breck's discreet high-aim. Then, as the horses thundered within contact proximity of one another, Bose abruptly lowered his lance, aiming to the right of Breck's body and parallel with the green and yellow lance still pointed at his head. Thrusting the tip forward, he braced it against the armor protecting Breck's upper arm and, using their forward momentum to his advantage, shoved his weight into the butt of his lance enough to dislodge Breck's aim. Using his might, he continued to propel the lance forward, even as the two destriers shimmied and reeled from the recoil of contact.

With Bose's strength and weight behind his thrusting lance, Breck's arm was dislodged from its socket before he realized what had happened. Dazed and in a good deal of pain with a useless limb, Breck hit the soft dirt of the lists as the crowd in the lodges went mad with approval.

Even on the outskirts of the joust field, opposing knights praised the tactics of de Moray as the man turned at the end of the joust barrier, reining his charger in the opposite direction for an uncharacteristic pass before the delirious throng of admirers. Tate and Farl whooped like a pair of wild men, shouting accolades of Bose's skill as their powerful liege thundered a wide sweeping arc in the direction of the lodges. As Adgar and Artur congratulated each other with less boisterous means, Morgan simply stood by the wooden barrier surrounding the field and smiled.

He knew why the man had emerged victorious, the matter of honor and knightly skill a secondary motivation as much as he would profess to pretend otherwise. For the comfort and assurance of a certain young lady, Bose had been willing to chance a great deal on his skill and talents.

A lady he was currently riding to greet. Summer was on her feet once more, her hands clasped against her breast and a miraculous smile on her lips. The multitude of guests and allies screamed and cheered, favors and tokens of esteem raining to the trampled joust field as several squires and servants rushed about to collect the silken veils and copper pences.

Bose, however, ignored the tokens of esteem as he came to a halt before the beaming young woman. Far removed from the panicked young lass he had left just moments before, his lopsided smile made a weak return as he dipped his head gallantly at the lady's feet.

"As I vowed, my lady," his deep voice was a hoarse rumble. "I have unseated my opponent. Now, I will hold you to your promise; my head is sorely in need of your nurturing aid."

Summer smiled. "I would be pleased to t-tend you, my lord," she replied softly. Near the center of the colorful joust barrier, Breck was being helped to his feet by several green and yellow clad servants as a cluster of grooms attempted to capture his spirited charger. Summer tore her gaze away from Bose's weary orbs long enough to cock an arrogant eyebrow in Breck's direction. "As you declared, you were quite efficient in unseating him. Did you, in fact, b-break his arm intentionally?"

Bose tried to shake his head in a negative gesture, but his ears were ringing and any movement of his head simply amplified the bells. "His shoulder is merely dislodged from the socket. Had I wanted to break his arm, I most certainly could have. He is lucky that I did not take his damn head off for the fear he has caused you this day."

Summer's cheeks flushed a pretty pink, her heart swelling with admiration and appreciation for the bloodied, exhausted knight. It was amazing how a few brief moments and a quick pass along the colorful joust barrier had served to ease her anxieties. She opened her mouth to continue the conversation when she sensed a warm, lingering body behind her, not surprised when she caught sight of Genisa's lovely blue gown.

"A brave course, my lord," Genisa said sincerely. "Much like the course in Chichester last January when you boldly unseated Sir Alwain Parham. Although others said the swift parry with your lance was considered an unfair maneuver, Stephan fully supported your actions.

He said that if you had not brought your lance up when you did and clipped Sir Alwain's shoulder, the man would have taken your head off."

Summer managed to spare her sister-in-law a genuine look of surprise; for a woman who could hardly remember the most important of details from one moment to the next, she was certainly knowledgeable when it came to a joust that happened five months ago. However, considering the tournament circuit was her husband's vocation, it wasn't particularly surprising that Genisa endeavored to know something of his chosen profession. In faith, it was nearly all she knew and she took great pride in her knowledge.

"I thank you for your kind recollection and support, my lady," Bose replied, listening to the cheers of the crowd die down as the heralds prepared for the next bout. As his surge of reprisal and determination wore thin, however, his gripping fatigue began to take firmer hold and he realized he would not be able to remain astride his charger much longer; the sooner he lay down and allow his wound to be tended, the better he would feel. Moving from Genisa's pretty face to Summer's beautiful expression, he found the thought of her soft hands grazing his flesh to be most inviting. "If you do not mind, my lady, I shall send one of my men to escort you to my tent. I do believe, at this moment, that it would be wise of me to seek my pallet immediately before I embarrass myself and topple from my horse."

Summer's gentle smile faded. "Are you f-feeling worse, my lord?"

He drew in a deep breath, gathering his reins. "Nay, my lady, not worse, but it would be inaccurate for me to say that the mere thought of lying flat on my back for the rest of the day was an unpleasant prospect."

He appeared drawn and ashen and Summer was once again greatly concerned for his injury. She gathered her skirts and leapt to the trampled field below.

"I shall escort you, my lord," she said firmly, looking up to him astride the tall warhorse. "Mayhap you should walk. 'Twould be b-better than falling off your horse and completely humiliating yourself in f-front of your devotees."

Bose smiled weakly, already moving to dismount even though riding to the tent would be quicker and far less strenuous. But he could hardly allow the lady to walk alone and found himself moving wearily to complete her bidding. The moment he hit the ground, however, a weak male voice from the lodges abruptly made itself known.

"Summer," Edward was on his feet, swaying dangerously from the effects of too much alcohol. "I will not allow you to accompany this... this knight back to his tent, unescorted. I believe Stephan has warned you against him."

Summer paused, her gaze lingering on Bose a moment before turning her attention to her unsteady father. "Stephan is wrong about him, Father. Moreover, as Sir Bose's f-favored lady, 'tis my duty to tend his wound."

Edward eyed her angrily, an expression that drew a good deal of surprise from Bose; certainly, a father should not gaze to his daughter as if she were his mortal enemy. Much to Bose's dismay, that seemed to be the precise gist of the baron's expression and he felt a tremendous surge of protectiveness toward the beautiful young woman.

Edward, however, was too far gone with his wine to notice Bose's dark expression as he focused on his defiant daughter. "Stephan has deemed this man unsuitable, Summer. You will listen to your brother and return to the lodges immediately to view the remainder of today's bouts."

"I will not," Summer said firmly. "I am Sir Bose's f-favored lady and it is my duty to tend his wound."

With that, she turned her back on her drunken sire and began to move away from the lodges. Furious that his youngest child would disobey him, Edward slammed his chalice to the table beside him, missing the table completely. The gold-encrusted goblet spilled to the wooden floor of the lodges, bleeding red alcohol across the slats as the drunkard baron wobbled to the edge of the platform.

"Summer du Bonne!" he shouted. "You will return this instant or I shall have my soldiers throw you in the vault for your insolence! Do you comprehend me?"

Summer kept walking. Bose, unmoving where she had left him standing before the lodges, watched her walk away with a straight, confident back. He wondered just how far she was going to push her father and indeed contemplating the potentiality of her own sire seeking to punish her for her defiance by locking her in the dungeon.

Should the possibility occur, he realized that he would not allow the execution of such an action and the situation would rapidly deteriorate. Therefore, with the desire to avoid an ugly situation, he endeavored to take the initiative.

"Summer," he called softly, pleased when she came to an immediate halt. But the expression on her face was not the soft, sensual expression he had come to appreciate. It was hard and stubborn. Oddly enough, he liked it a great deal; the woman possessed a measureable amount of courage and he found himself smiling at her plucky display. "Come back, my lady, and obey your father. My men are fully capable of tending my wound, even though I shan't enjoy their attentions nearly as much as yours."

She frowned, retracing her steps with a good deal of reluctance. Just as she moved into Bose's proximity, thundering hooves from the opposite side of the field rumbled toward her and she turned in time to note Stephan's colorful arrival. Shield slung over his left arm, his visor was raised as he focused curiously on his sister.

"What are you doing in the lists, Summer?" he demanded, looking to Bose and cocking an eyebrow. "And why are you still here? Your bout is over, de Moray. Get out of here and allow my sister to suture your hard head."

The corner of Bose's lips twitched at the attempted humor, his jaw ticking with the stress of the situation nonetheless. "We seem to have a problem, Stephan. Your father...."

"He demands that I not tend Sir B-Bose's wound," Summer interrupted Bose's tactful reply. "H-He says he shall throw me in the vault if I do."

"That's not what I said!" Edward shouted from the platform, oblivious to the audience they were coming to attract. "I will throw you in the vault for your stubborn defiance, not for the fact that you wish to tend Sir Bose's head. 'Tis your disobedience I would punish!"

Stephan growled low in his throat, a gesture of disbelief and intolerance. Casting his sister a long, if not somewhat supportive glance, he reined his charger around Bose and toward his weaving, sweating sire.

"Father, I believe it would be acceptable for Summer to tend Sir Bose," he said quietly yet forcefully, the tone he always used when dealing with his weak-willed father. "As for her insolence, you must understand she has experienced quite a bit of upheaval since yesterday. I believe we discussed this very same subject this morn and you agreed with me completely."

Edward's angry expression faded as he listened to his son's statement. Stephan always managed to calm him, convince him all was right within the world. "And... and I did, of course. But the fact that she demands to be a part of world that will not have her does not excuse her foul manners," wiping at his dripping brow, he began to appear somewhat uncertain. "And Sir Bose... Stephan, did you not tell me that the man is a known murderer? I do not understand your change of heart. This morn you were completely unwilling to...."

Stephan put up a hand, silencing his father's prattle. "I know," he said quickly, quietly. "But I must confess that I was wrong. Please allow Summer to tend the knight and I shall explain the entire situation after my bout."

Edward's face was calm once again, looking somewhat dazed as he diverted his focus from his son's earnest face to his daughter's eager expression. Confused and drunk, he was in no position to repudiate his son. If Stephan said he was wrong, then Edward would certainly not dispute him. With a faint nod of his head, he reclaimed his chair without another word.

Summer let out a faint sigh of relief, looking thankfully to her eldest brother. He smiled weakly.

"Get him off the field, Summer," he said quietly. "My bout is next and I'll surely run the both of you down."

The bottom of her persimmon colored gown stained from the damp, dark dirt of the arena, Summer moved toward her brother. "Please, Stephan," she said softly, reaching out to touch his armor with her soft hand. "Does this mean you have changed your mind? Is it acceptable for Sir B-Bose to carry my favor?"

Stephan gazed at his sister, finding he was no longer able to keep his attention from Bose. Piercing black eyes glimmered with warmth and appreciation and at the moment, Stephan knew there was no need for further words on the subject; Bose understood the depths of a man's honor and duty when it came to his family and he realized Stephan had acted in the only manner possible given the circumstances.

"Tend his head, sweetheart," he said, touching her honey-gold hair briefly before lowering his visor. "Send for Genisa if you require assistance."

With that, he was gone, thundering to the opposite side of the field where the heralds and squires were awaiting his presence. Summer watched him cross the field, deeply thankful at his apparent change of heart. More than any other requirement, Stephan's approval was a necessity to her future happiness. And that fact that he had come to approve of Bose meant more than she could express.

Tearing her attention away from her brother, she caught a glimpse of Genisa's triumphant smile from her seat in the lodges. Edward, drunk and eagerly awaiting his son's bout, had quickly forgotten about his daughter's situation and Summer turned away from the scene, her golden gaze coming to rest on the injured, exhausted knight.

"I have needle and thread in my tent, my lady," Bose said softly, extending his elbow. When Summer latched to him firmly, his smile broadened and they proceeded toward the edge of the field. "I will be the envy of every man here with your fine stitches embedded in my scalp."

"I promise to make them very small," she said as they approached the edge of the field. Immediately, she noticed several knights appraising her openly, the very same knights she had viewed the day before in Bose's camp. "However, I will confess that I have never s-sewn a man's head before."

He smiled, experiencing a surge of pride as the men about the field witnessed the Gorgon with a beautiful woman on his arm. "A simple task, truly. You need only remember to take care and not pierce my brain."

She turned to him, scowling gently. "If I pierce your b-brain, mayhap it will allow a measure of foolish knightly pride to escape. Never again will I see you riding helmless in a joust."

He laughed loudly, startling Tate and causing his other men to look at him with wide eyes. Never in their lives had they known Bose to laugh aloud like a carefree child. In fact, he felt very much like a carefree youth; powerful enough to challenge the angels, fortunate enough to defy God himself.

"I promise, my lady," he snickered softly as they cleared the lists. "Never again."

CHAPTER NINE

ER NAME WAS **Margot**.

That was all Summer knew of the elderly woman who had gazed at her with such venom that Summer was certain the lady was hexing her with a curse. Even as she knelt over Bose, sewing the substantial gash bisecting his scalp, she could feel the heated stare of the old woman and her equally vicious lady-in-waiting.

Bose had tried to convince the finely-dressed woman to leave the tent while Summer stitched his head, but the lady had been openly defiant, soliciting an uncomfortable argument as Summer stood by, respectful and silent and uncertain.

When it appeared obvious that the old woman had no intention of vacating the tent, Bose had left Summer in the company of an older knight, a distinguished looking man who had introduced himself as Sir Morgan Skye. Disappearing into the privacy of the black and white tent with the older female, Summer could hear their angry dialogue from her position outside the shelter. The fact that the woman's lady continued to gaze at Summer as if she carried the plague did nothing to alleviate her discomfort.

The elderly woman's haughty servant aside, Summer grew increasingly embarrassed as she listened to a good deal of hissing from the old woman, intermingled with Bose's deep, rumbling replies. She could not make out any definitive words nor did she understand the gist of their disagreement, but several moments later Bose re-emerged from the tent appearing somewhat paler and drawn of expression.

Ordering his knight away, he gently pulled Summer into the tent with hardly a word spoken. Indicating the supplies lain out on the floor by his pallet of furs, he pulled off his mail hood and lay down in preparation for her healing hands.

That had been an hour ago. As the elderly lady sat against the wall in grim silence with her arrogant woman hovering by her side, Summer had sewn tiny stitches into Bose's scalp, not daring to speak a word as she worked. Bose lay completely still, his eyes closed, and Summer seriously wondered if he had fallen asleep, as if a constant prick to his head was nothing to be concerned over.

But his patience and tolerance had eased Summer's discomfort and allowed her to complete the job in rapid time. An hour later, Bose had a beautiful row of silk sutures planted on his head and Summer paused after securing the last stitch, gazing down at his pallid, still face. Smiling faintly at her perfect patient, she found herself staring at the sharp angles of his face, the square plane of his jaw. The three scars that ran along his cheekbone were longer than she had originally observed, going well beyond the hairline and into his scalp.

"Are you finished?" the bird-like woman from the corner croaked, startling Summer from her train of thought. Turning to the woman, she was hardly able to open her mouth before Bose was sitting up, his black eyes blazing.

"I told you that you could remain in my tent only if you were perfectly quiet," he very nearly snarled. Turning from the old woman's challenging features, he called to the nearest servant hovering outside of the tent. When the man appeared, he waved him in. "The Lady Margot has a desire to seek fresh air. Escort her outside and demand my squire to take her and her woman to the vendor area."

"I have no desire to venture to the vendor's shelters," Margot growled, looking between Bose and the lady. "Surely you do not expect me to leave the lady alone and unescorted."

Bose cocked an eyebrow. "You have remained as proper escort throughout the time she has tended my wound, as you so graciously pointed out to be your proper duty," rising to his knees, he sighed heavily as the world rocked a bit and his aching head throbbed. "But the time is past and my wound is properly sewn. Your presence is no longer required and I would see you removed."

Shocked at the tone in his voice, Summer was disturbed by the air of hostility between him and the older woman. Obviously, there was a good deal of animosity and Summer abruptly rose, setting the needle and other items to a small maplewood table.

"T-Truly, my lord, her removal is unnecessary," she said, hoping to ease a strain she did not understand. "Your wound is tended and there is no longer any reason for me to stay."

Margot, verging on a wicked rage, was caught off-guard by the stammer. "You stammer," she said bluntly, focused directly on Summer as if Bose was non-existent. "A terrible defect. I am surprised your family allows you to mingle with normal people, sputtering and gasping as you do."

Summer's cheeks flamed a bright red and she lowered her gaze, a terrible embarrassment filling her. Knowing that her shame only served to accentuate her flaw, she struggled to calm herself as she formed a carefully worded reply. Before she could bring the necessary words forth, however, Bose was leaping madly to her defense.

"Damn you, Margot," he hissed. "We all have flaws, although some are more pronounced than others. The fact that you are a bitter, nasty shrew happens to be your particular defect and if I had any wisdom at all, I would not allow you to associate with normal people, either."

Margot looked to her son-in-law, unaffected by his mounting rage. Her eyes took on an unnatural gleam. "I understand a great deal now; you have simply taken to the lady out of pity. You were always exceptionally soft-hearted, Bose. Especially to those beings who are weaker and far more impaired than the general populace."

Summer felt as if she had been slapped; her chest ached with humiliation. Her first instinct was to run from the tent and sob until she could sob no more, but that would not solve the dilemma. Obviously, the old woman was attempting to belittle her, to unbalance her in front of a man she apparently held little affection for. Bearing that in mind, she struggled not to succumb to her usual reaction of tears.

"I am sorry you f-feel that way, my lady," she whispered, feeling Bose's hand as he attempted to grasp her. "If you will excuse me, I will take my leave."

Bose's warm grip had her firmly by the arm as she endeavored to leave the tent, holding her still. Even if his hand was reassuring and strong, his gaze upon the frail old woman was anything but pleasant.

"Get out," he rumbled, his baritone voice quaking the very ground beneath their feet. "Get out before I do something you'll regret."

Margot continued to maintain her even expression, though there was something in Bose's tone she had never heard before. Defiant as always, however, she refused to be intimidated. Especially when she was rapidly coming to realize that the stammering lady meant more to Bose than mere female attendance.

"Lora would not allow you to speak with me that way," she snapped. "How dare you threaten me!"

Still maintaining his grip on Summer, his onyx orbs flashed. "'Tis no threat, I assure you. Get out and stay out of my sight if you value your life."

Margot's thin eyebrows rose in outrage; she refused to allow the man to gain the upper hand. "Do you think to replace my daughter, Bose?" she demanded. "Do you think to replace my daughter with another woman you can just as easily kill with your massive seed?"

Bose was losing his composure, so easily provoked by Margot's guilt-strewn ramblings. He released Summer, unaware that he was frightening her tremendously. He simply wanted the old woman out of his sight and he did not care who he terrified in the process. The moment he moved for the vicious elder lady, however, Summer found her feet and bolted from the tent before he could stop her. His fury diverted by the lady's flight, he attempted to move after her when Margot was suddenly clinging to his arm, her sharp claws batting at his face.

"You bastard!" she cried, drawing blood on his chin. "How dare you flaunt your whore in front of me. How dare you think so little of

Lora's memory that you would sate your lust with another woman!"

His emotions soaring, Bose grasped the elder woman by the arms and thrust her away from him. Margot stumbled back, yelping with surprise that Bose had actually prevented her from demonstrating her rage; usually, he simply stood by while she beat and scratched him until the seizure passed. But not today; today, he had actually stopped her, and she found that prospect terrifying.

Even as she struggled to sit from her crumpled position, Bose was quitting the tent. Margot sat up, screaming her curses upon his deaf ears as went in search of her daughter's replacement. Even if he hadn't indicated as much, already, she knew. She knew the end of her tyranny was near. She was losing him.

C8

FOR ALL OF the grunting occurring within the green and yellow tent, one would have believed childbirth to be imminent. To Breck, of course, the pain was similar as the physic popped his shoulder back into the socket and bound the arm. And with every grunt of anguish, the hatred toward de Moray deepened.

"Christ!" he hissed as the physician completed the last of the bindings. "Do you see what the man has done to me, Duncan?"

By the edge of the shelter, Duncan gazed at his brother with a mixture of uncertainty and support. "You nearly took off his head, Breck. Surely you expected the man to seek vengeance."

Breck curled his lip at his brother, his forehead beaded with sweat as he struggled to find a comfortable position on his pallet. "A completely unfair maneuver," he grumbled. "Did you see how he literally shoved me from my charger? I had no chance to recover."

Duncan sighed faintly; the maneuver would have been considered legitimate had Breck himself executed it. Although he was supportive of his brother as a faithful sibling should be, there were times when his older brother was wrong and selfish. But if Duncan wanted to continue living under the protection and wealth of the House of Kerry, he would keep his opinions to himself.

"It was because of her, you realize that," Breck's voice was considerably calmer as the poppy elixir provided by the physic began to take effect. "I have never seen de Moray even speak to a woman much less accept her favor. She must be terribly important to him."

Outside of the humid tent, Duncan could hear the heralds calling an end to the third bout. He was next, competing against Sir Adgar Ross, one of de Moray's men. Shifting on his muscular legs, he was far more eager to attend his round than listen to his brother's prattle.

"She is a lovely woman," Duncan said evenly.

"She stutters," Breck said, his own speech slurred as he turned to look at his brother. "S-S-Stutters. Other than to deflower her, I suspect de Moray has no other interest. Even when he beds the wench, he shall have to put his hand over her mouth in order to fool himself into believing he's indulging in a woman of perfection."

Duncan cocked an eyebrow in mild surprise. "No wonder we've never seen her attend the tournaments, supporting her brothers' cause. They have been keeping her hidden so no one will know of her imperfection."

"Exactly. A tragedy, really. She is quite beautiful. But as worthless as a two-headed goat to a marrying man," suddenly, Breck's brow furrowed and his expression turned quite serious. "Duncan... do you suppose de Moray intends to marry the woman?"

Duncan cast him an odd look. "How would I know that?"

Breck matched his brother's expression, exceeding it. "You discovered who she was, did you not?"

"It wasn't difficult. A pence to a servant and they'll tell you anything you wish to know."

Breck eyed his brother a moment, feeling the root of an idea take hold. A simple idea, truly, but one of the most magnificent consequence; to defeat de Moray on the field was a near impossibility. For four years Breck had tried, and for four years he had failed. De Moray was immovable, powerful, and the wound to Breck's arm fully proved the fact. There was no way to best the man in the tournament arena.

But as time and history had proven, when men succumbed to the female sex, their weakness was revealed. Since Breck could not seek revenge for losses dealt by Bose by exhibiting superior strength or talent, logic seemed to indicate that a far more powerful means would be to somehow seek vengeance upon the lady.

An idea he had nurtured once before. But a concept that had gained a good deal of support and as he gazed to his younger brother, the seed of evil thought took deeper root and began to grow.

"Find out if de Moray has pledged for her," he told Duncan. "See if you can determine what his intentions are."

Duncan cocked an eyebrow. "And what if he has?"

"If so, I shall have to alter my plans somewhat. But if he hasn't...."

"If he hasn't pledged? Then what?"

Breck's gaze lingered on his brother a moment. "Then I will."

It was not the answer Duncan had expected and his eyes widened dramatically. "What are you saying? That you would marry de Moray's lady? God's Blood, Breck, you just finished telling me that she is defective. What would you do...?"

Breck held up a sharp finger, quieting his brother's babbling query. "De Moray does not believe her to be defective. In fact, I would hazard to guess that he is extremely fond of her," scratching his chin, he sighed heavily as his train of thought settled deep. "I wonder if Lord du Bonne knows of Bose's reputation and how he is said to have killed his wife."

Duncan eyed his brother, uncomfortable with the plan he was developing. "If he doesn't, I suspect you will make him aware of the fact."

Breck drew in a long breath, feeling his pain ease with the physic's potion. Sleep, however, was near the surface and he struggled against it for the moment. "If I only had support for my petition," he murmured. "His wife's mother is said to have started the rumors of Bose's murderous instincts. I wonder if she would support my drive to claim the du Bonne sister before Bose sinks his claws into her."

The faint peal of a trumpet pierced the air, calling Duncan to his bout. He should already be there, mounted and weapons in hand and he silently cursed Breck for distracting him. Hastily gathering his helm, he abruptly moved for the partially-open tent flap.

"I have no idea where his mother-in-law is," he said, covering his bright red hair with the gleaming helm. "She is probably in London, far away from the man once married to her daughter. Moreover, I doubt very seriously she would rush to your aid in order to support your twisted sense of revenge against de Moray. You'd do well to forget this line of thinking, Breck. You are intending to tread on sacred ground."

Breck turned to his younger brother. "Sacred ground? How so?"

"By interfering between a knight and his lady," Duncan was as close to scolding as he could come. "You would only pledge for the woman to steal her away from de Moray. What happens if your pleas are successful and you are forced to wed? Then what?"

Breck sighed, scratching at his dirty scalp. "I'd have no real use for a flawed wife. The only reason I am considering vying for her hand is to damage de Moray far more than any injury I can inflict in the melee or tournaments," he sighed again, feeling the poppy potion pull at him. "I suppose I'd push her down a flight of stairs and be done with it. A double dose of revenge on de Moray; stealing his lady and killing her once we were married."

Duncan stared at his brother a moment, hoping it was the drugs speaking and not his true thoughts. Even for Breck, the deranged ideas were extreme to say the least.

"Why must you do this?" he demanded softly, baffled by the conversation.

In a drug induced haze, Breck's sinister orbs glittered. "De Moray must be made to respect and fear me, brother. He is the only knight on the circuit I cannot seem to conquer. The only knight who can best me in the melee or joust, victories that are meant to be mine. If this is the only way to weaken the man, then so be it. Mayhap if I weaken him enough, he shall simply fade away and once again I shall rein on the circuit."

The poppy concoction had nothing to do with this madness; Duncan knew that. The muddle spouting from Breck's lips was his own. It was frightening, considering he possessed the intelligence to carry out his threat.

"De Moray was father's friend, once," he reminded him quietly. "Father thought a good deal of him."

"And father is dead," Breck's voice was faint. After a moment, he sighed. "Tend your bout, little brother. Beat Ross in the joust or do not return to my tent; I would see his blood on your lance."

Duncan saw blood, all right. But it wasn't on his lance. It was on de Moray's sword.

ℭ

ONCE SUMMER WAS free of the tent, she took off running. Blinded by tears, she rounded the corner of the tent and plowed straight into a warm, armored body.

Morgan was shocked. "Good God," he gasped when her soft body rammed into him. Then he saw her face and the tears in her eyes. "What's the matter, my lady? What's happened?"

Summer tried to speak. She tried to pull away, too, but he was unwilling to release her. Instead, he shifted his grip and put his arm about her shoulders in a protective, comforting gesture.

"Where's Bose?" he asked gently, his naturally calm manner comforting. "Did you quarrel with him?"

She shook her head, sobbing. With a sigh, Morgan glanced in the direction of the tent and, seeing that Bose was not directly on the lady's heel, suspected that something was indeed wrong between them. Getting a good grip on the lady, he led her away from the tent and toward the gnarled old oak in the distance, a favorite landmark for residents and visitors alike.

Summer allowed him to lead her away, too disturbed to summon the effort for protest. Moreover, the older knight's embrace provided a certain measure of reassurance and comfort and, for the moment, she was willing to submit.

"Now, now, it cannot be all bad," Morgan's voice was soothing as they approached the old oak. "Can you tell me what happened? Or must I find Bose and disable him without knowing the reasons behind my chivalrous vengeance?"

His humor brought a slight amount of relief to her tears, almost a giggle to her lips. As they reached the long branches of the sprawling tree, she struggled to reclaim the power of her speech.

"I-I-It's not him," she managed to sputter. "T-T-The lady was very c-cruel."

Morgan stared at her, noting the stammer but attributing it to her weeping. Grimly, he nodded, coming to somewhat understand why Bose had not followed the lady as she ran from the tent. He found himself wondering if he should return to the shelter to pick up the pieces Bose was undoubtedly creating from a frail old woman. It was a punishment dealt that should have come about long ago.

"So you have met Margot," he said softly. "What did she say that has you so terribly upset?"

Summer looked to him, then, and her severe weeping made a return. She tried to answer him but, unable to do so, simply shook her head and turned away. His gaze lingered on her curvaceous back, noting the sweet curve of her torso far more than he should have.

"S-S-She c-called me i-i-imp...."

"Impaired," Bose's voice came from behind them. Morgan turned as his liege wandered up, his face ashen and his black hair stiff with perspiration and blood. "Morgan, would you kindly leave us?"

Hesitantly, Morgan nodded, casting Bose a lingering glance. "I do not understand, Bose. Why would she...?"

"B-Because I stammer," Summer suddenly turned away from the tree trunk, her face flushed with anger as well as humiliation. "She said I was impaired and said that Sir B-Bose was only interested in me out of p-pity."

It had taken a good deal of effort to spit out that lengthy sentence and Morgan grew weary simply listening to her. But he also experienced a measure of shock with the revelation of her affliction; Bose had made no mention of the fact and, naturally, Morgan was surprised.

"You know that's not true," Bose said quietly. "I have absolutely no pity for you whatsoever."

Her sobbing slowed as she continued to wipe at her face with the back of her hand. After a moment, she snorted ironically. "Nay, you surely do not. I have never met anyone who p-p-possessed less compassion for my flaw."

Bose held up a correcting finger. "Ah, I said I did not pity you. But most certainly I hold a good deal of compassion. You speak of two separate emotions."

"They are the same."

"They are not by my definition. Pity means charity, and in my opinion you are the last person in the world to warrant charity. But compassion means tenderness and understanding, two qualities which I would hope to possess. Especially where they pertain to you."

Sobbing lessened, Summer stared at him with emotion brimming in her golden eyes. Morgan, his gaze lingering on the beautiful young woman, suddenly felt as if he were intruding on a tender moment. As if abruptly remembering he had been asked to leave, he turned on his heel when a soft voice halted him.

"Sir Morgan," Summer's voice was soft, the extreme stuttering fading as she calmed. "Thank you for your kind escort. I am sorry we've not had a chance to become b-better acquainted."

Morgan turned to the lady, casting Bose a long glance as he replied. "A feat that will be made impossible by my liege's meddlesome presence, I imagine. But fear not, my lady; I suspect we will have further opportunity in the future."

Bose actually managed a weak grin. "Think not to steal her from me, you aging rogue. I shall fight you to the death."

Morgan cocked an eyebrow, knowing he was jesting but suspecting it was the truth all the same. "I know," he said, turning away from the two of them. "I saw what you did to Breck Kerry."

Bose snorted with weak humor, returning his attention to Summer as his knight strolled away. His smile faded as he gazed into her pale face, eyes red-rimmed and a catch in her breathing. Moving closer, he nearly blotted out the sun as he hovered over her.

"I am terribly sorry about Margot," he said softly, struggling for words. "She hates me so much that, unfortunately, you have fallen within the scope of her venom. I can never apologize enough for the insults she has dealt to you this day, but know that just the same I will endeavor to try."

Summer shook her head, wiping the last of her tears away. Leaning against the tree trunk, Bose's massive body was disturbingly close as her heart began to race again with excitement. He had that effect on her.

"It wasn't your fault," she replied, her voice nearly a whisper. "B-But I must say, you seemed quite willing to tolerate her insolence."

His eyebrows briefly drew together. "I would not exactly call my attitude toward Margot tolerant."

Summer stared at his mouth when he spoke, enjoying the odd, wonderful shape to his lips. "I gathered from her words that she is your wife's mother. If you do not tolerate her, then why do you allow her within your p-presence?"

He lifted a resigned eyebrow. "As much as I am loathe to admit the fact, she is a member of my house. I left her at Ravendark three days ago, but she followed me to Chaldon because…," he suddenly paused, gazing into her eyes as he broached the forbidden subject of Lora's death. "Because yesterday was the fourth anniversary of my wife's death. Margot was angry because I opted not to spend my time bemoaning my loss, instead, choosing to attend Lance's tournament. Even though I left her at my keep, she nonetheless pursued me and is determined to see that I grieve properly."

Summer watched his expression as he spoke, the anguish, and was deeply moved. Reaching up, she gently stroked a stubbled cheek; it was a bold move, but she simply could not help herself. It was as if he needed to be comforted.

"W-What was her name?"

His black eyes glittered like the crisp night sky; literally, she could see the stars within. "Who?"

"Your wife."

His gaze never left her beautiful face. "Lora."

She smiled faintly, still touching his scratchy skin. "A very p-pretty name," she whispered. "What was she like?"

He thought a moment, recollecting his wife without the pain and sorrow that usually accompanied such thoughts. "She was about your size with her mother's pale blue eyes. And she possessed a head full of wavy auburn hair, a mane she complained over incessantly."

Summer's smile broadened. "Why did she lament her hair?"

The corner of his mouth tugged, his heart leaping wildly against his ribs as she touched the curving edge. "Because she claimed it had a life of its own and she could not control it. Once she threatened to cut it all off and probably would have had I not stopped her."

Summer laughed softly, running her finger along his lower lip in her increasing exploration of his face. "I know how she feels. There are days when I would shave my head as well."

In spite of the decidedly erotic gesture that nearly drove him to his knees, he managed to smile.

"God's Beard, don't do that," he breathed, not knowing if he was referring to her beautiful hair or her sensual touch. As he braced his enormous arms on either side of her slender, luscious body, Summer continued to toy with his cleft chin and Bose was gazing so intently into her porcelain features that he failed to remember the course of their conversation.

"What else?" she asked.

He stared dreamily at her a moment before abruptly responding, as if he had only just understood her words. "What do you mean?"

"About Lora."

"Oh," he blinked, struggling to focus. "Well, she had freckled cheeks and a nose that wriggled when she spoke. And she had a silly giggle that could veer out of control quite rapidly."

Summer pictured the lady in her mind, curious about the woman he had once been married to. As she pondered the mental picture presented, both hands came up to his face and she stroked his stubbled neck with a distant expression.

"You cared for her a great deal."

"Indeed. She was my wife."

"D-Did you love her?"

He nodded. "I did."

Summer smiled. "I think it wonderful that you married a woman you could love. Most men b-believe love to be a fool's fantasy."

He shrugged faintly. Shifting on his massive legs, he somehow moved closer and Summer realized he had come very, very near. Her heart was pounding in her ears and excitement surged through her veins as he focused on her.

"Men believe that love will weaken them, that it is a woman's emotion," his voice was faint. "I used to think so too, once. But I know better now."

He was so close she could feel his hot breath on her face, causing her limbs to tremble with desire. As an innocent maiden who had only just learned of the excitement of a man's touch, the prospect of a stolen kiss was nearly beyond her comprehension. But she knew that Bose meant to kiss her.

Softly, as not to frighten her, Bose's head dipped low and his smooth lips consumed her delicious mouth slowly. God help him, it had been so long since he had kissed a woman that the first brief second of contact ignited his senses and immediately, he realized his slimly held control was vanished. A kiss was better than he had remembered.

Drawing back briefly, he licked his lips and was consumed with such a surge of desire that he was unable to control it. Removing his arms from where they were braced against the tree, he swept Summer into his powerful embrace and clamped his mouth over hers. In that moment, he was lost.

Summer gasped as he hungrily devoured her lips, licking and stroking and suckling until she was limp in his embrace. Unable to support her own weight, Bose lifted her from the ground and propped her against Grandfather's oak, his mouth ravishing her as if he had no intention of stopping. She tasted far too delicious to stop.

Summer was becoming accustomed to his tender suckles, his heated tongue as it toyed with her own. His delightfully masculine lips were driving her to the brink of madness and back again and still, she wanted more. Hands moving to both sides of his scarred, rugged face, she ceased being an inactive participant to his seductive attack and took the offensive.

Through his haze of blinding desire, Bose was surprised to feel Summer's response against his powerful assault. Her hands were on his face, in his hair, and the surge of lust building within him threatened to explode in all directions. His thick arms wound about her once again, pulling her away from the tree as he somehow managed to stagger to the other side of the trunk, using the massive oak to shield their activities from the eyes of the curious. Falling to his knees, he took her down with him.

God, her body was so beautiful. So round, so full, so womanly. And her breasts... they were directly below his seeking mouth, calling his name with a silent scream. Whether or not he wanted to restrain himself from a more intimate action, he realized that his hands had a mind of their own.

Summer gasped softly with surprise as his fingers delicately moved over the crown of her breasts, tracing the puckered nipples beneath the persimmon colored silk. Hearing her soft groan of astonishment, feeling the hard pebble of delight straining against the smooth material, was nearly more than he could endure. His pulsating manhood was already painfully engorged, reminding him of exactly how long it had been since he had indulged in the intimacies of sex. But taking his pleasure with the lady was simply out of the question. As much as his physical needs might desire the action, his emotions were still firmly in control and he refused to bed the woman without first coming to a great many conclusions.

He knew what he was coming to feel for her, the power of his interest and mounting adoration. And as his thick fingers gently roved the silken flesh just above the neckline of her gown, it did not take a good deal of deliberation to realize that he simply could not stomach the thought of leaving her behind once the tournament was concluded. Clearly, the past two days between them had established a great deal and Bose was only now coming to realize the extent of his attachment to the beautiful young lady. He realized that he intended to claim her, permanently.

Oddly enough, the thought did not bring about the tide of guilt he expected. From the moment his lips had claimed Summer's, the fact that he was kissing another woman only four years after his dear wife's death was suddenly no longer a factor. He had expected waves of shame. For everything he had anticipated to feel in light of Lora's passing, he was amazed that the guilt had not consumed him. In fact, nothing in his life had ever felt so right.

He pulled Summer closer.

CHAPTER TEN

T HE FEAST THAT eve was a boisterous, loud celebration. Even if the grand hall of Chaldon was crammed to the rafters with knights and ladies and nobles alike, the massive room was not large enough to accommodate everyone. Spilling over into the upper bailey, through the open gates and into the lower bailey and encampment of knights below, it seemed as if the entire world were celebrating the past two days of merriment and games.

The massive hall was abundantly lit, reeking of burnt meat and sweaty bodies as a small orchestra of minstrels played from the gallery high above. A pair of mummers worked the room in their jingling hats and pointed shoes, older men who were quite affectionate with one another and on more than one occasion sent the knights into groans of displeasure and disgust.

Amidst the bustle and revelry, Summer sat between Bose and Stephan at the massive head table, her eyes wide at the festivities going on about her. Stephan insisted that the very same party had progressed the eve before, an event Summer had missed due to her wanderings. Even though Summer did not regret her actions of the previous night, she was nonetheless sorry that she had missed such an overwhelming spectacle.

The table at which she sat was crowded with Bose's knights, her brothers, and several other knights from various households. Far down the table, Lady Margot sat in grim silence attended by her peevish lady, while seated several feet behind the chatty group, Edward was well into his second bottle of wine. The chair he lounged upon was a great carved piece, inlaid with semi-precious stones and cushioned with silk that Genisa had embroidered.

Summer thought he looked somewhat like a king, overseeing the activities of his frivolous vassals. He acted the part, too, hardly moving but to bring his chalice to his lips. He just sat and watched. Even though the man was somewhat quiet and inconspicuous, Summer could not help but feel a bit wary; when her father drank heavily, there was no knowing what would spout forth from his mouth.

But she tried to enjoy herself nonetheless, clad in a lovely scarlet and gold gown borrowed from Genisa. As the other knights around her laughed and gorged and sang, she found herself increasingly interested in Bose's crew of somber warriors. Except for the young knight with the lovely auburn hair, the entire collection seemed to be far more concerned with their own private dialogue than mingling with the rest of the group.

That went for Bose as well. He hardly spoke a word to the other men at the table, instead, only focusing on Summer or his own loyal knights. Stephan managed to wrangle a somewhat involved conversation out of him regarding the latest style of armor worn by the Teutonic knights, but little else. For the most part, he was silent as he devoured his venison and beef; under the table, however, his massive hand rested on Summer's knee in a discreet display of his growing affection.

"Summer!" Lance shouted from several chairs down. He was quite drunk and quite happy. "You did not see my bout. Where did you go after you left the lodges with de Moray?"

She nearly choked on the food in her mouth, her cheeks flushing. "I-I...," swallowing hard, she reached for her goblet of wine. Bose watched her carefully, stepping in to answer for her when she appeared to be having a good deal of difficulty forming an answer.

"My head required a good deal of stitches, Lance," he said evenly. "The lady took great care in tending my wound and stayed to keep me company while I rested."

Summer took another sip of wine, wondering how much penance Bose would perform in Hell for lying. She had only spent a brief amount of time sewing his wound; the rest of the day had been spent behind Grandfather's oak, learning the tenderness of his kisses and indulging in the discovery of lover's dialogue.

An afternoon that she would have been willing to continue for eternity had the setting sun not prompted Bose to end their clutches so that he might return her to the keep. The separation had been difficult, but he had promised to dress quickly for the feast and return within the hour. Leaving Summer standing on the ramp leading into the broad keep of Chaldon, Bose had returned to his tent faster than he could ever remember moving. Throbbing head and all, he did not want to be away from her for a minute longer than necessary.

Throughout the feast he had remained by her side, introducing her to his knights and placing his big body between her and any man foolish enough to show a measure of interest. The only men he would allow to speak with her were her brothers, and Stephan seemed to find Bose's strong protectiveness amusing as well as oddly comforting. His doubts of the man were fading and he realized he was growing comfortable with de Moray's suit. He was forced to admit that he'd never seen his sister happier.

Even at this moment, Bose continued to answer for Summer as if he had been doing it all his life. Genisa noticed it, too, seated on the opposite side of her husband, and her gentle smiles in Summer's direction were approving. But Lance was still distrustful of the mighty knight and as Bose replied on his sister's behalf, he scowled at the man.

"She can speak, de Moray," he slurred, his expression sweet once more as he looked to his sister. "Well? Are you planning on missing my bout tomorrow as well?"

Summer swallowed hard, forcing herself. "Nay, Lance, I shall be there. I am truly sorry I missed your round today, b-but I was... b-b-busy."

"I would not be so eager for your bout on the morrow, Lance," Ian sat on the opposite side of Genisa, muttering into his goblet. "The heralds have already drawn lots and you, my dear brother, go against Tate Farnum."

Lance cast his brother a drunkenly wry glance, looking to Tate far down the table between Farl and Artur. The auburn-haired knight, hearing his name mentioned, looked to the man he would face on the morrow's joust and the two men exchanged salutes and threatening expressions.

"You joust like a woman, Farnum," Lance said, his voice muffled as he drank deeply from his goblet. Rising from his chair, he plopped his taut buttocks onto the table to better see the man he was insulting. "'Twill be a pleasure to do away with you."

Tate lifted his cup. "The wine is making you mad, du Bonne. I shall knock you to your arse and take great delight in your humiliation."

Lance gave him a sarcastic twist of the lips. "I have defeated you more times than you have managed to best me, loverboy. Keep that in mind when I send you to the ground yet again."

Next to Tate, Farl sighed dramatically, his bushy red mustache twitching. "I have a better idea. I'd like to see your bout end in hand to hand combat as the two of you bash each other's brains to a pulp."

Artur and Adgar gave a quiet "here, here" in agreement, sending Summer into giggles. Lance, distracted from his mortal enemy by his sister's snorts, looked to his rosy-cheeked sibling.

"How dare you show humor at his insult," he muttered. "You should be begging my forgiveness for having missed my bout rather than supporting McCorkle's slander." His eyes suddenly narrowed as he made contact with his sister's golden orbs. "In fact, you missed Stephan's and Ian's bout as well whilst you were off tending de Moray's big head. Well? What do you have to say for yourself?"

Summer met his gaze steadily, a twinkle in her eye. "You won, did you not? Why are you lamenting my absence as if it somehow jinxed your chances?"

Lance's scowl returned. "Because it was your duty to be in the lodges, supporting your flesh and blood."

"She shall have the opportunity tomorrow," Ian said, his lips twitching with mirth. "She shall watch every second of your brutal battle to the death against Farnum."

Lance looked to his smirking brother. "And what do you find so amusing? At least I have a sporting chance against my opponent. You'll be lucky if you survive the first pass against yours."

Summer looked to her middle brother. "Who are you c-competing against?"

"Me," Bose said quietly, smiling faintly when she turned her attention to him. She returned his smile, preparing to reply when Ian reached across both Genisa and Stephan to tug at his sister's arm.

"Plead for mercy, Summer," he said softly, with unmistakable humor. "Beg him to place himself in the path of my lance so that I might unseat him. Be a good girl and do this for your darling brother."

Summer's eyes glimmered mischievously at her brother before returning her focus to Bose. Tate and Morgan, seated next to Bose, saw Summer's expression and shook their heads with defeat.

"Ian is as good as the victor," Tate announced loudly, demanding more wine from the nearest serving wench. "God's Blood, look at her face. How on earth can he refuse?"

"And the Gorgon falls like a mighty tree," Morgan lamented with mock-sorrow. "Felled by the will of a beautiful woman."

"She has not asked me yet," Bose said calmly, his eyes twinkling at Summer's devilish expression.

Her smile broadened, sensing the game afoot. Feeding off the humor and attention, she grasped Bose gently by the arm, her hand trailing to the fingers toying with his chalice.

"Would you allow Ian to win if I wished it?"

Her voice was soft, infinitely tender. Tate and Morgan, now joined by Farl and Adgar and Artur, laughed with varied degrees of humor as Bose remained focused on the young lady he had spent the better part of the afternoon kissing. And he knew, whether or not she was jesting, that his answer would be the same.

"I would."

Bose's knights continued to chortle loudly at his expense, listening to Lance's high-pitched delight join in their amusement. The loud laughter had attracted the attention of other knights on the opposite side of the table, interested expressions focusing on the frivolity. If Bose noticed the additional attention, he did not react. In truth, he had eyes only for Summer as she smiled beautifully in reaction to his response.

"Truly?" she squeezed his hand. "You would do this for me?"

He fought down a threatening smile. God's Beard, it was difficult to look into her smiling face and not respond in kind. "I would do anything for you."

Bose's knights roared their approval, clapping loudly as if Bose had just accomplished a mighty feat. Lance clapped too, heartily, as Ian paid particularly close attention to the conversation; in faith, he had only been jesting when he had asked Summer to use her influence against the fearsome warrior. And even though he did not truly believe the man to be serious in his reply, it was increasingly apparent that he was responsive to Summer's pleas and Ian's hope began to mount. Mayhap he had a chance tomorrow, after all.

Summer was acutely aware of his softly-uttered words. She leaned closer to him, tugging on his sleeve.

"You say you will do anything for me?"

"Indeed."

"Promise?"

"I do."

She did not hesitate. "Then knock my b-brother on his arse."

The entire table exploded with boisterous laughter. Lance turned to Ian, slouched in his chair and awash with a miserable expression, to slap the man heartily on the shoulder in a show of sympathy. Summer moved away from Bose, her lips still creased with a devilish smile, to regain her chalice of wine.

"Bravo, Summer," Stephan said with quiet mirth. "I applaud a woman who refuses to misuse her power."

Summer's smile broadened in response, casting a glance to her forlorn brother three seats away. Ian looked to his treacherous sister between the splayed fingers of the hand over his face, grimacing in reaction to her smirking expression.

"You've doomed me, Summer," he lamented as Lance patted him on the skull. "By tomorrow this time, I shall be only a memory."

As the other knights about the table agreed, Summer's expression softened with mock pity toward her condemned brother.

"But you are so strong and skilled, Ian," she insisted with mock conviction. "You've told me so. And the only reason Sir B-Bose has managed to best you in the p-past is because he's cheated. Isn't that what you've said?"

The throng hovering about the table groaned and chortled as Ian turned shades of red. Summer merely smiled, loving the attention and the fact that she was succeeding in humiliating her too-confident brother.

"That's not what I said. I... I told you that Sir Bose bested me because he is the most powerful knight in the entire realm."

The bid to avoid Bose's wrath was met by cheers and drunken salutes; there was not one man about the table willing to disagree. The snickering laughter was directed at Ian, knowing the man was struggling to retain his hide.

Through the laughter and revelry filling the smoky air, Stephan seemed somewhat removed from the dialogue as he watched his baby sister sample her first true taste of public life. Her smiles, her rosy cheeks, and her lack of concern for her imperfect speech struck a chord deep within him.

Stephan and his brothers had shielded Summer for her own protection. And as Stephan lived and breathed, he knew his father had kept her isolated for very different reasons; Edward liked to pretend that he protected his daughter out of fatherly concern when, in fact, his eldest son knew full well that his father hid the youngest du Bonne sibling and her stuttering as one would conceal a disease.

Glancing to his drunken father now and again, Stephan could not help but wonder why Edward had allowed Summer to mingle with the masses. Mayhap the man was past the point of caring any longer, a factor Stephan seemed to have a good deal of trouble accepting. Or mayhap Edward permitted his daughter to attend the feast with de Moray in the hopes that the man would become smitten enough to take the girl off his hands.

Summer was indeed proving to be witty and beautiful, radiant and sweet. Her stutter was hardly evident and if the knights and ladies about the table noticed her occasional stammer, they certainly had not indicated as such. They were as enchanted with her as de Moray was and from the expression on Bose's face, Stephan suspected that enchantment did not quite encompass all of the knight's thoughts.

"Do you see how Bose looks at Summer?" Genisa's breath was suddenly hot on his ear, distracting him from his thoughts. As Stephan nodded faintly, his wife squeezed his arm encouragingly. "Your expression was the very same when we first met. I would wager to say that we are witnessing Summer's future husband."

Stephan eyed the dark knight a moment, moving to drink from his chalice. "Time will tell, love."

Genisa grinned, kissing his ear hotly. "It took you one week to pledge for my hand. How long do you suppose it will take Sir Bose?"

Stephan groaned softly, his male member already pulsing with life as his wife kissed him again. "God's Blood, Genisa, not… here. Later."

She laughed softly. "Sir Bose's expression has caused me to recollect the very first time we made love. In an alcove at my father's manse. Do you remember?"

Stephan groaned again, his palms beginning to sweat with the heat of desire. "Sir Bose's expression has provoked your lust? I find the fact that another man has managed to arouse you most disturbing."

"Do not," she breathed, suckling discreetly on his earlobe. "Be thankful. There is an alcove in the hallway near the kitchens, my darling. It is a perfect place for our passion."

Stephan did not reply for a moment, distracted from the thought of his sister's blossoming popularity by Genisa's desire. God's Blood, the woman was never satisfied. But, then again, neither was he.

Abruptly, he stood, thankful that his tunic concealed his arousal. Pulling Genisa to her feet, he mumbled his excuses to the table of guests and escorted his giggling wife from the table. Moving through the smelly hall, he directed her into a dark, seldom used corridor.

The alcove was deep and narrow, nearly completely concealed by a large dusty tapestry. Pushing his wife into the shadowed nook, he absorbed her wicked laughter with his demanding mouth, drawing at her flesh until her moans of desire drowned away the devilish mirth. Hiking her skirts to her waist as she fumbled with his hose, he lifted her against the wall and braced her writhing body with his hips.

With a soft shout of possession, Stephan filled his wife with the proof of his powerful passion. Thrust after mighty thrust, Genisa moved with him, her hands in his hair, her lips against his ear. She wondered fleetingly if Summer would ever feel the same power from mighty de Moray and suspecting that she soon would.

CƷ

"STEPHAN DREW DUNCAN Kerry in the fifth round," Lance was growing drunker by the moment. "I hope Genisa's lust doesn't drain his strength."

Ian laughed softly, knowing the current activities of his brother and sister-in-law and struggling to suppress the familiar pain the knowledge evoked. Controlling his emotions for Genisa had grown easier with time, a necessity for the sake of his sanity, until he was able to quite easily subdue the dull, anguishing ache. Still, not a day went by that he did not wish for Genisa to be his. And not a day went by that he did not envy his brother his good fortune.

But he refused to allow the familiar depression to envelope him at the thought of his brother bedding the woman that he himself was in love with. Instead, Ian found a good deal of distraction in the situation at hand and endeavored to focus on the conversation.

"I am surprised the young Kerry lad was able to best Sir Adgar," he said, shifting to gain a better look at the small, trim knight down the table. "A freakish occurrence that he managed to evade your shield."

Adgar leaned forward, his neatly groomed beard moving as he chewed. "Even more amazing that he managed to unseat me without trickery or unfair tactics. The lad caught me off-guard, pure and simple."

"Duncan is not like his brother," Bose said quietly, his gaze still riveted to Summer. "Fortunately, the lad possesses an ounce of compassion and morality. His older brother would do well to learn from him."

Hand resting on her chin, Summer listened to the conversation regarding the Kerry brothers with lagging interest. The other knights about the table had turned back to their ladies and wine, a peppering of varied conversations traversing the length of the heavy table. As she focused on a particularly loud knight who had fought quite brutally in the melee, a servant respectfully approached and whispered in her ear. Immediately, she stood up, much to Bose's concern.

"Where do you go, my lady?" he was already on his feet, preparing to escort her.

She smiled, patting his arm gently. "My father wishes to speak with me. Please sit and enjoy your wine," when he appeared hesitant, her smile broadened and she put a reassuring hand against his chest. "He oft grows frantic when Stephan is absent. He merely wishes to know where my b-brother has gone."

Bose cocked a black eyebrow, not wanting to let her out of arm's length. She patted his arm again in a comforting gesture, excusing herself from the table and moving toward her lounging father several feet away. Bose watched until she reached the portly, ruddy man before re-seating himself.

"Good Lord, Bose, she is not going to run away," Morgan mumbled from his left side, his voice muted as he took a long sip of wine. "You are acting as if she belongs to you."

Bose's searing black gaze snapped to his long-time friend, his normally expressionless face hard. After a moment, he turned away and drained the contents of his chalice.

"She does."

Morgan was not particularly surprised to hear his answer. "But you've yet to pledge for her."

"I will."

"When?"

"When you stop asking me a plethora of foolish questions."

Morgan's lips twitched with a threatening smile. Bose was never one to act on the spur of the moment, taking his time in concluding even the smallest decisions. This time, however, Morgan suspected time would not be on his liege's side. Considering the lady and her beauty, it was evident from the expressions of the knights throughout the room that she had an entire army of secret admirers.

"You'd better hurry," he said quietly, watching as a serving woman refilled his goblet. "She shall not remain unclaimed much longer."

The veins on Bose's temples throbbed. "You are correct in that assessment. Before the night is through, she will indeed be betrothed. To me."

Morgan looked to him then. "What of Margot?"

Bose blinked slowly, his black eyes gazing into the smoky depths of the bustling hall. "What of her? She has no say in my affairs."

Morgan did not respond for a moment. They all knew of Margot's attempts to control their liege through the memory of her dead daughter. And Bose knew it, too. Conceding the fact, however, was another matter. If the man wanted to pretend that the woman had no control over his life, then that was his business.

"Nonetheless, I suspect this afternoon will only be a foretaste of her reaction to your second wife," Morgan continued after a pause, catching a glimpse of the thin, vicious lady far down the table. "You cannot allow Summer to live her life at Ravendark absorbing the insults of a combative old shrew."

Bose sighed faintly. "Summer will come with me as I travel the circuit. She will never be out of my sight and she will certainly never be alone with Margot. You worry overmuch."

"And you are not being realistic. You cannot be with Summer every hour of the day, protecting her from Margot's venom."

Bose scratched his chin, increasingly irritated with the conversation and the truth of Morgan's reasoning. "Then mayhap I will send Margot to live in London. I'll buy her a manse of her own where she can live comfortably away from my new wife and me."

"She has a manse in London, Bose. She hasn't seen it in four years."

"Because it was where Lora was born and she cannot bear the memories. I'll buy her another."

Morgan sighed, unwilling to further pursue that line of dialogue. He was so involved in his thoughts that he was barely aware when Farl nudged Bose from behind, growling something Morgan couldn't quite hear. But it took less than a moment for Bose to bolt from his seat.

Morgan looked to see what had the man up. Lingering beside Edward's chair, a mere foot or so from a somewhat-wary Summer, was none other than the younger of the Kerry brothers, Duncan himself.

ℭ

"'TIS JUST A dance, my lady, truly," Duncan was saying earnestly. "One dance and I shall be forever grateful for your graciousness."

Summer gazed to the man with the red-gold hair, by far more handsome than his buck-toothed brother and infinitely more charming. But she was still reluctant to speak with him, unfamiliar as she was with his character, and impatiently waited for her father to send the knight along his way.

Edward, however, seemed quite content to observe her interaction with the youngest Kerry sibling. Now that his daughter had established herself as the belle of the feast, it was apparent that he had been wrong to assume that Summer's flawed speech would somehow jeopardize the du Bonne name. Edward was coming to see that perhaps there might be a bidding war for his daughter's hand. He was pondering the prospect when de Moray suddenly appeared.

"Be gone, maggot," Bose snarled. "The lady is in my company this night."

Duncan visibly shrank. Although he knew this moment would come, still, he endeavored not to appear too intimidated by the hulking knight.

"I meant no harm, my lord, truly," he said. "As far as I have been told, the lady is not betrothed, nor spoken for, and I was merely attempting to solicit an innocent dance."

Bose glared at the young knight; although he was a genuinely likable lad as compared with his brother, the fact mattered naught. Duncan was attempting to vie for Summer's attention and Bose was unwilling to tolerate the slightest advance from anyone.

"She is my favored lady, Duncan," Bose's voice was considerably less harsh. "If anyone is to dance with her this night, it will be me. Though I fault you not for your interest, there are plenty of young women about to occupy your attention."

Duncan cleared his throat, a nervous gesture. Breck had sent his brother to solicit a dance from the lady, knowing his own attempt would be quickly thwarted. Duncan was well liked by his peers and Breck knew there would be little valid reason to spurn the man's request for a single dance from Lady Summer.

All Duncan had to do was bring the woman to the floor, whereupon Breck would interrupt their cozy clutch and continue the dance in his brother's stead. It did not seem to matter that Bose had been the lady's shadow for the duration of the feast; all that mattered was that somehow, someway, Breck was able to pull the lady away from her admirer. Duncan was afraid of what would happen to him if he wasn't successful.

"I… as I said, I merely wished to solicit a dance. And as for the lady being your favored…."

"You may have your dance, young Kerry," Edward's slurred speech was faint but unmistakable. "Sir Bose is not pledged to my daughter by any means, nor has he petitioned for my blessing. Take your pleasure with her."

Summer and Bose looked to Edward with a good deal of shock and dismay.

"Take his p-pleasure with me?" Summer repeated with disbelief. "What do you mean by that?"

Edward eyed her, his veins flushed with the power of alcohol. "Just that. You wanted to sample the real world, Summer, and here it is before you. Sample all of it. With everyone who shows an interest. Find a man who will have you from the hordes of men leering at your beauty."

Bose reached out and grabbed her hand possessively, moving to return her to the table. It was all he could do to keep from blasting the callous, repulsive baron right between the eyes.

"Come along, love," he said, struggling to keep his voice calm. "We shall enjoy the rest of the evening together."

"Sir Bose," Edward's tone was suddenly firm. Summer and Bose paused in their trek back to the table, turning to note that Edward had risen unsteadily to his feet. Beside him, Duncan appeared most uncomfortable as the tension filling the air gained strength. "Regardless of your interest in Summer, she is still my daughter and she will do as I say. If I demand she dance with a man of my approval, then she will. And you have no say in the matter."

Bose knew his words to be truth. God help him, he knew the man's words to be correct and his stomach twisted at the thought of Summer dancing with another; even Duncan Kerry, as harmless as he was. He tore his hostile gaze away from Edward long enough to look into Summer's fearful orbs, knowing that it was essential that he keep his manner calm.

She appeared absolutely terrified and Bose knew if he showed any measure of rage, she would most likely collapse. Either that, or openly defy her father as she had earlier in the day, and Bose had no desire to see her ordered to the vault for another display of disobedience.

Therefore, it was with great misgivings that he forced a smile and patted her hand gently.

"Go and dance, love," he said softly. "Show me how beautifully you can dance and we shall continue to dance all night, just you and I."

Summer's eyes widened, as if she hadn't heard him correctly. Then her brows drew together with genuine puzzlement. "B-But... why do you agree? I do not want to dance with anyone but you."

He patted her cheek gently, looking to Duncan with a fading smile. "One dance, Kerry. And not too close else you will sorely regret your interest this night," practically thrusting Summer at Duncan, he turned to Edward. "I should like a word with you, my lord. Immediately."

As Duncan reached out to grasp Summer by the arm, Edward eyed Bose with disinterest. "Later, mayhap. At this moment, I'll not have my wine spoiled with menial talk."

Duncan was attempting to pull Summer with him, but she dug her heels to the ground like a stubborn old mule. She was intensely interested in the conversation occurring between Bose and her father and had no intention of leaving at the moment.

She suspected she knew why Bose was so determined to speak with her father; although Bose had never said a word regarding a betrothal, from the moment they had met up until the afternoon they had so recently spent locked within each other's embrace, there had never been a doubt in her mind that she had found the man to spend the rest of her life with. From the expression on Bose's face as he fixed on her father, she suspected he felt the same.

Edward, however, seemed uninterested in Bose's solicitation and repeatedly evaded the man's polite requests with a myriad of weak excuses. Summer grew increasingly frustrated as her father seemed intent to ignore her potential husband, frowning at Duncan when he continued his weak attempts to pull her toward the center of the writhing hall. Just as the tugging between her and Duncan appeared to be on the increase, a large body suddenly materialized at Summer's side.

Ian's face was grim, his focus on Bose and his drunken father. "Go with Duncan, love. I'll… I'll convince father to listen to your beau."

Summer's expression washed with relief and thanks. "Oh, Ian, would you p-please? Father is being most unreasonable and…."

"I know," Ian patted her shoulder, giving her a slight push in Duncan's direction. "Go and dance. I shall attempt to alter our father's attitude."

Summer continued to gaze at her middle brother, a strong, somewhat calm and even tempered man with a vicious sense of humor. He would have been a stunning and astute eldest brother had Stephan never existed; nonetheless, Summer considered herself extremely lucky to have two such devoted siblings. Three, actually; Lance was rather perceptive and intelligent when he wasn't wearing a pig mask.

"I thought you were unsure of Sir B-Bose's character and motives?" she murmured quietly, ignoring Duncan's gentle tow on her arm. "Moreover, why would you defend the man who will defeat you in the joust come the morrow, with my insistence no less?"

Ian's blue eyes moved to his sister briefly, a faint smile tugging at his lips. "He will defeat me with or without your insistence," he pinched her lightly on the cheek, his focus returning to his obstinate father and the massive man attempting to engage him in conversation. "Now, if you will excuse me, I shall endeavor to aid your lover."

Ian moved away, but not before Summer reached out to grasp his arm gently. Duncan Kerry all but forgotten, her golden eyes glowed at her devoted brother.

"He did not kill her, you know," her voice was barely audible. "B-Bose's wife died in childbirth. You mustn't believe what you've heard about him. He's quite wonderful and I do believe he shall make a fine husband."

Ian's expression softened somewhat, knowing that she believed in the hulking knight's innocence with all her heart. Ian's opinion was much like Stephan's; he was having a difficult time dispelling four years of rumors regarding the king's former captain. But from what he had witnessed this day between his sister and the mysterious knight, he was coming to think otherwise.

He smiled faintly. "As you say, love. But if you do not let me go, I may never get the chance to prove my belief in your convictions of your future husband."

Summer watched her brother go, immediately engaging his father in conversation with a firm manner and steady voice. Bose looked to Ian as well, an element of surprise across his scarred face as the middle du Bonne brother lent his support.

Duncan Kerry tugged again and this time Summer did not resist; all would be well with Ian supporting her cause. He was intelligent and tactful and Edward would have a difficult time spurning the reasoning of the two determined men planted before him; in fact, Summer was relying heavily upon her father's known weak-willed nature.

For once, it would be an advantage.

CHAPTER ELEVEN

THE FLOOR WAS filled with gay revelers by the time Duncan guided Summer onto the smooth stone. The ballad was light and quick and Duncan immediately took her into his arms at a proper distance and began whirling her across the room.

The organized dance had taken her to the far end of the room, well away from the head table. As the music flowed through the stale air of the packed hall, Summer was startled when Duncan let her go and another body took his place. Only when a voracious arm went about her improperly did she look up from her feet, coming face to face with small blue eyes and a field of pock-marked skin.

"Greetings, my lady," Breck sneered into Summer's surprised expression, his green-tinged teeth emitting a foul odor. "My brother has indicated his fatigue and has graciously allowed me to finish his dance."

Shocked and disgusted, Summer yanked herself free of Breck's grasp, bumping into another woman in the process. Though she should have apologized to the well-dressed lady, she could only focus on staying clear of Breck's lecherous company.

"I-I...," swallowing hard, she backed away, narrowly avoiding another dancer as Breck advanced. "I am also fatigued. I am sure there is another lady who would b-be happy to dance with you."

"I do not want to dance with another lady," Breck insisted seductively. "I want to dance with you. The most beautiful woman in the entire room."

Summer succeeded in backing out of the group of revelers without further collision, nearly tripping over a chair flanking the crowded floor when she finally directed herself clear. She was well across the room from her assigned table and well away from those who would protect her from Breck's advance. Quickly noting that she was on her own until she could move within sight of the head table, she sought to steady her nerves.

"I do not wish to dance, Sir B-Breck," she said as firmly as she could manage. "If you will excuse me, Sir B-Bose and my brothers await."

She moved to evade him but he put out an arm, bracing it against a supporting beam and effectively blocking her escape. Summer wrinkled her nose at the repugnant stench of body odor reeking from the man's tunic, swallowing the bile in her throat as he smiled lasciviously.

"Sir Bose and your brothers have had the pleasure of your company all eve," he said. "'Twould be polite of them to share you with your other admirers."

A glimmer of impatience took hold. "I have no desire to be shared as if I were a c-common tart for the taking," she said snappishly. "Move your arm and be quick about it."

He cocked a red brow. "My, my, how unfriendly. Mayhap if you came to know me better, your hostile attitude would ease."

"I have no desire to know you b-better. Move aside or I'll call a guard."

Breck's first reaction was to flare; disobedience in a woman was intolerable and he banked the impulse to slap her. Instead, he forced himself to calm for the sheer fact that if he became angry, his goals would most certainly not be accomplished. Duncan had brought the lady directly into his fold; it was now up to Breck to take advantage of the situation.

"Forgive me if I seem overbearing, my lady," his manner was calm and sorrowful. "'Tis just that... well, the moment I saw you this morn in the lodges, I swore I had never seen anything quite so beautiful. And I suppose my aggressive actions are merely my emotional impulses gaining the better of my self-control. Truly, I never meant to offend or harm. I would simply like to share a moment of your time. Women don't usually take easily to me; I am not a handsome man. I have had to learn to be aggressive when dealing with women."

Summer listened to his speech. He seemed quite sincere and, being a bit naïve when it came to conniving men, she began to feel somewhat sorry for him. With a sigh, she eyed him closely; indeed, he was an ugly soul and Summer realized she had judged his character based on his pocked appearance and her brother's ramblings. After she had heard the horrid stories how the man had broken Stephan's wrist last year, it was only natural that she considered Breck Kerry an individual to avoid.

Had she believed her brothers' tales of Bose's murderous instincts, she would have never come to know the man with the golden heart and gentle nature. Aye, her brothers had been wrong about Bose. Mayhap they were wrong about Breck, too.

"Very well," she said quietly. "I am rather thirsty and I suppose we could share a c-conversation as I refresh myself."

Breck looked pleasantly surprised. Not merely surprised, shocked. Swallowing his astonishment, his arm dropped from Summer's path.

"I… God's Blood, I suppose we could sit at my table. I'll have a steward fetch wine immediately," as Summer moved hesitantly in the indicated direction, a brief glimpse of the courtyard beyond the open hall doors captured Breck's attention and he stopped her, his wickedly clever mind moving into the realm of more private, intimate surroundings. *By all means, man, get her alone!*

"Wait, my lady," he grasped her gently by the arm. "It is rather warm in the hall. Mayhap a walk in the night air would refresh you more than a goblet of tepid wine?"

Summer gazed to the yawning entry, the landscape beyond bathed in silver light. Drinking wine with the man in a room full of guests was one matter, but strolling alone with him in the moonlight was entirely another and her attempt to make amends for her judgmental attitude was fading fast. Even if the man truly possessed a heart of gold beneath his unattractive facade, he was stinky and aggressive and she simply did not like him. In the light or in the dark.

"I think not, my lord," she said truthfully. "I would share a goblet of wine and t-then return to my table."

Breck, however, would not be so easily dissuaded. "Come along, my lady," he grasped her arm firmly, pulling her toward the portal. "A walk beneath the stars will do wonders for your fatigue. We could even stroll to the stables and take a look at my charger. My father had him shipped all the way from Italy."

Summer tried to pull away from him, but his grip was tight. Whether or not she was willing, Breck seemed to be leading her directly for the exit. "I do not like horses, my lord. And I am entirely too exhausted to walk about the courtyard. P-Please, can we sit?"

Breck appeared not to hear her. He continued to drag her across the floor, oblivious to her attempts to break his grip. His boney fingers were bruising the tender flesh of her upper arm and Summer looked in the direction of the head table in desperation; she could scarcely see the end of it through the crowd, but noting that Bose's wicked mother-in-law apparently had a bird's-eye view of her situation. She swore she saw the woman smile.

Summer's slippers scuffed the stone as Breck pulled her through the opening and into the ghostly light. In the dusty bailey there were several crews of sentries and Summer's panic faded somewhat; should there be any true aggression on Breck's part, all she need do is scream for assistance. Therefore, she sharply yanked her arm free of the zealous knight's grasp.

"Unhand me," she said irritably, straightening her mussed gown. "I told you that I did not wish to walk with you."

Breck's face was hauntingly ugly beneath the moonglow. "I…I did not mean to offend. Oft times, ladies say no when in fact they mean the opposite. It is simply a matter of making a firm decision on the lady's behalf."

Summer's expression was lined with annoyance. "When I declined your invitation, I meant it. I w-would return to the hall this instant."

"But…."

"*Now.*"

Breck eyed her, laboring to keep his irritation at bay. Defiant women went against the natural course of the universe and it was a struggle not to punish her for her rebellious demand. In lieu of physical retaliation, he settled for mental instead. It was far more painful if done correctly.

"Return you to de Moray?" he asked softly, with bitter amusement. "God's Blood, I cannot believe your father has allowed the man to pursue you given his reputation and dark history."

Summer immediately bristled. "I'll not hear you r-repeat the slanderous lies within my presence, for they are untrue."

Breck's expression washed with a good deal of forced pity. "I have been on the tournament circuit six years, my lady, well before the arrival of Bose de Moray. I have known the man since his appearance and I can only say that I have seen nothing to refute the common hearsay. Suffice it to say that Sir Bose carries a frightening reputation toward man and woman alike."

Breck's aggressive actions forgotten, Summer found herself outraged by his accusations. Unwilling to tolerate his slander, her small fists rested angrily on her hips.

"His reputation is the result of his mother-in-law's demented sense of vengeance and nothing more. Her daughter, B-Bose's wife, died in childbirth and the woman somehow b-blames him for the incident. He did not kill her, Sir Breck. He loved her."

Breck's gaze held even. "So he has told you. What did you expect? Did you truly believe he would tell you the truth of the matter, considering his interest in you?"

Summer's jaw went slack with fury. "How dare you say such terrible things! Clearly, you d-do not know him at all!"

"I have known him longer than you have," Breck was enjoying her anger. "I have seen him in action all of these years, Lady Summer. I have seen his moods and tactics and his interaction with others. Believe me when I say that the Bose de Moray you know is not the true man beneath. Certainly, I am only concerned with your safety."

Summer's breathing gained pace, her fury spreading like the ripples on the surface of a pond. Of course she did not believe the knight's lies for one moment. But for the fact that he was continuing to spout his defamation, she was growing increasingly agitated and her stammering began to worsen.

"You have n-no such concerns," she hissed, her cheeks reddening with embarrassment and rage. "You are a selfish, p-petty man and I'll have nothing more to d-do with you."

She turned sharply on her heel as Breck reached out, snatching her by the arm. Summer gasped as pain cut though her tender limb, his strong fingers biting into her upper arm. But far more than the pain, the fact that Breck had managed to pull her against his silk-clad chest disturbed her deeply.

"Listen to me well, beautiful lady," his foul breath was in her face, gagging her. "My concern is indeed for your welfare. Why else do you think I would risk de Moray's wrath by seeking to be alone with you? Truly, it was the only way I could attempt to convince you of his cloaking evil. You must understand that he will do or say anything to gain your trust and you must be aware of his tactics."

"As will you, I am sure," her voice was as quiet as it was spiteful. "Release me this m-moment or you will deeply regret your actions."

Breck continued to stare at her, his eyes sharp and glittering. "What will it take to convince you, my lady? Your own death?"

She tried to pull away but he would not release her. Angry, fearful and exhausted, she attempted to slap at him but he effectively quelled her weak attempts. When she continued to struggle, he shook her brutally to cease her squirming.

"Answer me," he hissed, his even tone vanished. "What will it take to convince you of de Moray's evil?"

"He is not evil," she grunted, wincing at the fierceness of his grip. "His mother-in-law is the evil one for spreading such lies. And you are evil for b-believing them."

Breck was coming to enjoy the smell of her rose fragrance; in spite of her speech impediment, she was a tremendously beautiful woman. Her comeliness was almost enough to cause him to overlook her defect, but truthfully not enough of a distraction. Even so, her soft body and delicious scent were most tantalizing.

"If I cannot convince you, at least allow yourself to explore the possibilities of the truth," he said. "Mayhap you should ask his dead wife's mother for the facts of the matter."

Unaware of Breck's lustful thoughts, Summer struggled not to vomit at the smell of his repulsive breath. "I will not," she groaned, striving to pull free of his grasp. "She is a b-barbaric, malevolent woman and she shall only fill my ears with more of her fabrications."

Breck stared at her a moment, a measure of curiosity taking hold at the implication of her words. "Then...then you have met her?"

Summer succeeded in pulling one arm free. "Unfortunately."

Breck seemed to be unconcerned with the limb she had released from his grip, peering strangely at her as she endeavored to free the other. Knowing from his brother's information that the isolated young woman had never traveled out of Chaldon's province, that factor alone led him to believe that the very woman needed to support his cause was not in London as had been speculated. She must be here at Chaldon.

"When did you meet her?" he asked.

Summer hissed with exasperation as she struggled to peel his fingers from her arm. "She arrived this morning." Realizing she would be unsuccessful in removing his hand from her arm, she slapped at the appendage in frustration. "Release me, Breck Kerry. I d-demand it!"

In the midst of her struggles, Summer never saw the action that sent Breck to his knees, finally releasing his hold on her arm. Suddenly, he was falling away from her as a great shadow blocked out the silver-cast moon, enveloped them both in an eerie darkness. Strong, gentle hands steadied her as Bose abruptly came into focus, his massive body coiled with fury.

Brushing her hair from her eyes, Summer was astounded as Bose delivered another powerful blow, sending Breck sprawling to the ground in a spray of blood. As he balled his fist for another punch, Summer found her tongue.

"Bose!" she cried. "Please… n-no more!"

Immediately, Bose's momentum came to a halt and he turned his focus to her. It was the most frightening expression Summer had yet to see on his face.

"N-No more," in spite of his dark countenance, she reached out to grasp his arm. "H-H-He… H-H-He…."

Bose unclenched his fist, straightening from his hovering position over a supine Breck. "Calm yourself, love," he said, his tender voice far removed from the threatening expression. "Take a deep breath and speak slowly."

Swallowing, Summer responded to his gentle tone and her grip upon his arm tightened. As Breck writhed about in the dirt, Summer pressed against Bose's massive torso, the warmth and power of his flesh calming and comforting her more than anything she had ever experienced. Smiling weakly, she was deeply relieved when he wrapped a massive arm around her.

"B-Breck is not to blame," she said quietly, hoping he would not become angry with her. "I accompanied him of m-my own free will. The hall was stuffy and you were b-busy with my father, and B-Breck offered to escort me into the fresh air."

Bose's smile faded. "Did you also give him permission to touch you?"

She shook her head, eyeing the battered knight as he pushed himself to his knees. Even if she did not want Bose to beat him senseless, she would not lie to protect his bold intentions. "N-Nay. Never."

Bose's tender gesture faded completely. Releasing Summer from his embrace, he motioned to his knights standing several feet away. As Summer came to understand that she was to be placed within the company of his men, she balked.

"Nay, Bose," she said, clutching him firmly. "No further punishment. Come into the hall with me now and we shall dance. P-please?"

He patted her cheek sweetly. "Indeed we shall after I have finished punishing Breck for his boldness against my betrothed."

Summer forgot about Breck. She stared at Bose, her eyes widening with understanding. "B-B-Be…B-B-Betrothed?"

The corner of his black eyes crinkled. "Indeed. Ian, in fact, was most persuasive. Far more than I ever believed him to be capable."

Summer's mouth popped open. "Truly?" she whispered. "Father g-gave his permission?"

Bose was dangerously close to forgetting his duty to punish the aggressive knight. All that mattered at the moment was Summer's luscious lips, her incredibly beautiful face, as he gazed deeply into dark golden eyes.

"A tentative agreement," he replied softly, stroking her cheek once more. "In his drunken state, it was all I was able to wrangle. Certainly, we shall speak more on the subject tomorrow after I have emerged victorious in the joust."

Summer could scarcely believe what she had been told. Just as Bose began to wonder if she understood his words, suddenly, she let out a whoop of joy and clapped her hands together in a gesture of pure delight. All laughter and silks and rose-scented perfume, she threw her arms around his neck and he joined her excitement, whirling her about in a joyous circle as his men looked on.

The smiles of de Moray's knights were wide enough to cheer God himself. It was the first true display of emotion their lord had allowed to surface in four years of grief. None of them had expected such a happening on the day they had arrived for Lance du Bonne's tournament; even if they returned home defeated and poor, they would always recollect the trip to Chaldon Castle with the fondest memories, for their liege had gained the grandest prize of all.

Bose spun Summer in circles, listening to her giggles of happiness, thinking the feel of her in his arms to be the most wonderful of sensations. He was so consumed with thoughts of a new future that he forgot about the collection of men observing his excitement. Before he could stop himself, his mouth was clinging to Summer's tender lips and she giggled softly in joy and ardor, her arms tightly about his neck as her feet dangled off the ground.

Somewhere in the midst of their bliss, however, Breck had managed to regain his footing with a good deal of effort. Grunting and off-balance, he watched de Moray and his lady with mounting hatred. Morgan caught sight of the beaten knight from the corner of his eye and turned to him.

"Clear out, Kerry," his voice was low. "If you've not vacated the bailey by the time I count ten, I'll finish what Bose started."

Breck drew in a deep breath through his nose, fighting the nausea and dizziness that threatened. Still, he couldn't help himself from his haughty retort.

"I had no idea you could count, Skye," he rumbled.

Before Morgan could reply to the jibe, Breck was wisely retracing his steps toward the grand hall of Chaldon. When he was out of sight, Morgan tore his gaze away from him long enough to pass a final glance at Bose and Summer as they continued to nuzzle and kiss.

"Mayhap we should return to the hall as well," he suggested with a faint smile. "Bose seems to have the situation well in hand."

Tate cocked an auburn eyebrow. "He's doing far better than the rest of us," he snorted softly, ignoring Farl's gentle shove on the shoulder. "In fact, I have yet to so much as speak with the lady I have championed for the better part of the tourney."

Adgar cast him a strange glance. "What's this you say? How can you be her champion if you've never met her?"

Tate smiled, a devilish gesture. "She is my secret lady, of course. Unbeknownst to her, I chose her on the day of our arrival and have yet to properly introduce myself. Considering she has been seated in the lodges with a bear of a man clad in fine silks, I have yet to work up the proper nerve."

Adgar's eyebrows rose in outraged recognition. "The lady in the blue silk gown with the golden wimple that…."

"…that looks like a Unicorn's horn?" Tate finished suspiciously.

Adgar's brows abruptly furrowed as realization dawned. "Indeed! She is *my* lady, Farnum. Choose another."

Morgan and Farl laughed uproariously, moving around Tate and Adgar as the two men squared off against each other like a pair of dominant cocks. Heading toward the cavernous entrance to the festive gallery, they left the two suitors to do their battle as they focused on more promising diversions awaiting them.

Between the laughter and shouting and harsh arguments, no one seemed to notice that Artur continued to stand and observe the interaction between Bose and Summer. Old and hard of hearing though he might be, the old man knew his nephew well enough to know that the man was far gone in love with the beautiful young maiden. Not that he could fault the man his taste, of course; flawed speech or no, Summer du Bonne was the most beautiful woman he had ever seen, Lora included, if Artur would allow himself to be so brutally frank.

So Bose had found a new wife. As wonderful as the event was, the fact remained that Margot was casting a long shadow upon the destiny of Bose's future union. Tearing his gaze away from the delighted pair of lovers, he turned toward the grand hall, alive with music and dancing and drunken bodies. Now was not the appropriate time to bring up his concern over Margot's menace, but he had little doubt that such a time would rapidly come to bear.

Passing one final glance at the couple locked in an amorous embrace, he followed the pair of Bose's arguing knights into the warm, stenchy hall.

⚃

BRECK HAD HARDLY taken a seat when a soft, bird-like hand touched him on the arm. Growling, he brushed the hand away and snatched a pitcher of wine from a passing serving wench, pouring himself a sloppy measure. Gulping the liquor, he sighed heavily as the fortifying warmth coursed down his throat.

"Does the wine lend bravery as well?"

The frail voice came from behind. Breck drew in another mouthful of alcohol, turning disinterestedly toward the source. A small woman, quite old, held his gaze a moment before he turned away, back to his drink. He had no idea who the woman was and did not care.

"He left a bruise upon your cheek, young lord," the woman spoke again. "Punishment for touching his lady?"

Breck swallowed another gulp of wine, smacking his lips before deciding, strangely enough, to look to the old woman once again. His gaze raked her shriveled, tiny form.

"What do you want, woman, and be quick about it."

The woman offered a thin smile. "I want what you want. To separate Sir Bose from his lady."

Breck stared at her a moment. "Why? So you can have him all to yourself? I'd hardly consider you to be of marriageable age."

The woman's eyes glittered through the smoky haze of the hall. Even though she was tiny and feeble and harmless in appearance, Breck could sense a terrifying darkness from her. His gaze followed her as she seated herself daintily beside him.

"I do not want to marry him, my lord," she said quietly, her expression steady. "He is already married."

Breck continued to stare at her, cocking a slow eyebrow after a contemplative pause. "I understand his wife is dead."

"In body, mayhap. But not in spirit."

The red-haired knight pondered her odd answer a moment as his impatience returned. "What do you want?"

The lady's weak smile transformed into a genuine gesture. "As I indicated, the same as you. You are interested in Sir Bose's lady, are you not?"

Breck licked his lips thoughtfully. "And if I am?"

"Would you do anything to obtain her?"

"Within reason."

The woman laughed softly. "I am not suggesting you fight Sir Bose for her, for certainly, you would lose. The man is unbeatable."

"I know. I have battled him several times in tournaments and am well aware of his skill," taking another swallow of wine, his small blue eyes took on a curious nuance. "Who are you?"

The woman's smile faded. "Who do you think I am?"

"I most certainly do not know who you are."

The aged lady stared at him, her smile relaxing until her thin lips were straight and true. "Tell me your name, sir knight."

"Sir Breck Kerry, Lord of Crestwood."

The old woman nodded faintly. "Sir Breck, if you desire Sir Bose's lady, then I will most assuredly help you."

Breck pushed his cup aside and sat forward. Leaning on the table, he studied the ancient, once-fine woman intently.

"Not until you tell me who you are."

"The perfect weapon by which to accomplish your desires."

"That tells me nothing. Are you involved in his household?"

"Involved, yes," the woman folded her translucent-white hands primly. "I am very close to Sir Bose and in a grand position to aid you in your quest for the lady's attention."

Breck eyed her, settling back in his chair and eyeing the odd old woman. "And how is it you know of my interest in the lady?"

The woman smiled again. "I saw you drag her from the hall, of course. And I saw Bose follow in a rage. I was standing in the entry when you came stumbling through, returning to your seat in a battered heap, and can only assume that Bose punished you for your interest in his whore. Am I incorrect?"

"Nay."

"Then accept my assistance. If you want her, I shall aid you."

Breck refilled his goblet from the pitcher he had stolen from the serving wench. "And how will you do this, providing that I am interested in your proposal?"

The mysterious lady drew in a deep, thoughtful breath. "Being exceedingly young and wise, I would assume that you will think of a

plan to obtain Sir Bose's lady if you haven't already done so. Tell me of your plan and I will tell you how I can help."

Breck swirled the ruby-red liquid about his tongue, eyeing the woman pensively. Not knowing who she was, he wouldn't say anything to her that could make its way back to de Moray.

"I have no such plans," he lied. "Even if I did, I certainly do not require the assistance of a helpless old crone. Return to your cave, witch, and leave me be. If I want the lady, I'll take her regardless of de Moray's interest."

The older woman snickered without humor. "A brave front, young knight, but a foolish declaration. You know as well as I that de Moray will kill you if you attempt any such bold action. You need my help if...."

Breck slammed the chalice to the table, spilling wine over the scrubbed wood. "Cease your foolery, woman," he hissed. "Tell me who you are or I swear I'll slit your throat and leave you for the dogs."

"Slit my throat and you shall not obtain the lady."

"To the Devil with the lady! My truer goal is to destroy de Moray as, I suspect, is yours as well. Certainly, you would not be here if it were otherwise."

The woman produced a sinister smile. "How true, my young lord. Place your trust in me and our goals shall become reality."

"Then tell me who you are!"

The lady reached for her own chalice of wine. She suddenly felt very much like celebrating.

"The answer to your prayers, Sir Breck," she sighed contentedly. "As you are, apparently, to mine."

CHAPTER TWELVE

S UMMER HARDLY REMEMBERED how she and Bose had reached her chamber. Between heated kisses he had asked instructions for navigating Chaldon's corridors and before she knew it, Bose had entered the keep and wound his way through the maze of halls. Summer's heavy oaken door loomed before them and without hesitation, Bose kicked the panel open and ushered them both inside.

Aloft in Bose's arms, Summer was aware of the familiar surroundings, the familiar scent of her possessions. Removing her face from Bose's neck, she blinked her eyes as if emerging from a deep sleep. Looking curiously to the dark knight, he met her gaze and smiled gently as he lowered her to the floor.

"Why are we here?" she asked, truly innocent of his intentions.

He continued to smile, stroking her hair. "Because it is quiet and private, and away from the Breck Kerrys and drunken fathers of this world."

She blinked again, regaining the composure that his heated kisses had shattered. Smiling weakly, she nodded in agreement. "I suppose so," unable to match his searing expression, she turned away, unconsciously moving toward her massive bed. "It is much b-better here, isn't it?"

He nodded faintly, watching the delicious curve of her back as she moved away from him. God's Beard, he knew he shouldn't be here, but he honestly could not help himself. The more he touched and tasted, the more he wanted to claim her in every sense of the word.

"C-Come here."

Summer's voice roused him from his train of thought. Realizing she was standing by the bed as she spoke, he nearly tripped over his feet in his attempt to reach her. Ever cool, customarily composed Bose de Moray was as giddy as a young squire and he nearly laughed at himself for his clumsy, eager actions.

Summer, however, did not seem to notice his ungraceful moves. As Bose reached the bed, she smiled sweetly and pointed to the pillow. Tearing his gaze away from her beautiful face, his black eyes located the source of her interest.

"Antony," his voice was soft as he reached down to stroke his former pet. Wriggling and twisting, Antony greeted his previous master by nibbling his massive fingers.

"He is rather fond of this p-pillow," she said, her hand joining Bose's against the gray and white fur. "In fact, he sleeps with me."

Bose sat on the edge of the bed and Antony scampered onto the massive lap. "As he used to sleep with Lora and I," he said, caressing his fuzzy friend. "After you and I are married, however, I shall find him a bed of his own."

Her eyebrows furrowed as she leaned against the canopy post, watching him toy with the playful creature. "Why would you do that? He will be comfortable with us."

Bose maintained a steady gaze upon the animal. "Because I do not intend to share you with anyone and especially not within the confines of our bedchamber."

She smiled. "Not even with Antony?"

"Nay."

"B-But you shared Lora with him."

"I had no choice. Antony was her pet well before she met me."

"B-But you allowed her to continue to sleep with him. Why not me?"

He frowned. "Because you show far too much affection for him. I'll not be ousted from my own bed by my wife's pet."

Summer laughed softly, sitting at the end of the bed and calling softly to Antony. The ferret immediately left Bose's lap and scurried across the heavy bedrug, writhing delightedly under his mistress' delicate touch.

"Do you hear that?" she crooned tenderly. "Sir Bose intends to oust you from our bed. What have you to say to that?"

Bose stared at her in surprise, noting that the stammer completely vanished from her speech as she spoke sweetly to the little animal. True, sometimes she could speak a complete sentence without stammering, but that was rare. Moreover, the way she spoke to the animal was different... so confident. He liked it. He wanted to hear her speak that way to him as well, for always.

Summer caught Bose's expression from the corner of her eye, a gentle quirk of a smile gracing his lop-sided lips. Distracted from Antony's frenzied play, she cast him a curious look.

"W-Why are you smiling?"

He continued to gaze at her a moment before leaning back against the heavy pillows, his smile growing. "Because I have listened to you speak to Antony without a stammer to be heard," when she looked bewildered, he laughed softly. "I told you that your speech was purely habit. You stutter because it is expected."

Summer watched the ferret as it scooted away from her, returning across the bedrug and attempting to make a nest in the mound of pillows. After a moment, she shrugged feebly.

"Y-You are speaking in riddles," she said weakly, knowing in fact that his theory made a good deal of sense.

Unable to match his argument at the moment, she rose from the bed in an attempt to move away. Bose, however, would have no part of her bid to put distance between them; reaching out, he snatched Summer by the arm and pulled her down onto the mattress beside him. Onyx-black eyes met with wide golden orbs.

"I am completely correct in my assessment and well you know it," his bass-toned voice was a growl. "You are conditioned to believe it is expected of you. But animals, like Antony, cannot judge you by your speech and you are completely relaxed when you speak to them. Consequently, you do not stutter."

She sighed with reluctance, watching his lips as he spoke. "B-But I always stammer," she said feebly. "Habit or no, I cannot help it."

"Aye, you can and you will," he said firmly, with quiet authority. "I do not want to hear you stumble over my name any longer. Look me in the eye, Summer. Look at me and repeat my words: Bose loves me, therefore, I will not stammer any longer in his presence."

Her brow relaxed with the astonishment. A lovely smile creased her face, a gesture of joy and fulfillment. Her soft hands moved to his face, touching his scarred, stubbled flesh, hardly believing of the words he had uttered with such nonchalance.

"B-Bose...."

"Repeat the words, Summer."

"B-But you said you loved me and...."

It was difficult not to become swept up in the light of adoration shining from her eyes, but Bose did his best to ignore her for the moment. He was attempted to accomplish something this night and would not be distracted. There would be time enough later to succumb to their emotions later. He shushed her softly. "Say the words, Summer. Say them to me and I will not hear you falter."

"B-But I do not want...."

He shook her gently, cleaving her plea. "Say them."

Ever obedient, Summer forced away her joy for the moment; Bose was demanding she speak flawlessly and she struggled to complete his bidding.

"B-Bose loves me..."

"Again without the stammer. Bose loves me, therefore...."

She nodded faintly, swallowing as she labored to concentrate on his order. "Bose loves me, therefore, I w-will no...."

"Look into my eyes, Summer, not at my mouth when you speak. Look into my eyes and repeat the words flawlessly."

Her eyes came up to his piercing black orbs, feeling the magnetism and power draw her deep. Her body relaxed, her mind calmed as the magic of his gaze enveloped her. Summer's smile returned and she curled against his mighty torso, pressing close. Gazing deeply into eyes the color of a moonless night, her gentle hand continued to toy with his cheek.

"Is that what you truly wish to hear?" she asked softly. "W-Would not you rather hear of my love for you as well?"

His gaze held even a moment before, slowly, breaking into a tender smile. "I shall spend the rest of my life hearing of your adoration. For now, I wish to hear my words repeated by your utterly delicious lips. Say them, love. Say them and mean it."

Her smile broadened, her lids seductively heavy as her gaze raked his rugged face. "Bose loves me, therefore, I will not stammer any longer in his presence." When he did not respond immediately to her perfect declaration, she cocked a well-shaped brow. "Was that not satisfactory?"

Bose hadn't reacted immediately to her flawless statement because, truthfully, the seductive expression on the woman's face had nearly drained him of his concentration and self-control. But he had heard her nonetheless, and his gentle smile grew in intensity as he pulled her more closely against him.

"Completely, love, completely," he said with sincere emotion. "It was not so difficult, after all."

She continued to stroke his cheek, her smile fading. "It is not diffi-cult when I speak to you. B-But I doubt the same will hold true when I speak to others."

He squeezed her tightly, an encouraging demonstration of his sup-port. "All in time, love. With practice, you will forget this nasty habit that has plagued you since childhood."

A delicate finger traced one of the three barbaric scars bisecting his right cheekbone. "Do you believe in Fate, Bose?"

"I believe in God and the Devil. Why do you ask?"

She maintained a delicate touch upon his scars, pausing a moment before answering. "Because I believe Fate has brought you to me. Of all the knights in England, the one man w-who would understand my affliction has come into my heart and I cannot sincerely describe my joy."

He gently touched her chin. "Not affliction, love, habit. An affliction is a disease or physical defect, such as leprosy or a missing limb. You, my fair lady, possess no such ailments. You are the most perfect creature God has ever created."

A faint blush mottled her ears, spreading to her cheeks. "You are my f-future husband and forbidden to think otherwise."

He smiled and she touched his lips as the uneven display split his face into two halves. "Every man who sees you believes as I do," he shifted her in his arms, reclining on his back and pulling her onto his mighty chest. "As for God and Fate, my lady, I believe that both have kept you sequestered for all of these years, waiting for the event of my arrival. Knowing that I was the only man worthy of your beauty, your spirit, and the only man intelligent enough to break you of your habitual stammer."

She tore her gaze from his mouth, lifting a delicate eyebrow at his arrogant statement. "My, my, how confident we are in God's Master Plan. T-Tell me, if you would, how we are to explain our introduction to our children? Do we tell them that God and Fate brought us together by magic?"

He stared at her a moment, his smile vanishing with unnatural speed. Summer could see the faltering of expression, the flash of pain, or mayhap panic, in his eyes and it puzzled her. Both hands to his cheeks, she endeavored to force him to meet her eye.

"W-What's the matter? What did I say?"

He shook his head, unwilling to elaborate on the apprehension that filled his veins the moment she mentioned their prospective children. God's Beard, their entire introduction and courtship had been such a whirlwind of emotion and activity that he had never truly been given the chance to linger on the potential of offspring. And given a moment to reflect, he realized the very thought scared him witless.

"Nothing, love," he replied. "Nothing at all."

Struggling to distract both her and himself, he kissed her firmly on the lips. But the effort wasn't hard fought; the moment she responded to his seeking mouth, he forgot about everything but his growing feelings for her.

Genisa's scarlet and gold gown was coming off. Summer felt the stays as they loosened, the silken material as it slid over her shoulders and down her torso. Bose's warm, calloused palms were against her breasts, bare flesh to bare flesh, and she again groaned softly with the wonder of it. When his lips left hers and moved tenderly to a swollen nipple, Summer did not protest the action.

An afternoon of private touches and awesome discovery had done well enough to prepare her for the event of his mouth upon her breast. He had fondled her a great deal beneath Grandfather's oak, stroking her through the confining material of her gown and listening to her soft grunts of pleasure. But he hadn't merely touched her breasts; his seeking, curious hands had moved about her entire body, snaking up her skirt and caressing the silken flesh of her thighs. The true jewel of his search, however, had remained untouched during the course of their time together.

A looming discovery that caused his hands to shake with anticipation as his scarred, course fingers danced underneath her skirts. Suckling her breasts, his hands skimmed her shapely legs, moving beyond her knees and lingering in the moist warmth between her thighs. Pushing her legs apart gently, he continued to blaze a trail up her silken thigh until the delicate brush of kinked hair tickled the tips of his fingers.

Beneath him, Summer lurched with surprise and Bose's head came up from her beautiful breasts, his eyes glazed with desire. She met his gaze, her half-lidded expression fearful and curious at the same time. He smiled faintly.

"Do not be afraid, love. I'll be gentle."

She blinked as if pondering his statement. "I-I… I-I am not. But you did n-not touch me… earlier, b-beneath the tree, y-you did not…."

He shushed her softly, stroking her cheek with infinite tenderness. "There is no need to be nervous, love. Relax and take a deep breath. That's my good girl."

A faint flush mottled Summer's cheeks as she did as she was told, calming the severe stammer that always accompanied an attack of nerves. After a moment, her half-lidded gaze of desire transformed into a more lucid, serious expression.

"There is so much I do not know," she said softly, her fingers toying with his hair. "The ways of men and women… I know the physical aspects of coupling, but that is where my knowledge ends. You've been married before and…."

"And I fully intend to teach you everything I have learned if you will allow me," he interrupted her quietly. After a moment, he removed her fidgeting hand from his hair and kissed the palm gently. "I will not continue if you do not want me to. I apologize if you believe my actions bold, for certainly, my sole intention was to demonstrate my feelings for you and nothing more. I never meant to frighten you."

She watched him as he nibbled on her hand. "I am not frightened," she said softly, a half-truth. "B-But this is all happening so fast that I can scarcely comprehend all of it."

He smiled, reading her uncertainty and deciding not to force himself on her this night. If all went according to plan, they would be wed shortly and he could spend the rest of his life teaching her the finer arts of lovemaking. Until then, however, he was perfectly content to wait. At least, he would make an attempt to maintain a proper patience. But, God's Beard, the wait would be a difficult one.

Pulling her skirts down, he shifted his massive frame so that he was looming over her, well removed from the temptation of her forbidden zone. Summer met his gaze, seeing the beads of sweat upon his brow and not unaware they were the results of a passionate fire raging wildly out of control.

"Forgive me for spoiling your passion," she said softly. "I certainly did not mean to."

He shook his head, kissing her delicious lips. "You did not," he whispered against her mouth. "'Tis proper that we should wait for the marriage bed, of course. If your brothers demand bloodied sheets that I am unable to supply, I suspect you will be a widow before your next birthday."

She giggled softly, returning his gentle kisses. "You may continue to touch my breasts if that will help control your lust."

He cocked an eyebrow, passing a lingering glance at her beautifully full breasts pressed against his chest. "I… I do not believe that to be a wise action, but I thank you for the invitation."

"B-But why?" she was genuinely puzzled by his rejection. "I thought you wanted to touch them. This afternoon, your hands scarcely touched anything else."

He sighed, scratching his chin as he pondered the proper words to explain himself. "Believe me when I tell you that touching your breasts will not bank my passions, love. Touching them will only stoke the fires."

Her brow furrowed. "I do not understand."

He sighed again, clearing his throat for good measure as he groped for the correct wording. "You see… Summer, love, your breasts arouse me terribly. Here," he took her hand, putting it to his groin. Through his breeches, Summer could feel his rock-hard arousal and her eyes widened. Meeting her astonished gaze, he nodded faintly. "Do you feel my want for you? A want that will only be sated when I join my body to yours. If I continue touching your breasts, the want will build and build until I explode. But if I refrain from touching you and we change the subject, the want will naturally fade."

"And you will n-not explode?"

He grinned. "A figure of speech, love. But I most certainly will wish I could explode if my loins grow any harder."

Her warm hand lingered on his pulsing bulge a moment longer before removing it, seemingly lost in thought. After a moment, she shook her head with wonder. "T-This is all so new to me. I have seen dogs mate, of course… and once, I happed upon a soldier and a serving wench in the alcove near the kitchens. There was a good deal of grunting and squealing and…" she shook her head again. "When we mate, you will spill your seed into my womb, will you not?"

He nodded, amazed that she was thinking so clearly and clinically about a most personal subject. Even this afternoon, when he had touched her breasts and explored her body in a limited fashion, she had showed surprisingly little resistance or fear. Certainly, the subject of physical interaction between a man and a woman was hardly a worthy focus of conversation for an innocent young maiden, but she was obviously unembarrassed by such discussion and he endeavored to answer her inquisitive questions honestly.

"I will," he replied. "That is how children are conceived."

"I know," she responded softly. "Kermit told me."

"Who is Kermit?"

He swore he saw a flash of pain in the darkly gold eyes. "He was my father's steward until his d-death last year. He taught me everything about life and schooled me in various subjects," suddenly, a mischievous sparkle appeared in her eye, quickly replacing the tinge of sorrow. "I swore that I w-would name my first born son after my dearest friend and tutor. I rather like the name Kermit de Moray."

He cocked a disagreeable eyebrow. "And I do not. Hardly an appropriate name for my…."

Abruptly, he found himself unable to complete the sentence. *Hardly an appropriate name for my son.* Once again, feelings of anxiety descended upon him as he allowed himself to imagine Summer conceiving a child, enduring a horrific pregnancy implanted with a babe far too large for her small frame to carry. An infant the size and power of his illustrious father, bringing yet another de Moray wife to ruin and death.

Bose struggled to erase the terrifying visions. Gazing into Summer's inquisitive golden eyes, he decided that her life was worth far more than that of a potential heir. Above all else, Summer would live a long and prosperous existence by his side and although they would be without a son to carry on the de Moray name, he would still retain the one individual without whose love he could not endure. Above all else, he could not lose his wife.

"You are lost to me, darling," Summer's voice was soothing, sweet. "You have c-chosen another name for our son?"

"Nay, love," he shook his head, forcing aside disturbing visions of pregnancy and birth. "No... no other name."

She smiled, willing to believe that even if he had selected another name, he would bow to her wishes nonetheless. "Of course, you and Lora had c-chosen a name for your child. What was it?"

He suddenly pushed himself from the bed, running his fingers through his black hair in an agitated gesture. Smile fading, Summer sat up from the mattress and covered her breasts with her unfastened bodice. Realizing she had upset him with her reference to his dead wife, she hastened to ease his anger.

"I am sorry," she said quietly. "I did not mean to make light of Lora's death. P-please forgive me."

He immediately held out a quieting, apologetic hand, turning to face her. The dim light cast from the crackling hearth gave her a glowing, ethereal appearance and his heart leapt wildly at the sight of her, more pain and anguish and bewilderment filling his mind than he had ever conceived possible.

"You did nothing of the kind, love," his voice was tight with emotion. Again, he ran his fingers through his hair. "I... I suppose the excitement of our relationship has finally caught up to me, too."

If she suspected his lie, she did not express her reservation. Instead, a timid smile creased her lips and she replaced her bodice, rising from the bed so that Bose could re-secure the stays. Obediently, silently, he helped her dress and took her in his arms when she was properly clad. Smelling her fragrance, feeling her warmth, helped clear his head tremendously.

"I suppose I should leave you to retire," he said hoarsely, his face buried in her hair. "You have had a most trying day."

Head against his shoulder, Summer inhaled deeply the fragrance of his distinct musk, finding it exceedingly masculine and comforting.

"As you have also," removing her face from his flesh, her fingers gingerly traced the stitches in his scalp. "Let there be no more w-wounds come the morrow's joust. I have had my fill."

He smiled, his black eyes twinkling. "Aye, my lady. I shall endeavor to do my best."

"See that you do." When his great head dipped low, capturing her lips tenderly within his own, she melted against his searing touch and a soft moan escaped her mouth. "Good Lord, Bose, I can h-hardly stand the thought of not seeing you 'til morn. And what will happen when the tourney is over? When will I see...?"

A heavy rap shook the chamber door, vibrating the wall with the force of the blow. Summer gasped with surprise while Bose, consummately undisturbed, made sure his dagger was within easy reach before moving to the bolted panel.

"Who comes?" he demanded.

There was a slight pause before a strained, decidedly familiar voice wafted from the other side. "Open the door, de Moray. Immediately."

Bose passed a glance to Summer, not surprised to note her uncertainty and, he thought, chagrin. "It's Stephan!" she hissed.

Prepared for a harsh tongue-lashing, Bose unbolted the door and opened it. Not only was Stephan at the door, but Ian and Lance were hovering in the corridor as well and Bose stepped aside, ushering them into the chamber.

Stephan's expression was grim as he eyed the massively dark knight. He paused a moment before speaking. "I am sure you will understand my position when I say that I am uncomfortable with this situation. Betrothed or not, my sister is not yet your wife and I will not have her reputation sullied by the actions of an aggressive suitor," before Bose could reply, Stephan looked to his flush-faced sister. "Well? What do you have to say for yourself? You know better than to allow a man into your bedchamber, Summer."

Swallowing hard, Summer wrung her hands in unconscious apprehension. "I-I... t-that is, we've done n-n-nothing but speak, S-Stephan. S-S-Sir Bose has been a perfect g-gentleman."

Bose sighed sadly, noting the strong return of her stammer where for the past several minutes the habit had been virtually forgotten.

"I was just leaving, Stephan," Bose said quietly, eyeing Lance and Ian. Ian seemed remarkably composed whereas a drunken Lance was torn between concentrating on his scowl and making certain he remained upright long enough to ensure his sister's reputation. "I simply escorted my lady to her chamber and was preparing to bid her a good sleep."

Truthfully, Stephan did not seem overly furious that his sister had been found in a compromising position with her future husband. If anything, he seemed to be enforcing the strict code of chivalry and morality simply because, true to his words, his sister was technically still an unwed maiden. Since the moment Summer and Bose were seen entering the keep in one another arm's, the rumors had been flying fast and furious and Stephan, newly returned from his rendezvous with his wife, had collected his brothers and moved to correct the potentially damaging situation.

"So you have managed to solicit a betrothal contract out of my father," Stephan's voice was quiet. Approving, even. "Ian told me of his reluctance in granting your request. Rest assured that I shall speak with him come the morn, when his alcohol has evaporated and his mind is sane once more."

Bose bowed his head slightly. "Your assistance would be tremendously appreciated, Stephan."

Stephan simply nodded, returning his focus to his sister. He softened. "Congratulations, sweetheart. You'll make a fine wife."

She smiled timidly. "T-Thank you for your support, S-Stephan," she said softly. "However, there seems to be a problem already; B-Bose does not like the name Kermit."

The statement brought a laugh from Ian and a belated chuckle from Lance, once he realized through his drunken haze what had been said. Stephan smiled broadly, casting Bose a long gaze.

"Poor man. I have a feeling he will agree to your demands regardless of his personal opinion," when Bose shrugged weakly, a glimmer of mirth in his eyes, Stephan's own smile faded as the reality of the situation once again came to bear; certainly, he had no intention of leaving the couple as he had found them. For appearance sake, it was best that Bose retreat for the evening. "As you can see, my lord, my sister has safely reached her bedchamber and is eager to retire. I thank you for your escort, but your presence is no longer required."

Realizing that he was being dismissed, Bose again nodded faintly and looked to Summer, her golden gaze warm and tender. Reluctant to leave her but knowing it was best, he moved quietly for the door. In the archway, however, he paused, once again meeting Stephan's brilliant green orbs.

The silent words of approval and understanding were unmistakable. Stephan had as much as voiced his approval and Ian had all but forced Edward to accept Bose's marriage request. Slowly but surely, the du Bonne brothers were accepting him for their sister. Four years of rumors and vicious lies notwithstanding, Bose was pleased to realize that the truth had finally triumphed.

"Good eve to you, Stephan," he said steadily. "Lance, I would suggest you retire immediately lest you provide Tate with a supreme opportunity for victory come the morrow. And Ian...," when the largest du Bonne brother met his gaze, something of a faint smile playing upon his lips, Bose smiled in return. "I will see you on the morrow as well. The second round, I believe."

"I shall be ready, my lord," Ian replied as if he held no fear of the man and his talents.

Bose held his gaze a moment, a knowing smirk on his lips, when Summer suddenly moved into his line of sight. Putting her arm about Ian's waist, she looked to Bose with an imploring expression.

"Mayhap you should consider allowing Ian to emerge triumphant on the morrow, Bose," she said seriously, nary a stammer to her speech. "After all, had it not been for my brother, you and I would not be betrothed."

A perfectly executed sentence. As the trio of brothers looked to their baby sister in astonishment, Bose merely smiled. "Indeed, my lady, I completely agree with the latter portion of your statement. As for the first," he tore his gaze away from her long enough to look at Ian. "I shall have to think of another way to thank your brother for his support, considering I promised you I would win the joust."

Summer returned his smile. "As you say, my lord."

Before Bose could reply, Lance staggered before his sister, weaving dangerously. "Summer!" he gasped. "You… you did not stutter at all!"

She looked to him as if his notation hardly warranted consideration. "Indeed, Lance. What did you think Bose and I were d-doing in my chamber, hidden away from the world? He was helping me with my speech. I'll become better, with practice."

Stephan, his mouth open with incredulity, moved to stand beside his drunk, equally amazed brother. "He was helping you?" he repeated, baffled and delighted and utterly awed. "I do not understand. By what magic did he do this?"

Lingering by the door, Bose endeavored to enter the conversation. "No magic, Stephan. With a good deal of patience and encouragement, anything can happen." Winking to Summer when she met his glittering gaze, he moved to quit the chamber. "Good sleep to you, love. I'll see you on the morrow."

He was gone, leaving three puzzled but delighted men and one besotted lady and all of them believing that the Gorgon, indeed, could conjure his own private magic.

❧

"YOU HAVE INTERRUPTED my sleep this night to rehash old rumors and hearsay that I am already well aware of?" he questioned the red-headed knight with a good deal of annoyance, his head aching and his vision swimming. "I allowed you into my chamber based on your declaration of an emergency regarding my daughter. If you consider a betrothal to Bose de Moray an emergency, then vacate my chamber at once and stop wasting my time."

Breck and Margot stood respectfully in Edward's lavish bower. Breck struggled not to rant or shout in the face of the drunken baron, but if he was to accomplish his goal this night, then it was essential that he remain calm. God's Blood, his scheme was coming together with such grace and blessing that he could scarcely believe he had reached his final obstacle, ultimately able to confront Edward du Bonne and plead for his daughter's hand. And with the support of Lady de Ville, he had little doubt that morn would see him a pledged man. But the necessity to remain calm was imperative if he wanted to achieve his intent.

"You do not seem to realize the seriousness of the situation, my lord," he said steadily. "Bose de Moray is a murderer. Somehow, he has managed to convince your daughter and your sons of his innocence, but I can prove without a doubt that he did indeed kill his wife. Do you desire your daughter to become another victim of his murderous character?"

Edward snorted, spraying spittle from his thick lips. "She shall not become a victim. Stephan and Ian are quite convinced of de Moray's innocence and I have complete faith in my sons' judgment. Now, if you will excuse me...."

"Bose is a silver-tongued devil, my lord, quite capable of persuading the most intelligent of men." Margot entered the conversation and when Edward looked at her, she bowed her head respectfully. "I am the Lady Margot de Ville. My daughter was married to Bose de Moray, and four years ago almost to the day he took her life in a violent burst of blood and agony. If you do not want your daughter to meet with the same brutal end, then I suggest you listen to Sir Breck."

For the first time since the arrival of his unwelcome visitors, Edward's disinterest in the dialogue faltered. Scratching the flea bites on his neck, he focused on the frail-appearing lady with a mounting sense of morbid curiosity.

"I was told she died in childbirth," his tone was considerably less strained.

Margot smiled thinly. "A convenient title for a mortal mistake. I saw my daughter's body, my lord, and you will believe me when I say mere childbirth could not have wrought the scope of damage I witnessed. She was torn asunder, destroyed by a man who has little regard for the value of life. Surely you do not wish for your daughter to succumb to the same torment."

Edward maintained as steady a focus as he was able through his alcohol-induced state, absorbing the woman's words with increasing distress. Always particularly pliable to the suggestions and motives of others, it was natural to find himself willing to listen to her sincere reasoning. In fact, he had always found it most comforting to have others form his opinions and decisions for him. This night was no exception.

The dirty nails scratching his neck moved to his chin. "Of course I do not want my daughter to meet with her death. But she will be another man's wife to do with as he pleases and if the death of his wife is his preference, then so be it."

Breck's brow furrowed slightly; even he found himself curious at the callous reference to something as fragile as a woman's life. For a man who was supposed to have sired a particularly beautiful, if not flawed, woman, the baron certainly lacked the usual fatherly compassion. For the first time during the conversation, Breck found himself wondering if the argument presented would prove to be persuasive enough to force the man to recant his verbal betrothal with de Moray.

Margot, however, was undeterred by Edward's attitude. Being a wise, instinctive woman, she could sense a great deal of indifference from the baron with regard to his daughter, a woman with a disturbing flaw and little marital value. But she could also sense a feeble-willed, foolish man who seemed to be easily swayed. And it was that portion of the man, the frail-minded, spineless idiot that she intended to target.

There was a small chair opposite the baron's position. Moving forward, Margot deposited herself neatly upon the embroidered silk. Hands folded primly, she pondered her next move.

"Since you obviously care not for your daughter's well-being at the hands of a murderous fiend, then allow me to present a different aspect to the situation," taking a deep, delicate breath, she maintained steady, convincing eye-contact. "Suppose you allow your daughter to marry Sir Bose and she inevitably meets her end as I say she will. Have you considered how your friends and allies will look upon you, having knowingly allowed your daughter to enter into a less than desirable situation? They will not think kindly of your carelessness, my lord."

Edward, not surprisingly, was listening to her. "They... they will believe me negligent? Foolish, even?"

Seeing the man's interest peaked, Margot realized she had hit upon a strong idea and she endeavored to continue before the baron had a chance to question her reasoning. "Indeed, my lord. They will whisper behind your back, speaking harshly of the senseless father who had been too blind and too witless to see beyond de Moray's facade when all who have ever been acquainted with the man know of his sinister reputation. Without a doubt, you'll be made the laughing stock of Dorset."

Margot was pleased to note the deep furrowing of Edward's bushy brow, the faint flush mottling his ears. Shifting in his chair with mounting discomfort, he opened his robe somewhat because he was beginning to sweat.

"I...I had never considered such an aspect," he said finally, his tone weak and sincere. "My only thoughts, of course, are to marry my daughter to a wealthy and powerful knight. Certainly, I never thought I'd be rid of the girl considering her flawed speech. Mayhap... mayhap the excitement of her first true suitor has shadowed my judgment."

Margot nodded sympathetically, her expression as cold as ice. "Of course, my lord. Your reaction was completely understandable. And your sons, too."

"My sons?"

She nodded firmly. "Certainly they believe as you do. Never imagining that their defective sister would find a husband, they agreed upon the first man who showed a measure of interest. And they eagerly believed his lies because of their desire to see their sister wed."

After a lengthy, contemplative pause, Edward slowly shook his head. "I cannot see that their desire to see Summer wed would override their judgment. Especially Stephan's. The man is exceedingly intelligent and introspective."

Margot's gaze was even as she digested his words, coming to suspect that the baron relied heavily upon his eldest son's discretion. From the clues delivered throughout the conversation and from the obvious weak-minded stance of the nobleman slouched before her, it was logical to conclude that the baron did not make his own decisions. Someone made them for him. At this moment, that someone would be Margot.

"I am sure he is, my lord, but even a wise man can be fooled by a clever opportunist," she replied softly. "Bose is such a man. I assume that your daughter will come with a substantial dowry?"

Edward stared at her blankly a moment, as if he had never considered the very idea. After a pause, he nodded unsteadily. "I... I will provide her with a good dowry, of course."

"And Bose is well aware of the fact. By selecting the imperfect daughter of a wealthy baron, he is assured of your eager response to his marital petition, thereby guaranteeing him a substantial inheritance. After your daughter falls victim to an unfortunate 'accident', he will simply move on to the next hapless woman and collect her dowry, too."

Edward's features relaxed with the naked truth of understanding, seeing the lady's logic quite clearly. "So he seeks to obtain my wealth!"

"Indeed. And the entire province will look to you as a fool for providing it so freely."

Beads of sweat peppered Edward's brow, the true focus of Bose de

Moray's scheme coming to bear. Of course! Great Gods, why hadn't he seen it earlier? For certain, there was no other reason why a man of Bose de Moray's standing and power would pursue a flawed woman other than the fact she was directly related to a good deal of wealth. Wealth de Moray desired.

Wealth he would have the moment he married Summer. Edward found himself thinking of his sons, wondering why they had been so naive to the man's terrible scheme. They professed to love Summer; if so, why had they been so entirely eager to marry her to a man whose true desire was to claim her sizable dowry? Even if de Moray had been able to convince him of his proper intentions, still, Edward wondered seriously why Stephan hadn't seen through the facade.

Lost in his train of thought, Edward was nonetheless aware of Margot's patient presence and Breck's fidgeting silence. Drawn from his deliberation, he wiped at his moist brow and focused intently on the lady's pale blue eyes.

"I appreciate your candor and wisdom, my lady, in helping me to see the truth of the matter," clearing his throat, he once again shifted listlessly in his chair. "My greatest fear now is how to properly break the betrothal contract between my daughter and de Moray without incurring the involvement of the church."

Breck, his agitated movements quelled with the encouraging response, fought the urge to sink to his knees and thank God for his mercy. Unable to keep the smile from his face, his glee and triumph was instantly quelled by a withering expression from Margot.

Restraint, young Kerry. Margot's silent demand went properly heeded and when she was positive Breck was not going to break out in a dance of victory, she returned her attention to Edward with her customary composure.

"Allow me to see the contract, my lord. Mayhap there is a provision providing for the annulment of the contract should either party find fault or discomfort with the proposal."

Edward shook his head. "There is no written contract. My permission was verbal, in the presence of a witness."

Margot struggled not to smile herself with the baron's weary, wit-less response. "Then the contract is not binding in the least. Unless your sanction has been put to paper, the church cannot involve itself because a verbal contract is not considered legally valid," passing a long glance at Breck, she continued with careful consideration. "If I may suggest, my lord, in order to avoid a good deal of trouble and crisis on the part of de Moray, I would like to propose that you immediately betroth your daughter to another knight to permanently remove her from de Moray's grasp. Surely the man cannot compare his verbal consent to a legally binding and written document."

Edward's gaze was distant, pensive, as he seriously considered Mar-got's suggestion. As Breck loomed into view, far more sedate than he had been only moments before, Edward's attention shifted to the pimple-faced knight and, suddenly, an expression of understanding creased his aging face.

"You, Kerry?" It was a question as well as a declaration. "You've shown a good deal of interest in my daughter. Would you be willing to marry her were I to provide her with a tremendously attractive dowry?"

A faint smirk played upon Breck's lips; he simply could not help himself. For all of the pain and humiliation, planning and strategies were finally coming to a positive conclusion and he could hardly believe his fortune. There was more than one way to defeat a Gorgon.

"'Twould be my pleasure to accept your daughter's hand, my lord," Breck hoped his quaking voice did not bely his excitement and disbelief. "In fact, the sooner we are wed, the better for all concern. The sooner de Moray will lose interest."

"Indeed," Edward rose unsteadily from his chair, weaving danger-ously as he stumbled to the chamber door. Opening the panel, he ordered one of his soldiers to summon a lesser steward. Summer, of course, was his chief steward, taking care of the affairs of his estate and handling scribing duties since Kermit's death. Edward was positive, however, this was one scribing duty she would most definitely reject.

When the soldier fled down the hall, Edward closed the door and staggered heavily toward a crystal carafe filled with wine. Pouring himself a healthy draught, he swallowed half the goblet before returning his attention to the two successful conspirators.

"I shall have the contracts drawn up tonight and witnessed," he said, his voice hoarse with fatigue and emotion. Taking another swallow, he smacked his lips loudly and fixed Margot in the eye. "I'll not allow Bose de Moray to murder my daughter and make me the laughing stock. You were most gracious to supply your reasoning this night. And I thank you as well, Sir Breck, for being most clear-headed and persistent in your opinion."

Neither Margot nor Breck replied to Edward's heart-felt thanks, repressing the urge to look to each other in triumph and glee. It was as good as they had hoped for and better. By tomorrow, Breck would be legally bound to Lady Summer and Bose, disheartened and spurned, would be forced to return to Ravendark empty-handed and defeated. Returning to Lora's memory where he belonged.

Edward lost himself in his wine. Without asking or without invitation, Margot confiscated a second pewter chalice to match the baron's and joined him in his liquor as Breck stood silently by, contemplating his unbelievably good fortune.

Once and for all, the Gorgon would be vanquished.

CHAPTER THIRTEEN

B OSE WAS NOT afforded the opportunity of escorting Summer to the lists the next morning. Rain, mists, damp winds and all, she and Genisa were planted in the assigned du Bonne box just after sunrise, eagerly awaiting the commencement of the joust. The three du Bonne brothers had escorted the anxious ladies to the field, convinced the women would proceed without them or not.

Therefore, dressing hurriedly and with varied degrees of alcohol-induced aching heads, Stephan, Ian and an ill-looking Lance were the first contenders to arrive at the lists. Even the heralds, immaculately dressed in du Bonne red and white, were tardy as compared with their liege's sons.

In spite of the excitement surrounding the last phase of the jousting competition, the dawning day had emerged dank and stormy. A nasty squall had blown in over the course of the night, wreaking havoc on the tents converged near the lists and raining muck and misery on the unfortunate occupants. Several knights, with their tents collapsed by the harsh winds, had found refuge in the grand hall of Chaldon.

Summer did not care about the weather. She did not care that the lodges had been somewhat damaged by the bitter winds or that even as she sat upon her sturdy chair clad in amber silk and brown rabbit, the ensuing winds hurling off the stark Dorset coast were enough to set her teeth to chattering. All that mattered on this glorious day was that Bose would win the joust, and she, as his betrothed, would be permitted to publicly reward his victory.

A victory that would come at the price of her three brothers; Summer tried not to linger on that single most disturbing fact. Even as Stephan and Ian and Lance set to a round of early practice against

several sturdy dummies secured to the joust barrier, Summer applaud-
ed loudly for them as if she were truly supportive of their endeavor.
Stephan bowed gratefully to her praise, Ian staunchly ignored her, while
Lance tried to yell at her but found the action far too painful with his
aching head. Grumbling and cursing, he simply shook his fist at her.

Bose had made his presence known shortly after Summer's arrival
to the field. Astride his great charcoal charger, he had reined his
frothing beast alongside the raised platform and proceeded to deliver
the tenderest of kisses to Summer's gloved hand. As Genisa watched in
smirking silence, Bose removed the gloves and kissed every finger on
Summer's warm, delicate hands, igniting a fire in her cheeks that had
yet to abate.

A fire of pride and delight she took great pleasure in as the lists
filled with the competitors that would duel to the finish for honor and
glory. The lodges rapidly filled with spectators, ill with the previous
evening's overindulgence yet utterly excited for the conclusion of the
joust. As the wind howled and the mist turned into a driving rain, the
crowd in the lodges grew vocal with their demands to commence the
games.

Summer and Genisa were deeply involved in every aspect of the
practice bouts and Summer listened intently to her sister-in-law's
knowledge of the sport. Regardless of her original opinion of the
tournament, the fact that she was now betrothed to Bose de Moray
brought about an entirely different aspect to her convictions. Certainly,
the man was to be her husband and it was only right that she know and
appreciate his chosen profession.

The fact that time and experience had eased her earliest view on the
games was a contributing factor, too. Aye, the melee was a horrid
display of brutality and blood, but it was also a grand spectacle of skill
and strength. And the joust, as shocking and vicious as it could be, was
also a tremendous exhibition of power and talent. True, she was still
uneasy with the experience of her first tournament. But she was
learning to love it, too.

Especially when Bose was on the field as he was at this moment. Summer watched him like a hawk, noticing that he hardly used his reins to guide the charger, using pressure from his thighs instead to direct his temperamental beast. He had already completed two excellent runs at the dummies fastened to the joust barrier, the second pass seeing the stuffed dummy completely torn from its mountings. The crowd went wild, Genisa cheered loudly, and Bose had approached the lodges, lifting his visor for a congratulatory kiss. Summer had bestowed one gladly.

Edward was nowhere to be found as Summer openly lavished affection upon her chosen knight. Bose proceeded to lift Summer from the platform, placing her on his massive saddle and parading from the field as the crowd cheered and hollered their approval. Stephan, not to be left out, tore another practice dummy to shreds and demanded a kiss from his own wife as Ian, keeping his distance from his competition, eyed his sister and the dark knight as they cuddled and conversed quietly at the edge of the field.

Only Lance was left to weakly protest Summer's amorous treatment, basing his argument on the previous night's reasoning that she was not yet a married woman. But Bose threatened him with the prospect of pain should they eventually face one another in the joust and Lance immediately shut his mouth.

Finally left alone by the three over-protective brothers, Bose was reluctant when it came time to return Summer to the lodges. As the gray clouds lightened with the rising sun, the heralds sounded the first trumpet of competition to indicate the games would commence shortly. Dutifully, with obvious affection, Bose returned his betrothed to the lodges and cast her a saucy wink as he returned to his men.

"Oh, Summer," Genisa sighed dreamily as Bose thundered back across the field. "I am so happy for you, darling, truly. Bose will make a wonderful husband."

Rosy-cheeked and deliriously happy, Summer nodded faintly as she watched her betrothed leave the lists. "I can hardly believe the truth of the matter. It's as if… as if I am living a dream."

Genisa observed her sister-in-law closely, noting the absence of her usual severe stammering. Stephan had made mention of the fact earlier that morn, amazed with the concept that Bose had seemingly eased his sister's stuttering speech. True to her husband's word, Genisa had been aware of Summer's improved articulation from the very moment of their morning salutation and from that point in time, Genisa realized that the youngest du Bonne sibling had matured before their very eyes.

"I know how you feel," she responded belated to Summer's dreamy declaration. "For months after I married Stephan, I would stay awake at night simply to watch him sleep. As if I was afraid I would awaken in the morning and realized his presence to have been a dream."

Summer smiled, turning to her lovely sister-in-law and knowing Stephan's feelings had been much the same. "You love being married."

Genisa laughed softly. "I love *him*, Summer. As you love Bose."

Summer met the woman's bright blue gaze a moment, feeling the wonder and magic of new sensations grip her. Like nothing she had ever known before. "In three days I have lived a lifetime," she murmured softly. "My one regret is that Bose will take me to live at Ravendark, away from my family. 'Twill be difficult to reside in his home and not my b-beloved Chaldon, unable to share my future happiness with those I love."

Genisa's smile faded and she touched Summer on the arm, an affectionate gesture. "I felt much the same, Summer. You forget that I have seven younger sisters who cried hysterically when Stephan took me away. I was uncertain about life at Chaldon, too, until I met a shy young lady who soon became my very best friend. You must trust that you will find a wonderful new way of life at Ravendark, darling. Have faith in the joy of your destiny."

Summer absorbed the wisdom of the words coming from a usually dense and silly young woman. In the past three days, she had come to know much about Genisa du Bonne that she had never suspected to exist. A depth to the woman seldom, if ever, seen. After a moment, her broad smile returned.

"You are sounding more like my brother every day," she said, placing her gloved hand over the warm appendage clutching her arm. "I shall m-miss this wise woman I have come to see over the past few days. A woman I should like to know better, I think."

Genisa chortled again, wondering when next she would see her beloved sister-in-law after Bose de Moray whisked the lady away to the distant keep of Ravendark.

"There will be time enough," she replied, noting the heralds had cleared the lists and were preparing to announce the first bout. "I suspect your wedding to Sir Bose will not be for a few weeks yet. By that time, you may be so utterly weary of my newly-discovered wisdom that you'll be ready to leave Chaldon and never look back."

"I doubt it," Summer, too, noted the activity of the heralds with mounting anticipation. "However, when next I return home, I should expect to see an heir in your arms. I have waited two years for you to produce a child and I refuse to wait any longer."

Genisa shrugged faintly, her smile fading. "When God decides to bless us with a child, I shall be entirely joyful," after a pause, she sighed pensively and her smile faded completely. "I do not think Stephan has recovered from my miscarriage last year. He was convinced I carried a son."

Summer's smile faded as well, remembering the pain of Genisa's failed pregnancy like a stab to her heart. She remembered her brother crying for hours by the darkened hearth in the grand solar, cursing God for the death of his child in one breath and thanking him for the spared life of his wife in the next. Summer recollected his pain, recalling Bose's anguish along a similar subject as well. Stephan had merely lost his child; Bose had lost his entire family.

Genisa caught a glimpse of Summer's dour expression. "Do not worry for us, darling. I did not mean to imply that Stephan still aches with regret for what could have been. He's quite happy and there will be more…."

Summer shook her head, fighting off the gloom that intimidated her soul. "I k-know," she whispered. "It's just… Bose lost his wife and son in childbirth. I c-c-cannot imagine what would have become of S-Stephan had he lost you, as well."

Genisa noticed the return of Summer's stammer as her emotions threatened to overwhelm her. When she was calm and content, the stammer was noticeably less. But when her sentiment or feelings flared, the stutter returned like an evil addiction. Digesting that particular bit of observation, Genisa endeavored to push the gloom of death out of the conversation.

"Fortunately, he did not," she said with forced courage she did not feel. Speaking on the subject of failed pregnancies, especially her own, greatly depressed her. "As for you, my newly betrothed darling, I expect the next time you return to Chaldon that it would be with a child in your arms as well. Mayhap our children will grow up together."

Laboring to cast aside her darkened mood, Summer smiled weakly. "Mayhap," suddenly, she emitted a soft giggle. "I t-told Bose of my plans to name our firstborn son Kermit."

The depressing atmosphere instantly vanished as Genisa joined Summer in her laughter. "Sir Kermit de Moray! What a wonderful name!"

"He hates it."

"So do I! What a wonderfully horrid name!"

Summer and Genisa screamed with laughter, drawing the attention of few in the lodges. When Summer suggested the name Percy for Stephan's first-born son, Genisa laughed so heartily that she nearly hyperventilated. Chortling and snorting as their good humor made a bold returned, the two women were unaware when Edward and another figure approached, claiming the chairs made available by hovering servants.

Summer's laughter was cleaved as a foul-smelling odor swept her, followed shortly by a warm body seated indecently close. Turning with shock to the source of the warmth and smell, she was immediately confronted with small blue eyes and a pock-marked face.

Breck smiled lasciviously. "Greetings, sweetling. How delicious you look today."

Stunned and instantly angered, Summer indiscreetly moved her chair away from him. "I will thank you for not sitting so c-close to me, my lord. Since our encounter last eve, I would b-believe our contact to be ended."

"Ended?" Breck's eyebrows rose in conjecture, looking to Edward seated far over Summer's shoulder. When the man did not respond to his queried expression, Breck returned his attention to his newly betrothed, laughing softly in disagreement. "Our association has not ended, sweetling. It has only just begun."

Disgusted and unnerved, Summer struggled not to pinch her nose in obvious repulsion to the man's smell. "My future husband says it is ended. P-Please leave before I am f-forced to summon him."

Breck sat back in the chair, making himself comfortable and eyeing Summer with a good deal of indifference. "Summon de Moray if you feel it necessary. But I have the law and the church on my side and may do with you as I please."

Summer eyed the man, her anger and disgust melding into a wide mass of confusion and mounting apprehension. "W-What are you talking about?"

Breck looked lazily to his dirty nails, selecting the proper finger to chew. "Ask your father. 'Tis his right to tell you, after all."

That statement brought a blow of terror slamming into Summer's abdomen. The moment he brought her father into the conversation, the general confusion and fury felt for the repulsive knight transformed into a premonition so sinister that she could barely comprehend it. Turning toward her father, she fixed the fat man with her awesome golden gaze.

"What would you tell me, Father?" she asked.

Amazingly, Edward was not drunk this morn. In fact, he appeared rather clear-eyed and alert as he met his daughter's gaze. He matched her expression a long moment before looking away, his eyes wandering over the colorful lists.

"You are officially betrothed, Summer," he said. "To a man of my choosing."

Summer's heart did a wild dance against her ribs as she fought to control her breathing. "I know. B-B-Bose informed m-me last eve that you gave him your permission that we might b-be wed."

Edward turned to her then, a flash of anger and defiance in his faded blue eyes. "The man you speak of caught me at a disadvantage last eve, as I was completely drunk with fine wine and unable to ponder the necessary factors relating to such a decision. With Ian as his accomplice, I could do little more than agree for fear of my life."

Summer sat forward in her chair, her white-knuckled hands gripping the arm rests. "You cannot possibly m-mean to insinuate that B-Bose and Ian threatened you. You are speaking of your own son."

"And I am speaking of a man who murdered his wife in order to obtain her dowry!" Edward roared. Slamming his hands against the heavy oaken chair, the entire platform vibrated with his fury. "There will be no wedding to de Moray, Summer. As of this day, you are officially pledged to Breck Kerry and I have the necessary documentation to prove it. Nothing Bose de Moray can do will ever break the contract enforced by the Holy Church."

Instead of flying into a hysterical rage, Summer stared at her father as if the man had completely lost his mind. All of the color drained from her cheeks, leaving her a ghostly shade of gray. As the rain continued to pour and the wind continued to wail, Summer rose steadily from her delicately carved chair. Her eyes, her expression, never wavered from Edward's perspiring face.

"You are mad," she hissed. "I'll n-never marry Breck, father. You promised Bose...."

"A verbal sanction and nothing more. There was never any firm agreement between us."

"Ian was there. He w-witnessed the bond. If you go back on your word, I'll never forgive you. *Never.*"

Edward was unconcerned with his daughter's feelings. The only matter of concern was the fact that she had been informed of her true betrothal and he suddenly felt the need for the soothing comfort of his fine wines. Motioning to his servant, the finely-clad man brought forth a lovely crystal carafe and began to pour. Handing the matching crystal chalice to his lord, the servant was abruptly covered with the burgundy liquid as Summer viciously slapped the alcohol from her father's hand.

"You will not ignore me!" she commanded, her fury rising in spite of her attempts to control it. Moving toward her father, she put herself between the startled servant and her equally startled sire. When she spoke, her voice was a hissing whisper.

"You have ignored me your entire life, Father, but no longer," she said. "When I was young, I liked to believe that you kept me safely shielded because you were concerned for my mental well-being. But as time and age has matured my wisdom, I have c-come to realize that you kept me isolated not because you loved me, but because you were afraid of what others would think of your flawed, defective child. Therefore, you kept me sequestered like a freak. Not shielded as a loved one."

Edward refused to meet her gaze, a peculiar shade of red mottling his cheeks. The heralds were ready to begin the bout, politely waiting for the signal from the baron that would commence their duties, but no signal had been forthcoming as of yet. The entire field hovered with anticipation and confusion as the games were unexpectedly delayed.

"L-Listen to me and listen well," she murmured. "I do not know what has c-compelled you to betroth me to a man you were determined to defend me against only two days ago, but know this; I do not recognize my b-betrothal to Breck Kerry. You gave your word to Bose, and Bose is who I shall marry. There is nothing on this earth that will prevent our union."

Edward's reaction was one he would have reserved for anyone who had disobeyed his command, much less his daughter. Grabbing her by the arms in a surprisingly brutal display, he thrust her at the household guards maintaining watch in the stands.

"Take her to the vault. Take her there until I decide what's to be done with her."

The joust commenced.

☙

"IAN!"

The middle du Bonne brother heard the piercing cry, knowing the source of the delicious voice before he turned in the obvious direction. Genisa was racing across the trampled grass at the edge of the joust arena, all silks and hair and feet of fury. A lazy smile crossed his face at the sight of his sister-in-law as she rapidly closed the gap between them.

"God's Blood, Genisa, what's amiss?" he asked casually. "You look as if you've seen...."

"Summer!" Genisa nearly crashed into him as she came to an unsteady halt, gasping painfully for every breath. "Your... your father ordered her to the vault. Where's Stephan?"

Ian cocked a slow eyebrow; the most collected of the three du Bonne brothers, he was sluggish to excite or rouse even when the situation dictated immediate action. Quite simply, his character was difficult to disturb and Ian had learned a long time ago that calm heads often prevailed over panicked flight.

"Calm yourself, love," he admonished softly. "What do you mean by saying that Summer has been ordered to the vault? Who would...?"

"Your father!" Genisa gasped, frustrated that Ian was refusing to take heed. "He ordered Summer to the vault when she rebelled against... against Breck Kerry."

Ian's brow furrowed, his smile fading. "Breck? God's Blood, what's he got to do with this?"

Nearing the heady edges of despair as a result of Ian's lack of action, Genisa could hardly control her panic and irritation. "For Mercy's Sake, Ian, we must find Stephan. Summer is in terrible trouble!"

Growing increasingly concerned with the confusing situation Geni-

217

sa was attempting to convey, Ian grasped his sister-in-law by both arms to calm and steady her. "Stephan is preparing for his coming bout. If Summer is in trouble, mayhap I should go and speak with father. Mayhap...."

Genisa shook her head sharply, bordering on tears once again, Ian failed to take her seriously. Why did the man have to be so damn composed and stubborn? "Good Heavens, Ian, if you've ever loved me, you'll go and find Stephan and tell him what's happened. There is no time to lose with this meaningless chatter!"

His warm manner and calm expression faded. Genisa met his gaze steadily, realizing he looked very much off-guard as the meaning of her words sank deep.

"What... what do you mean?" he whispered. "If I have ever...?"

She swallowed hard, laboring to ease both her panic and his awkwardness. "Please, Ian, I did not mean to sound trivial. I... I was simply attempting to motivate you. Summer is in trouble and...."

"If I have ever *loved* you?" he repeated, ignoring focus of her apprehensive message. "Where did you ever get an idea like that?"

Genisa continued to gaze into his eyes, feeling guilty that she had carelessly broached a subject she and Stephan had agreed long ago to be off limits. Staring into Ian's face, she could see more than ever that it was true. It had always been true.

"From you, darling," she whispered, her respiration calming dramatically at compassion for Ian's plight. Completely off the subject of Summer's imprisonment, she touched Ian's hand gently. "From the moment we met, I could see it in your eyes and feel it within your heart. But fear not, Ian; your secret is safe with me. No one shall ever know by my lips or by Stephan's."

He visibly blanched. "My brother... does he...?"

She nodded faintly, her soft fingers silencing his lips. "It matters naught. He's never faulted you your feelings," as Ian fidgeted and cleared his throat nervously, completely removed from the commonly controlled man she had come to know and love, Genisa realized now was not the appropriate time to continue the exploration of such personal sentiment. When, or if, the time ever presented itself again, perhaps she and Ian could clear the air between them.

But not now. There was a more pressing crisis at hand. "Go now," Genisa removed her fingers, seeking to divert the knight's unsettled attention. "Find Stephan. Tell him Summer's been taken to the vault and he must go to her immediately."

Ian continued to gaze at her a long moment, wanting to linger within her presence, wanting to put as much distance as he could between them. In faith, he wasn't at all sure what he was feeling; but the fact of the matter remained that Genisa knew his well-kept secret. And so did his brother. A fantasy that wasn't his own any longer and he somehow felt ashamed.

Turning on his heel, Ian went in search of his brother to tell the man of their sister's apparent confinement and wondering if he shouldn't apologize for his treacherous feelings in the same breath, expressing his sorrow for having coveted his brother's wife.

Or he could pretend the conversation never took place. For the sake of his heart, Ian liked that idea best of all.

CHAPTER FOURTEEN

S TEPHAN SAW BOSE'S figure before he ever saw the face. He knew he would be coming and in faith, Stephan was glad. He could not handle the situation alone. He needed help.

"Get her out of the vault, Stephan. *Now.*"

Bose was still several feet away as he issued the order. Stephan pushed himself from his leisurely position against the wall, moving forward to greet the man within the bowels of Chaldon's darkened labyrinth.

"Ian and Lance are with her and she is perfectly safe and comfortable," as Bose came into the weak light, Stephan was not surprised to note his menacing expression. In fact, Stephan had never seen a more deadly countenance and he hastened to calm the man before he exploded into a fury of fists and steel.

Bose's jaw ticked as he replied. "I would hardly call the stanky intestines of Chaldon's dungeon a safe and comfortable atmosphere. You will release her immediately."

Stephan nodded in agreement, putting his hands against the man's chest as he made an attempt to move past him. "Of course I agree with you, but we must confront the overall problem, not simply my sister's captivity. Calm yourself, Bose, so that we might rationally discuss this situation."

Bose was beyond rational thought. He was very nearly to the limits of his control and struggling further not to wrap his hands around Stephan's neck as the man sought to delay his retrieval of Summer. From the very moment a du Bonne soldier had entered his encampment spouting word of Lady Summer's captivity in the vault, Bose had defaulted his round to Ian du Bonne and made immediate haste for

Chaldon's keep with nothing but murder on his mind.

What Bose did not know, of course, was that Ian had forfeited his round to de Moray several minutes earlier after receiving word of his sister's fate from the hysterical Genisa. As Stephan sent a soldier running for de Moray's tent, the du Bonne brothers were already moving for the castle to make sense of the situation before Bose arrived and tore the place to shreds.

Shreds or worse; the ramblings of a breathless soldier was the extent of Bose's knowledge on Summer's imprisonment. He did not know where her father was and he frankly did not care; all that mattered was that he collect Summer and leave Chaldon immediately. If the brothers du Bonne supported his endeavor, then he would be forever in their debt. And if they interfered with his intentions, he would kill them on the spot.

Considering he had no desire to kill Summer's eldest brother, he forced himself to calm at the man's request. But it was a difficult battle. Looking into the Stephan's eyes, Bose drew in a deep breath for strength and patience.

"There is nothing left to rationally discuss, Stephan. Your father passed beyond the boundaries of rationality and common sense when he ordered his daughter to the vault for a reason that has eluded me."

Stephan met Bose's gaze, emitting a heavy sigh before turning away, pacing aimlessly toward the moldering stone wall. "Get hold of yourself, man. There is far more to this story than my father's reasoning to banish Summer to the vault."

Bose could have marched past him at that moment and torn the place apart in search of Summer. But something in Stephan's tone forced him to pause.

"Tell me, then. And be quick about it."

Stephan kicked at the wall distractedly, composing his thoughts and praying the notification of such news would not send Bose over the edge. Drawing a deep breath, he turned to confront the onyx-black eyes.

"My father betrothed Summer last night."

"I know, Stephan. I was there."

Stephan shook his head. "I am not speaking of his verbal consent to you." God's Blood, he could hardly stand to look the man in the face as he spoke. He felt as if he were about to destroy de Moray's entire world. "'Twould seem that after my father had a chance to mull over his oral agreement with you, he changed his mind and decided to officially pledge my sister to Breck Kerry."

Bose's features did not change expression. When he managed to speak, however, his tone was hoarse. "Who told you this?"

"Summer did," Stephan said softly, feeling the man's pain as it radiated forth from his piercing black eyes. "When she refused to obey his directive, father ordered her to the vault."

Bose continued to stare at him. Several moments passed with virtually no movement or reaction when Stephan began to notice the tick in Bose's cheek growing stronger. And his complexion, so recently tinged a furious red, seemed to drain of all color leaving him pale and wax-like. As Stephan braced himself for an eruption of anguish and temper, Bose seemed quite unwilling to summon the energy. In fact, if Stephan hadn't known better, he would have sworn the man to be verging on a smile.

"Then you are telling me, in essence, that your father has broken his word to me?"

Stephan nodded faintly. "So it would seem."

"And you have not confronted him with this information?"

"He's still in the lodges, viewing the conclusion of the joust."

Bose shifted on his thick legs, his eyes like smoldering coals within his ashen face. "Surely he has come to realize that you, as well as me, have yielded our bouts and fled the field. Surely he suspects we have gone to free Summer from her captivity."

Stephan looked entirely serious. "My father believes only that which he is willing to accept. He believes my brothers and I to be loyal to him, therefore, I am positive he has faith in our willingness to enforce his decision. In fact, he's threatened to disown us several times for the slightest of infractions and based upon the fear that we are disinclined to relinquish our inheritance, he has no reason to believe that we have come to the vault for any reason other than to comfort Summer until she is released. And to prevent you from doing anything foolish."

"Is that what you intend to do? Stop me?"

"Nay. But my father will believe so. He will demand so."

Allowing Stephan's statement to digest, Bose sighed heavily in the first real display of sentiment. "God's Beard, Stephan. Is your father truly such a tyrant that he would manipulate the lives of others at his whim?"

Stephan shrugged faintly. "Not really. But he is a fool. A weak-minded, irresponsible fool who believes the world to be within his grasp."

Bose's gaze was steady in the weak torchlight, moving from thoughts of Edward du Bonne to the true motivation behind the man's altered mind. Not an entirely shocking reason, he realized bitterly. "I had no idea Breck's interest in Summer would include challenging me for her hand. Do you suppose he confronted your father and convinced him that Summer would be better off as Lady Kerry?"

"Possibly. Father was terribly drunk last night, as you know. It's possible that Breck managed to convince him to disregard his verbal consent to you in favor of Breck's offer."

"And I would suspect that Breck's proposal was more of an attempt at revenge against me. I dealt the man a righteous pounding last eve for touching your sister and, naturally, I would assume he is eager to seek retaliation."

Stephan slanted him a glance, a blond eyebrow cocked in thought. "We know that Breck is ruthless and unscrupulous on the tournament field. 'Twould seem his tactics do not stop on the turf of battle, but rather dictate his entire existence."

"An eye for an eye."

"Or in this case, stealing what is most precious to you simply to retaliate for a proper punishment dealt."

Bose drew in a deep breath, steadying himself as the information of Summer's betrothal sank deep. In faith, he found he wasn't particularly surprised; based on his observations of the baron, such a change of heart had not been out of the realm of possibility and he found himself cursing his lack of initiative not to have insisted the verbal consent be immediately put to paper. Breck's vicious attempts at vengeance aside, there was truthfully no one to blame but himself for the circumstance.

"Do you suppose your father has written the contract already?" he asked quietly.

Again, Stephan shrugged vaguely, feeling distinctly weary and drained now that the shock of volatile emotions was beginning to wear thin. "Where my father is concerned, anything is possible. Summer, unfortunately, was far too hysterical to further elaborate on what I have told you." Receiving no immediate reply, he eyed Bose a moment; the man was oddly calm in the face of such monumental upheaval. Stephan focused on him intently. "You seem remarkably composed with the turn of events, Bose. Might I ask what you are contemplating?"

Bose did not reply for a moment, seemingly lost in thought. After a lengthy pause, he lifted his broad shoulders in a resigned gesture. "The subject is in little need of further deliberation. I must do as I must."

Not strangely, that statement unnerved Stephan. Pushing himself off the wall, he eyed the massive knight with a good deal of apprehension. "What does this mean?"

Bose continued to stare at the cold stone floor in a moment of contemplative reflection. When he lifted his gaze again, some of the color had returned to his cheeks. "It means that Summer is mine, no matter if your father or Breck Kerry says otherwise. I am leaving today and she is going with me."

Stephan had suspected his answer; therefore, he wasn't particularly hostile in response. Maintaining a steady gaze, he paused before Bose and regarded the man carefully After a lull in which he rapidly pondered all possible options, he found himself emitting a heartfelt sigh of his own true emotion.

"Although I should prevent you from doing such a thing, I find in my heart that I cannot," his voice was a hushed murmur. "I know how my sister feels about you and when I look in your eyes, I can see that you care deeply for her as well. Summer has known very little happiness, Bose. With you, she is far more joyful and content than I have ever known her to be and for that, I shall be ever grateful. All I ask is that you be kind to her, always. She is a terribly fragile soul."

Bose's features softened somewhat, knowing Stephan was speaking from the very depths of his heart. He loved Summer, too, as much as a brother could love a sister and the fact that he would be assisting in her abduction outweighed the legal and moral rights of the betrothal his father had created.

As Bose struggled to relay his tremendous relief and gratitude of Stephan's support, his future brother-in-law slapped him on the shoulder in a display of comfort.

"Come along, Sir Bose," he said with forced levity. "My sister is moldering away in a dank nasty cell and I doubt she shall stay confined much longer before she begins climbing the walls."

Bose allowed Stephan to direct him down the corridor. Pleased that he was calmer, better able to deal with an undoubtedly hysterical lady, his sense of humor made a weak return. "You realize, of course, I am prepared to risk everything for your stubborn, willful sister."

Stephan cocked an eyebrow. "That is your misfortune. I tried to warn you off at the onset of your interest, but you would not be dissuaded. Some of us must learn our lessons the hard way."

That remark brought a slight smile from Bose as they descended a flight of slippery, moss-covered stairs. "I suppose I shall have to take my chances," he replied. "What will you tell your father when he realizes I have spirited your sister away?"

Several du Bonne guards lingered ahead, partially obscured in the weak torchlight. Stephan's voice was hardly a whisper as they closed the distance. "Tell him that I assisted you and convince him it was in

Summer's best interest. He shall listen to me; he always does."

"You may come and live with Summer and I should he throw you arse-first from his keep."

Stephan fought off a smile. "Ah, a delightful situation; supporting your wife's penniless brother and his chatty wife."

This time, Bose held back a threatening smile. "I can see that this abduction plan is coming to lead in ugly directions. Mayhap I should reconsider my scheme."

"Too late. The time to act is now if you truly wish to take her."

The subject abruptly sobered as Stephan's words rang true. Bracing himself for the battle that was yet to come against six du Bonne guards, Bose's humor fled in light of the approaching situation. Even if Stephan calmly ordered the release of his sister, it was quite possible that the guards would refuse to obey based on the fact that their orders had come from Baron Lulworth himself.

Obviously, Bose was prepared to do whatever was necessary to obtain Summer's release and with the support of the three du Bonne brothers, he sincerely hoped his goal would be bloodlessly achieved if at all possible. If not, then he was properly remorseful that there were those foolish enough to oppose his wants.

The matter of gaining permission to enter Summer's cell was an uncomplicated task, as Bose suspected it would be. As the ancient iron door creaked open, his senses were assaulted by the smell of mold and rot, urine and feces. Anger and disgust twisted his stomach to imagine Summer lingering within the bowels of such an unholy place, but he shrugged off the surge of emotion, knowing that she would be free of the appalling conditions soon enough. As he entered the cell, his gaze fell on three figures near the far wall, huddled on the ground and speaking in hushed, fearful tones.

The sharp stab of relief and recognition was quickly joined by feelings of immense appreciation as he realized that Ian, unwilling to allow his sister to touch the stanky floor, had seated his armored body upon the dank stone and pulled the miserable woman onto his lap. Lance, kneeling beside his brother and sister, seemed quite content to pet Summer's blond head as if she were a wayward dog.

Lost to their quiet conversation, the noisy cell door jolted them from their dialogue and even as Bose focused on the huddled group, Summer's golden eyes were riveted to him and, with a small cry, she bolted to her feet. Racing the length of the vault, she propelled herself into his arms.

Bose held her tightly enough to break her, breathing in her rose scent with the greatest of pleasure.

"Did they harm you, love?" he demanded into her hair. "Are you well?"

She nodded faintly, trapped by his massive hands and arms. "T-They did n-n-not harm me," she gasped. "B-But my f-father has b-b-broken our b-betrothal and…"

The return of her sharp stammer was indicative of her fear and emotion. Bose shushed her quietly, kissing her silent so that she would not upset herself further. "I know, love, I know. Stephan has told me everything."

Her eyes were as wide as the heavens as she met with his calm onyx gaze. "He has already drawn up a c-c-contract with B-Breck Kerry. Oh, B-Bose, what will we do?"

Bose maintained an even expression as he absorbed her words, his composure weakening as her stammered meaning sank deep. "Did he tell you that he has already drawn up a legal contract?"

She nodded fearfully. "He said I c-c-cannot marry a murderer."

Bose continued to stare at her a moment before closing his eyes tightly, briefly, as his composure slipped yet another notch. He had been quite calm until Summer had made mention of the written betrothal agreement; now, however, he could feel his control draining away yet again as the gist of the situation became clearer. If what Summer said was true, then Breck possessed a legal foothold.

He gathered her into a fierce embrace once more, fighting to clear his swirling thoughts. "Not to worry, love. We shall leave Chaldon this day and be legally married. Contract or no, Breck cannot dissolve our union once the church joins us in matrimony. After we are married, there is nothing he or your father can do."

"Leave Chaldon?" she gazed up at him, puzzled and agitated. "B-But I am a prisoner. How can I leave if…?"

He kissed her again, realizing his lips were quivering with the force of his emotion as he slanted over her delicious mouth once, twice. Only when she was properly silenced did he speak.

"Trust me, love. Trust that I will do what is best for the both of us."

Summer could only bob her head in agreement, fearful and sickened with the turn of events. Of course she trusted him; she had always trusted him. Now, when it mattered most, she possessed the utmost faith in his abilities to see them clear of a most distressing situation.

Noting that she was calming somewhat with his soothing logic, Bose cast her an encouraging wink and swung her possessively into his arms. Turning to face the collection of grim brothers, his black eyes sought Stephan.

"She will not spend another moment within these moldering walls," his voice was like thunder. "Stephan, do what you must to evacuate us from this cell. Summer and I have an appointment with a priest and considering what she has told me of Breck's written contract, we surely cannot delay another minute."

Stephan eyed the dark knight a moment before his gaze moved to Summer. Reaching out, he clasped her hand tenderly.

"I am well aware of the time frame, Bose," his voice was soft with emotion. Looking to his equally emotional sister, it was difficult to fight off the lump forming within his throat.

God's Blood, life had been so unkind to her, cursing her with an embarrassing imperfection and a careless, emotionless father. But he could see, within Bose's arms, that Summer had finally found the happiness and joy she had been denied and Stephan realized he would do everything within his power to assure their ultimate unity.

He forced a weak smile. "It may be some time before I see you again," his tone was tight with sentiment. "If I am to help Bose whisk you from Chaldon, then you will promise me something."

Tears clouded Summer's eyes as the reality of the situation came to settle; Stephan was fully prepared to assist Bose in liberating her from the vault, going against his father's directive in the process. But more than the fact that Stephan was willing to disobey his foolish sire, the reality that he was prepared to face the consequences for the sake of his sister's happiness gripped her deeply. When she sobbed softly, Stephan kissed her hand swiftly and released it.

"Answer me. Will you promise me one thing?"

She nodded, unable to speak for the tightness in her throat. Stephan's weak smile broadened. "Then hear me well; you will not name my nephew Kermit."

Laughter abruptly bubbled forth, spilling over along with the tears. Wiping at her eyes, Summer looked to Bose suspiciously before refocusing her attention on her brother. "Did Bose put you up to this?"

"He did not. I must protect my future nephew as I see necessary, even from his mother's lack of good taste. Any lad named Kermit is bound to suffer a life of humiliation and embarrassment."

Summer's smile faded as she fixed upon Stephan's bright green eyes. "Then I would know his pain well."

Stephan's smile faded as well, a measure of remorse joining his other powerful emotions. "No more, sweetheart. Bose will see to it."

Summer looked to Bose again, feeling the warmth from his black eyes fill her very soul. She touched his cheek lovingly, turning once again to her brother.

"I suppose I always knew father kept me sequestered because he was ashamed of me, not because he loved me. And the fact that my birth killed our mother did nothing to ease his resentment toward me." When Stephan's features softened with regret and compassion, Summer merely smiled. "I entertained the thought that my three brothers kept me shielded because they were embarrassed of me as well, but I knew better. Thank you, Stephan. Thank you for appointing yourself my mother and father and for loving me in spite of my imperfection. Thank you for protecting me because you adored me, not because you were ashamed of your defective b-baby sister."

Lance could not hold back the weak sobs that overcame him. Ian put a comforting hand to his younger, far more emotional brother, echoing the younger man's sentiment yet too reserved to allow such an exhibition of feeling. They had all known Edward's reasoning behind Summer's isolation, each man hoping silently that the sweet young girl never came to know the truth.

Stephan, his eyes full of glistening tears, moved forward and kissed his sister tenderly on the forehead.

"Given the chance, I would do it all again," he whispered. "Be happy, sweetheart. For the first time in your life, truly be happy."

Summer dashed away her rolling tears, smiling with appreciation, adoration, at her beloved eldest brother. As the heady moment deepened, Stephan was aware that there was little liberty for such emotion. Time was of the essence and there was a tremendous goal yet to be accomplished; clearing his throat of the emotional lump, he turned to his weepy brothers.

"As you have managed to deduce, Bose is taking Summer from Chaldon before Breck Kerry can sink his claws into her," motioning to the closed cell door, his composure made a rapid return. "I am going to attempt to gain her release by non-violent methods. If my orders are rejected, however, we must be prepared to disable the six sentries guarding the door. Lance, your responsibility will be Summer's safety should it come to a battle. I suspect Bose, for pure size and strength alone, will serve us better in a fight and you will be left to protect our sister."

As Bose set Summer gently to the ground, Ian and Lance nodded grimly; as usual, they would obey Stephan's orders without question. Loyal to their eldest brother far more than their moronic father, there was little question that they, too, were willing to face the potential consequences.

"What would you have me do, Stephan?" Ian asked quietly.

"Stand with Bose. I shall capture the senior sentry's attention and attempt to reason with him. If the man resists, then prepare to quash any refusal to Summer's removal. Understood?"

As Ian nodded obediently, Bose removed a dagger from a fold in his armor and placed in within his left gauntlet. "Once we are free, my men must be notified of my actions, for I suspect the baron's grace will be extremely limited to those under my command. They must be instructed to fold camp immediately and return to Ravendark."

"We shall see to it, Bose," it was the first time Lance had addressed his future brother-in-law by his Christian name. "We shall cover their retreat if we have to."

Bose looked to the youngest, most volatile du Bonne brother. His black eyes glittered with warmth. "I would trust their back to none other, Lance. Thank you."

Lance, feeling the genuine camaraderie between himself and a man he both feared and respected, lowered his gaze in a purely baffled gesture; only yesterday he was loudly insulting both Bose and his men and now he found himself preparing to defend them to the death.

Stephan wasted no time. Fixing the sergeant in the eye, his features were grim. "I am taking my sister from this place," he said firmly. "She will be released to my custody and I shall inform my father of my actions. Your men may disburse themselves to their regular duties."

The sergeant, a seasoned soldier with a heavy Scots accent, appeared rightly off-guard. "My orders are tae keep her here until yer father decides what's tae be done wi' her, Sir Stephan."

Stephan's green eyes were like shards of ice. "As I said, I shall inform my father of my actions and you shall not be to blame. I am giving you an order to disburse."

The soldier was visibly torn. Licking his lips, he passed a long glance to the curious men behind him as he struggled for an answer. "My... my orders come from the baron, Sir Stephan. I would gladly accept yer order had yer father not instructed me personally."

Stephan drew in a long, steady breath. "Then you are prepared to disobey me?"

After a long, deliberative moment, the sergeant nodded hesitantly. "I must, m'lord."

Stephan's gaze was hard. After a tense pause, he cocked a deliberate eyebrow. "Very well," stepping aside, he gestured to Bose directly behind him. "Are you prepared to disobey Bose de Moray as well?"

Six pairs of eyes stared at Bose as if he were the Devil himself. They knew well of the man and his reputation and there wasn't one warrior among them willing to obtain first-hand knowledge of the man's temper and tactics. More than the threat of the baron's wrath, the very idea of facing Bose de Moray in mortal combat was enough to cause them to rethink their stringent stance.

"But… but the baron's orders…." the sergeant sputtered.

Sensing their intimidation, Bose was wise enough to use the advantage. Ducking through the doorjamb, he planted himself beside Stephan, his black eyes blazing and his massive fists working.

"Is the strict obedience of the baron's orders worth a broken neck?" his voice was a growl.

Eyes wide, the sergeant stepped back, tripping over another man's feet but rapidly regaining his balance. Quickly reconsidering his view, it occurred to him that if Stephan du Bonne was willing to accept all blame for his sister's release, then certainly it would be within the best interests of all if the girl were freed without contention. And for the fact that Bose de Moray was willing to fight them all for her freedom, certainly the baron's wrath did not seem quite so frightening.

"We've duties tae attend tae, m'lord," spinning on his heel, he waved his arms sharply to the gaggle of men-at-arms behind him. The collection scattered, leaving Bose and Stephan smirking triumphantly in their wake.

When the hall was vacant, Summer emerged into the corridor, gazing down the dimly-lit tunnel as if she could hardly believe what she had seen. But she soon caught the humor too, and she turned with twinkling eyes to the snorting, armored men behind her.

"You did not have to fight them," she announced with a mixture of disbelief and glee. "Bose, they were simply terrified of you!"

"As they should be," he said with mock-seriousness, removing the dagger from his gauntlet and replacing it in the folds of his armor. "Thank God the confrontation was bloodless, at any rate. I was afraid they were going to force me to follow through with my threat."

Summer shook her head with a combination of disapproval and pride as Ian and Lance snorted their endorsement of their future brother-in-law's imposing presence. For certain, they were not the only men afraid of the mighty knight.

"I suspect the rest of your escape will be less simplified," Stephan said, his humor fading as essential moments began to tick away.

"Indeed," Bose's smile vanished as well and he grasped Summer by the hand, tightly, as if to never let her go. "My charger is tethered near my tent. We shall have to make it there as inconspicuously as possible. All we need is for Breck or Duncan Kerry to spot us and…."

"Duncan is competing against Morgan in the seventh bout," Ian said, already moving down the torch-lit hall as a distinct sense of urgency took hold. "With the second, fourth and fifth rounds canceled due to the du Bonne brothers' absence, I suspect Breck is currently watching his brother take the field. The sooner we make way to Bose's tent, the better."

"Let's waste no time," Bose was in close pursuit of Ian, pulling Summer behind him as Stephan and Lance followed. "I plan to make it to Salisbury by nightfall."

"Salisbury?" Summer asked curiously.

He glanced to her as he helped her mount the slippery stairs. "A mighty cathedral is being built there, only partially finished. But there is a rectory and my cousin is a residing priest. He shall marry us."

Emerging onto an upper level of the dungeon, Stephan's voice was faint. "You plan to ride all the way to Salisbury to marry my sister? Poole or Bournemouth is closer."

Bose did not reply for a moment as the group edged the darkened walls toward the light of freedom. "My cousin performed the funeral mass for Lora. I… I would like him to marry us."

Not strangely, the distance to Salisbury did not seem so terribly great any longer.

CHAPTER FIFTEEN

"TELL ME WHERE your liege took my daughter and I shall be merciful."

When Morgan did not reply fast enough, another crushing blow caught him in the kidneys and he sank to his knees, a small grunt of pain the only outward display of his agony. When Breck prepared to deliver another kick to the man's already-bruised midsection, the baron extended a sharp hand.

"Answer me, Sir Morgan. Where did de Moray take my daughter?"

Breathing heavily from the anguish of broken ribs, Morgan's gaze was unwavering. "As I told you, I do not know. Why are you so concerned with their disappearance if your daughter is betrothed to the man? Mayhap…."

A powerful boot to his side sent Morgan to the floor. Breck loomed over the struggling man, his pimpled face flushed with anger. "She is not betrothed to de Moray, she is betrothed to me. Your liege stole my bride and I fully intend to prosecute him for thievery!"

Gazing up at the irate young knight, Morgan's countenance was confused. "Thievery? What… what are you talking about? As of last eve, Bose was betrothed to the Lady Summer."

Breck sneered, unsympathetic to the knight's misery. "A verbal contract and nothing more. After Lord du Bonne was presented with the true characteristics of his future son-in-law, he wisely decided to betroth his daughter to a finer man. Me, in fact."

Morgan appeared even more confused. "You? God's Blood, Kerry, how in the hell did you manage to convince the baron that you were a finer man than Bose?"

"With my help, Sir Morgan," Margot sat against the distant wall, far removed from the torture at hand and sampling another bottle of the baron's fine Bordeaux. She'd been settled behind Morgan, out of his line of sight and he had been unaware of her presence. As he struggled to catch a glimpse of the familiar, hated voice, Margot merely sipped her wine in satisfied warmth. "It was necessary that Baron Lulworth be told of Bose's murderous and greedy tendencies. He agrees with Breck and I completely. Do you not, darling?"

Edward did not look to the woman who seemed to have overtaken his house and hold within the past several hours. From the moment she had convinced him of her son-in-law's dark character, she hadn't set foot from Chaldon. Confiscating the largest unoccupied guest chamber in the upper hall, she had moved in as her severely wimpled lady ordered all of Lady Margot's possessions removed from de Moray's tent and relocated into the newly-selected bower.

Margot had come to see that the baron was not only petty, selfish and vain, but he was exceedingly dimwitted and moronic. Whereas Bose's intelligent mind could be manipulated by his tremendous sense of grief, Edward could be exploited purely for the fact that he seemed to lack a will of his own. And with the man's sons conspicuously absent, tending to the tournament and their sister's social affairs, Margot saw the opportunity to draw yet another man into her venomous web. She had found another victim to occupy her twisted attention.

A process that was already beginning as Morgan Skye lay upon the cold stone of the foyer, beaten and bloodied by an irate Breck Kerry. Arrested on the joust field when word of Bose de Moray's abduction of Lady Summer had reached Edward's ears, hordes of du Bonne soldiers continued to lay search for the rest of de Moray's men. The three remaining knights and Bose's aged uncle, however, were yet to be found and Edward had vocally suspected his absent sons having something to do with the knights' disappearance.

"Indeed," Edward replied to Margot's question. "My daughter cannot marry a murderer, a man only interest in obtaining her family's wealth. Again I ask you; tell me where your liege has gone and I will be merciful."

Morgan managed to regain his balance, still on his knees. The expression on his face, however, was solid. "Bose is not a murderer. Margot knows as well as I that her daughter perished in childbirth, yet she seems intent to spread lies to the contrary. Lies that would destroy Bose all to satisfy her twisted sense of revenge."

As Margot's expression visibly darkened, Breck slapped Morgan across the mouth and nearly sent him toppling over again. "Enough of your distortions. Everyone knows Bose de Moray killed his wife in order to gain her inheritance. The fabrications you weave are simply to mask the truth in defense of your liege."

"I do not hide the truth. But Lady Margot does."

"Lies!"

Morgan turned to the flush-faced knight, a corrupt man that seemed to be growing more corrupt and vile by the moment. His countenance, his demeanor, in spite of having been righteously beaten, remained entirely cool. "Why do you want her so badly, Breck? What is the Lady Summer to you other than another merciless conquest?"

Breck seemed to falter, the sinister light in his small blue eyes flickering unstably. "She is... she is the most beautiful woman in Dorset and it is only right that she be my wife," apparently recovered from his moment of uncertainty, his features hardened once more. "No more foolish prattle to avoid the subject, Skye. Where did Bose take my bride?"

Morgan sighed, weakly, seeing that he was about to meet with more abuse as a result of his honest answer. "As I have said at least a dozen times, I do not know. I was not even aware of the lady's imprisonment and I certainly have no knowledge of where Bose would take her. He has friends all over this country."

Breck was preparing to strike him again when Edward, in a surprising show of power, firmly stopped him. Sulking and angry, Breck moved away from Morgan and paced like a caged bull, muttering to himself in a gesture of madness. The baron tore his eyes away from

Morgan long enough to watch the pimple-faced knight tear a hole in his fine Persian rug with the heel of is armored boot.

"Logic would dictate one of two possibilities, young Kerry," he said quietly. "He has either taken my daughter to the nearest abbey to marry her, or he has taken her directly to his fortress. In either case, I would suggest we start looking for him at the seat of his power. Eventually, I would suspect, he will have to return home."

Rising from her cushioned chair, Margot set her chalice to a small engraved tray and made her way toward the baron. "How brilliant of you to anticipate his plans, my lord. Ravendark is just outside of Salisbury; if your men ride hard, they can be there by tomorrow morn."

Breck, not to be left out of the conversation, ordered the nearest sergeant to ready a company of men to ride to Ravendark. As the soldier fled the solar, he moved toward Margot and Edward.

"I will have de Moray captured and returned to Chaldon for trial," he said decisively, focusing closely on Edward. "I am an outsider to Dorset, my lord. Who is your liege?"

Edward looked to the young knight, seemingly not as excited about de Moray's capture as he should have been. In fact, he had been rather quiet and distracted throughout the entire interrogation with Morgan Skye and except for his clear-minded suggestion as to how to trail the fugitive and his captive, seemed to once again lapse into a sluggish demeanor.

"The Marquis of Cerne, Lord Bruce Eggardon," he replied quietly, almost lethargically. "He resides in Poole."

"Then we will send word to Poole as to the circumstances and charges," Breck acknowledged. "After de Moray is captured, I would see Lord Eggardon preside over his trial and sentencing."

"I cannot believe that you would actually prosecute Bose for thievery when it was he who was betrothed to the lady first," Morgan had been silent throughout the entire conversation, but no longer. Now on his feet, bound and bloodied, his liquid brown eyes were rolling with fury. "If there is to be any manner of punishment dealt, Baron Lulworth, you should be the one to receive it. Had you not broken your word, none of this would have happened."

Breck moved toward the battered knight, reeking of rage as he once again balled his fist for yet another painful blow. "This is none of your affair, Skye. If you would simply tell us…!"

"Touch him again and I will kill you."

All present in the room heard the rumbling, thoroughly threatening voice. Breck stopped short of Morgan, turning in the direction of the hazard directed at his intended action; certainly, when he discovered the origin, he was not surprised in the least. Edward's expression, however, was writ with astonishment and glee as he rose from his chair, his gaze fixed upon the latest entrant to the cast of players.

"Stephan!"

Stephan entered the lavish solar, still clad in his ceremonial armor from his waived joust bout. His handsome face was exceedingly grim as his massive boots met with the hard stone of the chamber and behind him, Ian and Lance were equally imposing and grim. In fact, Edward had never seen his sons appear so determined.

"Where have you been, Stephan?" Edward demanded, moving away from Margot and toward his powerful sons. "We've been looking for you everywhere. Do you know that de Moray has taken Summer?"

Stephan eyed his father, never more ashamed of the man as he bore witness to the activities of the room. "I know. I helped him."

Edward gasped. "You… you *helped* him? Why in God's name…?"

"Because you were wrong and foolish to have broken your word to de Moray. He loves Summer and would provide her with an excellent life." Struggling to maintain his composure, Stephan's gaze was heavy with shame and revulsion as he continued his scathing statement. "God only knows how Breck Kerry managed to convince you that he was a far better prospect than Bose de Moray, but I will tell you this; break the contract you have established with Breck or I will leave this place and you will never see me again. Do you understand?"

All of the color drained from Edward's face, his fat features resembling pallid dough. "Stephan! You cannot mean…!"

"I can and I do. Break the contract or I leave."

"You are not thinking clearly, lad. My decision was based upon my concern for Summer's best interests and you had no right…"

"You've never given a second thought to Summer's best interests. You've done your best to make sure she had little interest or life or pleasure because you were ashamed of the flawed daughter Edwina died giving birth to. Now do as I say; my patience wears thin."

"Sir Stephan," Margot's voice was cold. "Your attitude toward your father is most disrespectful. He is merely concerned with your sister's very life and you have no right to berate him for his decision."

Stephan looked to the slender woman, something of a sneer lingering upon his lips as he studied her intently. "I do not know who you are and I have no interest in speaking with you. Be gone, woman. This is a private family matter."

"Nay, Lady Margot, please stay," Edward quickly intercepted Stephan's harsh orders. Hastily, with a hint of panic, he looked to his son. "Stephan, this is Sir Bose's mother-in-law. The mother of his dead wife. She has convinced me that de Moray is a murderer and merely after our family wealth. As he killed her daughter, so shall he kill Summer unless we stop him."

Stephan stared at the woman, digesting his father's statement. After a moment, the sneer vanished from his lips and a disturbing glimmer came to his bright green eyes.

"So you are the one," he murmured, almost thoughtfully. "The woman who would destroy Bose for your daughter's unfortunate death. Odd, Bose never mentioned that you had come to Chaldon for the tourney."

Margot met his nearly-confrontational expression. "Not particularly when one considers that he virtually ignores me. And as far as my daughter's untimely death, 'twas an unfortunate occurrence only in that I was foolish enough not to have prevented its happening. I am determined that your sister should not meet the same end."

"If she conceives, there is a distinct possibility that she will," Stephan countered softly. God's Blood, he hated the woman already. "However, she is willing to take the chance. Just as your daughter was willing and you have no right to accuse Bose of murdering her simply because of her failed attempt to bear the man a son."

Cracks began to appear in Margot's cool demeanor. "What do you know of it?" she hissed. "Bose forced my daughter into marriage, obtaining her ripe dowry and then pumping his seed into her until she became pregnant. He knew she would die from his over-large child and he was completely without conscience on the matter. He left her to bear the child alone, to die alone. Only when it was over did he return to claim her money and flee London as the thief he is. Do you care so little for your sister that you would see her meet with the same fate?"

Stephan seemed to calm as Margot appeared to agitate. "A woman in childbirth is as a knight in battle; one has little choice but to see the event through and if Death claims your soul, then it is God's will. Surely you realize that seeking vengeance on Bose will not bring your daughter back."

The corner of Margot's lips twitched menacingly. "You foolish, foolish bastard," she seethed, struggling to control her usually-collected dignity. "You know not of what you speak. I am attempting to help you and you are too ignorant to heed my warning."

"'Tis not a warning you give but fabrications instead. Bose de Moray is no more responsible for the death of his wife than you are."

Margot's face was an odd shade of yellow as she endeavored to rein her hurling emotions. "How fortunate your father is wiser on the matter than his eldest son. Edward agrees with me, as befitting his brilliant intelligence."

Stephan's gaze passed between his father and the aged lady, suddenly sensing an additional dimension to their relationship that he had been unable to detect only moments earlier. The tender tone in which Margot addressed his father was infinitely disturbing, far more when he realized Edward, for as pliable and foolish as he could be, was apparently caught within her spell. And Stephan, better than anyone, knew how responsive his father could be to a strong-willed person.

Therefore, his reply was careful and succinct. "My father may be the wiser and more brilliant, as you have so erroneously phrased his character, which brings to bear the very fact that Edward du Bonne does not rule Chaldon and her vassals independently. He has help. *My* help."

Stephan's point was clear and Margot could see a considerable adversary in Chaldon's mighty heir. A man to match both her wit and cunning, and she began to see an apparent flaw to her master scheme to control the du Bonne wealth through the baron's weak-willed personality. Clearly, Stephan could interfere with such goals. But no matter, she decided quickly; Stephan du Bonne or no, she would not rethink her plans for the moment.

A thin smile creased her lips. "I am sure you believe yourself to contribute to Chaldon's stability, but even you must concede the fact that Edward alone is the baron and not you. Only he has final say in all matters. And your father has deemed it wise that your sister marry Breck Kerry and not Bose de Moray, a murderer who has apparently swayed your inexperienced and foolish mind."

Stephan, oddly enough, seemed to be enjoying the woman's venom. Green orbs riveted to the small, twitching female, he moved to within a few inches of her, gazing down upon her small, taut and oddly-colored face. He could nearly feel the hatred, the bitterness, reaching out to clutch at him and he somehow imagined an invisible struggle between his own soul and her embittered one.

"Do not toy with me, bitch," he growled. "I can guarantee it shall be your last action upon this earth."

Margot paled, but she met his gaze unwaveringly. Stephan was positive he read a challenge in the faded blue eyes as he turned away from her, returning his attention to his thoroughly uncertain father. The man was being torn between two strong-willed, powerful factions and truly had no idea as to the consequences or effects of his swayed conclusions.

"Father, I demand you order this woman and Breck Kerry away from Chaldon. They have managed to wreak havoc with your thoughts and mind and I'll not stand for their presence any longer. Do you understand me?"

Edward nodded faintly, unsteadily. "But… Stephan, Breck has every right to remain as Summer's betrothed. And the Lady Margot is my… er, guest for a time. Surely there is no harm in their presence while this matter is cleared up?"

"Breck means to have Bose tried for thievery, Stephan," Morgan's voice was soft. Although he should not have interfered in Stephan's verbal battle, he felt the man needed to know the extent of the situation. "He has assembled a company of du Bonne men to ride to Ravendark and return Bose for judgment."

Stephan looked to Morgan, feeling sickened at the sight of the needlessly battered man. His agony was his fault, of course, for having been too preoccupied helping his sister escape instead of informing his father of his actions before the circumstance began to grow in unattractive directions. While Ian and Lance had rounded up Bose's men, including Tate, Farl and Adgar, and directed them from Chaldon, Stephan had been busy stealing Bose and Summer from Chaldon's well-guarded courtyard.

No one had been able to lend concern to Morgan's whereabouts until Stephan caught word of his arrest on the tournament field. Truthfully, Stephan never believed his father capable of beating a man in anger and continued to have difficulty believing the evidence before him; however, the agitated presence of Breck Kerry made Edward's apparent willingness in the matter obvious. Breck had somehow convinced the baron that pounding the truth from Bose's closest friend was the only answer and, true to form, Edward agreed. As long as someone else made the decision, his father was willing to comply.

"I forbid a company of du Bonne soldiers to take Bose prisoner," Stephan was speaking to his father. "I shall disarm every man myself if I have to. Not one of my troops shall…."

"Then I shall send my men," Breck replied, his confident manner evident. "You have no power over my soldiers, Stephan. They'll return Bose for trial and you will have absolutely no say in the matter."

Stephan looked to Breck, knowing his words to be true. After a moment, he shook his head slowly. "What in the hell has Bose ever done to you that you would attempt to destroy him in such a manner? Have him tried for thievery when you know very well that he and my sister were betrothed before you somehow convinced my father to break his word? God's Blood, man, what form of demon are you?"

Breck's expression was amazingly steady. "I am very fond of the woman and have no desire to see her come to harm. Marriage to de Moray can only result in her death, as you have heard most convincingly from Lady Margot's argument. What form of idiot are you that you refuse to believe the evidence?"

Stephan rolled his eyes in exasperation, not particularly surprised when Lance leapt to his defense.

"Bank your tongue, pock-faced whoreskin!" he cried. When Ian attempted to restrain him, the youngest brother broke free and moved toward the red-haired knight with menace. "God's Toes, I should have killed you last year when you broke Stephan's wrist. Indeed I wanted to, but Stephan forbade both Ian and I from delivering retaliation. I wish to God I hadn't listened to him, for we most certainly would not be having this conversation right now."

Breck was quite cool. "You would have murdered an innocent man, Lance. What happened to Stephan was a misfortunate accident."

"Rubbish!" Not surprisingly, ever-calm Ian had all he could take from the bold-faced liar. "Breck, you are without a doubt the most unscrupulous bastard on the circuit and Stephan's broken wrist was certainly no accident. One more word from your twisted mouth and I shall kill you myself."

Stephan held up a silencing hand before the argument grew out of control. "Enough, all of you," he snapped in a genuine show of irritation. Looking to his father, he could see that Edward was quickly succumbing to a deeper degree of confusion and uncertainty as the chaos of the room spread. Struggling to maintain his calm, he met his father's wavering eye. "Call an end to this foolishness, father. Allow Summer and Bose their peace."

Edward sighed, torn between the lies and truths presented before him. In faith, he simply did not know what to believe anymore and his indecision was evident. Clearly, he should believe his son, for the man had long been his source of wisdom and stability. But Lady Margot's words of humiliation in the eyes of his family and vassals alike had struck a chord deep within his heart. If Bose killed Summer, then all of Dorset would laugh at the foolish baron too blind to see beyond the man's dark facade. More than Stephan's declaration that Bose was an innocent, Edward could not seem to take the risk that once again, his son was correct.

"Great Gods," he sighed after a lengthy hesitation, running a fat hand through his oily hair. "What Bose did was wrong, Stephan. He stole Summer."

"He stole what you had rightfully given him before the introduction of this foolishness. Moreover, he did not truly steal her; I handed her over."

Edward shook his head slowly. "It was not your right."

Stephan paused a moment; nay, it had not been his right to deliver Summer into Bose's waiting arms. But he had done so nonetheless and possessed absolutely no regrets in the action.

"You are correct in your statement," his tone was considerably softer. "It was not my right. But it was the right thing to do."

Edward scratched his head as a soldier entered the room, muttering something to Breck. Breck replied softly, sending the man off again. His steady gaze met with Stephan's equally hard expression.

"I have ordered your men disbanded, du Bonne," he replied. "My men will be assembling within the hour and we shall ride for Ravendark Castle."

There was nothing Stephan could do. Bose's detour to Salisbury to marry Summer would allow Breck's men to reach Ravendark first, and when Bose and Summer arrived at the fortress after their union they would be riding straight into the waiting arms of Breck Kerry. His mind began to work furiously, searching for a response to Breck's action.

"Father, I request permission to assemble a company of men and ride to Bose's aid," he said without a hint of desperation, turning to face his father once again. "After all, Bose is entitled to our support as Summer's new husband. It is our duty to aid him however possible."

Before Edward could reply, Margot answered for him. "And risk a conflict with the Lord of Crestwood? You are speaking of unrest, Sir Stephan, something that could scar your life and the lives of your children. To be at war with another house and hold is a serious matter and you must consider the long-term repercussions of your intention to interfere."

"She is correct, Stephan," Edward's voice was barely audible. As if he was embarrassed for agreeing with someone other than his son. "I cannot risk the peace of Chaldon in such a fashion. Summer will marry Breck and Bose shall be tried for thievery."

Stephan stared at the man, realization dawning that, for the first time in his life, Edward had rejected Stephan's advice. A sickening feeling gripped at him, something he was unable to easily shirk. As if, for the first time in his life, Stephan realized his father to be beyond his control and counsel. As if, for the first time, Edward seemed to be possessed by something as unrecognizable as it was frightening: the control of an outside influence.

"Give me control of the men or I walk from Chaldon," Stephan's voice was equally tight. "And I take Ian and Lance with me."

Edward visibly cringed, a healthy sweat peppering his brow. "Nay, Stephan, you must not! You cannot leave me!"

"Give me control or I leave."

"But Stephan...!"

"*Do it!*"

Edward began to quiver. Hands to his head, he caught a glimpse of Margot's stern face from one side, Breck's from the other. With Stephan's demanding presence directly before him, the strain was too much to bear as he felt his mind and emotions torn in a thousand different directions. He crumpled with emotion and stress.

"I cannot… I cannot allow a murderer to…."

Stephan turned and walked from the room. Ian and Lance followed.

CHAPTER SIXTEEN

"**B**Y THE POWER given me by the Holy Church and his most Holy Excellency the Pope, I do hereby declare you to be husband and wife. Go in peace."

Summer, sniffling miserably with the terrible chill contracted within the dank bowels of Chaldon's vault, sneezed into the soft linen rag Bose had secured for her from a sympathetic priest. And that very same priest, Dag de Moray, closed the book of Mass and Ceremonies and laughed softly when she sneezed again as Bose attempted to kiss her.

"Were I you, cousin, I would refrain from any contact with your new wife until she overcomes this illness," he teased gently. He had done little else but taunt and humiliate Bose in a good-natured sort of manner since the very moment of his younger cousin's arrival. "God only knows your sneezing will bring down the very walls should you contract her ailment."

Bose kissed Summer regardless of his cousin's jibes, disengaging himself just before she sneezed yet again. Smoothing her mussed hair, he smiled tenderly at his new wife.

"My poor love," he crooned softly. "A bit of sustenance and sleep will make you feel better."

Summer nodded faintly, sniffling and wiping her red-tinged nose. "Oh, B-Bose," she breathed through her mouth. "I have n-never felt so completely awful. I would forget the evening meal altogether and go directly to bed."

While Bose tried to convince her that eating would be in her best interest, Dag removed the scarlet mantle of office and handed it to a hovering neophyte. Nearly as large as his massive cousin and possessing the same onyx-black orbs, he eyed the newly-wed couple with a good deal of confusion.

Confusion with the fact that a cousin he hadn't seen in four years suddenly appeared on his doorstep, demanding to wed an extremely beautiful woman with a running nose. Hardly a word of greeting and even less conversation, Dag agreed to marry the couple without the usual counseling or money-exchange simply because it seemed so important to Bose. In fact, the couple had arrived less than an hour before and, already, they were man and wife.

It was obvious, however, that marriage agreed with them. Bose's brusque manner had calmed considerably and the lady, ill and weary, seemed to be in somewhat better spirits as well. Aye, Dag was confused. But he was also happy for the sake of his cousin. The last he saw the man, he was on his knees beside his dead wife's crypt, praying for God to take his own miserable life.

Therefore, his last impression of Bose hadn't been entirely pleasant. But the reappearance of his cousin after four long years with a beautiful woman in tow had managed to somewhat erase the sorrow and concern previously held. Even now, as Bose gently wiped his new wife's nose and kissed her forehead tenderly, Dag could not ever remember witnessing a man more in love.

And his curiosity was obvious, increasing by leaps and bounds as the situation multiplied. Straightening his robes, he moved from the dais to confront the newly-joined couple.

"Congratulations on your new wife, Bose," he said, meeting Summer's watery-eyed gaze. "And to you, my lady. God give you the strength to deal with my obstinate, moody cousin."

Summer smiled, a lovely gesture in spite of her red nose and pale face. Dag returned her smile, increasingly eager to press Bose for the details of the entire circumstance. Indeed, who *was* the lady? Where did she come from? And, more importantly, where was her family and were they in fact aware of the marriage? All questions that would have to wait for now, Dag knew. But he was also determined not to be put off forever.

The sooner the lady was cared for, the sooner he could discover the facts. Gesturing toward a small corridor, he indicated the couple to follow.

"You may have my room for the night, Bose," he said, grasping a torch as they entered the dim, confining hall. "I'll have food sent to your wife. You and I can partake of the meal in the dining room, as I should like to know what has become of you over the past four years."

Bose had to duck his head as they passed into the corridor; he was far too tall to stand his full height. "I shall eat with my wife, Dag. We must retire early so that we will be on the road to Ravendark before the sun rises. You and I can catch up on times past at a later date."

Summer sneezed violently into her kerchief, the loud sound echoing off the walls. "N-Nonsense, Bose. Your cousin hasn't seen you in four years. I insist that you spare the man some time; after all, he's just married us without question or payment. 'Twould be polite to tell him what he has gotten himself into."

Bose shook his head. "But you are ill, love. I must make sure you eat and rest."

She gazed at him with as much steadfastness as she could muster within her exhausted body. "I am n-not an invalid. I can eat and rest without your overbearing presence."

His eyebrows rose at her snippy reply. "Is that so? God's Beard, when did you become so petulant?"

Dag came to a sudden halt. Bose, still focused on his wife, failed to note his cousin's abrupt stop and plowed into the back of him. Dag grunted with the force of the blow, eyeing his cousin with a good deal of feigned hazard. "Clumsy oaf. And I agree with your wife; you *are* overbearing."

The priest opened a small, well-scrubbed door as Bose pretended to be hurt by their slander. "I sense that I am an unwelcome burden to you both. I suppose I should simply be along my way and leave the two of you in peace if that is your general consensus of my nature."

Summer's laughter was abruptly cleaved by a resounding sneeze.

Sniffling and moaning miserably where she had been smiling not a moment before, Dag peered at the young woman with genuine concern.

"My lady, your health is in serious question. Curse my damnable cousin for forcing you to travel in your condition."

Summer smiled weakly. "I was f-fine until a few hours ago, truly."

"You are most certainly *not* fine now," Bose pushed into the dim room beyond the open door, hardly able to stand his full height as he scanned the meager surroundings. "So this is your chamber, Dag? I can see that your sect strictly adheres to their vow of poverty."

Dag grunted in agreement. "Indeed. But it is warm and dry and I am sure your wife will find it more comfortable than the back of a charger," turning to Summer as she blew her nose loudly, his black eyes raked her intently for the simple fact that he had never before seen such an incredibly beautiful woman.

The curiosity that had been growing steadily suddenly grew wings and took flight; he found himself quite determined to know the lady's history where it pertained to his cousin and was eager to begin the interrogation. "My lady, I shall have food sent to you immediately. And water to wash with, if you so desire. I am sorry we do not employ women servants that would assist you in this task."

Summer wiped her nose, trying very much to be gracious in spite of her throbbing head and aching body. "F-Food shall be sufficient, Father. I doubt I would have the strength to wash, even with assistance."

Dag smiled faintly in a gesture reminiscent of his cousin. Bose, however, was still reluctant to leave his wife alone, even for a single moment. "Are you sure, love? Would not you like me to stay and help?"

"Help with what? Eating or bathing?" when Dag snorted humorously, Summer merely smiled at her concerned husband. "I'll be fine, my darling. I fear I will not be much company this night and I b-beg you to sup with your cousin. The man is desperate to know about me."

Bose emitted a weary sigh, knowing it would be of no use to argue with her; if he had realized one particular characteristic of a woman over the course of his first marriage, it was the fact that argument, in any form, was futile. A lady usually received her heart's desire and Bose could easily see that this relationship was to be no different. Worse, in fact.

"Very well," he grumbled, displeased with her request. "Eat and retire, then, and I shall join you as soon as my cousin has finished raking me for information."

Summer nodded, kissing his cheek quickly and narrowly avoiding sneezing on him. "There is no hurry," she said, moving to shirk the heavy brown cloak that had seen rain, tournament, dungeons and marriage this day.

Bose removed the garment from her shoulders, laying it across a small table and noting for the first time the lovely amber-colored garment she wore. It molded to her body perfectly and he suddenly felt the unmistakable flames of passion lick at him; after all, 'twas the eve of their wedding and it was his legal right to claim her as his wife, body as well as soul. But Summer sneezed again and Bose was forced to realize that his new wife might not be in the best frame of body and mind to receive his husbandly attentions.

Still, more than an overwhelming need to discover all of the ripe passion her sweet body had to offer, the fact remained that he must brand her as his wife for the simple reason that it was necessary in order to fully consummate the marriage.

Summer sneezed yet again, jolting him from his train of thought. Swinging into action, Bose propped his cousin's thin pillow against the wall and gently pushed Summer down against it. Wrapping the clean but worn woolen blanket about her legs, he smiled at her pale, pathetic face.

"I shan't be long," he promised again. "Eat what you are given before retiring, please. If I have returned and your food is untouched, I shall wake you and feed you every bite."

She pursed her lips at him, a cantankerous reply cut short by yet another sneeze. Kissing her on the forehead, he followed his cousin from the room.

The cramped corridor reopened into the large room that served as a sanctuary for the priests, the very same room where Bose and Summer had been married not moments before. Directly to the left was a smaller room, used for dining, and Dag led his massive cousin into the smoke-tinged room. Indicating for the weary man to sit, he served him bread and cheese personally.

"Tell me of your new wife, Bose," Dag could hardly contain himself as he poured his cousin a hefty draught of sour wine. "From where does she come?"

"Dorset," Bose took a long, healthy swallow of the foul wine before tearing into a hunk of the coarse brown bread.

Dag scratched at his shaved head before following his cousin's dining actions. "How did you come to meet her?"

"At her brother's tournament."

"And when was that?"

"Three days ago."

Dag stopped eating. "Three *days* ago?" he swallowed the lump of bread in his throat. "God's Blood, Bose, three days ago? What… what of her family? Do they know…?"

Bose put up a silencing hand as his loud cousin worked himself into a fit of disbelief. "Calm yourself, Dag," his tone was quiet yet firm. "I apologize that I did not explain myself clearly when I first arrived, but it was imperative that the lady and I be married immediately. When you hear my explanation, you will agree with my reasoning."

"God's Blood!" Dag hissed, throwing his mauled bread to the plate. "You stole her! Or… Christ, even worse, you've bedded her already and must make amends to her enraged father!"

Bose shook his head in a quieting gesture. "Hush yourself, man. You are exactly as Uncle Rickard used to be, quick to the temper and emotion before you've been dealt the gist of the information."

"My father was a wise, controlled man and I'll not hear you say otherwise. Simply because your father, Uncle Garret, was as cold as a new snow, you have no right to accuse my father of erupting emotions like a foolish woman."

Bose emitted a weary, grumbling sigh. "My father wasn't cold; he simply controlled his emotions better than most men. And I did not come here to argue with you over our fathers' distinctive personality traits. I have come for your help and counsel, Dag. You more than anyone have understood my feelings and emotions over the years and I need your wisdom now more than ever."

Dag cooled with amazing speed, his expression a mixture of uncertainty and sympathy. After a moment, he sighed heavily. "I have not always understood you, though I have tried," even his tone was considerably softer. "Very well, cousin. Tell me what you've done and I shall remain calm. At least, I'll try."

"Promise me."

"A tentative pledge is the best I can do."

Bose took a mouthful of bread, chewing thoughtfully as he spoke. "When I first saw the Lady Summer du Bonne, I thought her to be the most beautiful woman I had ever laid eyes on. And in my attraction to her, I felt extremely guilty in that I believed myself to have somehow betrayed my feelings for Lora. But as time passed, I came to realize that I needed to live life for the present, not allow myself to exist in the grief and remorse that had consumed me for four long years. Therefore, with a great deal of thought, I pursued the lovely young lady and eventually, her father verbally sanctioned my plea for her hand."

Dag had resumed his meal as well, listening intently. "Then why did you come to Salisbury in the dead of night, demanding I wed you and your lady immediately?"

"Because a young knight, an unscrupulous warrior who has been a nemesis upon the tournament circuit, also had his attention drawn to my lady. Somehow, he managed to convince her father that the rumors regarding my murderous reputation were true, which turned the tides of marriage in his favor. Summer's father broke his word to me and officially betrothed her to my competition."

Dag swallowed the bite in his mouth, setting his chunk of bread to his coarse wooden plate. His movements were slow, pensive. "The rumors Margot spread? The hearsay meant to ruin you?"

"The same."

"So you decided to force the father to his honor his vow," again, Dag sighed heavily with confusion and wonder. "Bose, I have never known you to act foolishly or rashly. Why must you start now with the abduction of a woman who does not belong to you?"

Bose's onyx-black eyes glittered in the weak torchlight. "Because I love her. And because I need her."

Dag realized he had lost his appetite and pushed his plate away, meeting his cousin's gaze. "Enough to risk potentially severe repercussions for your actions?"

"All that and more."

After a moment, Dag looked away, shaking his head slowly. Bose leaned forward on the table, resting his elbows on the scrubbed top and resting his chin on his folded hands.

"You do not agree with me?"

"I did not say that," Dag's voice was soft. Scratching his shaved head yet again, he met his cousin's searching expression. "I remember at Lora's funeral, how you spent hours kneeling beside her crypt while your mother-in-law hurled curses at you the likes of which I have never heard before," again, he shook his head out of pure bafflement. "What of the old woman, Bose? Does she still live with you? Will she continue to live with you and your new wife, providing of course that her legal betrothed does not have you executed for stealing his woman?"

Bose shrugged faintly. "Margot will not live with us. Out of respect for Lora, I will purchase her mother a manse in London where she can live peaceably. Had I not loved her daughter so, I would just as soon see the woman cast to the streets."

"And what of your wife's betrothed?"

For the first time, Bose's expression hardened. "After tonight, there is nothing he can do. The church will not annul our marriage no matter if Breck Kerry is Summer's legal betrothed or not. Once the union is sealed, they cannot interfere."

"Breck Kerry? God's Bones, Asa Kerry's son?"

"The same. He's nothing like his father, God rest his soul. A more vicious, petty lad you will never meet. Which is why it was imperative Summer and I be married immediately, before Breck could legally wrangle her from me."

Dag sighed slowly, a fatigued gesture. "So you took advantage of my position. You used me to sustain your improperly acquired ends."

"I needed you."

The priest did not reply for a moment, eyeing his cousin with disapproval. "Had I known this information upon your arrival, I would never have married you. You cannot use the church as a weapon against those who will not obey your bidding, or as a safe haven in which to hide from those intent to prosecute you. Have you for one moment considered what affect this will have upon your wife? You have forced her into facing a great danger all because of your reckless action."

"There will be no danger once we reach Ravendark."

"And what do you plan to do? Barricade yourselves within your fortress for the rest of your lives? A foolish plan."

Bose's composure was slowly weakening. Dag had always been exceedingly wise and forthright, and he suddenly found himself wondering if his cousin wasn't correct. Had he acted impulsively? Of course he had. But for Summer's sake, the action was necessary.

"I would rather live isolated at Ravendark with my wife than pursue a life of freedom with only my guilt and loneliness to keep me company," he leaned forward, fixing his uneasy cousin in the eye. "Being celibate, I do not expect you to understand my motives where it pertains to a woman. But know this; I love Summer with everything that I am and I will continue to love her until the end of time. There is not a man or god in Heaven and Earth that will separate us, her father and Breck Kerry included. Do you understand my words?"

Slowly, Dag nodded. "I do."

"Then know that I have never been more serious about anything in my life," Bose sat back, moving to stand. His appetite was vanished as well and he felt a tremendous need to hold Summer in his arms. "You have done me a great service this night, cousin, and I shall be ever grateful. If you will prepare the necessary documentation, I should like to take it with me when I depart. Good eve to you."

"Bose," Dag stood up quickly as his cousin sought to vacate the small, smoky room. "Please... I did not mean to sound condescending. If you are truly happy, then I suppose that is the only matter of import. But you must agree that the circumstances surrounding this happenstance are a bit... shocking."

Bose paused, the shadows from the dank room enveloping his massive form and creating an even more imposing aura about him. Piercing black eyes met with those of the same obsidian shade.

"Nonetheless, what I have presented to you is the path I have chosen to take. Whatever has occurred and whatever is yet to be, there is no stopping the chain of events I have created. Your support in the matter is welcome. Your cynicism is not."

"I did not mean to be cynical. Incredulous is a more apt term."

Bose continued to linger in the shadowy doorway, the sanctuary beyond dark and foreboding. Beyond the chapel lay the narrow corridor, and within that corridor resided his wife. After a moment, he scratched his dark head and looked away from his cousin's inquisitive, concerned expression.

"Be incredulous if you must. Be awed still. But do not fault me my emotions, Dag. That which I thought I had lost was returned to me by the beautiful woman you saw standing beside me this eve and I swear to you that I will die before relinquishing her."

Dag moved toward his massive cousin, knowing the man well enough to know that he did not profess his emotions easily. With a heavy sigh, he lay a meaty hand upon the knight's armored shoulder.

"Then I am pleased you have found love again," he said softly. "Pray forgive the unthinking words of a man who has never before known the pleasure. It was not my intention to be judgmental, Bose. Merely unbiased."

"I realize that," Bose replied, his hard stance softening. "But to hear your reasoning merely confirmed the knowledge I had so attempted to ignore. I have little doubt that Edward du Bonne and Breck Kerry will come for me, and I have little doubt that I will know minimal peace from this day forward."

"What of Henry?" Dag asked softly. "He is extremely fond of you. Surely he can intervene somehow."

"Mayhap," Bose shrugged, his thoughts once again drifting to his ill wife. "I should not like to burden him with my self-invited troubles."

"He will be angry if you do not."

Again, Bose shrugged weakly. If only for Summer's sake, he had indeed considered the possibility of contacting the king purely for the fact that the man could force Baron Lulworth and Breck Kerry to cease their pursuit of the stolen couple. If, indeed, the two slighted men chose to harass the newlyweds, and Bose had no reason to believe that they would not. Still, until such a time approached that royal intervention might be necessary, Bose was determined to handle the situation himself. For certain, he would endeavor to try.

"Mayhap," he repeated belatedly. "In any case, my wife awaits me. Thank you again, Dag, for your services and support this eve. I knew I could depend on you to aid me."

A measure of Dag's normal overbearing character returned and he snorted loudly. "Aid you in what? Ruining that beautiful girl's life? Out of my sight, Bose, before my superiors discover what I have done. After I am defrocked, I shall be forced to come and live with you and your beautiful bride and that shall be your punishment for your impetuousness."

Bose scratched his chin, grinning. "Summer's eldest brother made the very same threat as he covered our escape from Chaldon Castle. 'Twould seem my fortress is to become a haven for disgraced relatives."

"It is your own fault," Dag gave him a shove into the dim chapel beyond. "Go to your wife, Bose. Go to her and pray that she never comes to resent you for forcing her to marry you."

Bose's smile faded as he took his cousin's advice seriously. "I already have."

Dag watched his mighty cousin as the man approached the mouth of the narrowed corridor. Before the knight could disappear completely, he called softly to him.

"Bose?"

Bose paused in the open portal, his face barely visible in the weak light. "What is it?"

Dag did not reply for a moment. "Your wife… I meant what I said. She is the most beautiful woman I have ever seen and I find that in spite of the circumstances, I envy you your fortune."

Bose nodded faintly. "She is all my dreams and more."

Dag listened to the bootfalls fade down the hallway. For an endless amount of time he continued to stare at the dim corridor, his mind a vortex of thought and emotion. For all he had discovered this night, he found himself extremely apprehensive.

In the alcove off the sanctuary was a small room laden with various supplies dispensed to worn and weary travelers. Grabbing a heavy, beaten cloak, he set it aside and clutched a torn, disheveled satchel. Making sure there was no one to observe his actions, he set out for the kitchens to collect a few supplies.

To the Devil with his cousin's stubborn pride; if he would not ask for Henry's divine assistance, then most certainly Dag would. He had known Henry once, too, when the lad was very young and Dag was still a knight in training. They had bonded and been friends, once.

Aye, Henry would want to know what had become of his favorite captain and Dag was determined to tell him personally.

☙

SUMMER WAS SNORING when Bose returned to the cramped room. A thin spirit candle flickered by the side of the small bed, casting little light upon the gloomy room. On the floor beside the bed, a tray of food lay virtually untouched and Bose smiled faintly as he recalled his threat. Truly, he would not awaken her to force her to eat. But he would awaken her for another reason.

With a loud snort and a sniffle, she suddenly rolled onto her side, her beautiful hair splayed about the bed like an abstract halo. Quietly, Bose removed his armor, allowing the pieces to fall gently to the floor. Stripped to his linen tunic and hose, he proceeded to remove his damp boots, wondering if the horrid smell alone would be enough to wake her. Finally dislodging the tunic, he sat carefully on the bed beside her.

God's Beard, she was so very beautiful. Reaching out, thick fingers toyed with the silken strands of hair, loving the soft feel against his skin. The same hand stroked her hair a few moments before moving to her head, tracing the hairline about her face, caressing her cheek. Never in his life had he been witness to a more sensual, exquisite creature.

"If you were still married to Lora, you would not be touching me at this moment," her muffled voice was faint, yet alert.

Bose cocked his head, watching the dim light play off her porcelain skin. "No, I would not."

Summer rolled onto her back, her golden eyes half-lidded with sleep. "I am a wicked, wicked woman, Bose. P-Please do not... do not hate me for thinking terrible thoughts."

"And what thoughts are those, love?"

She blinked as if deciding whether or not to answer him. After a moment, she simply shook her head. "I cannot tell you. You will hate me."

"I could never hate you. What were you thinking?"

Tears suddenly sprang to her eyes and Bose shushed her softly, wiping the moisture away. "What's amiss, love? Why do you cry?"

"B-Because," she wept softly.

"Why?"

She tried to roll over, away from him, but he would not allow it. Instead, he lay on the small bed beside her and drew her against his naked chest, her faint rose scent filling his nostrils. "Tell me. Why do you weep?"

She sniffled and sobbed, sneezing and spraying his skin with moisture. He held her tightly, somehow suspecting what her answer would be but wanting to hear it from her lips all the same. *If you were still married to Lora, you would not be touching me now....*

"B-B-Because I-I... I-I...."

"There is no need to be upset, love. Calm yourself and speak slowly."

She swallowed hard, her hands against his taut chest. After a moment, small fingers began to caress his dark skin timidly. "I was thinking that I am glad for Lora's death," she said softly. "If she was s-still alive, I would never have known you. Or loved you. Although my thoughts are not m-meant to be evil, I nonetheless feel wicked for believing that I should thank her for her passing. For her kindness in providing her husband to a woman she has never met."

She waited for an explosion of fury, but there was none forthcoming. Instead, his embrace actually seemed to tighten and she could feel his lips against her forehead, warm and tender.

"I am a firm believer in the old proverb that states all events happen for a reason," his voice was barely audible. "I remember Dag telling me on the day we buried Lora that God is in control of our lives, not us as we would like to believe. God had allowed Lora to die for a reason, though at the time I surely could not imagine what that reason could be. Mayhap... mayhap you were the reason."

Her head came up, golden eyes melding with onyx-black. The tears faded as she gazed deeply into his rugged face. "Do you believe that?"

He met her gaze, his eyes raking her delicious features. "I do," he whispered. "God looked into the future and realized what my dilemma would be upon meeting you. Certainly, I would not have been unfaithful to my wife even if you are the most beautiful woman in all of

England."

She smiled faintly. "G-God was thinking of me, too. I would still be living an isolated life had you not been introduced into my world. Mayhap God realized that I needed you more than Lora did."

Bose sighed, thinking of Lora far more objectively than he had in four years. "Lora needed my level head, my wisdom. She could be rather mindless at times."

"As can I. 'Tis a female trait, I think."

He grinned in agreement. "I remember the day I met her. She was attempting to lower herself from a window to escape her mother's wrath. Apparently, Lora had a secret lover and Margot heartily disapproved. But the rope she was lowering herself on was made of linen sheets, tied together on the ends. Clearly, a woman cannot tie a knot as a man can and one of them inevitably came loose. She landed on top of me."

Summer giggled. "She did? P-Poor thing. Did she injure herself?"

His eyebrows rose. "You think only of her health? What of mine? She could have injured me terribly."

She continued to giggle. "So sorry, my darling. B-But we women must support one another. I would have lowered myself from a window to meet my secret lover regardless of who I landed on, too."

"You did more than that. You were a willing accomplice in your lover's secretive plans to abduct you from your home."

Her smile faded as she realized the truth of his words, the seriousness of her actions. His warm skin, beneath her fingers, drew her attention and she found her gaze wandering his muscular, naked torso. Bose pulled her close once again, his gentle lips finding her forehead, her cheeks, and her nose. Summer closed her eyes as his seeking mouth drew closer to her honeyed lips, feeling the heat of desire burn deep into her belly.

The palms of her sweating hands moved up his chest, her fingers digging into his shoulders as his mouth claimed her own. Moaning noises sounded deep within her throat as Bose pulled her into a crushing embrace, smothering her with his maleness. Kiss after kiss, their desire burned hotter and hotter until Summer abruptly found herself beneath him, the small bed groaning dangerously under their combined weight.

Straddling her luscious body, Bose fumbled with the stays of the amber-colored gown, listening to his wife's gasps of passion in between loud, pathetic sneezes. When the bodice of the garment came free, he removed the gown completely and set to work on her silky-soft shift. Easily, it dislodged and before Summer realized her state, she was completely naked beneath him.

The warmth from his over-heated body shielded her from the chill of the room, protecting her. Bose fumbled about again, his mouth still attached to her neck, and it wasn't until he lay upon her completely that she realized he had removed his hose. Naked and warm, he drew the coarse woolen blanket about them both.

Her legs were sandwiched between his massive thighs as a quivering hand gently traced her torso. When the searing kisses to her neck ceased, Summer opened her eyes to realized Bose was openly inspecting her nude body.

"Bose?" she whispered, disappointed that he had halted his scorching kisses. "What are you...?"

"God's Beard, you are beautiful," even his voice quivered with awe and desire. Moving to her breasts, his hand moved in a gentle circle as his eyes sought her curious gaze. "I am sorry this event could not take place in a comfortable bed with all the time in the world for foreplay and discovery. What I must do, I must do immediately, for every moment that passes is another moment that our location could be potentially discovered. If your father breaks down the door before I have had a chance to claim you completely, 'twill be ammunition for his cause."

She smiled faintly, her hand to the three parallel scars on his cheek that fascinated her so. "W-We have all night, do we not? Stephan will not tell where we have gone."

He kissed her hand. "I trust your brother completely, but my charger's tracks are distinct. If Breck and your father are intent to follow our trail, it will lead them here."

Her smile faded. "Then… t-then they could be upon us?"

"Possibly. And I cannot take the chance that they would separate us before I have consummated the marriage."

Her face darkened somewhat at the thought of being isolated from Bose. And with that thought, fear such as she had never known blossomed within her chest, consuming her, drawing her clean of all control. Throwing her arms about his massive neck, she pulled him close against her in a fit of possessiveness and desire.

"Then do it," she murmured against his ear. "Make me yours, my darling. I am not afraid."

His hands moved to her breasts, his lips to her shoulder. Summer surrendered to him completely, wanting to know the power of his touch, to feel the magic of his emotions. Two days of discovering passion and desire paved the way for a sensation that seemed to grow in intensity with every successive touch, every progressive kiss. The more he caressed and lingered, the more she wanted.

His heated mouth was upon her nipples, drawing them into stiff little pellets. He suckled her, bit at her, until Summer was panting with the heat of her unrestrained desire. Sneezing onto the hands that held his dark head captive against her breast, she made little attempt to stifle her delightful moans against his onslaught.

His hands moved to her slender thighs as his mouth continued to work her nipples hungrily. Gently prying her legs apart, he shifted his weight and settled between them. As Summer instinctively wrapped her legs about his slender hips, his calloused fingers moved to her delicate virgin core.

As before, she started slightly when she felt his probing touch, forcing herself to calm as he whispered tender words of comfort. Her natural apprehension banked somewhat as he invited her to watch his actions, acquainting her with her own body, its responses and reactions to his touch. Summer watched with a calming mind and increasing fascination as Bose gently traced the dusting of dark-gold curls between her legs, telling her how pretty the thatch appeared to his hungry, amorous eyes.

She blushed steadily as he murmured softly on the beauty of her private junction, tenderly stroking the thick lips until she gradually came to relax. Twice, he reached up to grasp her hand, insisting that she join him in his exploration, but she balked and giggled uncontrollably. Smiling at her natural embarrassment, he continued to touch her as only he was capable.

God's Beard, it had been so long since he had touched a woman in this fashion that he realized he had nearly forgotten the pleasure of it. His massive fingers raked the patch of dark curls, the scent of her feminine musk tantalizing his nostrils and feeding his desire. As Summer watched, he dipped his great head to deposit sweet, loving kisses along her groin. Planting a deep kiss directly on the center of the hedge of delicate ringlets, he laughed softly when Summer leapt in maidenly shock.

"Easy, love, easy," he murmured. "There is more to come."

She nodded uneasily, smiling timidly into his lust-glazed eyes. Widening her already-spread legs, his hands stoked the back of her thighs and caressed the rounded curve of her buttocks before gently probing the glistening petals of her womanhood.

God's Beard, she was slick as rain and he sighed raggedly as his finger slipped into her easily. Summer gasped softly, her eyes closing to the initial surprise and wonder of his intimate action. Bose groaned low in his throat as he withdrew his finger gently, slipping two into her with little resistance. She gasped again and suddenly, he could hardly stand the excitement; as his control began to splinter in the wake of her obvious readiness, he mounted her with as much care as he could muster.

His throbbing member was hard and heavy as he pushed against her, gliding in effortlessly until the ruby-red tip of his phallus was buried. Holding himself aloft from her body with one arm and gripping her tightly about the waist with the other, his black eyes met with her wide golden orbs and he smiled weakly, all of his strength and concentration centered on his careful, slow entry. She smiled in return, biting her lip in anticipation of his breach, expecting the pain and discomfort that would accompany such an action yet oddly eager to know the experience just the same.

Forgetting his control, his indecisiveness, Bose collected her delicious body into his embrace and drove his eager member deep into her yielding body. Listening to her soft gasps of shock, he kissed her deeply and passionately until she ceased to whimper. Holding her tightly, he coiled his buttocks and drove into her slowly, again and again, introducing her to a world of passion. Summer stayed with him, clinging to his lips, moaning softly with each successive thrust, and Bose felt his climax approach with blinding speed.

Abruptly withdrawing, he wrapped Summer's hands about his erupting member, gasping with ecstasy as he spent himself upon her hands and his cousin's mattress. Sweating and breathing heavily from his exertion, he observed his wife's expression as she watched the final surge of his orgasm die a lingering death within the palm of her hands.

"Good Lord," she whispered, watching the pearl essence run down her flesh. "Are you all right? What happened?"

Amidst his panting, he laughed and snatched the edges of the blanket, wiping off her hands. "My pleasure, love," when she looked puzzled, he laid her back to the bed and sought to clarify his statement. "My seed, as you called it."

Summer watched him as he resumed kissing her breasts, her torso. "But... but you s-seemed to be in such pain. Does it hurt you?"

He laughed again, reaching the dark blond curls matted with moisture. "Not at all," he said, descending upon her tender nub. "As you are about to discover."

Summer opened her mouth to question his odd reply when he suddenly came to bear on the jewel of her femininity, teasing it gently with his tongue. With a cry of surprise and a surge of pleasure, Summer's legs draped over his massive shoulders and she once again found herself surrendering to his wonderfully experienced touch. It was a matter of seconds before an explosion of stars pierced her brain, her loins and body wracked with euphoria such as she had never known.

"You have the power of life and death, husband," she murmured after the ripples faded. "I know not in which state I find myself."

Bose's pulled her into his powerful embrace, smiling weakly. "Alive, love. As you have made me more alive than I have ever been in my life."

Summer lifted her head, gazing at his relaxed, dozing face. "Then… then you were not d-disappointed by my lack of… that is, you have been married before and have had experience with this sort of thing. I have never even been kissed by a man until two days ago."

He peeped an eye open, peering at her charmingly disheveled face in the weak light. "Well and good that you have not. I shall be the only man to touch you. Ever."

Summer scratched her head, smoothing the hair away from her face. Bose closed his eye, thoroughly exhausted, yet noting from the shift of the bed that Summer was sitting up beside him. Opening both eyes this time, he observed her as she stared thoughtfully into the dim depths of the tiny room.

"What's amiss, love?" he asked softly, stroking her delicious blond hair. "Aren't you tired?"

She shrugged, shaking her head and wiping at her nose. After a moment, she sneezed again in the resumption of her chill symptoms that had miraculously seemed to vanish during the pcak moments of their pleasure.

"Did I n-not please y-you?"

The stutter had returned and he grew more alert, knowing its return to be an indication of her emotional level. Folding a massive arm behind his head, he gazed up at her exquisite profile.

"More than words can express. What is bothering you?"

Her lovely brow furrowed as she appeared to ponder his question, her reply. "I-It's just…I-I…" turning to face him, he could see the blush mottling her cheeks even in the weak light. "G-Genisa t-told me that when m-men spill their seed, i-it is inside a woman. I-If I p-pleased you, then why did you not spill inside of me? I a-am your wife, after all. 'Tis m-my duty to bear you s-strong sons and if you d-do not give me y-your seed, then h-h-how… h-h-how…."

He stopped her, his lethargy vanished as his black eyes focused on her intently. God's Beard, how could he tell her his reasons? That he was fearful of pumping her full of his massive seed, killing her as he had killed Lora? Gazing into her beautiful face, he knew as surely as he lived and breathed that if anything ever happened to her, he would be lost forever. There would be no reason left for him to live.

Reaching up, he cupped her delicate chin, loving and adoring her more than mere words could express but unwilling to divulge his truth. The truth was that he would deny her the chance to bear his child simply because he refused to face the risk of losing her.

"You're so young, love, so naive," he murmured, attempting to divert the subject. "Do you always adhere to what Genisa tells you?"

Summer shook her head, the light of uncertainty still in her eyes. "N-Nay. But I-I know…."

He sat up swiftly, kissing her firmly on the lips. "You must trust that I, for now, know more than you do where it pertains to sexual relations. Trust that there is more to this world than what Genisa has told you."

A nicely skirted answer to the subject, he congratulated himself as Summer deliberated his words. A few twisted words, a measure of confusion, and his wife was easily distracted. Eager to be clear of the subject, he wrapped his arms about her slender torso and drew her down on the bed beside him.

"Now," he said firmly. "I want you to sleep. We must leave before sunrise and I would have you rested."

Still pondering his mysterious, somewhat baffling words, Summer yawned and sneezed in succession. "A-Aren't we going to make love again?"

His eyebrows rose and he fought off a smile. "I could make love to you all night, but I doubt you would derive as much pleasure as I."

"G-Genisa and Stephan make love three and four times a night."

"And how would you know this? Wait – do not tell me; Genisa is quite free with tales of her personal habits, I would guess."

Summer pursed her lips wryly. "N-Not at all. Their bedchamber is next to mine and I can hear them."

Bose laughed softly, turning in the small bed and catching her against his naked chest comfortably. "Not to worry, love. When you and I are settled at Ravendark, we shall put Genisa and Stephan to shame with our continuous lovemaking."

Summer sighed, snuggled against her husband and feeling exceedingly weary. "I t-thought you said I would not enjoy making love more than once a night."

"I did not say that. I merely said that tonight might be an inappropriate night for such an event due to two very good reasons."

"A-And they are?"

"The fact that you are likely to be sore so soon after your fresh experience. And also because if your cries of passion grow any louder, I expect the priests listening at the door will be forced into an uncomfortable, if not embarrassing, physical situation."

Summer's head came up again. "They are listening to us?"

Bose pushed her head down. "Every word," he kissed her tenderly. "Go to sleep now, love. I'll wake you in the morn."

If Bose wasn't bothered by the eavesdropping of curious priests, then Summer supposed her outrage would be misplaced. After all, they were a newlywed couple and the men of God's Holy Order could hardly expect them to refrain from experiencing the intimacy of their union. With a heavy sigh, she burrowed deep against him.

"G-Good sleep, my darling."

"Good sleep, love."

Summer turned her head slightly, facing toward the bolted chamber door. "Good sleep, priests!" she called softly.

After a moment, footsteps that were making an obvious attempt at silence faded in both directions of the hall. Bose and Summer giggled until they could hardly stand the pain.

CHAPTER SEVENTEEN

T HE MORNING HAD dawned gray and misty, a perpetual coating of moisture gracing the landscape of Chaldon and her surrounding province. Within the castle herself, the last of the great houses were preparing to depart. In spite of the mysterious absence of the du Bonne brother and Bose de Moray for the final round of jousting, a young and virtually unknown knight had emerged victorious in the joust, endearing himself to the crowd with his gracious manners as he accepted his ransom.

Ransom taken from none other than Duncan Kerry. Even now, Duncan lingered in the misty shadows of the keep, watching the activity amidst the wet splattering that continued to fall. His usually lively face was grim, his skin pale and cold. Aye, his mood was as gray as the landscape and sky.

Just before sunrise, Stephan and Ian appeared, speaking to a small collection of men-at-arms. Duncan watched closely, the cold mist bathing his face, as the soldiers listened carefully to the two knights and then quickly disbanded. As Stephan and his brother split in opposite directions, Duncan made way to the oldest sibling.

"Stephan," he hissed, keeping close to the outer wall. "*Stephan!*"

Stephan, clad in durable battle armor and a heavy cloak, paused at the sound of his whispered name. Turning, his bright green eyes focused on the source and for a brief moment, his anger surged. But he banked, a control he had been forced to employ for the better part of the night. Even as Duncan approached, he found himself fighting the urge to wrap his hands around the young knight's neck; *any* Kerry neck.

"Stephan," Duncan was upon him, his handsome face anxious.

"What in the hell is going on? My brother left this morn and would not tell me anything. What's happened to Sir Bose and your sister?"

Stephan's gaze was hard as he stared at the knight, his jaw ticking faintly. "I should be asking you that question. Undoubtedly your brother told you of his plans to steal my sister from her betrothed. And when Bose fled Chaldon with his ladylove in tow, mayhap your brother alluded to his intentions to beat the truth of Bose's destination from Sir Morgan," he braced his powerful fists against his hips. "Or better still, mayhap he explained to you the fact that somehow, Bose's mother-in-law is involved in his corrupt plans. What, in fact, can you tell me, Duncan Kerry?"

Duncan's expression faltered and he lowered his gaze, emitting a heavy sigh. "He… he's been speaking crazy ideas for the past three days. I truly had no idea he planned to follow through."

Stephan's jaw stopped ticking. "Follow through with *what*?"

Duncan closed his eyes briefly, a painful expression. "God's Blood, Stephan, I know I should have come to you sooner… but, truthfully, I never believed Breck capable of carrying out his threats. He oft says things he doesn't mean, insane thoughts that just as quickly pass. I never thought…."

"Damnation, Duncan, what threat?"

Reluctantly, Duncan met Stephan's blazing green orbs. "The threat to destroy de Moray by using your sister against him."

Stephan could only stare at the man. "Why would he seek to destroy Bose? And, more importantly, how does he plan to utilize my sister against him?"

Duncan took a deep breath, praying that the man would not find reason to run him through once he had finished his explanation. "Ever since Bose joined the tournament circuit, my brother has taken every loss and every defeat against the man as a personal attack. He hates Bose for his talent, his strength, and has oft plotted to somehow eliminate him."

"Kill him?"

"Nay," Duncan shook his head. "Merely remove him from the circuit. When he discovered Sir Bose's interest in your sister, he believed he'd found his opportunity. Since he has been unable to physically ruin de Moray, he sought to ruin him through the lady."

The fog of confusion and fury that had plagued Stephan's mind since the previous eve began to dissipate. Of course, Breck had been unable to defeat Bose by the usual means, strength against strength, talent against talent; Bose was far too powerful in both arenas. Therefore, Breck had sought to weaken him on a far more serious level by using his emotions against him.

"So he petitioned for her hand, stealing her away from Bose by using the long-standing rumors against the man's reputation," Stephan's voice was remarkable controlled. "And the Lady Margot, being the source of the vicious rumors, is supporting his quest."

Duncan nodded faintly. "He told me she had offered to help him destroy Sir Bose."

After a moment, Stephan shook his head with disbelief; he wasn't sure if he should be furious or laugh at the foolishness of it.

"An embittered old woman and a sinister young knight join forces, convince my father that Bose is a murderer and should not be allowed to marry my sister, and my father agrees." He snorted ironically. "God's Blood, I can hardly believe what has happened. When I saw the old woman in my father's solar last eve siding with your brother, I could hardly believe her identity. As your brother saw support for his cause in her knowledge of Bose's past, the old bitch apparently also saw the weapon she had been seeking to destroy her son in-law once and for all. She is using your brother, Duncan. Just as he is using her, she is using him as well."

Duncan sighed, a weary gesture. "I have no idea how they found one another. I did not even know she had attended the tourney," scratching his damp head, his expression was pensive. "I am sorry for all of this, Stephan. As I said, I should have come to you earlier, but I had no idea he would go this far. What matters now is what I can do to help. How is Sir Morgan faring?"

Stephan was amazingly calm. The more the situation came to light, the more resigned he became and he ran his fingers through his blond hair, thinking. "Well enough after the pounding he took at your brother's hands. But more importantly than Morgan's health, Breck has gone to retrieve Bose and return him to Dorset to face charges of thievery. At this moment, my brothers and I ride to aid Bose. Unless you are God, I doubt there is anything you can do to prevent the trial that is sure to follow."

Duncan snorted, without humor. "Sometimes I wish I were God. Were I God, I could banish my brother to Hades and never have to worry about him ever again. Even if I were the king, I could...."

Stephan suddenly slapped his thigh, cleaving Duncan's sentence. "Of course! Damnation, I should have realized...what you said! *Henry!*"

Duncan looked to him curiously. "What about him?"

Stephan sought to explain. "Bose used to be young Henry's Captain of the Guard. Bose himself said that Henry was very fond of him and quite sorry to see him quit his post." Quickly, he turned to Duncan, jabbing a gloved finger at the man. "Do you truly wish to help?"

Duncan nodded hesitantly. "Then ride to London immediately," Stephan told him. "Ride to Henry and tell him of the situation and plead for him to intervene. With Bose's very life at stake, surely the king cannot refuse."

The excitement was catching. "I'll go," Duncan said, his pale cheeks gaining a measure of color as he realized his destiny to be at hand. "I will go to London and seek the king, I swear it."

"Good lad," Stephan slapped him on the back, feeling a genuine seed of hope where moments before there had lingered not a solitary grain. "Leave this instant. If you ride hard with scarcely a stop, you can make it by tomorrow eve. Stay no more than a day, for that leaves us very little time to preserve my brother-in-law's life."

Duncan eyed Stephan questioningly. "Your brother-in-law?"

Stephan nodded, steering the young knight in the direction of his partially-collapsed camp. "If all went according to plan, Bose married my sister last night."

Duncan was visibly surprised. "And how would you know this?"

Stephan smiled. "Because I helped them to elope. Surely you did not believe I would see my sister married to a man who broke my wrist. Now, off with you. The entire situation depends upon your speed and persuasion, Duncan. Make me proud."

Make me proud. Breck had never uttered such encouraging words and more than ever, Duncan was determined to do his very best for the sake of all concerned. Were it not for his brother, none of this would have happened. He needed to make restitution for the Kerry name.

"I will, Stephan," his voice was quiet. "I promise, I shall not fail."

Stephan met the soft green eyes, feeling a good deal of trust and compassion for the younger brother of a most evil warrior. And if the man's eyes were a window to his soul, Stephan could see that the soul was as clear as a bottomless mountain lake.

"I know," slapping him on the shoulder once more, he turned in the direction of Chaldon's stables. "Ride hard, Duncan. At this moment, I am bound for Ravendark to make sure your brother doesn't do anything foolish to my sister and her new husband should he be fortunate enough to ensnare them. If a trial is imminent, I'll delay it as best I can."

Duncan had never run so fast in his entire life.

CஒB

THREE MILES OUT of Ravendark, Summer found the day to be bright and lovely. Leaving Salisbury at dawn, she had been surprised that Dag had not seen them off; Bose, too, had seemed concerned with his cousin's lack of appearance but refrained from voicing his distress. The necessary marriage documents had awaited him and that was the only true matter of import.

So they pushed onward, traveling through the dark, misty morn as Summer slumbered lightly against her husband's armored chest. When the sun exploded upon the wide horizon and burned away the lingering haze, Lady de Moray found herself roused for the coming day by a husband weary of riding alone and silent as his wife dozed the time away.

Refreshed and free of the sneezing that had plagued her most of the night, Summer was unperturbed that Bose had aroused her to a clear morning and spent most of her time observing the scenery as soft conversation flowed.

"This is my property," Bose said from behind her, his visor raised and his stubbled face vigilant. "My men and I hunt in these woods constantly."

"Hunt?" Summer frowned. "What do you hunt? My b-brothers like to hunt, but I forbid them to kill anything precious or sweet."

He cocked an eyebrow. "That leaves very little choice."

She grinned, turning to face him. "Untrue. You have my permission to kill wild boar or opossum or skunk. But I forbid you to kill rabbit or deer."

"I like to kill deer."

"No longer. Sate your blood lust on a useless, ugly animal."

"Like Breck?"

Summer laughed. "We shall d-display his head above our hearth and throw the rest of the carcass to the dogs."

He grinned. "How barbaric, Lady de Moray. I like the idea very much."

She continued to smile, touching his scarred cheek. "'Twould be justice well served. Speaking of the Devil, how are your stitches."

"Itching," he grumbled, putting his fingers to his scalp as if she had reminded him of his discomfort. "I must wash my hair tonight of the sweat and dirt so that the wound does not fester."

"I cleaned it well enough so that it s-should not become infected," she said, catching sight of the delicate black sutures. After a moment, her gaze trailed to the three parallel scars that ran along his cheek, touching the thick, puckered skin. "I doubt the scar will be worse than these. How did you acquire them?"

"Margot," he replied without hesitation. "She did this to me on the day I learned of Lora's death. 'Twas her way of expressing her grief, I suppose, raking her nails across my face in anguish."

Summer's pleasant expression vanished, her eyes taking on a distinct countenance of horror. "Good Lord, Bose... she *scratched* you? I believed you to have encountered a wild animal or... or a terrible weapon of some kind. D-Do you mean to tell me that a frail old woman rent these scars across your face?"

He nodded faintly, kissing her hand when it came close to his lips. "She did. And I let her." When Summer's appalled expression focused inquisitively on his onyx-black eyes, he found he could hardly hold her gaze. "'Tis difficult to explain. It was as if I welcomed the pain, as if somehow I was accepting punishment for Lora's death. Accepting judgment for what I had done."

Summer's features softened. "We've had this discussion b-before," she said quietly. "You did not kill Lora. 'Twas God's will that she perished in childbirth and you must come to realize that."

He merely shrugged and looked away, but Summer would not be put off so easily. Her intelligent mind began to work. "Tell me, Bose; if C-Chaldon was under attack and I asked you to help defend her, would you do it?"

"Without hesitation. 'Tis my duty, as your husband."

"And you would do it gladly?"

"Of course."

Summer cocked her head. "And if you were killed, would it be my fault for asking you to fight?"

He could see where she was leading and he shut his mouth, refusing to answer her until she grasped his chin and forced him to look at her. Eye to eye, his stubborn stance melted in the wake of her searing golden gaze.

"Nay, love. It would not be your fault."

She cocked a well-defined brow. "But I asked it of you."

He sighed, knowing the answer she was expecting. "And I complied willingly."

She smiled. So did he. Gently, she kissed his smooth lips. "You see? Lora was willing to make the attempt, knowing it was her duty in life. And her attempt failed, but it had nothing to do with you."

He held her gaze a moment, sighing heavily and with great emotion. Grasping the back of her head with his free hand, he kissed her until she squealed. "You are far too wise for your own good, Lady de Moray," he murmured against her lips. "I realize that I will never be able to win an argument against you."

Summer smiled and his kissed her teeth. "Never," she agreed. "Your days of domination are ended."

Exhaling with contentment, Summer turned to face forward on the charger once again, eager to reach Ravendark and commence her new life. For certain, she had never felt so completely satisfied or needed, as a wife should be; the world that had eluded her grasp was finally hers for the taking and she was eager to know the progression of her newly content existence. Around her waist, Bose's arm tightened and she smiled, patting his gloved hand. He was anxious to reach his fortress, too, for more reasons than she could grasp.

"Do you s-suppose your knights are waiting for us?" she asked.

"If they left Chaldon when we did, undoubtedly," Bose could nearly see the tip of his northern turret in the distance. "In fact, I should have expected to meet a welcoming party by now."

Summer looked about, the heavy clusters of foliage and endless meadows beyond. "We are still a good distance out," she offered helpfully, noting Bose appeared somewhat perturbed when she turned to look at him. "T-Tell me, husband; what are Ravendark's sundry functions?"

Bose answered even though he was still on the lookout for his knights. "Aside from the fortune I have built on the tournament circuit, Ravendark has three small herds of cattle. We do adequately well selling beeves and hide."

"No textiles or sheep?"

"This isn't Yorkshire, Summer," he said with a faint smile. "The Wiltshire countryside is fairly devoid of lush lands and soil. But there is enough to sustain the cattle and whatever flocks the villeins cultivate."

She pondered his statement a moment, indeed noticing the chalky downs that covered the Wiltshire landscape. "S-Surely with all of this land, Ravendark can be made far more profitable by increasing her herds and expanding her interests. Have you ever given thought to raising goat for their milk and cheese?"

He raised an eyebrow, amused. "You mentioned that your father's steward schooled you in basic learning. Am I now to be the recipient of your grand knowledge of profit and fortune?"

She laughed softly. "I t-took over all stewardship duties when Kermit passed away last winter and I am rather proud of the fact that Chaldon has never run more smoothly. I can do the same for Ravendark too."

He nodded faintly, knowing she was an intelligent and educated woman but truly having no idea how deeply the vein of knowledge ran. Instead of feeling threatened by her mind as most men would have been, the idea of his brilliant wife taking charge of Ravendark and her holdings pleased him immensely. She pleased him immensely.

"I would be very interested in any and all ideas you might have on the subject, Lady de Moray."

Resting against her husband's mighty chest armor, Summer was flattered by his declaration of confidence; not all men were acceptant of a woman whose intellectual education neared their own.

"We make a good deal of cheese at Chaldon," she continued on thoughtfully. "Mayhap we could use the milk f-from your cattle to mass-produce cheese and sell it. If we make enough money, mayhap you can leave the tournament circuit altogether."

"And help you make cheese?"

She nodded, feeling his soft chuckle against her ear. "Blue V-Vinny cheese is delicious. It's indigenous to Dorset, you know. Why, the entire province is famous for its blue-veined cheese and...."

In the quieting trees flanking the dirt trail, a branch snapped loudly and Bose suddenly stiffened in the saddle, interrupting his wife's prattle as his entire body tensed with anticipation. He was already moving for his sword when the bleak foliage surrounding the roadway suddenly came alive with men on horseback, shouting and whooping in a most terrifying manner.

Summer shrieked, instinctively covering her face protectively as Bose deftly collected his shield, throwing it up in front of his wife in an effort to protect her from the onslaught. But the destrier startled as the roar turned deafening, rearing on its hind legs in fear. With both hands occupied, Bose had no chance to grab her as she fell to the dusty road in a heap.

"Summer!" he cried, using an impassioned tone she had never heard before. "Hurry, love, come to me! Come to...!"

His desperate plea was cut short as several men rushed him, bombarding him with their swords and battleaxes. Summer shrieked again, laboring to regain her footing as massive hooves threatened to crush her. Stumbling away from the action, she fell to her knees on the damp grass, ugly green stains ground deep into the fabric. She barely had a chance to regain her balance and her breath when gloved hands were grabbing harshly at her wrist.

"Ha!" came the triumphant cry. "Think not to escape me again, wench, for now I have you!"

Hair hanging wildly in her face, Summer managed to right herself, struggling ferociously against the iron grip to her arm. Through all of the twisting and gasping and restrained screams, her hair moved from her vision and she suddenly found herself face to face with Breck Kerry.

He smiled lewdly at her, a smile she had come to hate terribly over the past three days. Instinctively, without thought, she brought a clawed hand to bear on his pimpled face and with a powerful, vicious surge, raked her sharp nails across his reddened cheek in an act of self-defense.

Breck screamed like a woman, releasing his hold on her arm. Whimpering in panic, Summer stumbled away from him, struggling with every ounce of strength to reach Bose as he engaged several men on the chalky dirt road. Crying his name, fumbling in a blind panic, she was entirely focused on his armored charger when something grabbed her about the ankles. Falling heavily, Breck's bleeding, furious face loomed over her and she opened her mouth to scream at the terrible sight of him.

A scream of terror that never came as a blow to the head jarred her into blissful darkness. Heaving and panting, Breck grabbed his unconscious quarry by the arms, slinging her limp form over his shoulder. He began to shout Bose's name, struggling to be heard over the sounds of battle. But no amount of shouting would gain him the man's attention until Bose happened to turn in his direction, his panicked black eyes searching for his wife. He found her lying across Breck Kerry's shoulder.

His sword clattered to the ground. The shield did not and he fought off several heavy blows before Breck's order to cease was obeyed. Slowly, the mass of men came to an unsteady halt as all concerned focused on the red-haired knight bearing the lifeless lady. And none more focused upon the man's face than Bose himself.

The shield fell beside the discarded sword as Bose swiftly dismounted, shoving his fist into the face of a man who attempted to stop him. As the wounded soldier fell away, Bose's black eyes were smoldering as he focused on Breck.

"Give her to me." It was not a request; it was a command.

Shifting Summer's weight, Breck wiped at the blood on his cheek. "I have come to claim my bride, de Moray, and to escort you back to Chaldon to stand trial for thievery."

Bose maintained his advance on the small man, shoving aside another soldier who was foolish enough to get in his way. Ignoring the knight's statement, he extended his arms demandingly.

"Give her to me now."

Breck stumbled back, away from the approaching knight, tripping over his feet in the process. Bose seemed to lose a measure of his composure as Breck struggled to regain his balance, fearful that his wife would be dropped to the unforgiving ground below. He slowed his advance somewhat, but not entirely. He meant to regain Summer and was determined to accomplish his goal.

"Come no closer, de Moray, or I might not be able to keep your lover from falling to the ground the next time," his threat was confident. "There is no way to know what she would strike upon landing. Her head. Her beautiful face. Would you see her come to ruin?"

Bose's expression darkened as he slowed his pace. "You damnable bastard," he growled, an accusation and not a display of emotion. "You've no quarrel against her. Give her to me this instant."

Breck cocked an eyebrow. "Not until I extract a promise first."

Bose came to a stop. Standing a few feet in front of Breck, there was nothing more he could say or do to turn the situation in his favor. Already, the circumstance was out of control.

"What is it?"

Breck eyed him. "I will return her to you for safekeeping if you promise to return to Chaldon peacefully. Do I have your vow in the matter?"

"Aye."

"Any deviation will be swiftly met. Against the lady, of course."

"I gave you my word, Kerry. Now give me my wife."

Breck's eyebrows rose in genuine surprise. "Wife? Do... do you mean to tell me that you have actually married her?"

Bose regained some of his lost composure as Breck seemed to falter. "She was my betrothed before she was erroneously pledged to you," he said coolly. "Did you truly believe I would abduct her from Chaldon for any other reason but to marry her? To consummate our marriage so that you could never have her? A foolish belief if those were indeed your hopes, Kerry. I have done all of that and more."

Breck's red face washed a deeper shade of color. "I... I knew you left Chaldon to elude me, of course. But I also knew, eventually, you would have to return to Ravendark and therein would lie your capture." Taking a deep breath, he shifted Summer again upon his tiring shoulder. "After you are executed for your deed, I will annul the marriage and the lady will become my legal wife. And I shall take pleasure in erasing all memory of you upon her mind and body. Especially her body."

His men chuckled rudely but Bose refused to react. Consummately controlled, he maintained a steady expression.

"I have given you my vow to return peacefully to Chaldon," he rumbled. "You will give me my wife."

Still chortling with his lascivious thoughts, Breck shifted Summer's body from his armored shoulder and practically threw the woman into Bose's waiting arms. Cradling his wife to him tenderly, his heart sank when he noticed blood trickling from her left ear.

"God's Beard," he muttered, smoothing the hair away from her pale face. "She needs a physic, Kerry. I have a man who tends my soldiers and...."

Breck waved him off disinterestedly, more concerned with regaining his wandering charger. "We've no time to spare. The surgeon at Chaldon will attend her."

For the first time since the ambush, Bose's cheeks colored with his surging fury and concern. "For the sake of Mercy, Kerry, allow me to send to Ravendark for my surgeon. He is less than two miles away and I refuse to allow Summer to be carried over miles, injured, simply because you are intent to return me to Chaldon as soon as possible. She needs to be tended to immediately."

An obedient soldier had captured Breck's unruly charger, handing the reins to his smug liege. "If she is still breathing, she can make it back to Chaldon. Moreover, your surgeon will have his hands full when your men hap across the patrol I was forced to subdue. The patrol that was waiting for you, I suspect, to escort you home."

Bose's expression hardened. Momentarily diverted from Summer's injured state, he found himself disturbed by Breck's callous statement; no wonder a welcoming escort of soldiers had not awaited him as he approached the fortress. Kerry had disposed of them all in his murderous determination to capture their evasive liege. "Subdue? Or murder?"

Breck mounted his great beast. "I had no choice but to disable them. Not only would they have made your capture quite difficult, but they would have alerted the troops within Ravendark's walls to my presence. I could not take that chance."

Bose sighed faintly, with tremendous disgust. "Where are my men, Kerry? What have you done with them?"

Breck tilted his head toward the southeast. "In the woods beyond. Adgar put up an admirable fight, but he was simply overwhelmed by our number. A shame, truly. He was a fine knight."

Bose closed his eyes tightly, briefly, in a painful display of emotion. Adgar Ross, a knight whose intelligence and wisdom had been an immense source of comfort, had been a great asset to Bose's company of fighting men. Already, Bose missed the man and his quiet sense of humor and as the news filtered deep into his heart, the more enraged he became at the senseless, needless action.

"You did not have to kill him," his bass-toned voice was scarcely audible. "'Twas me you wanted. There was no need to take Adgar's life."

Breck gathered his reins, fussing with the leather straps. "Aye, it was completely necessary," he replied carelessly, gesturing for his men to escort the two captives to de Moray's subdued charger. "Mount up, Sir Bose. If we ride hard, we can make it to Chaldon come sunrise and be done with this unpleasantness."

Bose stared at the sinister knight, feeling the piercing jab of a collection of broadswords against his backside. Afraid Summer would be taken from him if he did not comply, he kissed her softly and gathered his reins as an escort of armed men surrounded him.

The horses began to move and Summer abruptly stirred, breaking Bose from his train of thought. Features etched with great concern, he

patted her cheek lightly in an attempt to bring her out of unconscious-
ness.

"Summer?" he whispered, kissing the hand that flailed against his
face. "Can you hear me, love? Open your eyes and look at me."

She sighed raggedly, batting at the left side of her head. "Bose?" she
murmured thickly. "What... what ha-happened?"

Her golden eyes rolled open, glazed and cloudy and he smiled,
partially with relief and partially to ease her dazed mind. "A small
setback, love. Nothing to worry over. We are returning to Chaldon."

The half-lidded eyes suddenly opened wide. "Breck!" she gasped,
her hand still to the left side of her head. "He f-found us! He grabbed
me and...Good Lord, my head hurts terribly."

A massive hand stroked her hair gently as Bose attempted to mask
his anxiety; a blow to the head, no matter how weak or insignificant,
was not a good thing and he struggled to contain his concerned
demeanor. "I know, love. I am sorry I could not protect you better."

Rubbing at her ear, she shushed him softly. In spite of her throbbing head, she was coming to think rationally and she sat up slightly,
the sway of the horse and the pounding inside her skull causing her
stomach to twist.

"You were correct all along," she murmured, glancing about at the
Kerry guards and swallowing her nausea. "Breck and my father were
indeed on our trail. But I d-do not see any du Bonne men. Where are
they?"

Bose shook his head, holding her tightly, protectively, as she endeavored to sit upright on his thighs. "There aren't any," his reply was
soft. "'Twould seem that only Breck and his troops have managed to
capture us. I'd be very interested to know where Edward du Bonne's
interests lie in all of this."

"Where my f-father is concerned, it is difficult to know," she shifted
slightly, attempting to find a measure of comfort as her upset stomach
and dismal thoughts took hold. "What will happen n-now?"

Behind her, she felt his heavy sigh on the top of her head. "Breck intends to return me to Chaldon to stand trial for thievery. You, I would assume, will be held at the fortress until my trial is over and the sentencing is carried out."

She did not like the sound of his response. Fighting off dread and panic, she clutched at the massive arm wound tightly around her waist. "Good Lord, B-Bose, what does that mean? What sentence?"

"Probably death."

Her body stiffened and he clapped a hand over her mouth before the scream could escape her lips. Mouth pressed close to her ear, Bose's breath was hot upon her flesh.

"Calm yourself, love. You know as well as I that Stephan will not allow this to happen. God willing, neither will your father when he sees the truth of the matter." When he saw the splatter of tears on his armored gauntlet, he squeezed her gently. "No tears, Summer. Please. I need you to be calm and brave for me, love. We've far too much ahead of us to allow emotions to interfere with our determination."

Although she sobbed softly once or twice, she nonetheless endeavored to dry her eyes. "You n-never said y-you would b-b-be ki...k-killed. You n-never s-said...."

He squeezed her tightly, silencing her stammering words. "But you knew it was entirely probable that I would be tried for the crime of abducting you, be it kidnap or robbery or thievery. But the fact that we have consummated our marriage will weigh heavily in our favor. If I am forced to answer to the charges and the magistrate rules in our favor, at the very worst I'll be ordered to repay your dowry to Breck in compensation for the loss of his bride."

She sniffled pathetically. "B-But if you are found guilty, they'll do what they do to all thieves. They'll... t-t-they'll execute you."

Bose did not reply, eyeing Breck as the man turned around and noticed that Summer had regained consciousness. When the pock-faced knight returned his attention to the road ahead, Bose endeavored to answer his wife's fearful statement. "You knew this from the inception, love. With all that we have undertaken, you've always known the potential consequences. Why panic now?"

"B-Because we weren't captured before. And b-because I believed you would return us to Ravendark before Breck or my father could find us. I suppose I never truly believed we would be facing these circumstances."

He was quiet for a moment. "Then I am sorry to have disappointed you," his voice was husky. "I suppose I was a victim of my own confidence. I, too, believed we could make it to the safety of Ravendark and thereby elude capture. Yet with everything that could potentially befall us, I believed my marriage to you to far outweigh the repercussions of our actions. You were the only matter of import."

Tears and nausea forgotten, Summer turned to face him. Pale and damp-eyed, her expression was nonetheless gentle and warm. "You did not disappoint me," she murmured, touching his scarred, rugged cheek. "You've exceeded my wildest dreams. But that does not prevent me from worrying over your fate."

He met her smile, kissing her gently. "We took a chance, love. 'Twould seem that Fortune did not favor us this day."

She kissed him again, feeling her throat constrict with emotion as her cheek rested against his stubbled flesh. But she fought the tide of sentiment, knowing he had asked her to be brave.

"F-Fortune has been favoring us since the day of our introduction," she whispered, her lips to his jaw. "Surely it will not disappoint us in our hour of need."

Bose did not reply and Summer lifted her eyes, studying his intent expression. His black eyes were focused in the distance, his features taut and unreadable. Curious and concerned, Summer turned in the direction of his focus and was mildly alarmed to see a rather large company of men bearing down on them. When she turned to question her husband as to the identity of the incoming riders, she was shocked to discover a smile upon his lips.

"B-Bose?" she intoned questioningly. "Who is it?"

He continued to stare at the approaching party, his smile broadening by the moment. When Summer prodded him gently, he tore his gaze away from the distant vision and gave her a saucy, hopeful wink.

"It's Fortune, I think."

Her eyebrows furrowed deeply. "Fortune? Make sense."

He nodded his head vaguely, his attention returned to the incoming tide of soldiers. "I have," he said quietly. "You said Fortune has been with us since the moment of our introduction. And he has arrived once more."

"Who has?"

Bose was silent a moment, feeling a good deal of relief in the cluster of recognizable soldiers and three very familiar knights.

"Fortune and his brothers," he said with satisfaction. "I believe, my love, that Stephan has arrived in time to escort us home."

CHAPTER EIGHTEEN

I N SPITE OF the fact that the day had dawned bright and clear, the mood of Chaldon was darker than the Devil himself. A sense of doom seemed to infiltrate man and beast alike.

On the second floor of the mighty keep, the anxiety was palpable. Summer felt the pain, and had ever since she had watched her husband taken away to the vault like a common thief. It was a pain that scorched every aspect of her even as her brothers attempted to comfort her and as Genisa cradled her.

Stephan had endeavored to prepare her for the extent of Breck's case and the support of Bose's mother-in-law to sustain his cause. The ride back to Chaldon, Summer and Bose had found themselves encircled by loyal du Bonne troops as the Kerry soldiers lingered about, suspicious and volatile, and none more suspicious and mistrustful than Breck himself. He was positive that Stephan and his brothers were preparing to steal his prisoners.

But there was no jailbreak and as the fortress of Chaldon drew near, the tension began to mount and the moment the party entered the gates of the massive courtyard, Breck took control of his betrothed's husband and ordered the man confined to the vault. It was a bad situation that grew worse when Summer dissolved into tears, clinging to Bose and refusing to release her hold. Breck had moved toward her, planning to disengage her himself until he was brutally halted by Ian. The biggest, most collected du Bonne brother practically strangled Breck before Lance and Stephan pulled him free. Breck then tried to retaliate and the situation grew out of control until the prisoner himself intervened.

Sedate and composed as always, Bose gently removed himself from his weeping wife purely for the sake of calming the situation. With dignity befitting his character, he had allowed Breck to lead him to the vault.

That had been the last Summer had seen of her husband. Edward had refused to allow her to visit him and Stephan had spent the entire night in deep, argumentative conference with his father and a triumphant Breck. A missive had been sent to Lord Bruce Eggardon the day before and a reply was expected shortly; therefore, there was nothing to do at the moment but wait.

Disheveled and exhausted from her night of hysterics, Summer had ignored the morning meal brought to her room and the serving wench who had politely offered to bathe her. Still clad in the amber silk, her luscious hair was ratty and unkempt as she gazed over the brilliant green fields of Dorset, noting the remnants of the lodges and tournament field in the distance with disinterest.

She was so consumed with her muddled thoughts that she failed to hear the knock at the chamber door. Genisa let herself in, slowly opening the panel to reveal her heartbroken sister-in-law. With a sigh of tremendous remorse, she quietly shut the door behind her.

"Summer darling," she said softly. "I have brought a fresh gown. I thought mayhap…."

"Nay," Summer's voice was as dull as her heart. "No gown. No nothing."

Genisa laid the lovely peach-colored surcoat across a carved oaken chair, moving timidly toward the grieving woman. She had no idea what to say, the words that would come forth to ease Summer's pain. Noting the hardened porridge upon the tray by the bed, she reached out to finger the uneaten loaf of bread.

"Cook made the honey and currant bread just for you," she said quietly. "She knows how much you love it. Why not try some, darling? Just a bit?"

Summer continued to stare from the window. Only one thought seemed to overshadow all others.

"Has Stephan seen him yet?" she asked, her voice hoarse. "F-Father refused to allow me to see him."

"Stephan has been with your father and Breck Kerry since last night," Genisa replied, feeling so helpless to ease her sister-in-law's ache. "Ian is with them, too, in support of Stephan. Lance spent the night with Bose in the vault, refusing to allow any of Breck's men to see or speak with him. The tension and hatred surrounding the situation is brittle to say the least."

Summer turned away from the window then, her eyes somewhat brighter as Genisa's information registered. "Lance spent the night with him?" she repeated, the first ray of hope since the previous night. "How sweet. Strange, he seemed to be the most reluctant toward my relationship with Bose. I s-suppose he's changed his mind."

"They have *all* changed their minds, Summer," Genisa noted that Summer seemed to be emerging from her dull state somewhat. "Come now, darling. Eat something and change your clothes, and we shall see if Stephan has obtained permission for you to visit Bose."

Summer's brow furrowed stubbornly and she shook her head, her dark-circled eyes dull once again. "I d-do not want to. I am not hungry and...."

"You do not want Bose to see you like this, do you?" Genisa pressed. "He's not seen you since yesterday. Do you want him to see a dirty, unkempt wife still in the clothing she slept in?"

Summer blinked in thought, a look of uncertainty creasing her features. As she moved woodenly away from the window and toward the massive posted bed, Antony emerged from his nest amongst the silken pillows and scampered into her comforting, soothing hands. Summer stared at the furry beast, stroking it as tears sprang to her eyes.

"Oh, N-N-Nise," she suddenly sobbed, collapsing on the bed. "H-He's in the v-vault and it's my fault! I shouldn't have...!"

Genisa sat beside her, drawing the weeping woman fiercely into her arms. "You did what you had to, Summer," she whispered sincerely. "You did what I would have done, what any of us would have done. Do not blame yourself for following your heart."

Summer clung to her, sobbing as if her heart was breaking. "H-He's put his life in jeopardy. How can I face l-life k-knowing that I have killed him?"

"He's not dead yet," releasing the hysterical woman from her crushing embrace, she grasped Summer's face gently but firmly. "Listen to me; you must trust that Stephan will not allow Bose's execution. Certainly, he was a party to your abduction and he will not allow Bose to take the wrath alone. I know it is difficult, darling, but please have faith. You must be strong."

You must be strong. Bose had made the very same request of her yesterday and, already, she was severely disobeying him. In fact, since the very moment her husband had been led away to the vault, she had been the antithesis of strength. Certainly not the qualities Bose expected from his wife. He had pleaded for calm and faith, and she had ignored his request for the most part.

Gazing into Genisa's eyes, Summer suddenly felt foolish and ashamed. Her family was rallying to her cause and she was repaying them by displaying her shallow and self-centered character. The longer she gazed into her sister-in-law's lovely face, the more powerful her embarrassment and sense of restitution became.

"Oh, Genisa," she whispered urgently. "I d-do have faith, truly. 'Tis simply that... this entire circumstance has me terribly unnerved. I never meant to convey my lack of belief in my brothers' cause."

Genisa smiled her charming, toothy grin. "I know," she said gently. "Stephan sent word to Ravendark this morn regarding Bose's imprisonment. His knights, save Morgan, should be arriving shortly to support you in your hour of need."

Summer sniffled, wiping at her damp eyes. "W-Why isn't Morgan coming?"

Genisa's smile faded somewhat. "He's here at Chaldon, recovering from Breck's beating. When you and Bose fled the keep, Breck arrested Morgan in the hope that the man would be able to tell him where Bose had taken you. Morgan, of course, knew nothing and was severely pounded until Stephan stopped the interrogation."

Summer's face was pale with shock. "Good Lord," she breathed. "W-Will he recover?"

Genisa nodded faintly. "He's already walking about, demanding to be allowed to join Bose in the vault. The only reason he did not come to you last night was because he and Stephan agreed you needed time alone."

Summer sighed faintly, sickened by the thought of Morgan's unnecessary torture. "'T-Twas probably good that he did not attempt to comfort me. I would have embarrassed myself with uncontrollable hysteria."

Genisa snorted softly. "Nonetheless, you have many, many people to support and love you, darling. You must remember that."

"I do," Summer said sincerely, wiping the last of the moisture from her eyes. Looking to the peach-colored surcoat strewn across the chair, she gestured toward the garment. "I-I do believe I shall take your advice. Help me to bathe and dress and we shall see if Stephan has been successful in gaining permission for me to see my husband."

"As you say, Lady de Moray," she replied with a twinkle in her eye.

The mood lifted as the two women procured water for bathing and began to arrange Summer's toilette. As Lady de Moray was preparing to disrobe for her bath, the door to her chamber suddenly burped and rattled with a great commotion and the ladies yelped with surprise. But their shock was quickly quelled a moment later when the door swung open and a very familiar, very annoying face made a staggering appearance. The pig masks, minus one, had returned.

"Aarrgh!" A pair of clawed hands scratched the air of the chamber menacingly.

Summer sighed heavily, shaking her head as Lance made a not-too-entirely appropriate appearance. Hands on hips, she frowned at her youngest brother.

"What are y-you doing?" she demanded.

Lance growled again, coming closer as if to accost her. Summer lashed out a foot and caught him in the shin, turning his growls to howls. As he grabbed his leg and collapsed on the bed in agony, she stood over him threateningly.

"T-There is no time for your foolishness, Lance," she scolded, joined by Genisa's disapproving support. "Why are you not with Bose?"

Lance rubbed his bruised bone. "I was," he groaned, his voice was muffled through the tanned leather. "I was with him all night, listening to his sickening tales of your wedding. For truth, I had to leave or become ill."

Summer pinched him and he yelped, holding his wounded arm as well as his assaulted leg. "God's Blood, Summer, cease your abuse. Your husband is safe and sound with Morgan to keep him company."

Her furrowed brow seemed to relax somewhat. "Morgan took your place with him?"

The pig mask nodded. "And I came to cheer you up. But it's not cheer you need, I see, but a spanking."

Summer's irritation with her brother fled; the man had spent all night in the vault with Bose, still, he was thinking of his sister in his childish attempts to ease her suffering. Truthfully, only Lance was capable of such foolish, tender gestures and she smiled, rubbing the flesh she had pinched.

"I am sorry," she murmured. "Was I terribly brutal?"

"Terribly," Lance pushed himself off the bed, continuing to massage his leg. "But I shall forgive you, considering the hell you have been through for the past few days."

Summer reached up, dislodging the pig mask so she could gaze into the eyes of her high-spirited brother. After a brief pause, she kissed him tenderly on the cheek.

"T-Thank you, Lance," she whispered. "For remaining with Bose in the vault. And for the pig mask. Both mean a great deal to me."

He grinned, pinching her chin lightly. "My pleasure, Lady de Moray," it was as close as he could come to a truly affectionate response without risking embarrassment. Glancing at Genisa's smiling face, he scratched his head wearily and moved for the door, his actions suddenly laced with fatigue.

"I suppose I should grab a bit of sleep," he mumbled, grasping the iron door latch. Casting a long glance at the two ladies, he gestured to the pig mask. "The next time I wear this, I shall not allow either of you to escape so easily."

Summer's expression was quite serious. "And I'll tell B-Bose if your threats are sincere. He shall protect me."

Genisa crossed her arms with equal resolve. "As Stephan will protect me. Your days of masking are over, Lance."

Although their threats dampened his enthusiasm substantially, the stubborn young lad in him refused to give in so easily. In spite of the circumstances clouding Chaldon, at this moment, the interaction between the youngest du Bonne brother and his two usual victims had never seemed more typical or more hopeful.

"Never!" he laughed wickedly as he fled down the corridor.

Summer could not keep from smiling. He had come to cheer her up and he had accomplished his goal.

Ↄ

"I W-WANT TO see my husband. You have no valid right to deny my request."

Seated before her father in the peach-colored surcoat, Summer was very controlled. Stephan, his face shadowed with a heavy carpet of stubble, stood slightly behind his sister in powerful support of her request and Ian, his blue eyes dulled with fatigue and lack of sleep, stood to her immediate left.

"The man who married you is a prisoner, Summer," Edward's voice was weak, his face pale and his lips an odd shade of blue. "He is denied the right of visitors."

"Why? L-Lance was with him all night. Why cannot I see him?"

Edward sighed, refusing to look at either Stephan or Ian as he squirmed restlessly in his chair. They'd been through this particular subject all night and Edward was coming to regret the very day he allowed Breck Kerry and Margot de Ville into his chambers. Since that moment, nothing had gone as planned.

"Lance was protecting your… husband from possible assassination by loyalist extremes from both sides," he replied weakly. "His presence was necessary."

Before Summer could reply, Ian cast his father a disbelieving look. "Lance spent the night with Bose to prevent Kerry's men from abusing him. Summer's husband has nothing to fear from the du Bonne soldiers."

"There is much tension and strife within the walls of Chaldon, not merely within the House of Kerry," Margot's voice was thin but firm. "Sir Bose is greatly at risk until his trial can be completed and justice is served."

Summer focused on the frail, bird-like woman seated slightly behind her father. Her golden eyes drew in the sight of the woman who had commenced four years ago with her sinister gossip in the hopes of destroying her grieving son-in-law. The longer Summer gazed upon the lady, the more her hatred for the woman grew.

"Lady Margot," she began evenly. "My request and conversation is directed at my father and I would ask that you refrain from entering this c-conversation. This is a family matter and your opinion is not invited."

Margot's expression held steady. "Instead of exhibiting your rude behavior, you should be thanking me for saving your life. I more than anyone is aware of Bose de Moray's murderous capabilities and it is by the grace of God that Breck intercepted your husband before he could seal you within Ravendark's impenetrable halls."

Summer stared at her, looking beyond the wrinkled, polished exterior, attempting to read the motives beneath. After a moment, she shook her head in a slow, puzzled gesture.

"Why are you d-doing this?" she whispered, experiencing a genuine need to know. "Why are you involving yourself in affairs that do not concern you? I am well aware of the rumors regarding Bose and I am well aware that they are fabrications. If I choose to marry this man, then it should be of little difference to you w-whether I live or die at his hands. It is my choice, lady; certainly not yours."

Margot rose from her chair. "It may not be my choice, but Bose de Moray had always been my concern. When you involved yourself with him, you became my affair as well."

"I do not want you involved. I want you to leave us alone."

"'Tis not your choice to make," Margot cast a glance at Edward. "Your father knows what is best for you and he has given his decision. As a respectful daughter, you should have obeyed his wishes."

"As your respectful daughter always obeyed you?"

It was an intentional jab to unsteady her confident manner. Margot looked to Summer once again, her thin lips pressing into a tight flat line. "My daughter was the pinnacle of female strengths and perfection, Lady Summer. Unflawed, as you are."

Summer could see the pure venom in the woman's eyes. But she could also see that her mention of Lora had struck a chord deep within the embittered woman's heart and she sought to pursue the subject.

She cocked her head thoughtfully. "Tell me, my lady; did your d-daughter love Bose?"

Margot's eyes narrowed, struggling not to appear too off-guard by the question. "That is none of your affair."

"When Bose became my husband, his relationship with his dead wife indeed became my affair. Now answer me; did she love him?"

Margot stiffened, drawing in a deep, steadying breath; all eyes were upon her and she was well aware that her calm conduct was necessary.

Her answer, when it came moments later, was quiet. "She did."

Summer cocked an eyebrow, feeling as if she were gaining headway somehow. She intended to make a point.

"T-Then would it be fair to ask that if she was indeed as perfect in mind and deeds as you profess, would she have approved of your hostile attitude toward her beloved husband?"

Margot struggled to remain collected, but with every successive moment her composure successively cracked. Stephan watched, Ian watched, Breck and Edward watched intently as the elderly woman downed a small chalice of wine before calmly answering.

"She would applaud my efforts to vindicate her death."

Summer watched the lady pour another swallow of wine into the glass goblet. "At the expense of the man she loved?"

Margot dropped the chalice half-way to her lips; the burgundy liquid erupted onto the wall, the floor, as the pewter bounced along the stone. Laboring to control her emotion, Margot faced her son-in-law's new wife.

"You know nothing of the situation," she hissed. "Certainly you see the circumstance as Bose has explained it, not how it truly exists. And your foolish questions allude to your naive understanding of the situation."

Summer refused to back down, not when the lady was growing increasingly agitated. If she were going to accomplish anything, she had to strive onward.

"V-Very well, then," Summer was in control. "Allow me to accept your explanation of events, assuming for a moment that Bose did indeed murder your daughter. Can you tell me, exactly, how he accomplished this task?"

Margot ceased to breathe for a moment, off-balanced by the calm question. Summer lifted her eyebrows questioningly when there was no immediate response.

"How, my lady? How did she die? D-Did he strangle her, stab her?"

"Nay."

"Did he beat her?"

"Nay."

Summer observed the woman closely, her thin lips pale and dry as she struggled to maintain her bold, aggressive gaze.

"Of course he did not," her voice was suddenly quiet-toned. "He loved her. He loved her enough to give her a son, which she died attempting to bring into this world. B-Bose did not murder Lora for profit or thrill. He was an innocent victim of her death, just as she and the son she carried were also hapless casualties. But you, unable to understand the will of God, found the need to fault him simply because there was no one else to blame. And in your grief, you attempted to destroy him. Just as Lora's death destroyed you."

By the time Summer finished speaking, Margot's face was as pallid as new snow. Her mouth worked a moment as if struggling to bring forth a rebuttal but the words sought refused to be heard.

"You do not know what you are saying," she managed to rasp.

Faintly, Summer nodded. "Aye, I know m-more than you would believe," she said evenly. "I know that you have spread vicious rumors in an attempt to punish your son-in-law for loving your daughter enough to bless her with a child. I k-know that you hate him and depend on him at the same time. And I know that you must be terribly jealous of me, as the second wife of your daughter's husband. P-Please tell me if I am wrong."

Control splintering, Margot labored to maintain her defenses. "You... you are wrong!" she spat, kicking aside the chalice on the floor as she advanced. "He killed her, murdering her with his massive child!"

"B-But it was not an intentional deed."

"It doesn't matter!" Margot shrieked; as she moved swiftly toward Summer, Stephan and Ian tensed, preparing to defend their sister against the raging old shrew. But Summer stopped them, holding up a quelling hand as the furious woman drew near. "Whether or not my Lora's death was intentional, Bose was responsible. He accepted that responsibility the day he married her."

Summer, not strangely, was quite calm. Confidence in her argument made her so. "I-I am sure if Bose had been able to foresee the future, the situation might have been different. Or mayhap it would not have changed. Regardless of his association to your daughter's death, what do you believe Lora would have done had she been foretold of the possibility of succumbing in childbirth? Do you truly believe she would have given up the opportunity to have a child simply because there was a chance that she would not survive the endeavor?"

Margot was visibly shaken, her thin face taut with rage and emotion. Blue eyes that were razor-sharp abruptly softened with uncertainty as she pondered Summer's logic. But years of belief in Bose's guilt were difficult to dissolve and she turned away, uncertain with the turn of the conversation and subject. Ever-aware of her audience, however, she knew she had to relay the fact that her duties and motives were correct regardless of Summer's reasonable words. Even if the flawed young woman had somehow succeeding in breaking down her wall of defense, it was imperative that Margot maintain her staunch beliefs.

"For Bose, she would have done anything. Just as you will," from quivering one moment to steady the next, Margot was shockingly in control once more. "He should have known that his child would have killed her for pure size alone. But his desire for an heir convinced Lora to jeopardize her life and she paid the ultimate price. He is without conscience, I say, as your abduction from the walls of Chaldon clearly support."

Summer stared at the back of the woman's well-coiffed head, seeing that she was unwilling to alter her ideas. If reason and calm logic had failed to convince her, then Summer doubted anything would. The Lady Margot would continue to exist, embittered and malevolent, until the day she died.

"I-I am sorry you feel that way, for certainly, you are wrong," she uttered softly, turning from the old woman and focusing on her father once again. "I would like to see my husband, Father. If Stephan and Ian escort me, would this be possible?"

Edward lowered his gaze, mulling over her request for the hundredth time and truly seeing no further reason why he should deny her. If anything, it might ease his sons' anger toward him and he was eager to lighten their disgust and fury. Coming to understand Margot's shaded occurrence of events as he had over the past few minutes, he seriously came to wonder if his disregard of Bose de Moray's petition was provided with any firm basis. He had been wrong.

Unfortunately, the situation was out of his hands. Bose had committed a crime by abducting Summer and as events were progressing, the circumstances were beyond his control. But there were some things he was still able to control.

"I would allow it, if Sir Breck is agreeable," he said weakly.

When Breck, collapsed exhaustedly against the wall several feet away, suddenly came to life at the mention of his name, Stephan and Ian cast the man menacing glares that would have made God himself unwilling to deny Summer's request. Breck met the challenging stares, although frankly too fatigued to summon the necessary energy to maintain the fight. It was of little consequence if Summer saw her husband, for certainly, she could do nothing to aid him beyond sweet words and tender promises. De Moray was a prisoner, Breck's prisoner, and the eldest Kerry brother found himself pleased with the control within his grasp.

"I would agree," he said finally, turning away and picking at his nose. "But only for a few minutes. And I would have my guards present during the meeting."

Stephan attempted to refute the last command but Summer hushed him, terrified that Breck would reconsider if the terms were challenged. Without another word to her father, the half-drunk woman in the corner or the repugnant knight pulling the mucus from his nose, she swept from the room with her mighty brothers in tow.

She was gone, leaving Margot and Edward and Breck bathed in an uneasy silence. As the soft hiss of the sea breeze infiltrated the lancet windows, Margot's thin voice pierced the air.

"She is wrong, Edward," she said softly. "Her reasoning is shaded with Bose's version of events. For certain, she is wrong and our cause is as strong as ever. Have no fear."

Edward, his expression dull, looked to the thin woman. "I do not fear. But I do question."

"Do not," she snapped, her confident composure making a customary return. "There is no need. We will not fail in our quest to be rid of Sir Bose. I promise you that."

Against the opposite wall, Breck looked to the lady curiously. "You have more information against him? Another strategy, mayhap?"

Faintly, Margot shrugged. Faded blue eyes met with those of small, questioning blue. "Indeed. As long as Lord Edward maintains his faith and truth, the results will be favorable."

Breck cocked an eyebrow. "What you mean to say is that as long as Baron Lulworth does as he's told, we shall emerge victorious."

Margot laughed softly, casting Edward a nearly affectionate glance. "He shall do as he's told. And I believe I have the final answer that will weaken any strength of Sir Bose's case."

"You do?" Breck moved away from the wall, toward her. "Do tell."

Margot merely smiled, a sly gesture. "An inebriated man usually cannot remember what has occurred during the course of his drunken state, can he?"

Jolted from his sluggish ignorance, Edward turned to the smug woman. "Make sense, Lady Margot. My memory has never failed me, wine or no."

Reaching out frail, boney fingers, Margot touched Edward's sallow hand. "It is about to, my lord," she whispered confidently. "It is about to."

☙

THE PEACH-COLORED SILK reflected the sun's rays beautifully as Summer and her brothers emerged into the dust-filled bailey en route to the vault. Her urgency and excitement growing by the moment, Summer kept a rapid pace toward the entrance to the underground dungeon just as a rider bearing du Bonne colors passed beneath the raised portcullis and thundered into the courtyard.

Stephan caught sight of the man, pausing in his pursuit of his eager sister. Ian paused too, causing Summer to rein her excitement for a moment as both brothers seemed focused on the red and white messenger. As the man was met by a few servants intent on collecting his frothing steed, he dismounted the weary beast and immediately made haste for his liege's eldest son.

Stephan waited with growing apprehension as the young rider approached, greeting him formally. "My lord Stephan," the youthful soldier was clearly out of breath. "I have ridden from Poole this day with a message from Lord Bruce Eggardon. Shall I deliver it to you now or within the presence of your father?"

Summer and Ian were suddenly beside their eldest sibling, their faces wide with anxiety. Stephan did not keep them waiting. "Tell me now."

The soldier nodded swiftly, attempting to catch his breath before he delved into his missive. "Lord Bruce has been feeling poorly as of late and will be unable to travel for several days. Expect him in six days, no less, and be prepared to begin the hearings immediately. He shall not have time to waste."

Stephan nodded faintly, dismissing the soldier as he turned to his brother and teary-eyed sister. When he saw Summer's composure crumbling at the thought of her husband languishing within the vault for the next week, he grasped her hands firmly and held them against his chest.

"No tears, sweetheart," he pleaded softly. "'Tis wonderful news, truly, and I will tell you why."

But Summer refused to allow him to continue, sobbing softly as Ian put a comforting arm about her shoulders. "Six d-days in the v-vault is n-not wonderful, Stephan," she wept. "He shall d-die in that place!"

"He will not," Stephan said firmly, lowering his voice so that his explanation would not be overheard. "I refrained from telling you about my hopeful prospects for Bose's freedom simply because you were entirely overwhelmed by the situation and I had no desire to baffle you further. But you must know now of the hope I have for Bose's release. And six days' postponement is the best possible news we could have hoped for."

She looked to him, sad and dubious. "W-Why do you say this?"

Stephan's expression seemed to glow with the knowledge of his clever scheme. "Before we rode in pursuit of Breck's trail yesterday morn, I sent a messenger to King Henry pleading for the king's Divine Grace in absolving Bose of the thievery charges. And my messenger was none other than Duncan Kerry himself. If anyone can convince the king of Breck's evil intentions, Duncan can. But it will take time, time that has apparently come as a gift from God in the form of six days' delay. Do you understand what I am saying, sweetheart? Eggardon's lag is very good news indeed."

She understood. Miraculously, the tears seemed to vanish and her expression took on the same warm glow that colored Stephan's features.

"D-Duncan went to s-seek the king's intervention?" she repeated with awe. "Good Lord, Stephan… d-do you suppose Henry will actually dissolve the charges?"

Stephan's lazy smile was nothing short of smug. "Breck and Father and Lady Margot believe they have the advantage. But they do not suspect that I would send Duncan to plead for Henry's intercession. We have the advantage, I say."

Summer's mouth was open in surprise. "Then Breck does not know of his brother's defection to aid our cause?"

Stephan shook his head. "He has apparently assumed Duncan to have returned to Crestwood. He's not made mention of the man nor asked for him."

A soft, warm body suddenly flew at him, all silk and hair. Summer giggled happily, hugging her brother tightly enough to strangle him. "Oh, Stephan!" she gasped, kissing his cheek loudly. "Y-You are wonderful! Absolutely wonderful!"

He hugged her tightly, his cheeks mottled with a tender blush. "I realize that, of course," he said with feigned arrogance, snorting with humor when she slapped him playfully. "Now, let's go and see your husband. I'll wager he can use a bit of good news, too."

CHAPTER NINETEEN

"**Y**OU MADE MENTION of Bose de Moray. Deliver your message and be done."

Duncan swallowed hard; nearly two days of a blistering pace had brought him to the halls of Windsor with the most difficult battle yet to come. It had taken another two days to seek audience with the king, pleading to anyone who would listen, demanding to speak to Henry on Bose de Moray's behalf. Scarcely anyone paid him heed, one soldier going so far as to kick him in the arse, until a small steward bearing food for the king's chamber crossed Duncan's path. Immediately, Duncan saw his chance to speak with Henry.

Not a wise choice, to be sure. Knocking the man on the head, he proceeded to steal clothes that were far too small for his large frame and, looking rather foolish in his confiscated clothing, made way to the king's chambers with tray in hand. The household guards, men who had once been under Bose's command, knew immediately that the tall attendant was far too well-bred for servitude and accused him of being an assassin. Looking down the end of a massive broadsword, Duncan began to frantically recite his purpose in coming. And the nearly-screamed mention of Bose's name had been enough to spare him.

As Duncan quickly discovered, the name of de Moray's bore a good deal of weight within the halls of Windsor and in little time he was waiting within a small private chamber, critically watched over by two suspicious knights. One man, tall and blond with piercing blue eyes, seemed particularly interested in his presence but Duncan ignored him nervously, wondering if he would indeed be provided the chance to relay his message to a king's advisor or if he were simply waiting for his own death.

After several hours of an uneasy wait, the blond knight escorted him into a lavish solar populated by a few men quite disinterested in the wide-eyed visitor. Urged on by the knightly escort, Duncan had made his way to the opposite end of the room where two men sat before diamond-paned glass windows. A game of chess sat between them, one man small and red-haired, the other man massive with a great shorn skull. As Duncan stood by with panting nervousness, the smaller man spoke without looking at him.

"You made mention of Bose de Moray. Deliver your message and be done."

Swallowing away his anxiety, Duncan focused on the finely-clad young man. "I have a message for King Henry. His former captain, Sir Bose de Moray, is in a good deal of trouble that requires the king's assistance immediately."

"What sort of trouble?"

The shaved-head man moved a pawn into position as Duncan answered the question. "He is accused of stealing a woman, my lord. He is set to stand trial for the crime of thievery and the necessity of royal intervention is imperative."

The fair-haired man did not look up from his game board, instead, moving a knight to capture his opponent's pawn. Only when the move was successfully accomplished did he look to the tall, red-haired knight in stolen servant's clothing. One droopy eyelid gave the youthful nobleman a dense appearance as he studied the oddly-clad warrior intently.

"There is more to this story than you are telling me. You will start at the beginning, please. And omit nothing."

With another swallow and a deep breath for courage, Duncan did as he was told. From the moment he was aware of Bose's interest in the lady until the very second he himself fled Chaldon in pursuit of the de Moray's pardon, Duncan made sure no detail was spared. The small man listened carefully, going so far as to ignore the game before him as he digested the messenger's words. When Duncan finished, the young man with the heavy-lidded gaze continued to linger upon the anxious knight as if attempting to ascertain the truth to his wild story.

"And you say it is your brother who's determined to press charges of thievery against Bose?"

Duncan nodded shortly. "Aye, my lord."

The young nobleman chewed his lips thoughtfully. "And your name?"

"Sir Duncan Kerry, my lord."

Several moments of unnerving silence followed before the thin young lord returned to his game board as if he had come to the conclusion that the tale presented had not been a message of the utmost concern.

"Your story failed to encompass everything this young knight is telling me, Dag," he said casually, moving his bishop. "You merely said Bose had acted irrationally and was in great need of my aid."

His large opponent watched the game before him, calculating his next move. "Obviously, Your Grace, this young knight is much closer to the problem than I am. If I'd known the entire situation when my cousin had come to Salisbury, I surely would have beaten a measure of sense into his thick skull."

Young King Henry snorted, his first display of humor. "What makes you believe you would have been successful? The Bose de Moray I knew was the epitome of stubborn confidence. Within his own mind the man can do no wrong."

Dag nodded shortly. "And within mine. Even if his actions were rash in stealing his ladylove, I cannot condemn them as incorrect. What remains now is exonerating him of the apparent charges against him." For the first time, the king's chess opponent looked to the red-haired young knight and immediately, Duncan saw a faint resemblance between the shave-scalped man and de Moray himself. Something about the black, piercing eyes drew his attention as the massive man studied him closely. "So your brother was the Lady Summer's betrothed?"

Duncan nodded slowly "Aye, my lord."

Dag cocked an eyebrow. "Bose called the man vile and unscrupulous. Is he?"

Again, Duncan nodded. "Aye, my lord."

Grunting in acknowledgement, Dag returned his attention to the game board just as Henry captured his second knight. Dag growled in frustration. "An unfair move, Your Grace. I was improperly distracted."

Henry smirked. "You are improperly skilled. Cease your moaning and accept your defeat as a true man would."

Growling again, Dag reached for his chalice of wine. Taking a healthy swallow, he moved his bishop forward with casual flair. "Then tell me, Your Grace; what is it you plan to do for my cousin? I would wager to say he is in a good deal of trouble by now and in dire need of your immediate assistance."

Henry nodded faintly, contemplating his next course of action. "I remember when I first met your cousin, Dag. The two of you were serving Hubert de Burgh shortly before he resigned his post as Chancellor. Whereas your cousin proceeded to swear fealty to me, you took your vows before the church. Do you remember?"

"I do," Dag replied, pretending to be more interested in the game than the conversation at hand. In faith, however, he was very much concerned with the conversation; he had spoken of nothing else for the past two days. But try as he might, he could not convince Henry of the seriousness of the situation; apparently, the king believed Bose impervious to bad judgment or the prosecution of mere mortals.

With the added support of the red-haired knight's stories, Henry was finally coming to grasp the seriousness of the situation and Dag thanked God for the unexpected appearance of the persistent Duncan Kerry. For certain, his prayers for an advocate to his cause had been answered and he continued to stress his point as non-threateningly as he could manage.

"I also recall how quickly Bose rose within the ranks, following in Uncle Garret's footsteps. He was Captain of the Household Guard at

the tender age of twenty-eight years and you relied upon him tremendously," a bushy black eyebrow slowly lifted. "Surely his loyalty to you
during that time has earned a measure of your Divine Grace?"

Henry sighed, moving a pawn and avoiding the question put to
him. "I wish he were still with me, although his successor is a brilliant
replacement," he directed his statement to the tall blond knight
lingering in the shadows. "You've long known my feelings, Olav. Bose
was a friend."

The silent knight with the sharp blue eyes nodded faintly. "He was
my friend as well, Your Grace. When he left, I would have gone with
him had you not convinced me otherwise."

"You mean had I not threatened your very life," Henry muttered,
laughing softly when Olav's agreed. "God's Blood, the man took my
finest knights with him when he departed; Morgan, Tate, Farl, Adgar.
Even old Artur. I was rather fond of the aged bastard."

Dag made a foolish move, purposely intended to end the game.
"Uncle Artur is a unique soul. Christ, he shall probably outlive us all,"
eyeing the king as the man countered the move, he pretended to study
the board. "And he will most definitely outlive Bose if you do not do
something to help him. Soon, I would suspect."

Henry studied the game board as well, drumming his fingertips on
the table. After a moment, he looked to Duncan, slightly calmer than he
had been upon first entering the stuffy chamber. "When you left, Bose
was still on the run?"

Duncan nodded swiftly. "Aye, Your Grace. That was four days ago
and I have no way of knowing what has happened in that time."

Henry returned his attention to the game as Dag foolishly left his
queen unguarded. "Four days is a long time," he said, easily capturing
his opponent's primary piece. "I do suppose I should ride to Dorset and
absolve Bose of these charges, which, as I would understand, are not
entirely righteous."

"They are not, Your Grace," Duncan said quickly, feeling his first
genuine surge of hope in four days. "My brother coerced the lady's

father into breaking his word to Sir Bose. She belonged to de Moray first and certainly, if there is anyone to charge with thievery, it should be my brother. He is attempting to take what does not belong to him."

Henry scratched his head wearily, motioning for the board and table to be taken away. When hovering servants cleared the debris, the king focused on Dag's serious face. "Although Bose may have the church on his side for his legal marriage to the lady, it would seem that his foe has the law in his support. He holds the legal betrothal contract, not your cousin, and has every right to prosecute for stolen property."

Dag knew this, nodding in agreement to the king's assessment. "But if the situation is as Sir Duncan presents it, Breck Kerry isn't interested in Summer personally. Simply the opportunity to gain vengeance against Bose by threatening what is most precious to him; his lady wife," with a sigh, he scratched his stubbled scalp. "Mayhap an agreement could be reached between the two men; monetary compensation for the dissolution of all charges. Or land compensation of some sort for the loss of a promised bride."

"Breck doesn't want money or land, my lord," Duncan interrupted softly. "He wants to destroy Bose by using the lady against him. He even told me that once he marries the lady, he shall simply do away with her because he has no real use for her. The only matter of import to my brother is defeating de Moray any way his is able. Since he cannot beat him upon the tournament field, he seeks to emotionally ruin him."

Henry stared at him, his droopy eye a distracting element to his overall commanding aura. "Why would he do this? What crime has Bose committed against this man that would cause him to seek such horrific revenge?"

Duncan shrugged faintly. "In truth, I believe it to be nothing more than professional jealousy. Breck considered himself the best knight upon the tournament circuit until the appearance of Bose de Moray. Now, he is lucky to run a close second. Third, even. And he cannot stomach the constant humiliation."

Henry pursed his lips thoughtfully, looking to Dag with equal seriousness. "'Twould seem that this situation deepens by the moment. Certainly your nagging requests that I ride to Bose's aid did nothing to fully convey the seriousness of the circumstance."

Dag cocked an eyebrow. "Fine, fine, so I nag like an old fishwife," he grumbled, causing Henry to smile. "And you ignored me quite soundly. The more you disregarded my prattle, the more I was forced to nag."

Henry snickered, moving to rise from his overstuffed chair. Duncan watched the king intently, a young man of twenty-eight years but wise beyond his age. Assuming the throne of England at the tender age of nine had the distinct ability to mature one too rapidly and Henry bore the characteristics of his premature development. His movements, his manners, were of an older, more experienced man.

"Although I can hardly spare the time to make the journey to Dorset, I shall endeavor to do so for Bose's sake," glancing to Olav still lodged against the wall, he issued his orders with the confidence of a man who had been giving commands for most of his life. "Prepare an escort immediately. I want a full complement of knights and soldiers assembled in the bailey within the hour."

"Shall I prepare a royal coach, Your Grace?"

Henry shook his head. "I shall ride. Ready my steed."

Olav bowed swiftly and was gone, leaving Dag and Duncan to sigh with relief. Two men who had never met until this moment, both in support of the same cause, were about to see the results of their determination and the thanks upon their weary lips ran far too deep for words. When Henry turned away from the two men and began to converse quietly with one of his advisors, Dag rose from his chair and faced an exhausted, but hopeful, Duncan.

Duncan openly studied the massive man, noting his ecclesiastical robes for the first time. He gestured toward the coarse woolen garment.

"Forgive me, Father. I did not know you were of the cloth and have addressed you improperly during the course of our conversation."

Dag shrugged faintly. "Do you think I shave my head in this fashion because I like it?" When Duncan grinned, Dag took a moment to scrutinize the knight more closely. "So you are Asa Kerry's youngest son? I knew your father once, very well."

Duncan nodded briefly. "As I have understood. My father was very proud of his service to de Burgh."

Dag smiled in remembrance. "We were all proud to have served the mighty chancellor to three kings. My calling, however, eventually took me to a higher court," he cocked an eyebrow at the younger Kerry brother, studying the man who resembled his strawberry-haired sire a great deal. "So tell me, Duncan Kerry; did you come of your own accord to seek Henry's help for my cousin or did someone send you?"

"The lady's brother, Sir Stephan du Bonne, asked that I come," Duncan replied steadily. "But I was more than willing, considering my brother has caused this chaos."

A bit more informed as to the young knight's appearance, Dag cast a long glance at the king. "I never thought he would go to Bose personally. I knew he would send a missive granting the man absolution, but I never truly believed he would personally ride to my cousin's assistance."

Duncan had always been in awe of the dark and mysterious Bose de Moray. But knowing that he had royal power at his command somehow validated the myth of the legendary Gorgon.

"The king obviously thinks a good deal of Sir Bose," Duncan said, scratching his arm where the too-small uniform chaffed him. "I had no idea de Moray held such power. I am positive my brother was unaware as well, for surely, he would not have moved against him as he has done."

Dag looked to the young knight once again, his black eyes appraising. "I do not even know your brother and already I am made aware of his foolishness. Pray that he has not harmed my cousin in our absence, for certainly, Henry's wrath shall be swift."

Duncan sighed heavily, watching as a roomful of men and counselors suddenly moved about with a sense of purpose as the king's travel plans were announced. "He deserves whatever Henry delivers, Father," he said softly. "I hold no pity for him."

Dag stared at the youthful knight. "Nor do I, lad," he rumbled slowly. "Nor do I."

ॐ

THE GRAND HALL of Chaldon was eerily silent considering the crowd of nervous people sitting in residence. The sun was preparing to set on the sixth day of Bose's confinement, the soft tendrils of orange light caressing the stone walls as the last rays of illumination faded into night.

Lord Bruce Eggardon sat on the dais usually occupied by the mighty du Bonne family, his chin resting wearily in his large hand. Once a proud warrior, years of declining health had taken their toll on the once-powerful man. His blond hair was yellowed with age, his faded green eyes lined with fatigue as his sharp gaze raked the room and surroundings. And most interesting surroundings they were.

The du Bonne party sat on the right side of the room; three brothers, the eldest brother's wife, and the very reason for the proceedings seated in the center of the group clad in a lovely pink surcoat. A beautiful girl, the Lady Summer, as Bruce had noted upon his arrival not an hour earlier. Being Edward du Bonne's liege, he'd never known the man had a daughter and as the details of the situation were again relayed to refresh his memory, he could recall thinking that Bose de Moray wasn't such a fool after all. In his opinion, the lady was well worth the risk.

Opinion or not, however, the fact remained that Breck Kerry was intent to bring very serious charges against Sir Bose. De Moray's men sat with the du Bonne siblings, massive men with grim faces who seemed as protective of the young lady as her brothers. And the Kerry Clan, joined oddly enough by Edward du Bonne, sat to the extreme left of the room. As if an invisible barrier divided the two opposing sides with razor-sharp intensity, Bruce was eager to be done with the unpleasantness.

Tearing his gaze away from the du Bonne and de Moray party, the Marquis of Cerne looked to his vassal, Baron Lulworth, and motioned the man forward with a flick of his wrist.

"Are we prepared to begin?" he demanded quietly. "I made it clear that I would not tolerate any delays. If you want the man tried, let's get on with it."

Edward nodded quickly. "He's being brought from the vault as we speak, my lord. We are quite prepared to commence."

Bruce nodded impatiently, accepting a chalice offered to him by his manservant. Smacking his lips as he swallowed the fortifying ale, his attention was diverted by the sounds of armor and distant voices. From the corner of his eye, he could see Lady de Moray rising to her feet and Bruce was aware the appearance of her husband was at hand.

Among the approaching red and white clad soldiers, a massive black-haired prisoner came into view dressed in simple breeches and tunic. Forbidden access to his armor, the enormous warrior appeared uncomfortable without it.

Nonetheless, the prisoner assumed his place respectfully before the Marquis of Cerne, his black eyes focused on the man who would preside over his trial. Breck Kerry stood several feet from the man accused of stealing his betrothed, his pimpled face taut with emotion as Bruce faced the two opposing factions with veiled impatience. In spite of his fatigue and failing health, the Marquess' voice was steady.

"Announce yourselves to me."

Breck was the first to speak. "Sir Breck Kerry, Lord of Crestwood. This man is accused of stealing my bride."

Bose's reply was even. "I am Sir Bose de Moray, my lord. The lady I married was betrothed to me before her contract to Kerry was established."

Bruce's gaze moved between the two men; he had met Breck upon his arrival to Chaldon, a high-strung knight with an unruly mouth. But he had yet to meet de Moray, the accused, and his first impression of the man was one of calm and control. His interest was directed towards the prisoner.

"You are de Moray?" he asked.

"Aye, my lord."

"The one they call the Gorgon?"

"Aye, my lord."

"Why do they call you this?"

"Because I fly the Gorgon banner."

"I will again ask why."

Bose sighed faintly, although no one could hear him. Still, there was some hesitance in his manner. "Because the Gorgon is a fearsome female demon from mythology," he said. "To me, it represents my former mother in law. You see, my lord, the time when I was beginning my career on the tournament circuit was a particularly vicious period in my association with the woman. My wife had just died in childbirth and Margot blamed me for her death. So I commissioned the Gorgon banner to represent her, as the one who made every attempt to ruin my life. She is still trying. The banner was meant as an insult but it has become my symbol."

"You draw inspiration from such a thing?"

"It reminds me daily to defeat the obstacles that have been given me."

In just those few sentences, Eggardon could see that the prisoner was sane and strong. Oddly, he was impressed by the man. After a moment, he gestured weakly.

"I will hear your side of this, Sir Bose." It was a polite command.

In spite of having spent the past six days in the dungeon, Bose was remarkably groomed and composed. Thanks to his new brothers-in-law, one of whom had remained constantly by his side as he awaited trial within the bowels of Chaldon, he had been provided with a good deal of comfort and luxuries – clean clothes, a fine bed, and his wife's constant presence. The only reason Bose hadn't asked for Summer's permanent company was because he could hardly stand to see her within the moss-ridden walls as it was. Every time she left him, her sneezes threatened to overcome her and his guilt was great for forcing her to endure his terrible conditions.

During this time, Bose had been informed of the entire circumstance regarding Margot's influence on Edward's change of heart and in truth, he wasn't surprised. There wasn't anything his mother-in-law would not do to wreak havoc upon him and he did not even find it remarkable that, somehow, she had aligned herself with Breck Kerry. A good deal became clear regarding the motives behind Edward's change of mind as Bose came to realize Margot's involvement.

But that did not matter to him anymore. Nothing mattered any longer but the love of his new wife. Facing Lord Bruce, he found that he was eager to be done with the idiocy at hand.

"'Tis very simple, my lord," his baritone voice was even. "I was given verbal permission to marry the lady in the presence of a witness. Before I was able to put the betrothal to paper, Breck Kerry used lies and coercion to convince Lord Edward to change his mind. Even though Breck possesses a written betrothal, it is invalid because the lady was already betrothed to me at the time. Claiming my right, I proceeded to marry her."

Bruce sighed faintly, mulling over the concise explanation. "You are saying, in fact, that Breck's written permission was given after your verbal sanction?"

"Aye, my lord."

"And you have a witness that will attest to this?"

"Aye, my lord. Sir Ian du Bonne will testify on my behalf."

Seated beside Summer, Ian immediately rose in support of Bose's claim but Lord Bruce gestured him to remain seated for the moment. Currently, he was involved in the meat of the prisoner's deposition and continued to focus on the massive knight.

"Even if this is true, Sir Bose, you realize that a written contract is far more binding than a verbal pledge."

Bose's expression did not waiver. "Lord Edward gave his word. I consider that as valid as any written pledge."

Bruce pondered the steady answer. "But if you did not have your witness, it would simply be your word against Lord Edward if he denies having given permission. Who is to say that the tale of a verbal sanction wasn't something you and your alleged witness invented simply to support your claim to an illegal marriage?"

The thought had never occurred to Bose. For the first time, he tore his gaze away from the Marquis and focused on Edward, seated next to Margot on an overstuffed chair. "Has the baron, in fact, denied giving me his sanction, my lord?"

Bruce looked to Edward as well, expecting an answer from the pale, overweight man. Edward, sensing that he had become the focus of attention, shifted uncomfortably in his chair and Bose was not overly astonished when Margot whispered in the man's ear encouragingly. In truth, nothing the woman did surprised him any longer.

"My lord," Edward cleared his throat, his gaze shifty as he struggled not to look at his disgusted, angered sons. "As I indicated upon your arrival, I was quite drunk on the night in question. Sir Bose... well, he says I gave permission. And so does my son Ian. But, quite simply, I cannot remember for certain what, in fact, happened."

Sighs of disbelief and concern arose among the listening gallery, including a loud gasp from Summer herself. Ian, his face taut with fury, rose to his feet once more and faced his father across the dimly-lit room.

"I was there, Father," his teeth were clenched. "You most certainly gave your permission for Bose to marry my sister."

Edward's expression was filled with desperation. Clearly, he felt as if he were arguing with an enemy and not a man whom he had sired. "So you say, Ian, but I was drunk that eve and... truthfully, I can recall very little. I do not know if...."

"Then you are accusing me of lying on Bose's behalf?"

"I did not say...!"

Ian let out a sharp hiss. "For the love of God, Father, have the decency to admit that you verbally pledged Summer to Bose. For once in your life, show your daughter a measure of fatherly support and concern. Admit that you betrothed her to Sir Bose."

Edward, breathing heavily with emotion, was genuinely distraught. "Ian... I cannot! I cannot recall...!"

Ian abruptly turned away from his father. Focusing on Lord Bruce, he endeavored to keep his manner controlled in the face of his father's treachery.

"My lord, I fear that my father is under the influence of Sir Breck and the elderly lady seated by his side, both of whom are determined to see Sir Bose and my sister meet with ruin," he said with control. "Upon the Holy Bible, I swear that my father sealed a verbal betrothal between Sir Bose and my sister well before his contract with Breck Kerry."

Bruce eyed the largest du Bonne brother, inclined to believe the young man's sincere statement. But the fact remained that Edward was apparently intent to deny he had ever give Bose verbal permission to wed his daughter. The betrayal and confusion deepened.

"Please take your seat, sir knight," he quietly bade Ian to sit, who did so with comforting assistance from his sister. In fact, Ian seemed more disturbed than the lady at the moment and Bruce watched the two siblings comfort one another before returning his attention to Bose.

After a lengthy lull, he sighed heavily. "Sir Bose," he began quietly. "Do you see the dilemma I am faced with? 'Tis your word and Sir Ian's word against Baron Lulworth's. Obviously, by the code of ethics and standards, I am forced to believe Lord Edward over the two of you because of his elevated station."

For the first time since the trial began, Bose emitted a heartfelt sigh of despair. Edward's denial was an element he had not expected, but one he should have been prepared for nonetheless. With Margot feeding her venom deep into the man's soul, there was no limit to the betrayal involved. Margot must have convinced Edward to disavow any knowledge of his permission to further bolster Breck's cause.

In spite of the unwelcome fabrication, his tone was characteristically steady. "Be that as it may, my lord, I have nonetheless married his daughter. And not even you have the power to dissolve our union regardless of the charges or circumstances against me."

It wasn't an arrogant declaration, simply a statement of facts. Lord Bruce was experiencing more fatigue by the moment as he removed his gaze from Bose, focusing his attention on Breck. Immediately, his manner seemed to harden.

"And you? What do you have to say to all of this?"

Breck, smug and vile, drew in a deep breath before commencing his testimony. "My statement of the situation will be simple as well, my lord. Whether or not Sir Bose has the church or witnesses to support his cause, the fact remains that I alone hold the legal documentation that gives the Lady Summer to me. A legal document that permits me to charge Sir Bose with stealing my intended bride. In short, the man is a thief and I want him properly punished."

Bruce's expression was critical. "And are you aware of the punishment if he is found guilty?"

Breck nodded confidently. "Death, my lord."

Between Stephan and Ian, Summer whimpered softly as the tears she had been struggling to control suddenly spilled forth. Immediately, her brothers turned to comfort her, sensing the trial was heading for the worst possible verdict. The three brothers were praying feverishly for the appearance of Duncan Kerry, bearing a missive of absolution from Henry himself. For certain, it seemed as if the arrival of the youngest Kerry brother was their only surviving hope and they clung to their faith desperately.

Bruce was well aware of the emotional turmoil within the du Bonne encampment but his gaze remained focused on Breck. For lack of support toward de Moray's claim, he truly had no other choice but to agree with Breck's assessment of the situation; according to the law, Bose had indeed stolen what did not belong to him and by all accounts had to be punished. But Bruce would not make that final decision before he had viewed the very document upon which a man's very life hinged.

"Show me this contract," he muttered. "I would see it for myself before we continue."

Breck immediately gestured to a Kerry servant, who fled the hall. Meanwhile, the trial was on hold and Bose turned to Summer; lodged between her protective brothers and surrounded by his own knights, she seemed terribly vulnerable and amply shielded all at the same time. Without asking permission, he went to his wife.

Artur was holding her hand as he approached, attempting to calm her fears. But the comfort of seven men and her sympathetic sister-in-law could not compare to the loving arms of her husband and Summer threw herself against Bose, weeping uncontrollably into his soft linen tunic. Massive, warm arms calmed and weakened her at the same time.

"Calm yourself, love," he crooned, his voice hoarse. "'Tis merely argument at this point. Nothing has been proven or decided."

She sobbed against his chest. "B-But m-my father s-says he… h-h-he did not…."

He shushed her gently, kissing the top of her head and glancing to the faithful men surrounding them; grim, emotional, torn expressions met with his even gaze and he found himself growing more despondent by the moment. He could not stand seeing his defeat in their eyes.

"I am sorry about my father, Bose," Ian's voice was faint with emotion. "I truly had no idea he would deny all recollection of his sanction."

Bose shrugged faintly, cradling his hysterical wife. "It matters not in the overall scheme. But I certainly wish Duncan would return from London soon; it would appear that time is becoming of the essence."

Wiping at her eyes, Summer looked up to her husband's rugged, scarred face. "H-He shall be here. He promised S-Stephan he would return with Henry's absolution."

Bose smiled encouragingly. "And he shall, love, he shall. But he had better hurry or I fear we shall be on the run once again."

Genisa, in tears beside her husband, touched his arm gently. "Should it come to that, you can steal away on one of my father's merchant vessels. They travel all over the world and Breck could never find you."

She had meant the suggestion seriously and Bose smiled warmly at her. "I thank you, my lady. Your offer shall be seriously considered if Duncan Kerry doesn't come through that door within the next few minutes."

A strong hand gripped his arm and he turned to Morgan's grim face. "We are all with you, Bose, wherever you go. You know that."

Bose's smile faded. "Aye, Morgan, I know that," his gaze was steady upon the man who had taken a severe beating on his lord's behalf. "Ever my loyal friends through good times and through bad, though it seems as of late we are mostly meeting with bad."

"You're cursed," Farl's bushy mustache twitched with humor, sending the small group into light laughter, including Summer.

As the mood lightened somewhat, Tate suddenly caught movement from the massive doorway leading into the grand hall and he nudged Morgan, who diverted his attention to see what was happening. As his expression slackened, the entire group turned to the commotion going on in the massive foyer beyond the gallery entrance.

No one was more riveted to the activity than Bose. His black eyes were sharp, his expression steady, when suddenly his features appeared to slacken. Blinking with disbelief, he released his wife and took a step in the direction of his focus as if hardly believing what he was seeing.

"God's Beard... Olav? Olav Swenholm?" he could not stop himself from pointing to the cluster of vaguely familiar knights populating the wide entry hall. "Morgan, do you see him? Isn't that Olav?"

Morgan looked equally stunned, but his shock did not prevent a shadow of a smile from creasing his lips, growing bolder by the moment.

"Aye, I see him, and several others I recognize," turning to Bose, he suddenly erupted with triumphant laughter. "I believe our prayers have been answered, Bose, and none too soon. Duncan has returned and he's brought the entire company of Household Guards with him. God's

Blood, man, you are saved!"

Saved wasn't the term Bose had in mind to describe the younger Kerry brother's timely, if not astonishingly accurate, appearance. Miracle would have better served the situation. The man sent to seek royal aid had apparently arrived.

And the armies of Heaven were with him.

CHAPTER TWENTY

F ROM DESPAIR ONE moment to joy the next, the entire group of de
Moray and du Bonne knights were awash with smiles of relief as
several knights clad in the crimson and gold of the royal house poured
into the grand hall. The noise of their armor pierced the air as the
presence of powerful men filled the musty room.

"Are those truly Henry's men?" Summer was still clinging to her
husband's massive arm, her eyes wide with amazement.

Bose made eye-contact with Olav and, once again, a rare smile
crossed his face. "Indeed they are, my love," he gripped her hand tightly
as the room filled with warriors in gleaming protection and well-clad
royal men-at-arms.

Olav passed before Lord Bruce with nary a glance to the astonished
magistrate; the knight's attention was focused on his former captain.
Immediately, he extended a gauntleted hand in greeting.

"My lord de Moray," he said with true warmth. "We came as soon
as we were able. A crazy priest, claiming relation to you, came spouting
tales of your criminal activities and we thought it wise to heed his wild
stories. Was he wrong?"

Bose maintained his smile, returning the man's affable greeting. As
the gist of Olav's declaration sank deep, he slowly shook his head.

"Dag," he muttered as if the revelation did not overly astound him.
"So my cousin rode to London, did he? I wondered why he did not see
my wife and me off from Salisbury."

"Most likely because he was determined to save your life," Olav was
grinning. "He spent two days in London pleading your case to Henry
before our king grew weary of the man's ramblings and agreed to
intervene if only to shut him up. We could not convince Dag to come

323

to Dorset, though. His priestly duties forced him to return to Salisbury, but he demanded we inform him of the outcome of your trial. In fact, I would assume that is the situation at hand?"

Bose nodded. "You've arrived just in time. Another hour and you might have found me in pieces."

"You came," Summer could not keep the awe from her voice as she spoke to the knight she had not yet been introduced to. "You truly came!"

Olav directed his smile to her, bowing in a graceful gesture. "For Sir Bose, there is nothing we would not do," he continued to scrutinize her closely, politely. "The Lady de Moray, I am to assume?"

"Astute as always, my friend," Bose muttered drolly, clutching Summer's hand tightly. "The very reason I am facing the block."

Olav cocked an eyebrow, his eyes lingering on Summer in an appraising manner a moment longer. "Well worth the gamble, my lord," behind the lady, familiar faces caught his attention and he found himself gazing into the pleasant expressions of men he had known very well, long ago. His eyes glittered with warmth. "God's Blood, is that motley crew still hanging about? Morgan, I thought you would be dead by now."

Morgan grinned. "I shall live to dance on your grave, Olav."

Olav snorted, preparing to insult his former squire, Tate, when more commotion at the entrance to the hall captured his attention. Small and wiry amongst the large armored knights surrounding him, Henry III entered the room in his usual aloof manner, ignoring the vassals and servants who immediately dropped to their knees before him in startled reverence.

Bose's eyes glittered as he studied the man intently. "God's Beard," he breathed, his surprise evident. "He came."

Olav watched the king emerge into the smoky chamber. "You were his favorite knight, Bose. Do you truly believe he would stay away during this time of crisis?"

Bose shook his head feebly, unsure how to answer, when Olav gestured the man forward. "Come along," he said quietly. "Our king has ridden all the way from London and is anxious to see you."

Bose did not release Summer as he followed the knight who held his former position. Pulled toward the small man lingering in the center of the room, Summer could scarcely believe her eyes; not only had Duncan returned, but he had returned with the king himself and she fought to control her shock as Bose guided her close to the king.

A king who was focused on Bose as if witnessing the return of an old, dear friend. His young face creased with a genuine smile as the massive knight and his lady fair bowed respectfully before him.

"Stand and face me, Bose," he said benevolently, his eyes reacquainting himself with the man who had once been his friend and Household Captain. "I see that we have arrived just in time to prevent your untimely demise."

"Indeed, Your Grace," Bose's baritone voice was warm. "I did not expect to be fortunate enough to warrant your appearance."

A reddish-blond eyebrow rose. "And why not? You seem to have involved yourself in a serious situation and I am apparently the only person capable of saving you," tearing his gaze away from Bose, he focused on the red-cheeked lady by his side. "Your wife, I presume?"

Bose nodded, presenting Summer to the king. "The Lady Summer du Bonne de Moray, Your Grace."

Summer bowed again, her knees shaking so terribly that she was afraid she would collapse. But she managed to right herself somewhat steadily, keeping her eyes properly lowered in the presence of young Henry.

He studied her carefully for a moment. "Very fine, Bose," turning away, he seemed distracted and fatigued by the circumstance and was eager to move forward. "All pleasantries aside, tell me who is presiding over your trial?"

Bose gestured toward Lord Bruce. "The Marquis of Cerne, Your Grace, the Lord Bruce Eggardon. He has been impartial so far."

Henry moved purposefully to Lord Bruce who, caught completely off-guard by the king's unexpected appearance, folded himself in a proper bow. When the marquis met the king's intense gaze, the older man's upper lip was slick with perspiration.

"Your Grace, we are… honored by your presence," he stammered.

Henry regarded him silently, once again turning to Bose. "And who is this man that would accuse you of stealing his bride?"

Bose tilted his head in Breck's direction. "That man. Sir Breck Kerry."

Summer had never seen anything but arrogance and determination on Breck's ugly features. At this moment, however, he looked terrified as the King of England brought him to focus. Pale and agitated, he bowed swiftly for the monarch's benefit.

Henry's expression was hard on the red-haired knight. "Approach me."

Like an obedient dog, Breck did as he was told. Standing before the king, he could feel the angry stares of the silent household knights surrounding them. He kept his gaze lowered as the king spoke.

"You have brought charges against the former captain of my Household Guard," Henry's voice was controlled. "By what right do you make these slanderous claims?"

Breck swallowed, his usually cocky demeanor vanished. "His wife is betrothed to me, Your Grace," he said hoarsely. "She was to be mine before…."

"She was pledged to Bose before you convinced her father to break his word and betroth her to you," Henry motioned to a group of men standing off to his right. A few of the royal advisors shifted, moved aside, to reveal a tall young man with golden red hair within their midst.

Breck's eyes widened at the sight of his brother. "Duncan!"

The youngest Kerry brother nodded coolly. "I have told him everything, Breck," he said quietly. "He knows of your evil plans. He knows the only reason you solicited a betrothal for the lady was to seek vengeance on Sir Bose, and he further knows that the only reason you are going forward with this foolish trial is to see de Moray completely destroyed."

Breck's jaw went slack with astonishment, his composure completely destroyed with the realization of his brother's apparent treachery. "You... you are my brother, for God's sake. How could you turn against me like this?"

"Because you are wrong," Duncan said, no longer fearing his brother's retribution. "The Kerry name used to stand for strength and respect years ago, before you received your spurs and began to destroy the family reputation. Father and grandfather spent their lives establishing a powerful honor which you have endeavored to shatter. I am ashamed of you and I'll not tolerate your corruption any longer. For the sake of our heritage, I cannot."

Breck stared at him. "So you would betray me simply because you do not agree with my ideals?"

"I do not agree with your morals or your ideals," Duncan was growing increasingly passionate. "I have stood by as you've disabled honorable knights with your sly tournament tactics, or spread rumors that have shattered the reputation or marriages of those we've come to know through the circuit. But no longer; this will end now, brother. It will end now before any further damage is done."

Breck could scarcely believe what he was hearing; the concept of his brother's betrayal was nearly too much to comprehend and as he opened his mouth to refute the treacherous man, the very servant he had sent to claim the critical betrothal contract abruptly returned to the hall. Holding the scroll high above his head, the green and yellow garbed attendant made his way through the sea of knights and vassals in an attempt to reach his liege.

"Here it is," Breck's sharp mannerisms were bordering on madness as he seized the vellum from the servant's clammy palm. "This will vindicate me and prove that my charges are not false. Bose stole my bride and this piece of parchment shall prove it!"

Henry reached out and snatched the contract from the agitated knight, examining the rolled parchment carefully.

"The betrothal contract between my wife and Sir Breck," Bose explained quietly.

Henry nodded in understanding, removing the bindings and unrolling the fine yellow hide. The room seemed to quiet abruptly, Breck included, as Henry slowly read the contents of the missive. As the tension mounted, the deafening silence was nearly overwhelming, and Bose could feel Summer trembling within his grasp. His hold on her tightened and he waited, with bated breath, for Henry to absorb the contents.

After a small eternity, Henry finally raised his eyes, glancing to the serious expressions around him.

"Where is her father?"

Before Bose could reply, Edward was on his feet with Margot directly behind him.

"I am the lady's father, Your Grace," his voice sounded feeble.

Henry caught sight of the frail, thin woman lingering behind the pallid-faced earl, recognizing her to be Bose's former mother-in-law. He remembered the vicious, screeching woman who had marred her daughter's funeral with her hysterics. Puzzled but not particularly surprised to discover she was at Chaldon, aligned with the opposition against her deceased daughter's husband, he simply shook his head. The situation involving Bose's trial was growing in unexpected ways and he was frankly too exhausted to pursue the woman's presence.

Shifting his focus to the baron, he met the man's polite reply. "Am I to understand that this written contract came after you broke your orated pledge of marriage with Sir Bose?"

Edward visibly paled. "I...I am told, Your Grace, that I verbally consented to a betrothal between my daughter and Sir Bose. But I had imbibed a good deal of wine that night and it is difficult for me to remember what, precisely, happened."

Henry gazed headily at the man, obviously displeased. "Then you are denying any such promise?"

"I cannot deny or confirm what I do not remember, Your Grace."

After a continued moment of scrutiny, Henry once again looked to the parchment in his hands. "But there was a witness to this pledge. Your own son, I am told."

"My sons have turned against me, Your Grace. As much as I am ashamed to admit the fact, they would most likely say or do anything to support Sir Bose's cause."

"Then you are saying, in essence, that your own son has conspired with Sir Bose in an attempt to convince you that in your drunken state, you pledged your daughter in marriage to de Moray?"

Edward shrugged uncomfortably, torn between Margot's silent insistence and his sons' angry expressions. "I am suggesting nothing, Your Grace. But the possibilities are obvious."

Henry sighed with disgust, knowing the laws of ethics and standards would demand the baron's word be considered over the views of two lesser-stationed knights. If Bose said the man had verbally sanctioned a betrothal contract between the mighty knight and his only daughter then, in fact, Henry believed his former captain without question. But the truth remained that Edward, by station, would expect to have the consensus of belief over a mere knight.

A slow burn of irritation began to take flight, fed by the king's exhaustion. Looking to Edward, he could hardly keep the contempt from his voice.

"Are you lying to me?"

Edward swallowed hard, feeling Margot's hand on his arm in a supportive, demanding gesture. "Nay, Your Grace. It was never… but I simply cannot remember giving the knight my verbal approval."

Henry's thin jaw ticked. "And you fully realize that the court is obligated to believe you over the testimony of two lesser knights."

Edward nodded unsteadily, his jowls quivering like great loaves of fat. "Indeed… it is expected, Your Grace."

The king stared at the rotund man a moment longer before emitting a heavy sigh. "You realize what you are endeavoring to create, do you not? You are preparing to sentence an innocent man to his doom with your less than truthful reply."

Edward averted his gaze, lacking the words to form a proper response. As he stammered for a reply, Henry's irritation seemed to cool. Regardless of the baron's fabrication, he was cognizant of what needed to be done. Even if Lord du Bonne was intent to play him for a simpleton with his evasive replies, Henry refused to concede the game. He knew how to win. Extending the unrolled missive to Olav, he cast the man a single directive.

"Burn it."

Edward's expression slackened as Breck's eyes threatened to spring from their very sockets.

"You cannot!" Breck's face was red with emotion. "The missive is my property and I'll not...!"

The crowd was distended, rumbling with tension as Henry moved toward the irate knight, surrounded by his household protectors. They were seasoned men who had little tolerance for those who would defame their king. Henry openly studied the challenger of his royal honor.

"Do you disagree with my actions, Sir Breck?" he asked, a red eyebrow cocked questioningly. "Pray, are they as unjust and unscrupulous as your own?"

Breck's lips worked, spittle forming on the edges. "The... the church has endorsed the betrothal, Your Grace," he hissed, struggling to recover his last vanishing remnants of control. "You cannot simply burn it as if it never existed. There are those who have...."

"Witnessed it?" Henry's tone was patronizing. "As Sir Ian witnessed Lord Edward's verbal sanction? As we have all seen, Lord Edward has denied making any such commitment. And because he is of ranking nobility, it is expressly understood that his word be believed above the testimony of two honorable knights. And I say that if I burn this ill-gotten betrothal, it has never existed. And, being king, I retain the right to be believed above the testimony of all."

No one dared say a word. Olav and several other household knights watched the betrothal missive burn to ash as Henry maintained a steady gaze on the three individuals who had been driven to destroy his former captain. His rage and vengeance was ripe.

"These charges against de Moray were foolish from the onset," his soft-pitched voice was a growl. "I was forced to set aside my royal duties and travel two days in the saddle to vindicate my former captain from a trio of vipers I would just as soon quash. My patience is severely stretched by your conniving scheme and I will hear no more of these plots. If I ever again catch word of betrayal or spite against de Moray, my wrath shall be swift and painful. Do I make myself clear?"

Edward, as pasty as tallow, managed to nod faintly. "I... I was merely attempting to protect my daughter, Your Grace. Sir Bose is known to have killed his wife and...."

"Did you take this woman's clouded word over the truth of the circumstance?" Henry would not allow him to finish his sentence, gesturing toward Margot; although visibly demurred, Margot met the king's gaze with her usual haughty resolve and Henry smiled, a thin and hateful gesture. "Bose de Moray's wife died in childbirth, pure and simple. And as a result, he left my service in order to flee the memories associated with his position. Is that clear enough?"

Edward had heard that explanation before, many a time, but he had allowed Margot's venom to cloud his mind until her truth was the only reality he was able to comprehend. Hearing the recount of facts from the king's own mouth, however, brought the subject to bear and he sighed heavily, turning unsteadily from the young monarch. The verity of the truthful circumstance somehow drained his strength until he could scarcely support himself.

Settling heavily in the nearest chair, Edward du Bonne, Baron Lulworth, was left to ponder what course his feeble mind and weak will had brought about. He had ruined the honor and trust of his own family. He had destroyed his life. The du Bonne honor he had been so zealous in protecting was now in ruins.

Henry's attention was drawn from the dejected baron as Breck loomed before him, his lanky body twitching with fury. The smoke from the cindered betrothal contract was strong upon the stale air, reminding the occupants of the room with every breath of the swift justice served. And none more so than Breck as he endeavored, one last time, to summon his confidence.

"The Church will have something to say about this, your grace," he said in a low, hazardous tone. "You are attempting to play God by interfering in the church's business. And it must not be tolerated."

Henry cocked an eyebrow. "God's Blood, you truly are a fool. Your statement sounds very much like a threat."

"It was indeed a threat, My King," Olav was suddenly between the two men, his massive hands gripping Breck by the arms. "All who threatened the king are immediately imprisoned and sentenced for treason. Is this not so, Bose?"

Until this moment, Bose had refrained from direct involvement in the dialogue as much as he was able; in truth, he was still reeling from the swiftness of the king's decisive deed and could do nothing more than hold Summer against him, struggling to absorb the truth of his monarch's actions. But gazing to Breck Kerry within Olav's mighty grasp, he knew well the advantage of ridding himself of a man who had been a mere hair's breadth away from destroying him. If only to protect Summer from the man's evil once and for all, Bose knew he had to be rid of him.

"Indeed," his baritone voice was commanding. "All who threaten our good King Henry must meet with the unavoidable consequences."

Roughly grasped by several Household Guards, Breck struggled furiously. "I never… I did not threaten him! I am innocent!"

"Just as Bose was innocent of thievery?" Henry pressed. "How terrible it is to be wrongly accused. I suspect you do not appreciate it, either."

Kicking and fighting furiously, Breck was wrestled across the floor by several armed men as the audience in the hall gasped and whispered.

"I did not threaten the king!" he shouted. "I swear to you... de Moray, do you hear me? You will stop this or I swear I will...!"

His words were cleaved when someone slapped an armored gauntlet over his mouth; clearly, Henry and Bose weren't the only men weary of the pimpled knight's blather. Bose continued to watch as Breck was carried from the hall by a host of warriors intent on doing their former captain a favor. Bose could hardly bring himself to comprehend the extraordinary turn of events.

The room went sharply silent as the sounds of struggle faded. Bose remained frozen to the spot, in awe of the events and endeavoring to bring forth the words of thanks. In the midst of his shock, he caught sight of Duncan from the corner of his eye, appearing somewhat morose in spite of the justifiable circumstances. When Duncan noticed de Moray staring at him, he labored to mask his remorse. Weakly, he shrugged.

"He deserves the king's judgment and more," he offered, his voice faint with sentiment. "Still, he is my brother and for the sake of our family relations, I am nonetheless saddened to see him meet with an unpleasant ending."

Bose's expression was steady. "I understand your dilemma, Duncan. But your actions on my behalf were brave and commendable, and I thank you deeply. I owe you a great deal."

Again, Duncan shrugged, his cheeks mottling a faint pink when he met Summer's golden gaze. "'Twas the least I could do, considering my brother was the cause of your misery," glancing to the three appreciative du Bonne brothers, it was obvious his purpose had been served and the time had come to take his leave. Bowing a brisk farewell to the collective group, his charming smile made a weak return. "I shall return to Crestwood with a clear conscience, good lords and ladies. And with somewhat astonishing memories of Lance du Bonne's tournament."

"Do not be a stranger, Duncan," Stephan said. "You will always be welcome at Chaldon."

"And at Ravendark," Bose said firmly. "We shall see you at the next tournament, I hope."

Duncan's smiled broadened. "In Banbury, I believe, come October," he suddenly cast Bose a long glance. "Does your appreciation encompass allowing me the opportunity to win the joust for a change?"

Bose cocked an eyebrow. "I fear my days as tournament champion are at an end. You must take your place in line of all the men I plan to allow victory in display of my thanks."

Relieved laughter followed Duncan as he quit the hall, lighter of spirit than the young knight had been in many years. Summer watched the warrior fade into the foyer beyond the grand hall, emitting a sigh of relief for the timely appearance of her husband's angel of grace.

"B-Breck can never hurt us again," she murmured. "How wonderful of Henry to do this for you."

Bose touched her cheek, exhilaration taking hold where there had once been astonishment. Then he turned to the king.

"Your Grace," his tone was strained with emotion. "I cannot adequately express my gratitude for what you have done this day. To simply declare my thanks seems terribly deficient."

Henry's pale eyes were warm. "There is no need, Bose. Consider this small intervention my own payment of gratitude for years of devoted service on your behalf."

Bose smiled faintly, his gaze locked onto the young king he had known very well, once. In fact, his attention was so diverted that he failed to notice Margot's movements on the outskirts of the crowd; pale-faced and maddened with the turn of events, Bose's former mother-in-law began fumbling in her skirts as if searching for something. For her, the situation was not over. She had one final trick up her sleeve.

Bose was speaking quietly with the king as Margot skulked through the crowd of advisors and knights just outside of his peripheral vision, her focus lingering on the beautiful woman by his side. Bose's own knights were speaking between themselves or listening to the conversation between Bose and Henry. Even Stephan's wife, the silly whore, was listening politely to Morgan's conversation. But all sounds, all commotion, seemed to fade as Margot drew close, the rustling of her skirts coming to a disarrayed halt as she drew forth the object of her quest.

Margot carefully, politely, pushed between two of the king's men-at-arms, a path suddenly clear between herself and the new Lady de Moray. As Bose continued to chat with the king, Margot gripped the hilt of the small bejeweled dirk as she made her way toward the golden-eyed lady. And then, there was only madness.

Bose hardly remembered how it happened. First he heard a shout, and then a scream as Summer fell against him. Suddenly Margot was gripping his wife by the hair, a bloodied dagger raised high in her wrinkled palm. With a surge of panic, Bose reached out, blocking the dagger Margot had aimed for Summer's neck. His own hand impaled by the small jeweled blade, Bose lashed out with his uninjured hand and grasped Margot around the throat, feeling the frail bones snap within his iron grip. As if the elderly woman was no more than a rag doll, the silk-clad figure was hurled across the room, crashing to the floor in a heap of blood and bone and dead, ancient flesh.

Bose stared at the twisted body, hardly grasping what he had been forced to do. As difficult as it was for him to comprehend, Margot was dead and he himself had killed her. But even more pressing than his mother-in-law's lifeless body, Summer was weeping hysterically against him and ignoring his own pain and shock, he turned to her with an uncharacteristic display of panic.

"Where did she hurt you, love?" he demanded, his voice hoarse. "Show me."

Coughing and sputtering, Summer gestured weakly at her arm. "H-H-Here," she swallowed hard, struggling to control her hysteria. "S-She stabbed my arm!"

Morgan and Tate were beside her, each man fighting the other for the opportunity to see the wound. Morgan finally peeled the material away, gently, a smile appearing on his face as he inspected the injury.

"'Tis a scratch, Lady de Moray," he said calmly, motioning Tate to locate a measure of linen to halt the bleeding. "See? She scarcely touched you."

Pale-faced, Summer looked to the wound with its stream of blood and thought it looked to be far more than a scratch. It certainly hurt worse than a scratch. But she resisted the desire to complain as she realized that her husband had been injured much worse. His face was equally pale as Stephan and Farl inspected his punctured hand closely.

"Y-Your hand, Bose," she murmured; even though he was injured and bleeding, still he managed to keep his right arm wrapped tightly about her. "She injured your hand."

He glanced at the clean puncture as Stephan accepted a strip of linen from a servant, wrapping the injury tightly. "Indeed," his voice was faint. Summer continued to observe him, wide-eyed and shaken, as his gaze found the distorted body several feet away. "God's Beard, I never... she forced me to do this. For Lora's sake, I never wanted to harm her no matter what she had done, although at times my restraint was difficult."

"You were protecting Summer," Stephan's voice was steady as he wrapped the bloodied appendage. "You reacted instinctively to a mortal threat by destroying it. You cannot condemn your natural actions."

Bose sighed heavily; the occurrences of the day were so staggering that all he wanted to do was leave this place of agony and betrayal and death. Even if the circumstance had ended in his favor, still, it had been a costly day both emotionally and physically, and he was eager to be done with it.

"I realize that," he exhaled slowly. "But still... it happened so fast. I simply cannot understand why she would do this; Margot was vicious and mad, but she was never suicidal. Did she truly believe I would not defend my wife against her attack?"

Tate returned with the linen for Summer's arm, confiscated from a jittery house servant. "Mayhap she had hoped you would not. You've always allowed her to physically demonstrate her rage without fear of discipline."

Morgan accepted the bandages. "She has always abused you, Bose, and you've let her simply because you accepted the abuse as your punishment for Lora's death. Margot was accustomed to your acceptance of her brutality. God's Blood, had it been me, I would have done away with the bitch long ago."

"And my acceptance of her violence led to her own death," Bose's bass voice was hardly audible. "She accused me of being a murderer. I suppose she was right. I murdered *her*."

Summer winced as Morgan tended her arm, drawing a sympathetic kiss from her husband. "You did not murder her, Bose," she whispered, closing her eyes to his lips against her forehead. "She was trying to k-kill me and you were merely defending your wife. It was an act of self-defense."

He kissed her again, emitting a quaking sigh. "God's Beard, I cannot fathom the twists and turns this day has brought. First Henry's arrival, then Breck's imprisonment, and finally Margot's attack… I can scarcely believe all of it."

"Believe it," Henry entered the conversation, having stood by in stunned silence since the event of Margot's violent endeavor. Looking from the crumpled body of the old woman to the injured Lord and Lady de Moray, he simply shook his head.

"Had someone relayed this story to me, I would have accused them of fabrication," he said what they were all thinking. "The events are too shocking to comprehend, Bose."

Bose nodded his head faintly. "Entirely, Your Grace."

He found himself looking to Margot's body once more, shaking his head with disbelief as he focused on the brutal woman who had been his first wife's mother. Henry, sensing the knight's internal conflict, was aware that Bose and his wife required a measure of peace and quiet to recover their composure.

After a moment, he placed a comforting hand on the shoulder of the man who had once been his mightiest warrior. His expression was kind as he focused on the bloodied knight and his pale-faced lady.

"It's all over with now," he said quietly. "We can thank God for the happening of events that have brought about this ending. I was glad to be of assistance."

Bose nodded faintly, a weak smile on his lips. "As am I, Your Grace," he said softly, feeling Summer's warmth against him. Glancing to her lovely, ashen face, his smile turned genuine. "Certainly, I have everything I want. No matter if I had to dance with the Devil to gain my ends, I find that in spite of the trials I had to face, the results are well worth the effort."

Henry acknowledged his statement with a vague smile, turning to his hovering advisors and demanding portions of food and ale to help him recover his wits and strength. As the king moved away and the observers of the trial, including Lord Bruce, found it necessary to disburse themselves in light of the final events, Bose turned to those around him with the utmost wonder and awe.

"It is truly over," he murmured, watching Artur as the little man moved to Margot's body and kick it as if to rouse the corpse. "God's Beard, it seems impossible that the situation is over and we have emerged victorious."

Stephan, with Genisa under his arm, moved forward and slapped his new brother-in-law on the back. "Indeed you have," he said, his tone light as the delight of the emerging future took place. "You have wed my sister and acquired three very protective, very meddlesome brothers. I would hardly call the acquisition of your wife's siblings a victory."

Bose smile grew. "At least you'll not have to come and live with me," glancing toward the edge of the room where Edward continued to sit in dazed silence, he nodded his head in the direction of the muddled baron. "What of your father? What will you do with him?"

Stephan looked to the fat, pallid man, the warmth in his expression fading. "He is still the baron," he said quietly. "I could petition Henry to become guardian of the baronetcy, but for now I believe I'll simply bide my time and see what the future holds. My father cannot live forever."

Exhausted and nearly ill with the events of the day, Summer leaned heavily on her equally pummeled husband. "T-Thank God for that," she murmured, feeling wicked for anticipating her father's demise. But for all that he had put her through, she could hardly forgive him. Turning to her husband, she met his gaze. "I wish to go home, husband. To Ravendark. I have had enough of Chaldon for this day."

Bose smiled faintly. "As you wish, my lady. I am eager to introduce you to your new residence."

She returned his smile, weary though it might be. "As I am eager to see it," abruptly, she looked concerned. "And we must not forget to collect Antony before we go. He'd never forgive us for leaving him behind a second time."

Bose's eyebrow rose in feigned horror. "God be merciful. We most certainly must not forget the very beast that brought us together."

"Even if I plan to share our bed with him?"

"We've already had this discussion and I have made my demands quite clear. I have shared one wife with him but I'll not share the other."

"I-I realize your feelings on the matter, darling. Now tell me; where would you prefer him, at the head or at the foot?"

He sighed. "The foot."

Bose's knights were already in action, moving to quit the hall and intending to prepare for their liege's departure. Lance and Ian kissed their sister in turn, bidding her a particularly meaningful farewell with the promise for a future visit to her new home. Only Stephan lingered, his wife cradled against him, gazing at his sister as if he were seeing an entirely different woman.

"Are you all right, sweetheart?" he asked her gently. "With every-thing that has happened, are you well?"

Summer removed herself from Bose's arms long enough to embrace her beloved eldest brother. Aside from Antony's aid, the man without whose assistance her relationship with Bose could not have occurred.

"I am f-fine, Stephan," she murmured, embracing Genisa tightly before returning to her husband's massive arms. "Thanks to both of you for your aid and encouragement. Bose and I are ever grateful."

The sun was nearly set upon the Dorset coast as the House of du Bonne and the House of de Moray parted company. As a soft sea wind stirred the cooling night air, the mood settling upon the Dorset and Wiltshire populace alike was one of hope, of joy, of a positive destiny.

No stronger faith and joy was felt than within the tight group of the Gorgon and his loyal men. Upon their arrival to Chaldon less than ten days ago, there was not one person among them that could have predicted the course of the next week and a half. The jaunt to Lance du Bonne's tournament had been a most successful endeavor for all concerned, and a most victorious venture for one.

The Gorgon, indeed, had triumphed.

EPILOGUE

Early March, Year of Our Lord 1236

"DO WE TELL him now or wait until he discovers for himself?" Tate and Morgan stood at the entrance to Ravendark's massive keep, eyeing their liege as the man rode in beneath the raised portcullis. The bailey was awash with activity, man and servant alike greeting their returned lord from his three day visit to Chaldon Castle following Edward du Bonne's death. The new Baron Lulworth, Stephan du Bonne, had been most grateful for his brother-in-law's wisdom and presence in a time of change.

It was a calming presence that nearly made up for the absence of the new baron's very pregnant sister. Even though she had three weeks yet to go, as Stephan's very own wife had another two long months, Lady de Moray's husband had forbade her to travel, even to her father's funeral. In her stead, Bose had attended the mass and mourned as he properly should. But his heart wasn't supportive of his actions. Simply his duty, as required of a good husband.

Not that Lady de Moray was particularly eager to attend her father's funeral. The past nine months had seen little progress in mending the father-daughter relationship that had been so damaged by the episode with Breck Kerry. Summer doubted that she could ever forgive her father for his treacherous actions. But for the sake of family harmony, she had tried. She was still trying.

But it was a new life she sought, a new life far away from her father and the horror of his doings. The memories of the first few days of her marriage had mercifully faded as Summer rapidly settled into her new role as Lady de Moray with delight. Bose, too had settled in to being a husband again, incredibly at peace with his beloved second wife. But his peace was short-lived; shortly after they had set up house in Ravendark, Summer announced her pregnancy.

It had been the longest eight months of Bose's life. His greatest fear had become reality and for the first few weeks of Summer's pregnancy, he was literally beside himself with panic. He knew his wife was aware of his terror, a terror that kept him awake at night, watching her sleep with tears in his eyes. But he kept his apprehension well-hidden, instead, finding delight in the kicking movements of his child or lending sympathy to a wife who seemed to cry with the change of the hour. All of this kept him distracted from the true panic that lay ahead; the birth of his first child.

A panic his knights refrained from mentioning because Bose was far more easily disturbed these days and they struggled to maintain a calm, even atmosphere in his presence. The subject of childbirth was off-limits in conversation, although it was difficult not to broach the subject naturally when Lady de Moray began to speak of her plans for the child.

A child that was apparently unwilling to wait for his designated time to be born. On this day as Morgan and Tate watched Bose casually dismount his charcoal steed, they began to nudge each other encouragingly.

"Go ahead, Morgan. You've known him longer than any of us. 'Tis your duty to tell him."

Morgan jabbed the younger knight with his armored elbow. "You can run faster than I can. Tell him quickly and run for your life."

A bushy red mustache joined the conversation; Farl strolled up beside the two twitching knights, having been on the battlements when his lord arrived home. His faded green eyes focused on the distant warrior. "Well? Morgan, we've agreed that you would tell him. You'd better do it before some fool inadvertently spills the truth."

Morgan sighed, watching his liege approach. The closer the man loomed, the more anxious the knights became.

"I do not know why we are acting as if something terrible has happened," he grumbled, though he knew very well the reason. "The child is fine, as is the mother. Moreover, it was Lady de Moray's demand that we not send word of the birth for fear that Bose would kill himself in his desperate attempt to reach home. Look at him," he gestured to his unconcerned liege as the man lifted his visor, his black eyes glittering at the three huddled knights. "He looks entirely calm. Pity I am going to have to destroy his state."

Farl cleared his throat loudly, turning to leave. "I have duties, gentle knights. Good day to you."

"If you leave, McCorkle, I'll tell Bose it was your idea to withhold sending word of his child's arrival," Morgan did not look to the knight as the man stopped in his tracks, groaning softly in protest. But he obeyed nonetheless, resuming his stance beside Tate. As Bose drew closer, the knights seemed to visibly shrink.

"I see that three days has seen nothing changed within my fortress," Bose said, removing his helm and scratching at his sweating scalp. "Is there anything to report?"

Farl coughed loudly, Tate pretended not to understand the question, while only Morgan seemed able to maintain his composure. But it was a desperately fought battle.

"Welcome home, my lord," he said. "How went the funeral?"

"Smoothly enough. As soon as Edward was buried, the man was forgotten," he fumbled to remove his gauntlets. "Stephan is finally in control of Chaldon and there is a good deal of gladness with his assumption of power. The new baron aside, however, I had the pleasure of meeting Ian's new wife for the first time. A pretty woman. Looks a great deal like Genisa, in fact."

Morgan nodded faintly, struggling for courage to bring forth what he knew he must when the opportunity was right. "Your wife was disappointed that she was unable to attend the wedding. In Banbury, wasn't it?"

Bose snorted. "As if I would allow her to travel over miles of territory in her condition. I thought she was going to knock my teeth out when I denied her."

"She is only now speaking to you."

He snorted again. "That will change soon enough when I tell her that Ian's wife is expecting, also."

Tate, having recovered from his bout with stupidity, leapt into the conversation. "But they were only married three weeks ago!"

Bose cast him an obvious look, sending Farl and Morgan in to snickers of realization. "Dare I say that he had to marry the woman, Tate. Already her belly is rounding."

Speaking of rounded bellies, Morgan thought. No better time than the present to broach the subject. Summoning the courage, he opened his mouth to reply just as Artur came shuffling from the keep with more speed than the old man had exhibited in years.

"Congratulations!" he shouted happily. "Your son is magnificent, Bose! Why are ye standing out here gabbing at these three? Yer wife's waiting for ye!"

Time came to a screeching halt. Bose stared at the old man as if he hadn't understood a word; the blank expression on his face was indicative of the level of shock. Morgan, Tate and Farl scrutinized the man closely for signs of collapse or fury, waiting with anticipation as news of the birth of his son sank deep.

"Bose?" Morgan muttered timidly. "Are you well? Can you speak, man?"

Bose swallowed, his black eyes still riveted to his ancient uncle. Artur drew close to the group, waving his good arm in agitation and unaware that he had blurted the news to his unsuspecting nephew.

"Why do ye stand there like a fool?" he demanded. "Summer knows yer here. Better go and see the lass before she comes down here. And she shall come, too, looking for ye."

As the old man chattered like a magpie, Bose suddenly emitted a harsh gasp that sounded more like a cry for help. His knights continued to watch him apprehensively, Morgan going so far as to reach out and steady his arm.

"You have a son, Bose," he said softly, a twinkle of mirth appearing in his eye as the expression on his liege's face provoked a sense of humor. "A strong healthy boy was born to you yesterday morn. And Summer came through without incident."

"I...," Bose tore his gaze away from the old man, looking to Morgan with a degree of shock never before witnessed. When his friend smiled encouragingly, the startled father seemed to snap out of his trance and he grabbed the older knight by the arms, hard enough to break bones. "I have a son? Summer has given me a son?"

Soft laughter could be heard from Tate and Farl, convinced that Bose was not going to tear them all to pieces for failing to relay the news in a more timely fashion. Morgan merely smiled into the ashen face.

"A fat little lad with your dark hair," he replied. "He eats constantly and screams loud enough to rupture my eardrums. He shall be a mighty warrior someday."

Bose's eyebrows rose as his shock wore thin, a faint mottle of color reappearing on his pale cheeks. "God's Beard," he mumbled, turning to look at a beaming Artur. "I had no... for God's sake, it's not time yet. The babe is not due to arrive for three more weeks."

"He is here nonetheless," Artur said over the knights' laughter. "Summer forbade us to send word of her birth, knowing how panicked and irrational you would become. She was afraid you'd kill yourself riding day and night to return home."

Bose took a deep breath, running a gauntleted hand through his wet hair. His eyes moved from the men surrounding him to the keep beyond. An unmistakable longing pulled at him, tightening his throat and squeezing his heart until he could hardly breathe. He could not stop the well of tears filling his eyes.

"I must see them," he muttered, pushing past the men in a blind rush to reach the keep. "Summer... you say she is fine?"

Artur was close behind, as were the other three knights. "As healthy and whole as the day ye left her," the old man replied steadily. "She began having pains on the night ye departed for Chaldon and by dawn she was holding yer squalling son in her arms. We hardly had time to work up a substantial worry."

"And my son is well?"

"Well, Bose. Well."

Bose did not know whether to laugh or cry. All that mattered was the fact that his son had been born, healthy and strong, and by the grace of God his wife had survived unscathed. God's Beard, he was desperate to hold her, to tell her how much he loved her and to thank her for her most gracious gift of a son.

Into the massive keep, even the servants were smiling broadly as their rushed lord mounted the stairs, followed closely by his knights. The closer he came to his wife and new child, the more tears and emotion threatened to overwhelm him.

As Bose entered the familiar second floor where the bedchambers were situated, he realized he could hardly breathe through the force of his feelings. Closer and closer he drew until finally he burst through the master chamber door. What he saw nearly sent him to his knees.

Summer was sitting up in bed, holding a swaddled bundle and smiling radiantly at her pale-faced husband. When the man seemed unable to move his feet in a forward direction, she held out a hand to him.

"Welcome home, my darling," she said softly. "Come and m-meet your new son."

Bose let out a ragged sigh as Artur gave him a shove, pushing him into the warm, sweet-smelling chamber.

"God's Beard, Summer," he croaked. "Why... why did not you send word? Why did not you demand I return home, to be with you while you...?"

"Because you would have been absolutely useless," she said, her eyes twinkling with mirth. "Look at you now; I am fine, the babe is fine, and still you look as if you are seeing ghosts. Believe me when I tell you that you would not have survived my night of labor."

Near the bed, Bose collapsed on the edge, staring at the small, squirming bundle in his wife's arms as if unsure of the truth of the matter. As if hardly believing all had happened as it should, a healthy wife and a healthy child. Summer smiled at his disbelief and patted the bed beside her.

"Do not sit so far away," she commanded quietly. "Come and sit with us."

Woodenly, obediently, he rose and moved around the bed, staring down at the two human beings most precious to him. After a brief, hesitant moment, he lowered himself carefully beside his wife and son.

"Hold out your arms," Summer commanded, preparing to hand over the child. "He shall not bite you, Bose. H-Hold out your arms, I say."

He extended his hands awkwardly, unsure of himself. "I have... I have never held an infant before, Summer. God's Beard, what if I drop him? What if I crush him?"

She laughed, listening to Artur and the knights titter. "He shall scream like a banshee if he's not comfortable. You w-worry overmuch, husband. Now fold your arms; that's right."

With a good deal of coaching, Bose finally placed his arms in the correct position and Summer neatly deposited the tiny bundle in the crook of his left elbow. Peeling back the swaddling, Bose was blessed with the first glimpse of his squirming, fat-cheeked son.

"Oh, Summer," he breathed, his uncertainty and surprise being replaced by awe. "He's marvelous. Absolutely marvelous."

Summer's eyes were filled with tears as she watched her husband's expression. "Indeed, darling," she stroked his clammy black hair, feeling her strength return by the mere sight and smell of him. "Since you refused to discuss names, I was forced to choose a proper title without your consent."

Bose watched the infant as he suckled on his fingers. "I apologize for my reluctance," he offered feebly. "I... I was afraid to. Afraid to hope that our child would not live long enough to be named and afraid that you would not live long enough to name it."

She shushed him softly, kissing his ear. "I know," she whispered. "There is no need to explain your fears to me, darling. But I refuse to hear any c-complaints should my choice not be to your liking."

"As long as it isn't Kermit."

She cocked an eyebrow. "Nay, husband, I have spared you such embarrassment of a first name. But have no doubt my son will bear the name somehow."

He smiled for the first time since returning home, his face soft with enchantment as he continued to gaze at the bundled infant. "Anything you choose is fine, love, truly. I swear I'll not dispute you."

Summer watched his features carefully as she replied. "I rather like your father's name, Garret, but I wanted to honor my brother as well. Stephan has meant a good deal to us both," gazing down at the fair baby's face, she ran her finger along a silken cheek. "Therefore, I have decided to name your son Garran. Master Garran Kermit de Moray."

Bose gazed down at the rosy face, more wonder and joy and contentment filling him than he ever thought possible. All of his fears, his pain and his sorrows were fading rapidly until he could scarcely recall the feelings that had been a part of him for more years than he cared to count. For within his arms lay the catalyst to a greater healing and sitting beside him on the massive bed lay the very key to his heart.

A key that would give him three more children in the years to come. All of the Gorgon's children would grow to see adulthood and one would live to fight alongside his mighty father. But for now, there was no more misery and no more sorrow. No more woes to plague him.

Finally, the Gorgon had found peace.

⟨ THE END ⟩

THE GREAT KNIGHTS OF DE MORAY SERIES

The Shield of Kronos

The Great Knights of de Moray Series is connected with Stephen of Pembury, the hero of The Savage Curtain. Bose is the great-grandfather os Stephen of Pembury.

The Savage Curtain

Bose de Moray also makes an appearance in The Thunder Warrior.

The Thunder Warrior

The heroine of The Thunder Knight, Douglass de Moray, is Bose de Moray's daughter.

The Thunder Knight

For more information on other series and family groups, as well as a list of all of Kathryn's novels, please visit her website at www.kathrynleveque. com.

ABOUT KATHRYN LE VEQUE

Medieval Just Got Real.

KATHRYN LE VEQUE is a USA TODAY Bestselling author, an Amazon All-Star author, and a #1 bestselling, award-winning, multi-published author in Medieval Historical Romance and Historical Fiction. She has been featured in the NEW YORK TIMES and on USA TODAY's HEA blog. In March 2015, Kathryn was the featured cover story for the March issue of InD'Tale Magazine, the premier Indie author magazine. She was also a quadruple nominee (a record!) for the prestigious RONE awards for 2015.

Kathryn's Medieval Romance novels have been called 'detailed', 'highly romantic', and 'character-rich'. She crafts great adventures of love, battles, passion, and romance in the High Middle Ages. More than that, she writes for both women AND men – an unusual crossover for a romance author – and Kathryn has many male readers who enjoy her stories because of the male perspective, the action, and the adventure.

On October 29, 2015, Amazon launched Kathryn's Kindle Worlds Fan Fiction site WORLD OF DE WOLFE PACK. Please visit Kindle Worlds for Kathryn Le Veque's World of de Wolfe Pack and find many action-packed adventures written by some of the top authors in their genre using Kathryn's characters from the de Wolfe Pack series. As Kindle World's FIRST Historical Romance fan fiction world, Kathryn Le Veque's World of de Wolfe Pack will contain all of the great story-telling you have come to expect.

Kathryn loves to hear from her readers. Please find Kathryn on Facebook at Kathryn Le Veque, Author, or join her on Twitter @kathrynleveque, and don't forget to visit her website at www.kathrynleveque.com.

Made in the USA
Columbia, SC
10 July 2018